THE CLIMATE OF COURAGE

THE
CLIMATE
OF
COURAGE

By
JON CLEARY

COLLINS
ST JAMES'S PLACE, LONDON
1954

*This book is fiction. Several of the incidents are based on
actual happenings during the war, but the relative chapters
are not intended as representations of those happenings. Nor
are the characters in the book meant to represent any persons,
living or dead, who took part in the war.
They too are fictitious.*

PRINTED IN GREAT BRITAIN
COLLINS CLEAR-TYPE PRESS: LONDON AND GLASGOW

To
BARRY

CHAPTER ONE

SYDNEY and home came towards them gradually, a slowly returning memory. The outer suburbs, shallows of the city, were behind them and now the familiar stations were rushing past. Granville, Auburn, Lidcombe, the names all at once were personal. Rookwood cemetery went past, the long rows of ghostly headstones stretching away to the pale morning sky, the dead arranged neatly for Judgment Day. The old jokes were made about digging up a friend and everyone laughed: laughter hung on the lips like a bubble, ready to burst at any moment. Strathfield, Ashfield, Summer Hill: there was a yell as each station went past, of recognition and greeting and excitement. People on the platforms waved, and even their fleeting smiles, out of sight almost as soon as they were seen, left an impression that warmed the men. They were coming home and every welcome counted.

A sergeant, his thick black hair blown into a frightened wig about his small head, his lean body still bent from the wind, plunged into the carriage from the outside platform. He slammed the door behind him and leaned back against it, laughing and his eyes quick and bright in the brownness of his thin smooth face. Men looked at him for a moment, for Greg Morley was the sort of man everyone looked at, always expecting him to say something that would make them laugh or take their minds for the moment from their particular problem; but he had nothing to say this time, still laughing to himself because of his inner good feeling, and the men went back to finishing the game of Five Hundred, to staring out the windows, to waiting for the end of the journey. Sergeant Morley slapped a man on the shoulder and moved on through the carriage, picking his way none too carefully through the litter of bodies and legs.

Morley at last came to a vacant seat. He dropped into it almost gracefully; every movement was quick but there was never any awkwardness. He was the battalion swimming champion and had been a State champion before the war; nearly all his life had been spent close to the sea and there was the fluidity of water in every movement he made. There was also some of the unreliability of water in him. Strangers meeting him would note the faded sergeant's stripes on his sleeves, there too long, and the purple ribbon of the Victoria Cross on his chest, and they would wonder that he wasn't an officer by now; then after a while they would be aware of the lack of stability in him and would reason that the Army authorities were also probably aware of it. Morley himself was aware of it, but it didn't bother him. Nothing bothered him, except getting home.

He took a cigarette from a packet, flipped it into the air and caught it between his lips. He was full of such small vaudeville tricks: he should have gone on the stage instead of on to the clerical staff of the Water Board. In the Middle East he had even made the Arabs laugh with his antics and more than once had stolen the show from a street magician. He loved to be the centre of interest, but no one, except possibly the street magicians, had ever resented his conceit. It was hard to resent anything about Greg Morley.

He lit the cigarette, then abruptly sat up straight. "Where are we now?"

The lieutenant beside him turned from the window. "Relax, she won't mind if you're a little late. Haven't you kept her waiting before?"

"Not two bloody years." His voice was quick and light: a laugh lived in his throat. "And I'll bet there's a Yank just waiting for me not to turn up."

"Two years," said Vern Radcliffe. "I'm going to notice a difference in my kids."

"Just so long as there's none in the wife, that's the main thing." Morley grinned, then impatiently dropped his cigarette to the floor and ground it out with his boot. "Sometimes I used to be scared that by the time we got back I'd be too old."

"You'll never be too old for that or anything else," said Radcliffe, and looked at Morley with affection. "You'll be one of those eternally young bastards."

Morley laughed again, glad and proud of his youth. He was twenty-five, but Radcliffe was right: he would never be old. Age never shows on water.

Radcliffe turned and looked out of the window. He was a thick-set man who looked short sitting down but would be of medium height when he stood up. His face was the type that is square when the man is in condition but is round when he falls into fat; the corners were a little soft now after the long lay-off on the journey home from Tewfik. His brows and moustache were thick and ginger and his hair lay like a heavy auburn pelt on his well-shaped head. He had a certain animal look, amiable but not finely bred. Some day when he had slowed down and all the corners were round he would remind people of a sleepy old bear. But now there was still strength and a hint of controlled quickness in him, something that appealed to women who met him; if later they were a little disappointed in him it was because they found there was also a good deal of caution in him. The unit thought him a good officer.

The train sped on: Sydney came up out of the past at fifty miles an hour. Stations rushed backwards out of sight: now there wasn't far to go on the journey towards home.

It had been a long journey, beginning almost two years ago, in the winter of 1940, when the last farewell had been said; and it had included an ocean twice crossed, a desert, mountains, and these last two days the hills and plains they knew so well. They had boarded the train at Adelaide and had passed through Melbourne, and every mile had brought another remembrance. There had been the wide brown paddocks, the horses curving away in white-eyed fright like the chargers on a carousel, the nude corpses of the murdered gums, the shifting grey billabong that had turned into a mob of sheep, and the drab towns whose only beauty was the friendliness one knew one would find in the houses. The last stage of the journey had been the shortest and yet the longest, but above all the best.

There had been little to see at night, but Australia had been there outside the train. Some had stared out the windows seeking the Southern Cross, but the engine smoke had blown like a cloud across the sky. The train's whistle had wailed across the dreaming countryside: somewhere an echo had been evoked in a heart and someone had felt the chill of sadness. Houses, windows of cats' eyes, had crouched in the lee of invisible hills; a town had spun away, spangled with lights, beautiful at last in the darkness. Then the world had fallen past the moon and there had been the pale landscape stretching away as far as the eye could see and the heart remember; the hand of home had reached out and touched the sleeping brain, and the men, disturbed, expectant and yet frightened, had turned over to face the darkness of the racing train. In the morning their loneliness and their fear had been forgotten in their excitement.

Now they were almost home. The city closed about them and everything was suddenly, startlingly familiar. A church, a bridge, even the posters on the hoardings were the same: Ginger Rogers smiled invitingly, Tooth's KB Lager was a Man's Drink; and the men wondered what had ever attracted them to brothels and arrack. There was the black smudge in the clear day, the railways workshops at Eveleigh overhung with their fog of soot; and for the first time the men saw them as a target and felt a sudden emptiness, as if they had seen an old friend stricken with an incurable disease. Redfern Station went by, the men's shouts echoing back as part of their own welcome; the tracks multiplied, spread out like the silver flood of a river; and at last there was the tall clock tower of Central Station, the landfall they had all been waiting for. The train began to slow.

"I'll lay five bob he pulls her up out here in the middle of nowhere. There! What did I tell you?"

"Hey, Mr. Radcliffe, go up and pull your rank on the engine driver. You must wanna get home as much as us."

Vern Radcliffe turned from the window and smiled at the smiling faces. Good humour lurked constantly at the corners of his wide mouth like another, intangible feature; sometimes his good humour had been taken too much for granted and he had had to convince a few of the men that he also believed in discipline. But not now: the men didn't need discipline this day. He smiled at them, then looked at Greg Morley, who shook his head and rolled his eyes downwards.

Radcliffe caught the hint. "Where's Sergeant Savanna?"

"Here, sir." Sergeant Savanna was stretched out on the floor, his head pillowed on a kit bag; he made no effort to lift his long bony frame into an upright position. "Always on hand for the call of duty."

Like Radcliffe and Morley, Jack Savanna had come out of the ranks of these men and some of the old relationship still remained. But when it was needed, he could be as tough as any permanent army N.C.O. He was a born leader who had continually held back his own promotion by getting into scrapes; his waywardness was not a result of weakness, like Morley's, but of a stubborn streak of rebellion in him. He had been reduced from a sergeant to a corporal twice, and had only been repromoted because he was so much better than anyone else available. But he had been born to lead revolutions, not the forces of tradition; had he been born a hundred years earlier he would certainly have had a say at the Eureka Stockade. He looked up at Radcliffe, one of the minor pillars of tradition. "You wanted me, sir?"

"Go up and tell the driver to get a move on," said Radcliffe, enjoying the feeling of good humour that pervaded the carriage. "Private Brennan wants to get home to his girl."

"Plural, sir," said Private Brennan. "I've got seven of 'em waiting."

"That makes it even more urgent, sergeant," said Radcliffe. Sergeant Savanna didn't stir. "Corporal Talmadge."

"Here, sarge." The tall man with the close-cropped, prematurely grey hair, turned from the window; there was no look of expectancy on his leathern face, he had another three hundred miles to go before he would see home. "Want something?"

"Go up and tell the driver to get a move on. Private Brennan wants to get home to his harem."

Corporal Talmadge hadn't been listening to the conversation, had been completely isolated from it by his own thoughts, but he moved immediately into the joking intimacy of the rest of the men. "Private Brennan."

"I might of bloody well known it." Private Brennan ran his hand resignedly through his fair curly hair as the carriage broke into the one easy laugh, the sort of laugh that comes from an inner spring of feeling and is ready to greet even the feeblest joke. "The flaming chain of command. Forget I mentioned it. I don't care if we're stuck out here all day.

The sheilas can wait. They been waiting two and a half years for me."

"Get a load of him! Six months longer than the rest of us. Tell us about your war experiences, dig. You were with the Sixth Div., weren't you, dig? The mob that lost the war in Greece, weren't you, dig?"

"I heard the bugle when they blew it the first time." Joe Brennan had gone to the Middle East with the first convoy of Sixth Division troops in January 1940, and had transferred to this Seventh Division battalion after the Greece and Crete campaigns. He was the only man in the battalion who had tasted the sobering bitterness of defeat, and he was that much a better soldier because of it: he would never again under-estimate the enemy. "They didn't have to send me an invitation like they did you mugs."

"They didn't invite us, they advertised. It was in the Positions Vacant column in the *Herald*. Good jobs, it said. Five bob a day and all found. Pensions if you survive, it said."

"I'd of been in sooner. I was looking around for a good job on the home front, that was all. But I was too late. All the bookies and jockeys had 'em."

"I was making three thousand quid a year, meself, at the time. But I chucked it all up——"

"Bull, you were on the dole like the rest of us!"

The chi-acking went on, anything to fill in the waiting minutes, long and unsettling as the minutes just before an attack. It was all the same, Radcliffe thought: farewell, war, return, all of it waiting and very little else. He had the sudden feeling he had been waiting all his life, that to-morrow was the only real ambition; from the slapping palm on the new-living buttocks to the gentle fingers on the new-dead eyelids, one spent one's time in waiting. He moved uneasily, all at once feeling impatient and a little afraid; then seeking reassurance, he leaned across Greg Morley and looked down at Jack Savanna.

"How do you feel?"

"Like a girl on her wedding night." Savanna's face, though long and bony like his body, was not unhandsome; when he smiled it was surprisingly boyish. The smile belied the eyes and the drawling voice; a natural faith struggled hard against an acquired cynicism. He had seen too much too young: the cruelty in the dormitory, the stranger rising confusedly from his mother's bed, his dead and bloody father; but some relic of childhood struggled through and made him liked even by those he insulted. "Although, being a bachelor, I can only use my imagination in choosing such a simile. You married wrecks would know better than I."

"Christ, I wish they'd get a move on!" Morley's voice was petulant with impatience.

"You expecting Sarah to be at the station?" Radcliffe was asking himself the same question: would Dinah be there, would she have changed? It was their first time away from each other and he was surprised how, now at the time for reunion, it had frightened him.

"Oh, she'll be there, all right." The petulance was gone from Morley's voice immediately: any mention of his wife could only have the effect of wiping out the mood of a moment before. He had always been ready to talk about her and she was as well-known as any film star or racehorse to his many friends in the battalion. Her photo had occupied pride of place in the pin-ups in the tent he had shared with three other sergeants, above a line of anonymous nudes and between Rita Hayworth and, the choice of the orderly-room sergeant, Tamara Toumanova. "She hasn't failed yet."

"Sure of yourself, aren't you?" said Savanna, and only Radcliffe detected the faint bitterness under the banter. "The conceit of the married man."

"The poor kid's probably been waiting there an hour," Morley said.

"God, listen to him!" said Savanna. "It's only you married bastards who believe women are so faithful."

"It's only we married bastards who *know*," Radcliffe grinned.

"How far out are we?" said Morley. "Can you see the platform from here?"

"Better strap him down." Savanna sat up, then slowly got to his feet, untangling his length. He was several inches over six feet and seemed to be all bone, though broad and heavy bone. Then one looked again and noticed there was also a good deal of muscle, and realised here was a man tough enough to battle a team of bullocks or a whole company of men. It was a shock to learn that in civilian life he had been only a radio announcer. He affected a thick Air Force type moustache and his blond hair was long enough to have begun to curl on his neck. He was a mixture the men had never understood. Several of them had seen him in civilian clothes while on leave before they had gone overseas, and he had been wearing suède shoes; but as Basher Hanna had said, there was no accounting for taste, for he had once known a bloke who wore gloves even when it wasn't cold. The men had never understood him, but they liked and admired him.

Not that Jack Savanna cared much what people thought of him. He stretched himself now, his bones cracking, then slapped Morley heartily on the back. "We don't want you jumping out the window and galloping up to the platform."

The carriage had quietened down. Some of the men had begun to put on their webbing and packs as long as twenty minutes before, and now they were beginning to feel the effects of trying to move in the cramped space with such awkward loads. Their kit bags, packed with souvenirs for the kids and dirty clothes for the wife to wash, added to the

to be, as far as the general public is concerned. I wouldn't have told you if I hadn't known what a close-mouthed bastard you can be. Anyhow, you'll discover it for yourself when you get out into the field as a correspondent. Things are so bad, I don't know how we're going to keep it quiet much longer. Right now they've got MacArthur to hold their attention. You'd think Christ had come back to earth."

"What's he like?" Vern said. "The boys haven't been impressed. His type of soldier doesn't go down too well with the Aussie, all that grandiloquent bull of his."

"Well, they'd better get used to the grandiloquent bull. He's here as boss."

"Blamey won't like that."

"Blamey will look after himself," Fredericks said with a grin. "I'm no admirer of him personally, but he's the bloke we want if we're to have any say in the way things are run. MacArthur reckons he has God on his side. He'll need Him, if he's to push Tom Blamey around." Then he tossed the two generals out the window and said, "How much leave have you?"

"Eight days. I report back next Monday morning to Ingleburn. Where we go from there, and when, I haven't the faintest."

"Righto, call me at home Sunday. It's still the same place, Macleay Street, and the number is in the book. You just need an American visa to come up there now, that's all. How are the wife and kids?"

"Fine. I'm like a stranger in the house, seeing them for the first time. I just sit back and admire the three of them, and feel bloody proud of myself."

"Good for you." Fredericks extended a plump hand across the desk; Vern had forgotten the strength in the plump fingers. "I'm glad to see you got back all right, Vern."

Vern said good-bye to Fredericks, promising to give a lot

of thought to the war corrrespondent offer, and went out to
the lift. It was operated now by a girl, instead of the World
War I veteran who had been there for years (had he gone back
into the Army? Some people didn't know when enough was
enough. But Vern had noticed when war first broke out that
the older men had rushed just as quickly as the young men to
enlist). The girl was a blonde who munched on bubble gum,
and gave him a franker stare than he had been accustomed to
from Australian girls before the war. She stood leaning on
the power handle, one hip thrown out in an attempt at dis-
location that was supposed to be provocative, a bubble now and
again hanging from her lips like an ectoplasmic burp. She
stared at him again as the lift bounced gently to a stop.

"Ground floor, loo-tenant."

"Thanks, babe," said Vern, and winked at her as he got out.
She smiled and watched him as he went out to the street, her
hip still thrown out, still blowing bubbles, one hand stroking
the blonde hair. Some of these Aussie boys weren't bad when
you came to think of it. Why, her sister Elsie had even married
one. . . .

Vern, unaware that he had almost been tagged as eligible,
had turned out of Elizabeth Street and into Martin Place.
He walked down and turned into George Street and was
walking against the crowd as he headed down towards the
harbour. The faces came swimming towards him above the
dark river of bodies. He looked for signs of worry or panic,
but there was none. True, some faces were unhappy, the eyes
a little dead and the mouths drooping in self-pity, but the
unhappiness was personal: a husband had been killed, a girl
had given back an engagement ring, there were bills to be paid
and no money. But there was no general mask of concern,
no nervous attitude that showed the crowd knew danger was
just around the corner. The Australian had always had the
reputation of being easy-going: to Vern's suddenly acute and

worried eye, he had never looked more easy-going than now. Vern walked on, beginning to have the first doubts that the country would have what was needed when the time came.

He skirted the wharves of Circular Quay and climbed the steps to the Bridge and walked out into the middle. He stood there and looked out at home. It was an Australian early autumn day, no hint of dying in it, and the upper sky was streaked with thin cloud that looked like the brushings of a white wind. The light was clear and fine, and everything, even the smoke from ships in the harbour, had an edge to it. The sun put a silver sheen on the afternoon air and everything glittered with the sharpness of a poignant memory.

Above him the arch of the Bridge reared against the sky, a heavy tracery of steel touched with sun that went in a single curving leap from pylon to pylon, and the pylons themselves towered like bleached medieval forts above the polished harbour. The coloured roofs of Milson's Point and Mosman stretched away over their hills with a pointillism effect that danced before the eyes. A ferry came across the water, its hooter protesting in a sharp moan at nothing at all, and an American naval launch went over towards Garden Island, spreading a cool white fan behind it. Beyond the island he could see the grey shapes of an American cruiser and some destroyers; he looked away from them, a reminder of how close the war had come to home, and up towards the city. The buildings were stacked in confusion on top of each other, their windows flashing like small explosions and the shadows stretching down between them like black bombing scars. Already, he thought, the war is giving me my similes: I'm half-way to being a war correspondent.

He turned and walked back along the Bridge, now and again turning his head to look back at the harbour and the city sprawled about the hills. It all looked good, better even than the memory that had changed almost imperceptibly, like a growing child, as time had dripped down out of the glass and the desire to come home had grown stronger.

Home was where people worshipped racehorses and took no pride in work and drove the seeds of their culture overseas; but he didn't want it invaded nor did he want to leave it ever again.

"They offered me a job to-day as a war correspondent," he said.

"Gee, that's wonderful, Daddy," said Jill, and hastily swallowed a lump of meat. "My, won't the girls at school like this! Someone glamorous in the family!"

"Thank you," said Dinah. "Let me tell you, when I was in the chorus I was called glamorous, seductive——"

"Ah, you're all right, Mum," said Michael. "But being a chorus girl isn't like being a war correspondent."

"I told one of the nuns the other day that my mother had been a hoofer," said Jill. "She said she'd say a rosary for you."

"That's nice," said Dinah. "Tell her in return I'll put on my tights and do a bit at the school concert." She stabbed at a piece of kidney. "A hoofer!"

Michael was looking at his father. "Where will you go, Dad? Up to New Guinea? Will you get your name on your stories? Heck, I hope there's a war on when I grow up——"

"If there is," said Dinah, "I'll see you get a nice soft cop in a reserved occupation."

She said it without any particular emphasis, but Vern looked along the table at her. She smiled at him, a smile as unreadable as a chorus girl's. "Go on, darling. Did you take the job?"

"I haven't decided."

"Ah, 'struth!" Michael carved at the air with his knife, disgusted with a father who didn't recognise opportunity when it knocked. "Someone else will get it if you don't hurry up! I bet everyone on the paper wants——"

"Don't you want it, Daddy?" said Jill.

She was eleven, small but well-built, with her mother's features and her father's colouring, but with the temperament of neither of them. She already had all the poise that Vern had spent years trying to acquire; a trick of retiring into herself that made her completely beyond and independent of what went on about her; and an intelligence that sometimes dismayed Dinah.

Vern looked at her, aware that, with her uncanny sense of feeling, she knew something was troubling him. "I don't know. It's not something I can just say yes to, just like that——"

"I could," said Michael. "Ask me."

Dinah was the first to admit that her brain was little better than a chorus girl was required to have, but like her daughter she could sense when anything was worrying Vern. "Righto, Michael, we'll ask you when you leave school, in six or seven years' time. Now get on with your eating and let's forget all about the glamour."

Michael grinned, his blunt dark face suddenly like his father's. "Ah, you're only jealous. How'd you like to be a lady war correspondent?"

"I'd rather be top of the bill at the Tivoli," said Dinah. " And by golly, I would have been if it hadn't been for you two coming along."

"Other women have had babies and continued their theatrical careers," said Jill. "Even hoofers."

"When you're married and going to have a baby," said Dinah, " let me see *you* do the can-can."

Vern again felt the sudden warmth that had come over him several times in the two days since he had arrived home. The children had developed amazingly in the two years he had been away, and his pride in them was like a heady tonic. But what pleased him more was the intimate, almost adult relationship they had with their mother. That, he realised, had come about because of his absence: she had encouraged it, perhaps unwittingly, to make up for what she had missed by his being away. The family seemed to have become tighter knit while he had been away, and yet he didn't feel out of it. Dinah had kept him a part of it, and he looked along the table at her now and loved her more even than in the lonely moments overseas.

Later when they were going to bed she took off all her clothes and stood in front of the big wardrobe mirror. She turned side on and patted her stomach. "Think I've got fat while you've been away? I went on a diet when I knew you were coming home, even did exercises. Hoofer's exercises."

Vern hung his trousers in the closet. "The belly's all right, but I detect a slight droop in the bosom."

"What do you expect at thirty-two? You wanted to marry a thirty-six inch chest. I remember distinctly that was the first thing you said to me after you'd asked my name. You said I had a magnificent chest."

"And I remember you shoved it out a little more." Vern had sat down and begun to take off his shoes and socks. "I had to stand back to make room."

"Well, the older I get, the tireder I get holding it up. But while you're home I'll make a special effort." She drew back her shoulders. "There, how's that? My God, you're lucky, you know."

He was, he knew that. Her bosom had deepened after the birth of the two children, but it was still firm and lovely. Her waist was slim and there was no thickening over the hips; they curved, then came in a smooth sweep to her long thighs. No birth wrinkles marred her stomach: her slightest movement brought exciting shadows to the firm modelling of it. And the face with its good wide bonework, short straight nose, dark sparkling eyes that could suddenly become lazy-lidded, all of it backed by the shining black hair, had remained vividly clear in his memory over the last two years. She wasn't strictly beautiful, but she was Dinah and there was no one else. He was lucky, all right.

"There are a lot of men who would give their right arm to get into bed with a body like this," she said.

"Good-o, try your luck some time. We'll collect right arms."

She had climbed into bed. "Come on! God, I've never seen a man so slow at getting into bed. Are you as slow as this in the Army? You must get in just in time to get up again for reveille."

"I don't have naked women in my bed in the Army."

"It's not making you move any faster now. Why the hell did I have to marry such a damned neat man? Drop your clothes on the floor and get in here quick!"

He got into bed and put his arms about her. There had never been anyone before her, and he was as excited now as he had been the first time. They had had no trouble discovering each other in those early days and their love-making had been successful from the start. But now he was trying to restrain himself. He hadn't yet become accustomed again to the idea of having his wife beside him in bed each night. It was like a second honeymoon: everything, the smoothness, the intimacy, the claiming surrender, was still a little unbelievable.

But now he was beside her she had suddenly quietened down. "Darling, what is it about the job as a war correspondent?"

"What do you mean?"

"You don't really want it, do you? Wouldn't it be a good job?"

"Better than I've ever had before," he said, and all at once was surprised how remote he felt from the newspaper office. Two years ago he would have been excited about the job, would have lain awake well into the night to talk with her about it. Now it was as if the job had been offered to someone else, someone he knew but wasn't particularly interested in. "Remember how ambitious I used to be? This could be the answer. I might finish up famous, make a lot of money——"

His voice trailed off and after a while she said, "So what's holding you back? Am I too dumb to see something?"

"No." He grinned in the darkness and patted her shoulder; sometimes she was more of a child to him than the two youngsters in their rooms down the hall. "Though I don't know if you'll understand when I do explain it to you——"

"Thanks," she said. "I'm not dumb, just a little backward."

But he hadn't heard her. "I don't know that I completely understand it, myself. Darl, I don't want the correspondent's job, because I want to prove myself to myself." She made no comment and he went on, "I've been an officer now for nearly two years. In another month or so my third pip will be through——"

"Captain Radcliffe," she said, testing it for sound. "You didn't tell me."

"I was going to surprise you. I know how rank-conscious you women are."

"I'm just surprised you're not a colonel by now. The Army doesn't appreciate you like I do. I think you're wonderful." She moved closer to him, if that were possible. "The hope of the nation."

"Thank you," he said, and patted her shoulder again. "Trouble is, I don't think I'm so wonderful. Darl, for two years now I've been responsible for other men and I still don't know if I'm big enough for the responsibility. I've never been tested. Every time we were in action in the Middle East there was never a time when a decision rested wholly on me. There was always someone there who out-ranked me, and all I had to do was carry out their orders. And what I don't like is that I was always glad they were there."

"Is that something to be ashamed of?"

"Maybe it is, maybe it isn't. I haven't thought about shame, because no one else knows about it. But I worry—am I good enough to be responsible for the lives of other men?"

"The Army must have thought so."

"One of the things you learn in the Army, darling, is that it is far from infallible. It has a greater talent for making mistakes than any other organisation yet devised. I could be one of its major mistakes."

She was silent for a while, then she said, "How you feel—is it really so important?"

He said nothing for a while, wondering if she would understand when he did tell her. Women had a greater sense of responsibility than men, but they also had a different perspective. There were certain things that a man saw in himself, questions that worried him and had to be answered, that a woman could never take too seriously. Honour, for instance. Women had a sense of honour, but they were rarely foolish or heroic about it: they were not so afraid of the alternative, dishonour, because they had a greater armour against shame. Would Dinah understand, or think him a fool, playing up to some schoolboy code?

At last he made the confession: "It's important to me, darl. More important than the job as a war correspondent. If I take that, I'll never know if I had what it takes when the moment called for it. I don't want to be a hero. I just want to know that I'm not a coward." He turned and looked at the dark mass of her head on the pillow beside him; in the darkness he couldn't see her face and (cowardly, he thought) it was better that way. "Do you understand what I'm getting at, darl?"

"Does a woman ever understand a man?" It was the answer he had half-expected. "I don't want to understand it, darling. If it's the way you feel, then it's all right with me." He could feel her fingers digging into his back. "I just don't want to lose you, that's all."

"I could be killed just as easily as a war correspondent,"
he said, and knew at once that he was being cruel; he ran his
hands gently over her. "Don't let's think about that part of
it, darl. I'm not going to shove my neck out to prove I'm not
a coward. I'm not searching for physical courage, although I
don't know that I have an abundance of that, either. It's
something else again, something I'd like to know I had, even
if I never have to use it but once."

"I said it a moment ago, Vern. If it's what you want, it's
all right with me. I told you a long time ago, all I want is
for you to be happy. And that includes every way, in the Army
or out of it."

There was no answer but to kiss her, to draw her to him and
take the love that he sometimes felt was more than he deserved.
Life had been a long climb over the rocks before he had met
her, and disappointment had lost its bitterness for him. When
he had met her he had expected something to go wrong with
their love as a matter of course, but it never had. It had been
a long time before the surprise had worn off that she loved him
completely and forever.

She murmured sleepily as he held her to him, and the bed
creaked as she moved closer to him. Outside in the street some
youths laughed as they came up the hill from the picture
theatre, and in the Hastings' house next door he could hear
the phone ringing peremptorily but in vain. A car went
swishing by and a cat cried mournfully at the night; the
phone next door stopped ringing and the youths had gone on,
and abruptly there was silence.

The sounds I've missed, he thought, and almost instantly
fell asleep with his face buried in his wife's neck.

Standing there in the bar, amid the loud foreign-sounding
babble of the hundreds of anonymous voices and beneath the
thick blue smoke climbing lazily to the ceiling like diaphanous

vines, he thought of the bazaars they had visited back in the
Middle East and their superior comments on them, and he
smiled to himself.

"What's so funny, chum?" said Jack Savanna.

"Just thinking."

"Well, quit thinking and start drinking. We're waiting to
order again."

Just before the train had drawn in at Central Station and
each of them had been whirled into the tight embracing circle
of his own welcome home, several of the men had arranged
to meet here in the Marble Bar this evening. In the confusion
at the station, embracing wives or girl friends at the same
time as they wished each other a good leave, saying hallo to
relatives while they shouted *See you in the Marble Bar!* they
had forgotten that the civilised drinking customs of the backward Middle East were now behind them. They were in
civilised Australia again with its backward drinking customs,
away from the Wogs and back with the wowsers, and one
just didn't join one's friends for a drink at the Marble Bar
or any other bar. Drinking in Sydney wasn't as simple as
that.

Vern had come in from the street, had looked about him,
seen Jack Savanna waving to him above the heads of the crowd
like a man calling for help in the middle of a riot, and had
prepared for battle. He had taken a deep breath, raised his arms
in front of him so that his elbows had stuck out like cow-
catchers, and had ploughed his way through the sweating,
yelling crush that is the Australian man in his leisure moments
after a day's work. Some day, perhaps, the blue laws that
closed all hotels at six o'clock would be rescinded. In the
meantime the wowsers, the narrow-minded of certain churches
and societies, went smugly on in their belief that Sydney was
being saved from further degradation by having limited
drinking hours. Vern arrived at the bar bruised, dishevelled

and feeling more degraded that if he had come by way of the sewer.

"With this sort of training," he had said, "we can't lose the war."

The second round of drinks arrived, dumped in front of them by the cheerful, durable barmaid. She had the hard brassy brightness of those women who would be out of a job if there were no men.

"Who's your friend?" she said to Jack Savanna. "Another boy from your unit?"

"This is Mabel, Vern," Jack said. Mabel smiled at Vern as if he were the only boy in the world, winked at him as if she knew all about him, then went away down the bar. Jack looked after her, then turned back. "Well, how's the leave going? How are Dinah and the kids, chum?"

"Fine." Vern sipped his beer, the good strong Australian stuff that made all the other beers taste like waste water. "What have you been doing?"

"Just taking things quietly," said Jack. "Sort of easing myself back into Sydney so the impact won't be too much for the population. But I'll have to start stepping out soon if I want to get something out of my leave. Celibacy shouldn't be one of the aims of such an occasion."

Vern turned to the two men nearest him, Bluey Brown and Dad Mackenzie. "What sort of leave are you having? Has celibacy been one of your aims?"

"I'm too bloody old," said Bluey Brown. "I'd like to know I had the choice of being celibate or not. I'm known as Old Impotence in our house."

Staff-sergeant Brown had been a First World War man, and had only got into the current show by putting his age back and because he had been a member of the same club as the battalion's first C.O. Vern knew that Bluey could have had a commission as the battalion quartermaster, but for his own

C

reasons he had preferred to be nothing more than an N.C.O. He was forty-eight, cheerfully plump, his red hair was now only a suggestion, like rosy cirrus clouds round the beaming sun of his face, and he was the most popular man in the whole battalion despite the fact that he was the company quartermaster sergeant.

Dad Mackenzie grinned, the smile as cautious as everything else he did. "Things have changed since we went away. The chookies seem much easier."

"Influence of the Yanks," said Jack Savanna. "I don't know that it is a bad thing."

"You wouldn't," said Vern. "I can't ever remember you supporting the morals of the community. You were always doing your best to bring about a lowering of them." He had known Jack before the war, when the latter had worked for the Australian Broadcasting Commission: not much more than casually, but enough to know that Jack was something of a rake. "Easy chookies, as Dad calls them, were always your meat."

"In this particular instance," said Jack, "I am trying to be impersonal. I am looking at the picture from a distance, as it were. I have a great interest in the future of Australian womanhood."

"He's a nephew of Dorothy Dix," Bluey Brown told Dad Mackenzie.

"Go on?" said Dad Mackenzie. "Legitimate or illegitimate?"

Jack hadn't heard the interruptions. "I think a leavening of the Americans' preoccupation with sex, their wonderfully uninhibited attitude towards it—at least while they're abroad—may do something towards breaking down the broad, if not admitted, puritanical streak in our national make-up."

"I haven't detected any broad puritanical streak in you," said Bluey. "Turn around and let's have a look."

"I have done my best to eradicate it," said Jack.

"You've been eminently successful," said Vern, then turned round to see Charlie Fogarty grinning at them. "Hallo, Charlie. What the hell's that you're drinking?"

"Shandy," said Charlie. "Three parts lemonade, one part beer. It saves the barmaid embarrassment."

"Meaning?"

"Some of them don't know if they ought to sell an aborigine grog, even if he *is* in uniform. This saves 'em having to ask the boss if it's all right."

Charlie Fogarty was the best-looking aborigine Vern had ever seen. He was tall and broad-shouldered and his smile was as wide and bright as sheet lightning. His voice was soft and musical, the voice of a man who belonged to broad sunlit plains and singing streams; it wasn't an apologetic voice, but Vern couldn't imagine its ever being dogmatic or insistent. He knew Charlie's story, it stretched behind him like a travelogue of Australia. The mission in the Northern Territory where they had made him conscious of his magnificent black body by putting it in white man's clothing; the cattle station in western Queensland; the abattoirs in Brisbane; the flour mill in Sydney; the army camp at Ingleburn—he was more Australian than any of them, but he was also more alien.

"I wonder how they'll treat you coves after this is over?" said Vern.

Charlie smiled again, not a trace of bitterness in his dark shining face. "I'm thinking of going back to the tribe. Then we're gunna bring in a Black Australia policy and kick all you white bastards out of the country."

"Speaking of bastards," said Dad Mackenzie.

They all turned, and for a moment Vern didn't recognise the burly figure in the tight blue suit pushing its way through the crowd towards them. Then suddenly he remembered the figure as it had been in khaki, remembered the arrogance and stupid discipline and petty spite of ex-Major Caulfield, and he knew this was going to be an awkward moment.

"Hallo, men," said Caulfield, and the smile on his face was as shaky as a scaffolding in a gale. The big red face with the dark freckles on the forehead and across the broad nose did its best to look friendly; but, as one, the five men turned back to the bar, picked up their drinks and stood in silence. Farther along, two other men from the battalion, Joe Brennan and Mick Kennedy, interrupted their close confab and stood looking silently at Caulfield. Vern, looking down at his drink, knew that Caulfield could hear that silence more than he could hear the hubbub of voices or the occasional shout.

Caulfield stood there behind them for a moment and Vern could only guess at the expression on his face; then he said, "Ah, come on, let's forget all about rank for just this once. Just call me Jim."

No one moved and Vern felt the prickle of embarrassment spreading through him: he had never had the defensive thick skin of a superiority complex. He was sensitive to other people's feelings, even to those he disliked. He could feel Caulfield's reaction almost as much as if it were his own when Jack Savanna turned slowly from the bar and said, contempt thick as spittle in his mouth, "Why should we call you *anything?*"

Jack raised his glass, looking at it and not at Caulfield, took a drink, and just as slowly turned back to the bar. Then Bluey Brown said, "If I called him anything, it wouldn't be Jim." He smiled at Mabel, the barmaid, who stood at the taps just in front of them. "You wouldn't like to hear me using bad language, would you, love?"

"Why, what've I done now?" Then Mabel caught sight of Caulfield clinging to the edge of the group like a giant limpet. "Hallo, is this another of your boys?"

"No," said Bluey. "He's one of our bastards."

Then Vern felt the touch of his arm and knew what he had feared had come. "Hallo, Vern. How's tricks?"

Vern could feel the others waiting to see what move he would make. He was the only one who, as far as the Army was concerned, could meet Caulfield on a social level: rank called to rank, the only caste system, outside of money, that Australians had so far had to contend with. Vern remembered with what resentment the Australians had viewed the *Officers Only* signs outside the hotels in the Middle East; and now here was Caulfield trying to strike up a conversation on an Officers Only basis.

"Hallo, Ape." It was the first time Vern had called him that, the name the battalion had given him two days after he had joined it; Vern, with a thought for discipline, had never referred to Caulfield by that name even in private conversation with the other men. He stood there looking at Caulfield, wondering why the latter had deliberately walked into such a situation, then suddenly he knew. Caulfield took the insult without a blink, as if he had been expecting it and was prepared for it. He had been slapped across the face with the past and he had taken it without any of the violent outburst that might have been expected. Vern knew then that he was lonely. The man had been invalided home six months before, after the Syrian campaign, and he had found that it was home no longer.

"Ah, we can let bygones be bygones, can't we?" He licked his thick lips and smiled tentatively. "I'm another bloke altogether now."

"A leopard can't change his spots," said Bluey. "Neither can an arch-bastard."

"A very true statement, staff," said Jack. "Your own?"

"Just made it up," said Bluey. "Inspiration."

Dad Mackenzie turned round and Vern was surprised at the fire in the heavy stolid face. "You were an officer and a gentleman, Caulfield, while you had a crown on your shoulder. An officer and a gentleman, by the King's permission." Dad Mackenzie's grandfather had been a Glasgow Scot and his grandmother a London Jewess, and he'd inherited all the caution of both races. But he had still been one of those who had suffered at Caulfield's hands, just as much as the reckless types like Greg Morley and larrikins like Mick Kennedy. There was no hint of caution now in Dad, just a quiet hatred that was more chilling than any display of anger. "The King doesn't know you like we do. You're not a gentleman, Caulfield, you're not even an officer, because an officer is someone who deserves to be in charge of men. You shouldn't even be in charge of dogs in the council pound."

There was another silence, then a drunken soldier stumbled out of the crowd and bumped into Caulfield. The latter spun round, anger in his eyes ready to be turned on anyone, but the drunk put his arm about him and hiccupped loudly in his ear.

"G'day, dig. Me ol' mate, me cobber. Everybody's me mate to-day. Ain't it a lovely day? It's a lovely day to-day, not t'morrer, like the song says. Plentya beer and lotsa people. 'At's what I like. It's me birthday, dig. Many happy returns. Thanks. It's me birthday and everybody's me mate. Hoo-ray."

He patted Caulfield on the shoulder, beamed droopily at the others, then stumbled on in search of another mate. Caulfield looked after him, then back at Vern and the others.

"You ought to have gone with him, Ape." Mick Kennedy spoke for the first time. He had always been one of the loudest in his hatred of Caulfield, and his voice now carried far enough to attract the attention of the policeman who had just come in the door. Vern saw the policeman look towards them, and he hoped Mick Kennedy wouldn't run true to form and start a brawl. But Mick looked as if he was quite satisfied to use his tongue this time instead of his fists. "He wanted to be your mate, Ape. You ain't in a position to knock back offers like that."

Caulfield suddenly threw away the air of friendliness he had brought with him, almost with an expression of relief, as if he had known from the start that it would be useless. He put his hands behind his back and rocked back on his heels; the pose was familiar to the men leaning against the bar, but it was out of place here.

"This is going to be good," said Bluey. "Company, shun!"

"Righto," said Caulfield. "So I made a mistake. I tried to be a good soldier, but it wasn't your idea of what a good soldier should be. All right. But there were some of you who weren't good soldiers, some of you who were up before me more times than I can remember, who weren't *my* idea of a good soldier. Some of you had rank, but I'll tell you now I only agreed to your promotions because there was no one else. But I'm forgetting that——"

"Generous to a fault," said Jack Savanna.

"——Those days and those mistakes are past." He stopped, suddenly lost, as if he had just realised he wasn't on the parade ground and that the men in front of him couldn't be dismissed. He brought his hands from behind his back and shoved the right one, with its stumps of fingers, into his jacket pocket. He had dropped his parade ground voice when at last he said, "I was hoping we could make a new start."

It was Jack Savanna who answered. Vern knew that, with his rank, he was the one who should have answered for the men and while Caulfield had been talking he had been searching for the words to reply to him. But now they wouldn't be needed. Jack, drawing himself up to his full height, his hat pushed back on his head, his sweeping moustache accentuating the curl of his lip, had taken over.

"I doubt that your brain, Caulfield, shrivelled as a piece

of old copra, could understand how we feel about you. You were all right as a soldier, perhaps—at least you had guts, which not all us of profess to have. But you weren't a man, that's our complaint. We know something of your background, that you spent fifteen years in New Guinea before you came into the Army, and perhaps that's to blame. I'm told that only missionaries and fools treat boongs as human beings —and you had some idea that everyone in the Army was a boong." Jack cocked an eye at Charlie Fogarty. "You will forgive my using the term *boong*, Charlie? I am trying to speak in this bastard's language."

"Go ahead," grinned Charlie. "In the tribe we'd call him a white boong."

"Stay out of this, darkie!" Caulfield snapped.

The men straightened up and Vern tensed, ready to step in front of Jack Savanna, expecting the latter to swing his fist into Caulfield's furious red face. He had seen Jack in action several times when he had lost his temper; time and place meant nothing to him if he thought a swung fist was the answer needed. Caulfield seemed suddenly aware that his incautious tongue had gone too far again, and he took a step back. He was pressed against the crowd as against a wall, his eyes flickering over the men without fear but expecting them to move towards him, and Vern waited for the moment to blow up.

"Sock the bastard!" Mick Kennedy snarled.

"Pull your heads in," Vern said, and tried to sound reasonable and not like an officer throwing his weight around. "He's not worth the strife it would cause. There's a copper over there."

"You're right, Vern." Jack Savanna was surprisingly calm. He looked again at Charlie Fogarty. "Although we'll hit him if you like, Charlie."

"Skip it," said Charlie, and looked at Caulfield with a dark, impassive face. He's got more dignity than the rest of us put together, Vern thought.

Jack turned back to Caulfield. "You're fortunate, Caulfield. But don't ever make a remark like that again while we're around. You've just illustrated what I was saying about your thinking everyone in the Army is a boong. It may surprise you, but to every one of us here, Charlie is just a man who's a little more sunburned than the rest of us. But you would never be able to see it that way. You have to be a man, Caulfield, to know how to treat men properly. And you never knew how to treat us. If the boongs disliked you as much as we did, then I shouldn't go back to New Guinea if I were you. Not now, when they could blame your death on the Japs."

Caulfield's face got redder, the freckles turning almost black, but before he had a chance to speak the men had turned back to the bar; and there was that little island of silence again in that sea of noise. Vern stood there waiting for the burst of temper that they all knew of old.

But Caulfield just muttered, "You'll be sorry for this," and when Vern looked back over his shoulder he had gone.

"I've been waiting to say that for two bloody years," said Jack. "In the circumstances I thought I was remarkably restrained."

"Too bloody restrained," said Mick Kennedy. "I'd of jobbed him if I'd been closer to him."

"I wanted to job him," said Bluey. "Trouble is, my days of jobbing people are over. Even with that bung hand of his, he'd have knocked me arse-over-Bluey." He looked wistfully into his glass. "You miss a lot when you get past forty."

" 'I'm another bloke,' he said." Joe Brennan almost spat into his beer. " ' Let's make a new start.' Christ, what does he think we are, lovers?"

"Now in the tribe," said Charlie Fogarty, and sipped his

shandy, "we would've pointed the bone at him, and he'd of been dead in a week. You blokes are too civilised."

Vern had been thinking of all they had had to put up with in the time Caulfield had been with them. The sarcastic arrogant way he had of talking to the men; the looking after his own comfort and ignoring that of those under him; the trivial rules instituted just to show his authority. The company after a while had called itself Caulfield's Boongs, and had put up with him with good-humoured resignation Then the good humour had begun to run dry and threats were muttered against him. On the trip to the Middle East he had headed the shark-bait list; but somehow he had landed safely in Palestine and had survived the months spent there and at Mersa Matruh. Then the battalion had gone into the Syrian campaign and he had had his hand mangled by a shell splinter, and he had been invalided home to the accompaniment of loud cheers from the men. Vern had never seen anyone hated so much, and now here was the man daring to come back and ask that the past be forgotten. Was he so thick-skinned or just blind or did he have more guts than the men, though reluctantly, had conceded him? And what had he meant by his remark that they would be sorry?

CHAPTER THREE

JACK watched Vern Radcliffe board the tram, waved at him, then turned away with the feeling of being lost that had kept recurring ever since they had first landed back at Adelaide. Vern had asked him home for dinner, and he had almost accepted. But then he had recognised the invitation for what it was, sincere but a spur-of-the-moment thought; he had thought of Dinah sharing the moments with her husband after two long years, and so he had told Vern he had a date.

Well, he'd better see if he *did* have a date. He crossed the road to St. James station, lined up outside the phone box and ten minutes later was dialling a number, conscious of the thick stuffy smell of the box and the belligerently impatient queue outside.

"Rita? This is Jack here."

"Jack? Jack who?" Her voice sounded the same, light and empty as her head.

"Jack Savanna. How many Jacks do you know?" They had once lived together for three months, but now she had forgotten him. He grinned to himself and patted his bruised ego.

"Jack *Savanna!* Well, Ah declare! How you been, huh?" Her voice *had* changed, after all: it had crossed the Pacific. "Long time no see, Jack, honey."

Why did I ring her? he thought, and thought what a trap was the telephone. In the old days, when one had to write

43

a letter there was always time for a second thought. But now: two pennies in the slot, a spin of the dial, and bingo! Why had he called her? Rita, with the blank pretty face, the pretty blank mind and the beautiful body—yes, that was why he had called her. "I've missed you, too, Rita, *honey*. How about dinner to-night, and afterwards we can talk about old times, huh?"

"Ah gee, Jack honey, if I'd only known! But I already gotta go out—I'm gonna see "—he could hear her two-stroke brain changing gears—"my aunt."

"Your ant? Are you interested in entomology now?"

She laughed, light and meaningless as a child's bell. "Still the same old Jack! Still making with the big words."

Serves me right, he thought, for having designs on her body. He hadn't taken her mind into account, and he was beaten before he had started. Suddenly the box seemed more stinking and stuffy than ever. Abruptly he said good-bye, hung up and pushed open the door.

"You been long enough, dig," said a sailor. "Who you been ringing, MacArthur?"

Jack hunched his shoulders. "Want to make something of it, matelot?"

"I gotta ring me sheila," said the sailor, and skipped nimbly into the box. He grinned through the glass, then turned to the phone, a red-headed, broken-nosed, freckle-faced Romeo who was sure of his girl.

Jack walked past the other people waiting to use the phone and out into Elizabeth Street again. It was a mild night with light still in the sky behind the buildings on the west side of the street. Right above him a few stars, poignant as tears, looked down at the city. A plane appeared from behind the towers of St. Mary's Basilica, a metal angel with winking red and green lights, heading north; it passed over the harbour, suddenly an angel no longer but a small black fly caught in the tangled skein of the searchlights. I should be on that, he thought, getting out of this bloody unfriendly city. And then was angry at himself for being sorry for himself.

He looked about him, aware now of a change in the atmosphere of the city he had loved so well. There was that air of electric nervousness that came upon all cities at this time of day during the war. In London and Cairo and Berlin, and in all cities within reach of the bombers, there would be fear behind the nervousness; here in Sydney and in Melbourne, probably New York too and San Francisco, there was just the hope of a good time. Girls stood waiting for their men, looking at other men, wondering if they were better prospects than their date for to-night: modesty had become a wartime casualty and had been replaced by the roving eye and the calculating mind. Couples walked arm-in-arm out of the great green bed of Hyde Park, flushed with love-making and stained with grass juice. An American sailor, his arm about a brazenly successful girl, stood on the kerb waiting confidently for the cab that would come to him past all the hailing Australian arms. The city had changed, all right.

He began to walk along Elizabeth Street, aimless and lost in the city that was his home, big Jack Savanna who was always so definite and self-possessed and impregnable. Then he heard the music coming across the park and suddenly he remembered the Anzac Buffet. There would be girls there, plenty of them, all dedicated to the enjoyment of the boys on leave. He turned and began to hurry across the park, almost as if he had to get there before the supply of girls ran out. He wasn't drunk, he'd had only four beers with the boys in the Marble Bar, but he suddenly had the pleasant lightness of feeling, that warmth that makes the world a good place that must be enjoyed to the full, and his low mood of the last quarter-hour had suddenly gone like the last light of day behind the buildings across the street. He was determined to enjoy to-night.

He saw the girl as soon as he entered the large hall where the band was bouncing out *Chattanooga Choo-Choo*. She was sitting in a deep chair, turned away from him, and all he could see was the smooth blonde hair, almost silvery and suggesting metal in its polished sleekness. He stood for several minutes watching the blonde head, waiting for it to turn and let him see the face that went with it. He had seen plenty of girls who looked like Miss Australia from the back and like the wreck of someone's grandmother from the front. To-night had suddenly become too good to spoil by being in a hurry. Then he saw an R.A.A.F. corporal coming from the other side of the room, heading for the blonde in the chair: the expression on the corporal's face, the way he was smoothing his hair, the hand straightening his tie, told Jack that the girl could not be too bad. He had to take a chance, otherwise he might miss out and spend the rest of the night kicking himself.

He beat the corporal by a good two yards, without appearing to hurry, lazy and casual, the approach that had been so successful in the past. " Would you care to dance?"

She looked up at him, and he could guess at the disappointment of the corporal behind him. She was even better than he had expected, much better: with the all-out war effort, beauty standards had been raised in the leave centres. Perhaps her beauty had frightened away most of the other men, because a girl as good-looking as this must surely be booked for the night and she was just waiting for her boy-friend to arrive. Her face was an original one: nothing about it had been borrowed from film stars or cover girls or beauty salons. The bones were strong yet fine, and her skin glowed like a golden peach bursting with sun. Her mouth was heavy, but the lipstick covered only the natural outline of her lips: the passionate mouth couldn't be wiped off with a handkerchief or a kiss. Her eyes were dark, too dark really for the colour of her hair, though the latter looked natural, and when she looked up at him they shone with a soft amused gleam under their heavy lids.

She nodded to the girl she had been talking to, and stood up. She was taller than he had expected, but not too tall; big though he was himself, he didn't like women to look as if they could swing an axe or carry a banner at the head of an army.

The silver-haired girl was wearing a light grey jersey frock with short sleeves, and it showed off the deep tan she still retained from summer. It also showed off her body. With the blonde sleekness of her head and the deep tan he had somehow expected her to be the athletic type, all the curves slim and firm and almost a little muscular. He had seen that type of girl in Russell Flint paintings and on the beaches, healthy and vital and always somehow a little disappointing, as if one knew all their passion had dried out with the exercise in the sun. But this girl was built like a *woman*, soft yet firm, and the sun had only kindled her passion.

"Do I pass?" She danced with a lazy sort of rhythm, as if her body was tired and she would rather be in bed.

He grinned, and they danced for a while, easily and well: they could have been old partners. "I'm Jack Savanna."

"Silver Bendixter," she said, and saw his eyebrows go up. "You have heard of me?"

"I used to read the Society columns in the Sunday papers in the Red Shield hut," he said. "One read anything and everything in the Middle East."

"Fame, fame." She shook her head slowly and a lock of the blonde hair fell down. When she looked up again she was smiling and he was surprised at how soft and young-looking her face had become with its unexpected dimples. "Are you sure it was me you read about, or my mother or my sister?"

"It could have been all three. The Bendixters are pillars of Sydney Society, aren't they?"

"Don't sneer."

"Forgive me. It's my proletarian upbringing." Then he said, "There was a fellow in our unit who knew you, or said he did. Tony Shelley."

"A stinker, if ever there was one, "she said calmly. "A rat, and a friend of my sister."

"I didn't like him, either." He twisted his head to look at the hand resting on his shoulder. "Are you engaged or anything?"

She held up bare fingers. "Or nothing. I'm completely unattached, if that will put your mind at rest. Were you thinking of proposing, or don't the proletariat propose to pillars of Society?"

"Oh, we do, by all means. It's the proletarian blood that keeps Society alive. But that wasn't why I asked."

She smiled. "Is something the matter, then?"

"Yes. A girl as beautiful as you shouldn't be unattached. I'm prying into your private affairs and I'm unashamed about it, but have you lost a man in the war?"

"No. I'm just unattached, that's all."

There was a faint note of bitterness in her voice, but he didn't comment on it. He decided he was going to learn all there was to know about this girl, and there would be time. He grinned down at her, liking the way her cheeks shadowed with the dimples as she smiled back, and he thanked his luck that dear dumb Rita had had a date with her "ant."

"In The Mood" finished, then there was "Dolores." After that a girl got up before the band and wailed that she didn't "Wanna Set The World On Fire"; and didn't. Songs hadn't been particularly inspired during the war, and everyone was still waiting for something resembling the great favourites that had come out of the last war. The dance tempo had become bouncier since Jack had last danced in Sydney, and the floor quivered like the bruised back of some great beast. A sailor and a girl, both chewing gum as if gasping for air, jived in a corner, completely isolated in their own little world of twisted limbs, vibrating muscles and communion of intellect. A girl and a soldier went by, he plodding in his heavy boots as if on a route march and she doing her best to avoid being crippled. By a doorway an Australian private and an American corporal were arguing, the Australian red in the face and the American looking as if he wanted no part of the argument.

After the fourth dance she said, "We're supposed to circulate. We girls, I mean."

"Do you really want to dance with someone else?"

She smiled and shook her head. "Would you like to take me home, or would that spoil your evening?"

"I haven't eaten yet. Have you?"

"Then we'll have dinner together at home. I'll get my coat."

By a miracle he managed to get a cab, and twenty minutes later they drew up outside the Bendixter home in a quiet street in Darling Point. They pushed open the big iron gates and walked up the drive. A line of poplars supported the night sky and behind the house there was the dark mass of other trees. The house itself shone faintly in the starlight, white and square like some huge tomb.

"Not a bad place at all," said Jack. "What is it, a branch of Parliament House?"

"It's nothing much," said Silver, "but we call it home."

Jack stopped and looked at the house. "It's top heavy. It looks as if someone got big ideas only after the foundations were down."

"Are you always so critical of the homes of girls you meet?"

"The only other girl I've taken home lived in a tent," he said. "She was a Bedouin I met in Gaza."

D

"I must be a disappointment. Your life's been so full of romance."

They went up the steps to a terrace and crossed to the front door. Silver took out her key.

"No butler?" said Jack. "Not even a maid?"

"Nobody at all. We have a cook and a maid, and a gardener who doubles as chauffeur. But they're all down at our place at Bowral at present. They'll be back to-morrow, when my mother comes home. In the meantime, there's just my sister and me—and God knows where she is."

Inside the hall, with the light on, Jack looked around at the sumptuous furnishings. "All this from a few mob of sheep, eh?"

"And timber and mines and shipping and a hundred other things." She tossed her coat on a chair and led the way out to the back of the house. "My dad was a fine man, but he couldn't help making money. He *liked* making it, but he made too much. In the end we were the only ones who knew how good and kind he could be. Nobody has any time for the rich in this country." She looked back at him as they entered a large gleaming kitchen. "Or am I offending a member of the proletariat?"

"You're talking to an ex-rich man's son," he said. "Your father would have known my old man. He was one of the biggest pearlers on the north-west coast."

"You lost everything only recently then?" she said. "Since the Japs came into the war?"

"No," he said, and felt the old sadness even after twelve years. "He committed suicide when I was sixteen. Things just went wrong."

She stopped and put her hand out.

He took it, and felt the warm sympathy in her fingers. He had noticed it several times in the hour he had been with her, a sudden softening in her that belied the polished sophistica-

tion of her looks. Being rich had spoiled her, he thought, but
not entirely.

A long time later they were sitting in what Silver called the
small living-room. It reeked of luxury, but on a small scale,
and Jack felt at home. He lay sprawled on the lounge, his shoes
off and his webbing belt thrown on the floor. She had taken his
coffee cup from him and put it on a small table with her own.
She lit a cigarette for him, lit another for herself, kicked off
her shoes, sat down in a deep chair and drew her feet up under
her.

"When did you last have some home life?"

"Too long ago. I'll tell you about it some other time."
He waved his hand, throwing the subject away as if it were
some foul thing that had unexpectedly clung to his fingers.
"Sit over here."

"There'll be time for that later," she said, and sat looking
at him for a while. "You'd be handsome if it weren't for that
damned great broom under your nose."

"This?" He fondled his moustache. "No other girl has
complained."

"Not even the Bedouin?" she said. "Why do you wear it?"

"Vanity. I liked to be noticed."

She laughed, stubbed out her cigarette and slid off her chair
on to the lounge beside him. "People notice you, all right.
I saw you as soon as you came into the Buffet. I wondered how
long it would be before you asked me to dance. If you hadn't
I'd have asked you."

"You'd have circulated, eh?" he said, and kissed her.

Then her sister came in. "Don't mind me, go right ahead!
I shan't peek."

Silver drew back. "My sister has a one-track mind. Mamie,
this is Jack Savanna."

They were sisters, there was no doubt of that, though one
was as dark as the other was fair. Mamie was not as tall as

Silver, but her body had the same womanliness and her face the same good bonework. Even the eyes and mouths were alike. But there was a looseness about Mamie that wasn't there in Silver; not only in the face and body, but one sensed it also in the character. Then he remembered it was Mamie Bendixter that Tony Shelley had known, and he was surprised at how glad he was. He pressed Silver's arm and stood up.

"My!" said Mamie. "So big!"

"In his stockinged feet too," said Silver. "Six feet three, all man, and I saw him first."

Mamie smiled up at him: there were no dimples and her smile was somehow not as soft. "Silver has a complex about me. She thinks I want to get my claws into every man I see."

"Don't you?" There was no rancour in Silver's voice: she sounded almost a little bored.

"Not all, sister dear," said Mamie. "Only those with red blood in them."

"We'll take a blood test of him later," said Silver. "Right now I'm just getting acquainted with his surface features."

"And they're not bad," said Mamie. "Except for his moustache."

Jack at last managed to get a word in. The only time he was defeated in conversation was when he was in the company of two females. It was gratifying to think that they might fight over him, but he had already made up his mind whom to crown the winner. He chipped in before Mamie began thinking she had got a foothold on him.

"Silver and I have already discussed the moustache," he said. "She also happens to have got her claws into me a couple of hours ago."

The smile stayed around Mamie's mouth, but died in her eyes. My God, he thought, she's a mean, vicious, dissipated bitch; I can believe everything they say about her. Without getting her name in the papers for anything more notorious

than having lunch at Prince's, she had become a legend of
sin in Sydney. Her own circle had known her for years, and
cab drivers too, and the odd anonymous men she had picked
up off the streets; in the last two and a half years, with men
talking among themselves as they did, she had probably become
known to half the Army, Navy and Air Force. She read his
mind and the smile widened, completely shameless.

"You've heard of me, have you, Jack?"

"He's in the same unit as Tony Shelley," said Silver.
"Dear drunken, perverted Tony."

"That's what we call him," said Jack. "Pervy B. Shelley."

For a moment Mamie looked as if she were going to stay
and fight. The smile changed almost to a snarl and the eyes
thinned dangerously. Then suddenly she changed the whole
expression to a yawn. "I'm tired. I've been out with a Navy
type who's been at sea for ten months, so he said. You'll be
around again, Jack, or are you staying the night? Good night,
then, and don't sleep in Mother's room. She's coming home
to-morrow."

Then she had gone and the room seemed cleaner and
fresher. Jack sat down and began to draw on his boots.

"Going?" said Silver. "Did that bitch of a sister spoil
things for you?"

"I don't like her," he said, buckling on his belt. "But she
didn't spoil things. She just somehow made me see you in a
new light."

"Better or worse?"

"Better. I'll be back again. I'm going to spend the rest of
my leave with you. Do you work at all?"

"Since the Japs came into the war, yes. I'm secretary to a
doctor friend of ours in Macquarie Street. Some people
wouldn't call it war work, but it depends on the way you look
at it. Sid Hugo is overworked, like all doctors now, and I do
my best to help him." She had spoken a little forcibly, but

suddenly she smiled and made a deprecating gesture. "I'm sorry, I'm always defending myself. It's a habit of the conscientious rich."

"Lunch to-morrow, then." They were at the front door now and he took her in his arms. "Is Silver really your name?"

"Don't you like it?" And when he nodded, she said, "Dad was nicknamed Silver, because of his hair and, I suppose, because of his money, too. When I came along and had hair exactly like his——" She looked up at him, frankly pleased. "I'm glad you like it, Jack."

"It suits you." He kissed her, and was aware of the passion in her. The night hadn't ended as he'd originally planned, but he had no regrets. The future, compared with the prospect of a few hours ago, looked better than to-night could ever have been. It was the first time he could remember meeting a girl and thinking beyond the next morning. "Good night, Silver."

It seemed that he had been saying good night to women and leaving them all his life and would be for ever. Even when he had been living with Rita they had both known that one night he would walk out and not come back. He could not do without women, but for as long as he could remember he had been frightened of their hold on him.

He had even been frightened of his mother's hold on him. Tenuous yet strong, like the line a fisherman holds. She had played him as one plays a fish: several times he had tried to escape, but she had always known how to bring him back.

"I wasn't cut out to be a mother, Johnny," she had said once, "but that doesn't mean I want to forget I am one."

"You're all right," he had said, knowing he was expected to say something. She had been a vain woman and would have liked him to say she was a wonderful mother: she was greedy for any sort of praise, even when she knew it wasn't true. But he hadn't been able to bring himself to make the lie an extravagant one. "When is Dad coming home?"

"Next week." She had turned to him, giving him the smile he had seen her give his father when she wanted something. "And I wouldn't mention that Mr. Garry and Mr. Phillips have been coming here, Johnny. Your father sometimes misunderstands things, sees them in the wrong light. So we shan't mention them, shall we?"

He had loved his father as he had never been able to love his mother. Big Pat had had boats going out of both Thursday Island and Broome, and had spent his time between both places, with four visits a year to Sydney. Then he would come down for a fortnight each time and be like a north-west storm, a Cocky Bob, blowing through the house. He had built a house on Thursday Island for them all, but Jack had been there only twice and his mother never at all. The house had never been a home, just an outpost where Big Pat slept and drank and (as his son learned later) pined in secret. The four visits a year to Sydney were like four Christmases to Big Pat's son.

Then Big Pat had come down from Broome on one of his visits and had arrived a day earlier than expected. He had called for Jack at school, persuaded the master to let him go early, and they had caught a cab and gone home, both of them happy as schoolboys, flushed with the thought of the fortnight ahead.

"We'll surprise your mother," his father had said, and he had seen no danger in it because he knew both Mr. Garry and Mr. Phillips were out of town. "She's probably in the middle of her afternoon beauty sleep. We'll sneak in and scare the day-lights out of her. Cripes!" He slapped Jack's knee, almost breaking it. "You've got no idea how I like coming home to you two! One of these days you'll find there's no feeling like returning home."

But his mother hadn't been having her beauty sleep. She was in bed, all right, but there was a man with her, someone he had never seen before. His father had said nothing intelligible, just let out a roar of animal rage, and plunged into the room, slamming the door after him. Jack had stood for a moment, sick and frightened, then he had turned and walked slowly down the hall to his room.

From the window there a few minutes later he had seen the stranger staggering down the drive, his clothes hanging on him in shreds, his hands to his broken bloody face, never looking back, an adulterer who hadn't known what had hit him. Five minutes later Big Pat had come into his son's room.

"I was wrong, son," he had said, and, unbloodied and unscathed, he had looked more broken than the man who had just gone stumbling down the drive. "You can't win, after all."

Then he had gone downstairs and locked himself in his study and begun to drink. Two hours later, when they heard the shot and Jack had burst the door in, he was dead. Big Pat lay among a litter of bottles and photographs and letters, and in a pool of blood that spread to touch the bottles and stain the photographs and letters. Jack would never forget that sight of the wreckage of his father's life.

His mother had looked in the room past him and then, the only womanly decent thing she had ever done, she had fainted. He had closed the door quietly on his father, stepped over his mother with only a hateful glance at her and left her to the care of the gardener and his wife, and had walked out of the house and down the road to the home of the doctor who had brought him into the world. Old Dr. Cotterell, who had known what was going on, had opened the door and from the look on Jack's face had guessed at tragedy. But his guess had been only half right. He had cried out in shock and grief when Jack told him Big Pat had killed himself and not his wife.

Jack had never gone back to his mother. At first, out of remorse, she had come pleading to him to return; then after a while her vanity had got the better of her again and she gave up chasing him. Big Pat had died in a hurry, without expecting to, probably without meaning to, if he hadn't been so blind with anger or sorrow or drink or perhaps all three. When it came time to settle his affairs it was found he had over-expanded and in doing so had borrowed right and left. He had left little but goodwill and a fleet of half-paid-for luggers that added up only to a man's dreams. In solid cash they meant very little.

Jack's mother had married again, not Mr. Garry nor Mr. Phillips nor the bloody stranger but a French woolbroker, and had gone to live in Paris. Whether she was still there, he didn't know nor care. Whatever the Germans did to her couldn't be worse than what she had done to his father.

And so because of his mother and because he would always remember his father's last words—*you can't win*—he had spent his life running away from women. Well, not running away from them immediately, but only when he had begun to fear they were getting a hold on him.

Good night, Silver, and she had five more days in which to strengthen her hold on him. For she did have a hold on him, he admitted, even after only four hours and two kisses. And sitting on the ferry edging its way past the wartime boom defences in the outer harbour, going over to Manly where an understanding cousin had lent him his flat for the eight days of his leave, he further admitted that perhaps this time he wouldn't be so keen to run away. The war, that had ruined so many futures, had begun to make him think of his.

This return to Sydney, to the welcome that wasn't there for him, had made him realise for the first time just how lonely he was. His father had been right, there was no feeling like returning home. But one needed a welcome, if the feeling was to mean anything.

They had lunch the next day at Prince's. They sat close to a

table that was fast becoming famous as the command post of
certain American war correspondents covering the New Guinea
front, and behind a table that was already famous as the command post of a genteel lady who covered the Society front.
Gay young things were being industriously gay, keeping one
eye on each other and one eye on the door in case a photographer
appeared. Matrons pecked at their food like elegant fowls, also
eyeing each other and waiting the advent of a photographer.
Two suburban ladies from Penshurst, having a day out in
Society, sat toying with their food and wishing they had gone
to Sargent's, where they could have had a real bog-in for less
than half the price. Aside from Jack and the American correspondents, there were only one or two other men in the place,
and they looked as uncomfortable as if they had been
caught lunching in an underwear salon. Australian men still
hadn t learned to be at ease when outnumbered by women.

Silver told Jack she had to go to a meeting that night. "It's
some sort of bond rally that my mother has organised for
business girls. David Jones' have lent their restaurant. Everyone has tea and sandwiches, then this war hero gets up and says
something. After that, the idea is that the girls all rush up and
buy war bonds."

"I thought they'd rush up and lay themselves at the feet of
the war hero. It has better possibilities, I mean as a spectacle."

"Well, anyway, that cuts out dinner to-night," she said.
"Unless you want to wait until after the meeting."

"I'll come along and eat tea and sandwiches. Maybe
afterwards, just to set the girls an example, I'll rush up and
throw myself at the war hero."

That evening, shortly after the stores had closed, he met her
outside David Jones'. They went into the big gleaming store
and, in a lift crammed with chattering females who looked
with an appreciative eye on Jack and a critical one on Silver,
they went up to the restaurant floor.

As soon as they entered the large high-ceilinged restaurant Jack saw the war hero. "You mean he's the one who's supposed to inspire these girls to save their money for war bonds? He's never saved a penny in his life! I've kept him in spending money ever since we joined the Army on the same day."

"Who is he?" said Silver. "My mother's a bit on the vague side. She couldn't remember his name."

But before Jack could tell her, the war hero had broken away from the group around him and come plunging towards them. "You old bastard, Savanna! What are you doing here?"

"After you speak, I get up and say a piece," said Jack. "They want the girls to get both sides of the question. You, you bludger!" he said elegantly, and shook his head disgustedly. He turned to Silver. "This is Sergeant Morley, V.C. Miss Bendixter."

He was glad to see that Silver remained cool and didn't gush. "My, we are honoured to-night. A real live V.C. winner."

"I'll say this for him," said Jack. "Most of them don't stay alive."

Greg Morley's black eyes were bright with light and his thin face was flushed under its tan. He's just like a big kid, thought Jack. Even the thin brown face had a suggestion of boyishness about it: the features seemed thrown together above the mobile mouth, as if they had never settled into a mature countenance. He was good looking, but in a way one could never remember: there was a suggestion of impermanence, of possible change, about his face, as if when one saw him next he might have changed beyond recognition. And his face, like a young boy's, showed every emotion.

"I'm glad I stayed alive for this," he said, throwing an arm towards the room, laughing with a mouthful of bright white teeth. "I'm lapping it up! You should have been a hero, Jack."

"God forbid," said Jack. "Is Sarah here?"

"She's over there with the mob," Greg said. "I've got my own bodyguard of Army Public Relations blokes, War Loan johnnies, a photographer from D.O.I. The works, all for Greg Morley!"

"What are you going to talk about to-night?" said Silver.

"God knows." Greg couldn't have been more cheerful: he wasn't a modest hero to be frightened by public adoration. "They've written it for me. All I have to do is deliver it."

"What are you doing next week?" said Jack. "*Hamlet?*"

But Greg couldn't be dented. "Come and meet Sarah and the old duck who's organising this. You'll love her, Jack. Doesn't know a bee from a bull's foot about the war, but you'd think she was Lady Blamey."

"My mother," said Silver with mock reverence, but Greg had already left them, plunging back towards his bodyguard and the centre of interest. One of the bodyguard detached himself from the group and came towards them. He ignored Silver and looked up at Jack.

"What are you doing here?" He was a lieutenant with neat wavy hair, a soft round face and an air of authority he was just trying out. "This is a bond rally for business girls, not the Anzac Buffet. You won't find what you're looking for here."

"When you speak to me address me by my rank," said Jack, and wondered how many bonds it would sell if he smacked the lieutenant here and now. In the past he had several times felt like hitting officers, but had been restrained by second thoughts for which he had later despised himself. But if this officer went too far, there mightn't be a second thought this time. "And speak to me again like you just have, and I'll drop you down the lift well. Pips or no pips."

The officer's round face seemed to get even rounder, and his air of authority almost choked him. "What's your name and Army number? I'll fix you, my friend——"

Jack looked down at him from his full height, past the bristling moustache that stuck out like the horns of an angry bull. "Just step aside, mister, and allow me to escort Miss Bendixter through to join her mother."

The lieutenant stepped back, his mouth open but empty of words, and Jack and Silver moved on across the room. "You would have hit him, wouldn't you?" Silver said. "Or thrown him down the lift well."

"Certainly. Don't you think he asked for it?"

"I suppose so. But *here*! Do you always choose such crowded places for your assassinations? And when you're with your lady friends? I felt a little like some floosie from Paddington."

He stopped and looked down at her. "For that last remark, I should drop *you* down the lift well. I don't know why, but one thing I hadn't expected from you was snobbishness."

She said nothing for a moment, and he thought she was going to walk away from him. Then she put her hand in his and suddenly he was aware of a new intimacy between them. It was as if they were old lovers who had patched up a quarrel, and there was none of the awkwardness that would have been natural in view of their short acquaintance. "I'm sorry, Jack. That was something I should never have allowed myself even to think. My apologies to the girls in Paddington."

Then a grey-haired handsome woman, better dressed than anyone else in the place, came steaming towards them. "Silver! My God, I thought you were never going to arrive!" She looked up at Jack. "So this is our war hero! So big and handsome, too! We should sell a hundred thousand pounds' worth of bonds to-night. I wish all our heroes were like you. What did you win?"

"The Melbourne Cup," said Jack. "Only man ever to do it. It's always been won by a horse before."

Silver patted her mother's arm. "This is not the war hero, darling. This is Jack Savanna."

"Oh, he's with you?" said Mrs. Bendixter, and it was a long time since Jack felt he had been so neatly dropped overboard. Mrs. Bendixter looked about her. "Then where is *he?* You'd think he'd be on time, even if he is a hero. Have you seen Smithy?"

A small pony-faced woman materialised out of nowhere. She wore an expression of dedicated enthusiasm: the war had been the first cause big enough in which to lose herself. When peace came she would need rehabilitating as much as the men who had fought on the battle fronts.

"You wanted me, Mrs. Bendixter?" Even her voice was enthusiastic, a thin reedy trumpet blowing the national anthem. "Such a crowd! We should sell enough bonds to-night to buy at least one bomber!"

"All we need," said Jack. "One more bomber, and the war is won."

He felt Silver kick his leg and when he looked down at her she was frowning severely at him. But Miss Smith's attention had been hauled in by Mrs. Bendixter.

"Where's this war hero, Smithy? We must get started soon. We have to go on to a bridge party after this for the war widows——"

"Orphans," said Miss Smith, glowing with charity. "And it's not a bridge party, it's a musicale."

"A musicale? Well, that's good. I can doze off. My God, I'm *so* tired!" Mrs. Bendixter put a hand to her forehead, suffering from war fatigue. "Well, where is this man? Hasn't he turned up yet?"

"He's here, Mrs. Bendixter! You've already met him. Sergeant Morley, the thin dark boy——"

"The boy with those lovely teeth! Why didn't someone say so? My God, if I wasn't here to organise things, they'd never get started!" Mrs. Bendixter turned round as a newspaper photographer came up. "Hallo, you're from the *Sunday*

Telegraph, aren't you? Take me full face this time. Last week I was in profile and I looked like General MacArthur."

Then Greg Morley came back, dragging a pretty girl with honey-coloured hair after him. "You remember Sarah, Jack! Look after her, will you? I've got to go up and do my act now."

Then he had gone plunging away, surrounded by his body-guard, the whole group moving towards a platform at the end of the hall, headed by Mrs. Bendixter with Miss Smith in close tow.

"Looks like Queen Victoria and the Prince Consort," said Jack. "Is there no band?" Then he took Silver's arm. "Sarah Morley, this is Silver Bendixter."

Sarah smiled and shook her head in wonder. "Your mother puts up with this sort of bedlam often?"

"Every day," said Silver. "She loves it."

"So does your husband," Jack said to Sarah. "Look at him up there. Clark Gable never felt more at home."

Greg was up on the platform, beaming round at the thousand or more girls below him. Mrs. Bendixter was speaking, reading from a typescript that Miss Smith had shoved into her hands, but she was standing too close to the microphone and her voice was just wave after wave of almost unintelligible blasts. Nobody minded, because nobody had come to listen to Mrs. Bendixter anyway. And Jack somehow felt sure that Greg at the microphone would be as practised as any crooner.

"His life is complete," Sarah Morley said. "He's waited all his life for these past few days."

"I suppose you've been besieged by the newspapers?" said Silver.

"And radio, and the newsreels, and the magazines, and war loan committees. It's like being married to a public property, a new statue or something." There was no spite or rancour in Sarah's voice: it was as if she had succeeded in detaching herself completely from the whole business. She looked at Jack. "The surprising thing is, he's terribly modest with me about it all. He hasn't told me a thing about what he did to get the V.C. All I know is what I read in the papers. Was he really as brave as they said?"

"He was." There was no mockery now in Jack's voice: he had seen the incident and he knew Greg deserved the honour he had got. "We'd been held up for an hour by these two machine-gun posts. They had us as nicely taped as I ever hoped to be taped. We were stuck behind some rocks on the bank of the Litani River." As he spoke the whole rocky sunbaked Syrian countryside came back to him, and he felt suddenly nostalgic. The campaign had been tougher and more important than the outside world, for some political reason, had been told. The Vichy French had fought with the same whole-hearted hatred as the Germans had in the Western Desert. But after the armistice, camped among the olive groves in the shadow of the sharp-ridged mountains, bathing in the warm Mediterranean, loving the dark-eyed Lebanese beauties, when one could get them away from their hawk-eyed parents, Syria had become the first piece of territory worth fighting for that they had so far met. Jack had liked Syria and one day hoped to go back. "I didn't see Greg start out, I don't think any of us did, but the next thing we knew he was across the river and going up the opposite bank. He took those two machine-gun posts on his own. He threw in grenades and then went in and used his bayonet. We were still on the other side of the river and it was like sitting in the dress circle watching a film, the sort of film that excites you but that you don't believe in. When he'd finished he stood up, grinning all over his face just like he is now, and yelled back at us, ' Righto, what are you bastards waiting for?' It's the first and only time I've ever heard a man cheered while we were in action. Yes, Sarah, he was really brave."

"I'm glad," she said. "It makes me feel better for him."

"What do you mean?" said Silver.

"Nothing," Sarah smiled, her grey eyes looking a little tired. "It's been all a little confusing these past few days, married to Public Hero Number One."

"It can't have been much of a reunion for the two of you," said Silver. "I mean, no privacy. So little time to yourselves."

"It's been like spending our honeymoon on Central Station," Sarah said. "I'm afraid to take my clothes off for fear the doorbell will ring again."

"That wouldn't worry Greg, would it?" said Jack. "He'd welcome them all, naked or not."

Sarah nodded. "He was interviewed the other day by the *Herald* in his underpants. He was never what you'd call self-conscious. I must have had a too modest upbringing. I like to be fully dressed in front of strangers. Anyhow, we're escaping for a couple of days. We're going up to Katoomba to-night."

Greg had now begun to speak. Just as I thought, Jack said to himself. Bing Crosby, Clark Gable, Richard the Lion-Heart, all rolled into one. You'd think he'd been doing it all his life. Listen to the microphone technique, better than I could ever use it and I've had years of practice. Look at the charm flowing out like syrup out of a barrel. And just the right touch of modesty to season the devil-may-care attitude. I like the bastard and I admire him, but in a moment I'm going to be sick right in the middle of Mrs. Bendixter's bond rally.

"I'm going downstairs for a breath of air," he said. "I don't want any bonds to-day, thank you."

"I'll come with you," said Silver. "We can go and have dinner now."

"What about helping your mother?"

"She won't need me. It was just in case the hero was unmarried. Sometimes I'm expected to find him a girl, or

E

in the last resort go out with him myself. But Greg's all fixed." She smiled at Sarah. "Have a nice second honeymoon, Sarah. No photographers or visitors."

"Take your clothes off and leave them off," said Jack.

Sarah smiled at them. "I'll do my best. And thank you. I'll say good night to Greg for you."

They left Greg and his bated-breath audience and went down in the lift and out into Elizabeth Street. The air was pleasantly cool and the crowds in the streets had thinned out. A breeze came across the park, brushing the leaves like a restless child, and the moon struggled to free itself from a net of clouds.

"Sarah looked rather tired," said Silver, "as if she's been under something of a strain."

"Living with Greg under any circumstances would be a strain on a woman."

"Sometimes you sound as if you don't like him."

"I do like him." He had come to cherish the friendship of several of the men in the last two years, particularly Greg and Vern Radcliffe. He had been self-sufficient before the war, having no close men friends and needing none. But of late, knowing these men in arms with him, exchanging confidences with them, having them sometimes depend on him, he had become aware of a feeling of selflessness that had given him more pleasure than he could remember in his dealings with men before. At one time he had laughed at the Australian religion of mateship, the spirit of fraternalism that was evident in so many movements in the country's history. If he hadn't yet succumbed to it completely, he had at least stopped laughing. He had recognised it as one of the few things of constant value in a world of changing values. "I have a great affection for the irresponsible bastard. But that's his trouble, he's too irresponsible."

"You sounded like a good responsible type to-night, when you were going to sock that officer." She stopped walking and stared at him, then she moved on again. "I believe you would have, too. You're a queer mixture, Jack. Sometimes you sound too cynical to care about anything. And other times——" She made a hopeless gesture with her hand. "Remind me to think twice if ever you ask me to marry you."

"I've never asked anyone yet," he said.

"Oh, pardon me for being so forward!" She had regained her poise, was cool and slightly mocking again. "I'm so used to being asked, I just take it for granted."

He grinned, losing his dark mood. "Let's have dinner, before I take to beating you. I'm a patient man——"

"Like hell, you're patient," she said, and put her arm in his and smiled up at him: the dimples took all the cool mockery out of her face and made her young and lovely. He pressed her arm tightly against his body, feeling it like a soft link in a chain she was winding about him, and they walked up through the cool electric night, on the verge of love in the city that was just experiencing its first epidemic of lust.

When they had finished dinner she looked at her watch. "It's still only twenty-past eight, a young night. What would you like to do now?"

"Go to bed with you," he said, and somehow succeeded in making the words not so brutal and vulgar and selfish.

"With anyone else, that could have spoiled a lovely evening." She reached across the table and put her hand on his: in the pressure of her fingers he could feel her desire answering his. "But I'm not going to any cheap hotel room. I'm not like my sister. I have a distaste for the sordid."

"I have the loan of a flat at Manly." He signalled for the waiter and tipped that surprised worthy as liberally as any American who had come into the place: everyone benefited from love, even waiters. "We'll go down to the Quay and catch a ferry."

He kissed her as they rode on the outside of the ferry, with the cool breeze stirring her hair like wisps of spun silver, and with a quartet at the rear of the ferry serenading the moon with the Maori Farewell. Behind them the city was dark in its brown-out, and as they crept out past the defence boom he had a sudden shivering feeling of unreality. His arm tightened about her.

"It's hard to believe," he said. "In Alex and Haifa and Beirut, yes. But not here."

"I get scared stiff at times," she said. "What if we should lose the war?"

The ferry was rolling now, meeting the swell coming in through the Heads. They were on the lee side of the boat, looking back up the moonlit harbour. Other ferries, dark as their own, crept like cats from shore to shore. Against the far stars the Bridge was like some great night-beast in mid-leap. Only an occasional shaded car light showed, peering furtively, then quickly disappearing. Then ahead of them they saw the dancing tops of the pine trees that identified Manly.

"Don't let's talk about losing," he said. "There are more important things to think about to-night."

"Spoken like a true man," she said, and kissed him lightly.

CHAPTER FOUR

THIS trip to Katoomba looked as if it was going to be a waste of time. Greg lay on his back staring up at the ceiling and tried to remember what he'd imagined his homecoming would be like. Not the public homecoming, the photographers and the reporters and everyone congratulating him. That had been just as he'd expected it and there had been no disappointment there. But though he'd enjoyed it all, that wasn't what he had come home for. He had come home to be with Sarah again, to revive the past and all he had remembered in the lonely nights overseas; but the past hadn't caught up with him and sometimes, like now, he felt as lonely as he had ever felt in the Middle East.

He lay beside her now and said, "What's the matter, hon?"

"How do you mean?"

"You know how I mean. Have I got repulsive or something while I've been away?"

"No."

"You used to like it once. What's got into you?"

It was bright moonlight outside. A swathe of it, slanting through the window, lay across the bed. Sarah too was lying on her back staring at the ceiling, unmoving as if asleep, and he had the feeling she was hardly listening to him. The side of her face towards him was in deep shadow and all he could see was the silhouette of her profile. She had a good face, especially in profile: there was character in the nose and chin, a hint that she could be depended upon.

"I've been wondering how to tell you," she said at last. "Greg, I don't love you any more."

He heard her say the words quite distinctly and he knew what they meant: it wasn't as if she had gabbled something in a foreign language. But he was so totally unprepared for what she had said, she might just as well have not spoken at all. He just lay looking at her, listening with the back of his mind to a woman laughing somewhere in the hotel.

Sarah turned her head on her pillow. "I suppose that's a shock to you?"

He sat up, leaning on one elbow. "Don't joke like that, Sarah!"

"I'm not joking, Greg." Her voice was calm but definite: she had always known what she wanted to say. "I'm not in love with you any more."

He reached up quickly and switched on the bed lamp. "When did this happen, for God's sake? It's bloody sudden. You didn't say anything in your letters——"

"I didn't think I should tell you while you were away. Somehow it wouldn't have been fair."

"Why didn't you tell me when I first got back?"

"It would have spoiled the other business, wouldn't it? The fanfare, the publicity——"

"Are you narked about that? Is that the cause of the trouble?"

"I was out of love with you before you won the V.C.," she said. "I stopped loving you six months after you sailed for the Middle East."

He dropped back on the pillow. He felt words bubbling up inside him, but he suddenly felt too weak to say them. Somehow they wouldn't have meant anything. He just lay in silence, aware of his own heartbeats, till she spoke again.

"Aren't you going to say something?" Her face was turned towards him, but he didn't look at her. "Say something, Greg. Don't just lie there."

"What is there to say? You've said about everything there is. I could start swearing at you—that would come pretty easy. But what good would that do?"

He got up and walked across the room to the dressing-table. He picked up a cigarette packet, but it was empty. He could feel his hand shaking as he dropped the packet back on the dressing-table.

"Have you any cigarettes?" Even now he had to depend on her. He wished he could have done without a cigarette, but he knew he must have it. "I'm right out."

She took one for herself from the packet on the bedside table, lit it, then threw him the packet and the box of matches. He lit a cigarette, his hand still shaking, then walked across to the window. From here he could look down one of the many gorges of the Blue Mountains. The gaunt ridges were folded into a pattern of deep shadow and bright moonlight, and across the gorge a steep cliff-face shone like a wall of green ice. Down in the far valley the long beam of a car's headlights came and went, tentatively, like a blind man's tapping stick. The distant white beam only made the countryside more lonely.

"Hadn't you better put on your gown?" said Sarah. "There's no point in getting pneumonia."

He had been so used to her looking after him, he picked up the gown now and put it on almost automatically. "Is there someone else? How long's it been going on?"

"There's no one else." She was sitting up in bed now, propped against the pillow. One arm was folded across her breast, the hand holding the elbow of the other arm. She was smoking, much more calmly than he was, not attacking the cigarette as he was but almost enjoying it. "I've been faithful to you that way. Which was more than you were to me."

He didn't answer that.

"I'm sorry, Greg. Really. This hasn't been much of a homecoming for you."

"Yeah, that's the bit that worries me, the spoiled homecoming." There was sarcasm, but little edge of anger to his voice. He was still too let-down to feel anything but shock. His voice was carrying on automatically for him: it seemed to know the words for the part: "Do you want a divorce?"

"That would be the best thing, wouldn't it? Though I don't know what grounds we can have. Unless I leave you and you sue for restitution of conjugal rights, or whatever it is. Then the next step is desertion, I think. You can get a divorce on those grounds."

"You've got it all worked out, haven't you?"

"I've had plenty of time to think about it," she said. "Eighteen months."

He stubbed out his cigarette and went back and sat on the bed beside her. "Look, hon, are you sure you're right about this? What makes you so sure you don't love me? Maybe once you get used to having me around again, you'll find you're wrong."

She drew on the cigarette slowly. The action suddenly made him angry, the one small thing needed to root him out of his shock, and he snatched the cigarette from her. He dropped it in the ashtray on the table beside the bed, grinding it savagely with the ball of his thumb. She looked at him for a moment, her eyes and lips narrowing, and he waited for one of her cutting remarks, one of the few things about her that had sometimes annoyed him. Then she seemed to make an effort and the tenseness went out of her face.

"This is going to surprise you, Greg," she said. "But I've been thinking back and I wonder if I ever loved you. Really loved you, that is."

He wanted to hit her, all at once hating her, but he knew dimly this was one time when he had to control himself. He was on his own here in this, the biggest crisis their marriage had ever had, and she wouldn't help him as she had in the past. This was all his burden, and giving way to anger wouldn't help at all. "You're just making things up now. Why can't you be honest? Are you trying to hurt me or something?"

"I've already done that. I can see that. Why should I try and rub it in? I told you I didn't write and tell you while you were away because I wanted to hurt you the least I could."

"Well, what do you mean, you wonder if you ever loved me? Why did you marry me?"

"I did love you in a sort of a way, I suppose. But not in the way that keeps marriages together. I think that was the trouble, Greg. Getting married. If we hadn't married, I might have gone on loving you. The trouble with you, Greg, is you've never grown up. It often appeals to a girl when she hasn't got to live with it every day. It appealed to me, I'll admit. I always enjoyed seeing you, you were such good company. And you knew how to pay attention to a girl— even if you sometimes had trouble taking your eyes off other women." Then she said, "That was one of the main troubles, Greg. The other women. When you had gone I started to think about them——"

"You're not giving me any credit for having changed since those days."

"Have you?"

He was silent, unsure himself if he had changed, remembering how much he had looked forward to women's company when he had gone on leave to Tel-Aviv and Jerusalem and Beirut, and after a moment Sarah went on: "I don't want to have to look after you all my life, Greg. Always having to hold our marriage together. A marriage, a good solid one, shouldn't need holding together. It's not some jerry-built thing that any wind can blow over. Your mother and father's marriage, my people too, their marriages have never needed holding together. Some girls enjoy the mother role, I mean towards their husbands, but I don't. I'd like to be a mother, but I want children, not a grown man! And what if we did have kids, Greg? Could I depend on you to help me care for them? All your life, Greg, you've waited for things to fall into your lap, and when they haven't you've just turned around and borrowed off someone else." For the first time she lost her calmness, and passed her hand wearily across her eyes. When she took away her hand there were tears on her cheeks. "I tried, Greg, you've no idea how I tried! But it's just no use, no use at all."

It was the first time he had ever seen her weep: even when they had said good-bye two years ago she had kept a brave face. He had been glad of that then, because he knew he hadn't the armour to withstand her breaking up. Now she looked younger than he had ever seen her look, helpless for the first time, and he had an almost overpowering desire to take her in his arms. Instead he got up and began to walk about the room.

"I think it would have been better if you'd told me while I was away," he said.

"Why? You might have taken it much worse than you are now."

"Christ, how do you think I'm taking it now? Do you think it isn't hurting me as much as it would have over there?" His hand pulled at his hair; the mobile face was almost splitting with emotion. "I still love you, hon! Just because I'm back, doesn't alter or lessen that. Look at you now. You're half-naked. Do you think I can't remember what we've done together? Do you think I can shut my eyes and say I'm going to forget all that? I can remember you, every inch of you, and so long as you're around I'll go on remembering you. And unless I stay up all night, I've got to get back into bed with you now. If you'd told me while I was away in the Middle East, at least I wouldn't have had to do that."

"If that's all you're going to miss of me, the sex part——"

"Ah, God Almighty! Can't you see what I'm getting at? I remember everything else about you, too. You'd be surprised at the small, no-account things a man remembers when he's away. And likes to remember. It sounds silly now, but time and again I used to think about the day you fell in the water fully dressed at National Park. I used to laugh about that and feel good about it. It was something I loved about you, although it's hard to explain why. I'm in love with you, hon, and I want to stay in love with you. If I've talked about getting back into bed with you, it's because we both know it's the best way of showing love." He sat down on the bed again and twisted his face with his hands. "I realise now, that since I've been back I might just as well have patted your hand for all it meant to you."

"I'm sorry, Greg." They sat in silence for a while, both of them unaware of the cold night air coming in the open windows. Somewhere down in the gorge a night-bird cried, and on the terrace below their windows a woman giggled nervously. There was the sound of light running footsteps, high heels click-clacking on the cement, a man said hoarsely, "Come here, you little dope, I'm not going to hurt you!" then there was the sound of heavier running footsteps going away along the terrace. Then there was silence again and after a while Sarah said, "Shall we go home to-morrow?"

"Do you want to?"

"I don't know, I like it here. It seems a pity—but you say you can't go on sharing the same bed with me. I suppose you're right. It doesn't mean anything to me any more."

He took off his dressing-gown and slowly got back into bed. Already he felt a strangeness beside her, a restraint upon himself as if he mustn't touch her for fear she should scream. She was doing nothing to help him. Her nightgown was low cut at the neck and as she turned towards him her breasts, the breasts he knew so well and would remember, were almost completely exposed. He looked away from her and sought some relief in sarcasm.

"The double bed," he said. "The torture rack for about-to-be-divorced couples."

"We'd better go home to-morrow," she said. "I'll take some things and go and stay with Mum till your leave is up. When you go back to camp, I'll come back to the flat."

"There's no need for that. We've got a date on Saturday night. We promised we'd go to Bluey Brown's party."

"Do we have to go to that? Is it so important? Haven't you had enough of being fêted?"

"The party isn't being put on for my benefit. And if it were, I wouldn't be thinking about that part of it, believe it or not." The excitement of the last few days had been completely forgotten: he suddenly wished he was a nobody. "I just don't want people feeling sorry for a V.C. winner. I'll be the one who'll get the sympathy, you know that. I just don't want people calling you a bitch."

"I don't deserve so much consideration," she said slowly. "Is that what *you* want to call me, a bitch?"

He ignored the question because he had no answer for it: his mind was still in too much of a turmoil to begin thinking of calling her anything. "We'll go home to-morrow and I'll sleep in the spare bedroom. We'll keep up appearances till I go back to camp. You won't have to worry," he said bitterly, "you can lock the bedroom door at night. When I'm back with the unit, we'll see about getting a divorce."

"You're taking it better than I'd hoped," she said very quietly.

He reached up and switched off the bed lamp. He turned

away from her to stare at the dark wall before him, dark and blank as the future.

"You forget I'm a V.C. winner," he said. "Brave beyond the call of duty."

Next morning they went back to Sydney. The train wound its way down out of the mountains, threading its way through narrow culverts, skirting the edges of deep drops, passing small towns that had once been only holiday resorts and now were the dormitories of munition workers. The grey-walled gorges were as wild and deserted as they had ever been and the ranges still had the appearance of lonely sleeping beasts; but the Blue Mountains, once just a playground, were already caught up in the war. Munition works, stark and utilitarian and temporary-looking, money and materials thrown into tremendous sheds of death, were springing up all down the line. And from the train the roads seemed to be carrying little but military traffic.

The train itself was crowded, as much as it had ever been when returning from a holiday week-end. The authorities had cancelled all inter-state passenger traffic, unless one had a permit, and had asked people not to travel within the state unless their reasons were urgent. Everyone suddenly seemed to have urgent reasons for going somewhere: it was doubtful if so many people had ever moved so far so often. For the first time in years the New South Wales Government Railways looked as if they might show a profit.

By one of those unbelievable pieces of luck which seemed to be natural to him, Greg had managed to get two seats. From outside the carriage had looked packed as any cattle truck and almost as packed as any tram going home from a Saturday race meeting. They had just settled back in the seats when two young soldiers came plunging back into the compartment.

"Hey, those are our seats, dig! We just been out to get a cuppa tea. We've had them seats ever since we left Cowra."

Greg made no move. "I'm sorry, dig. I've got a bad leg——" He tenderly felt the wound he didn't have.

The youngster suddenly noticed the purple ribbon on Greg's chest. "That's all right, sarge. You're Sergeant Morley, ain't you? No, go on, you stay there. Me and me cobber'll be all right. I'll just get me kit bag. There. Well, best of luck, sarge. Look after yourself."

When the two boys had gone Sarah whispered, "That was cheap."

"I know," said Greg, smiling at the woman opposite, who was looking at him with frank admiration. "I feel like being cheap to-day. Cheap and nasty and don't-give-a-bugger-for-anyone."

He knew that yesterday he wouldn't have thought of taking the seats from the two kids, nor of putting on the cheap act about carrying a wound. But yesterday he had been another man, a friend to everyone; and to-day he was as badly wounded as any man who had ever stopped a bullet. But if he told that to Sarah, it would only look like another cheap bid for sympathy.

The woman opposite leaned across. "I heard the other young soldier ask if you were Sergeant Morley. You're the Victoria Cross winner, aren't you? That's the ribbon there, isn't it? I saw your photo in the papers earlier in the week."

"Yes," said Greg, all at once wishing he had taken off his ribbon this morning and carried it in his pocket. He glanced at Sarah, expecting her to look bored, but she smiled at the woman opposite. She moved her arm, linking it in his, and he knew then she was only keeping up appearances. For a moment he was angry, then with a sense of fairness that had once been foreign to him, he realised she was doing it for his sake. He pressed her hand, but there was no answering pressure.

"May I congratulate you?" the woman said, and smiled

at both of them. Then after a moment she said, "You were in the Middle East, weren't you, Sergeant Morley? I wonder if you ever knew my son, Lieutenant Updyke. Mervyn Updyke."

At any other time Greg would have said yes, he was a bosom friend of old Merv. It was the sort of opening he would not have been able to deny, would have in fact welcomed. He would have invented a series of fantastic and scandalous adventures that the absent Lieutenant Updyke would have spent months disclaiming. But all his capricious humour had been left back there in a room at Katoomba that he would remember for the rest of his life.

"No," he said. "I don't know him."

"He's with the Ninth Division," said Mrs. Updyke. "He was one of the Rats of Tobruk."

I should cheer at this moment, thought Greg, or at least bow my head reverently. He belonged to a division that called itself the Silent Seventh, since no one ever seemed to have heard of it. But the Ninth Division had been even more widely publicised than Phar Lap or Don Bradman. None of the other divisions' troops would have wanted any of the glory shorn from the Ninth's part in the siege of Tobruk, and indeed took pride in it; but too much mention of the Ninth had finally begun to have a purgative effect on the bowels of the other divisions. Particularly the Seventh, which had begun to wonder if people knew it was in the war.

"He's lucky," Greg said.

"Do you think so?" said Mrs. Updyke, missing the sarcasm. "I don't know. Why are those boys being kept over there? Why aren't they home defending their own country? They're not doing anything over there. My son wrote the other day that he'd been playing *football!* Football in the Middle East, with the Japanese right on our doorstep!"

"Was he complaining?" Greg had heard the complaint several times since he had been back and he had given up trying to explain what he understood of the pattern of this war. He knew that for months there had been German divisions poised on the Bulgarian border of Turkey, only prevented from moving south by their knowledge of the concentration of Allied troops in Syria. The Ninth Australian Division was there and would be brought home when ships could be spared to move it, provided, of course, that the Germans didn't move in the meantime. But explaining overall defence and logistics to a civilian, especially a woman whose only interest was in her son, was as difficult as explaining cricket to a G.I. from Nebraska.

"Well, no. No, he wasn't complaining. But then he never was one to complain. But then he doesn't know how desperate things are back here——"

"How desperate are they?" Greg said. "I've only just got back."

"Bloody desperate," said a man with a fat sad face and a pot-belly, "if the ladies will excuse the language." He leaned forward in his seat and thumped a hand on his knee. He looked about at the other occupants of the compartment, inviting them to listen to him. "We've never been in such danger. It's time all our boys were home to fight for us, instead of keeping the Germans from ill-treating the Arabs and the Gyppos. I've never been to Egypt, but I know people who have, and they say the Gyppos aren't worth saving, they've got no more time for us than they have for the Germans. And the same goes for Palestine. A young nephew of mine was there and you know what he wrote, if you'll excuse the language again, ladies? He wrote, I'm in the land where Christ was born, I wish to Christ I was in the land where I was born."

"By jove, that's original!" Greg all at once was grateful for the silly woman opposite him and the sad-faced man with his second-hand opinions. They were keeping his mind off Sarah, and as so often in the past when people began to annoy him, he felt the urge to pull their legs. "Did he really write that? You should send it to the *Women's Weekly*. They'd pay you for it."

Sarah pressed his arm, urging him to lay off, and he became aware of her again, like some lost limb that had begun to ache. Oh Christ, Sarah, he, thought and almost turned to put his arms about her and clutch her to him. But it was no use. He was on his own, and her arm linked in his meant nothing more than the gold ring on her finger. They were both symbols, and symbols had been among the most consistent casualties of this war.

He had never been on his own before. This was the first time he could remember when there was no one to turn to, no one who could help him. Trouble had been happening to him all his life; but he had always got out of it somehow: either by just ignoring it, where a more responsible man would have attacked it and tried to find some solution, or, when the trouble was such that it couldn't be ignored, by turning to someone who, if not exactly willing, had never refused him help.

Everyone in his family had always been ready to help him: Dad, Mum, his brother Don, his two sisters Emily and Jean. His father, who was a hard-working Presbyterian with definite opinions on everything, particularly loafers and irresponsible union leaders, had always been ready to help him, never recognising irresponsibility in his own family. He was a master builder who spent his days working like two men and his nights abusing the unionist termites, as he called them.

But unionists and politics hadn't interested Greg in those days. He had only glanced at the front pages of the newspapers, never read an editorial, and buried himself eye-deep in the sports pages. Europe was crumbling and Japan was re-arming, but lying on the beach at Dee Why those things hardly mattered. There were more important matters closer at hand:

F

girls and beer parties with the boys and surfing and training for the State swimming championships.

"I'm a traveller in men's overalls," the sad-faced, pot-bellied man was saying to Mrs. Updyke, "but I think I've sold my last overall for quite a while to come. We're going over to khaki shorts and trousers. That's the way it is right through the trade, not only in our trade but everywhere. Everyone going over to war work. It makes you wonder if we'll forget how to make peacetime goods." He belched behind his hand and shook his head until the dandruff rained. "I don't fancy spending the rest of my life selling goods to Army officers. Don't know their job, half of them. I tell you, I don't like the look of the future at all."

Greg looked at Sarah. "What are you going to do this afternoon?"

"I thought I might go out to Mum's. I haven't seen her for a couple of weeks. I'll stay the night."

"Are you going to tell her about us?" Mrs. Huntley had been one of the few people who had never fallen for Greg's charm: she had always treated him with a distant air of suspicion, as if she knew her daughter could have done better. Well, in a day or so she would be feeling as smug as hell, knowing she had been right.

"Not yet, I'll wait till you go back."

"Do you want me to come out with you? She may think it queer, my coming back after being away two years and you going out there to stay the night."

"Does it matter what she thinks?" They had both been talking in low murmurs, but now he could hardly hear her. Her voice had fretted away till it was just a soft breathing, like someone at the end of their tether. "Have we got to keep up appearances in front of my family, too? Isn't it just enough to satisfy your public?"

He said nothing, sitting with her arm still in his, looking

across at Mrs. Updyke and the sad-faced, pot-bellied man. When he had wakened this morning, after only a few hours' fitful sleep, it had been with the hope that during the night Sarah had changed her mind. But every growing minute of the day, every turn of the wheels carrying them back to the flat where their marriage had begun, convinced him that Sarah was finished with him. The last dregs of hope turned bitter within him and he felt empty and helpless.

"I never thought the future would be as black as this," the sad-faced man was saying. "This is one time when, if you'll pardon the language, ladies, we need all the guts we've got."

That afternoon, while Sarah went over to Dee Why to see her mother, Greg went into town to get drunk. He showered and got dressed as if for a regimental parade. He put on his hat, admiring the thick puggaree that he had had specially made for him by an old Arab in Beit Jirja, and carefully turned up the brim at the side. He took a last look at himself, then took the Victoria Cross ribbon from his breast, dropped it in his stud box, and went out to get blind, stinking un-remembering drunk.

He did it with a method that was unnatural to him, getting no enjoyment from it at all, taking a long time about it because he had never got drunk this way before, and at last he walked unsteadily out of the hotel and up through the crowded streets to Hyde Park. All the drunks go there, he thought. I'm not drunk, but I've tried, and I want to be with all the other drunks.

He found a spot free of drunks and lovers and shouting children, and lay down on the grass. Suddenly he didn't want to be with the other drunks, but to be alone. He lay flat on his back, his head pillowed on his hat, staring up at the clouds drifting across the sky. He could see nothing but the sky, but he was aware of the city all about him.

He loved this city with a passion that would have surprised people had he given voice to it. He had taken it for granted in the years before the war, but while he had been away he had become increasingly sentimental about it. It wasn't a city that had the tradition of London, nor the glamour of New York and Paris, nor the mystery of Cairo. As cities went, it was an upstart; but even so it had already developed a character of its own. It was a masculine city, for nothing feminine has yet been able to assert itself in Australia, but it was a young boy of a city. It had enthusiasm and ambition, it had a consuming love of sport, it had a desire for sin but little experience, it had pride and yet was lacking in confidence. It had grown too quickly and now was waiting impatiently for maturity.

It was not a cruel city, as so many cities are, and it gave itself freely to all its citizens. And to those who wanted to be its citizens. They had come from all corners of the state, and from other states, and from Britain and Ireland, and in the years immediately before the war they had come in droves from the dark corners of Europe. They had come from Boggabri and the high reaches of the Snowy River, from the Darling Downs of Queensland and from Gippsland in Victoria, from Yorkshire and Connemara and Berlin and Prague and Vienna. It wasn't a city as cosmopolitan as London or New York, but among its citizens were Chinese and Italians and Greeks and Syrians, none of whom wanted to return to the lands of their ancestors. It was a city of promise and it begrudged no one an opportunity.

It was a city with beauty, but not in the way that other cities were beautiful. It had no broad avenues like Paris, no imposing public buildings like London, no monuments to the twentieth century like New York. It had no sidewalk cafés, no cosy, friendly pubs, no shops that breathed romance. It had nothing as exciting as the Champs-Élysées, as dazzling as Fifth Avenue, as urbane as Regent Street. As a pattern of streets and buildings and parks and dwellings, it was mundane. And yet, sprawled about its glittering harbour, bordered by its bright beaches, humped here and there by its rolling hills, all of it under a sky that shone much more than it wept, it was a city of beauty.

It lent itself to the imagination and yet had no imagination. Its streets had been given names that, if they had once meant anything, had no meaning now. They had been named after British monarchs and statesmen: they had the dullest English sound: there was no Threadneedle or Cockspur or Half Moon Streets to lift one out of the rut. Only in its suburbs, Maroubra, Coogee, Turramurra, was there any imaginative note, and those districts had been named long before the city had been thought of.

There was no imagination in its entertainment. For twenty years it had looked at the same musical comedies, applauded the same stars in the same parts, till the sameness of its entertainment had become a joke even to itself. Even the visiting overseas companies weren't prepared to trust the city to experiment, knowing its reputation: one saw the same old ballets, heard the same music, made an occasion every time of Gilbert and Sullivan. Its only imaginative entertainment was to be found in its big park, the Domain, on Sunday afternoons, among the gospellers and health cranks and spiritualists and amateur politicians. And they were only what could be found in all big cities anywhere.

But whatever else it possessed, or lacked, it had the loyalty of its citizens. Whenever they got together, in crowds or groups or just couples, they were a part of the city and proud of it; and sometimes a man could be alone and feel as much part of it as the crowd passing him by. The Saturday afternoon crowds at the races and football, the artists and radio people grouped about their tables in the coffee shops, the young lovers strolling along the harbour front: they were the heartbeat of the city and knew it and were proud of it. They were not vocal about it, except to visitors from Melbourne, a less gifted city, and if anyone wrote a song or a poem about it, none of the other citizens knew nor cared; none of its history was celebrated in a way that took possession of the whole town; and its future was taken for granted but never broadcast. It was a bloody fine place, and its citizens could think of no better expression of pride or loyalty.

And why am I thinking about it? Greg thought. What do I care about its future or its streets or its pretty girls? I'm thinking about it only because I don't want to think about Sarah, the prettiest of all its girls. She came suddenly back to him, and then all at once he was drunk.

He lay in a stupor, tears running down his cheeks, and the forgetfulness he had been seeking had now come. People passed him by, looking at him disapprovingly, and none of them had pity. A bird perched on the toe of his boot and deposited its droppings on his gaiter. A dog came sniffing at him, then trotted on its way, disdainful and uncaring. The city had turned its back on him.

Dimly he was aware of someone sitting down beside him, talking to him, touching his pockets, but he had no way of telling who it was nor of speaking to them. A mumble fell out of him, but he had no idea what he'd been trying to say. Then the city fell in on him and the forgetfulness was complete.

When he woke he was in the back of a truck, and his right eye was swollen and painful. It was some time before he realised where he was, then he sat up and said he wanted to be sick.

A voice above him yelled, "Pull up, Les! The bastard wants to be sick!"

The truck came to a stop, someone helped him out, and he

was violently ill in the gutter. Then he climbed back into the truck, he heard a gate or door slam, and the truck started off again. He sat for a while with his head in his hands, feeling the lump over his eye, then he straightened up and looked out the back of the truck. He was looking at the receding roadway through a screen of heavy wire.

"Are we off to the pound?" he said. "Is this the R.S.P.C.A. cart?"

"Bloody funny." He turned and there was a big broken-nosed military policeman sitting opposite him. "A night in the cooler will knock some of the funniness outa you."

"That's all I need now," Greg said. "A night in gaol."

"You'll get it," said the M.P.

Greg felt the lump over his eye. "How did I get this?"

"I give it to you. Any complaints?"

"None at all," said Greg. "As a shiner, it feels like a good job."

"Bloody funny," said the M.P.

It was dark by the time the truck pulled up. Greg was pushed out through the wire gate by the broken-nosed provost. Another provost appeared out of the darkness and grabbed him by the arm, twisting it sharply up behind his back.

"No tricks like you played in the park, mug," the provost said. "Or you get the works"

"For Christ's sake, go easy!" Greg felt his arm was being torn from its socket. "I'm just a peaceful drunk. There's no need for stand-over stuff!"

The two provosts said nothing, but hustled him across the dark yard and into a room that at first looked like the office of a police station. Bars were on the windows and notices covered the walls. A warrant-officer sat at a desk reading a copy of *Man*, and in a corner a corporal was seated in front of a switch-board, slicing an apple with a jack-knife and reading an evening paper propped up against the switchboard in front of him. A barrier separated the sergeant-major and the corporal from the rest of the room, which was bare but for three chairs lined along a wall. Some rifles hung by their slings from a hat-rack, and something that could have been a strait-jacket was tossed in one corner. The room had no look of comfort or welcome: it was designed to discourage visitors from coming again. On the wall above the sergeant-major's head, like a picture of Justice, a little fly-spattered and dusty, was a photograph of General Sir Thomas Blamey.

"Well." The sergeant-major took a last look at the pneumatic girls in *Man* and put the magazine face down on the desk. "Another drunken defender of our shores?"

"Drunk and resisting arrest," said the provost who held Greg's arm. "We picked him up in Hyde Park and he kept slinging punches all the way across to the truck."

"Me?" Greg said, then flinched as the provost twisted his arm. "Jesus, look out, you'll break it!"

"You should speak only when you're spoken to, sergeant. That's how you'd have it with the men under you, wouldn't you?" The sergeant-major had a heavy blue-shaven face with a black moustache and dark bloodshot eyes. He had a trick of flicking his tongue over his teeth before he spoke, so that everything he said sounded cynical and disbelieving. "I suppose you really are a sergeant?"

"Am I supposed to speak now?" Greg said, and instantly realised his mistake: his arm was given another sharp twist.

"Let him go, Les," the sergeant-major said. The provost let go Greg's arm, and Greg began to massage his elbow and shoulder. "Yes, you may speak now, soldier. *Are* you a sergeant, a drunken bum like you? And what's your name and Army number?"

"Lance-sergeant Morley, G. W.," Greg said, and gave his Army number.

"Have a look at his pay-book, Harry," the sergeant-major said.

The broken-nosed provost went through Greg's pockets and came up with nothing. "Hasn't got a thing on him, except a dirty handkerchief."

"Come off it——" Greg said, and the broken-nosed provost slapped him across the mouth. Greg tasted blood and suddenly his temper blew up. He brought his fist up in a swing that would have hospitalised the broken-nosed provost had it landed. But the provost neatly parried it, stepped in and drove at Greg's stomach with a fist that seemed to have the weight and hardness of a rock. Greg went down, gasping for air.

"Pick him up, Harry," the sergeant-major said, without rising from his chair. "And watch those slaps across the mouth. We don't want any broken teeth littering the floor."

Greg straightened up, his stomach sore, and looked at the broken-nosed provost. "I should have recognised you. Harry Delvico, isn't it? You always could only beat blokes smaller than you."

"Bloody funny. You want more of the same?" The ex-heavyweight boxer raised his fist, but first cocked an eye at the sergeant-major. He had never been a top-line fighter, but because the country had been sadly lacking in good heavy-weights for years, he had managed to get more fights than he was worth.

"That's enough for a while, Harry," the sergeant-major said, then looked at Greg. "There's nothing in your pockets, soldier. And don't imply that the boys have frisked you. If you've lost anything, then it happened before you were picked up." Greg then remembered the voice talking to him just before he had lapsed into unconsciousness, and the hands feeling his pockets; but the damage was done now and these provosts wouldn't be interested. "Let's have a look at your meat-tags, soldier."

Greg was almost crying now, but he kept on. "His name is Vern Radcliffe. He lives at Coogee. It's a FX number. Get him. Get him, for Christ's sake!" Delvico twisted the arm, his broken-nosed face shining with sweat and sadism; and Greg suddenly screamed and went limp.

"The bastard's fainted," Delvico said, and dropped Greg to the floor. He stood looking down at the limp bloodied heap at his feet. "Some of these —— oughta never joined the Army. Always making trouble for themselves and everyone else."

"Do you think we'd better call this bloke Radcliffe?" said the corporal.

"Why?" said the provost named Les.

"Well, just in case. What if he did turn out to be this cove Morley he claims to be?"

"This bum?" said the sergeant-major and looked over his desk and down at the inert form of Greg. He flicked his tongue over his teeth with a loud sound. "Does *that* look like a V.C. winner?"

"No-o." The corporal hadn't wanted to be a provost in the first place, but he would never have got two stripes in another unit and he needed the extra money. "But maybe this Radcliffe will come and identify him. Christ, it may take us a week to get this bloke to give us his real name."

"That's a point. See if Radcliffe is in the book and give him a ring." The sergeant-major gestured to Harry Delvico and Les, and picked up his copy of *Man*, already half-way back to the overblown girls and the self-consciously naughty jokes. "Lock him up, and when he comes around give him an Aspro."

More than an hour passed before Vern Radcliffe arrived. Greg recovered consciousness just after he had been put in the cell, but he had lain quietly, glad of the respite from the thugs in the outer office. Once or twice one of the provosts came in to look at him, but he closed his eyes and breathed heavily as he had heard other drunks breathing in their sleep. They had left him alone and at last Vern had arrived.

Harry Delvico came to the door of the cell and swung it open. "Righto, on your feet! There's a Lieutenant Radcliffe out here says he'll have a look at you. We'll see how your story stands up now."

Greg got painfully off the stretcher on which he had been lying and followed Delvico down the hall. He stared at the thick neck in front of him and felt an almost overpowering urge to leap at it and wind a throttling arm about it. But sick and hazy though he was, he knew that Delvico was only walking ahead of him to tempt him into such foolishness, so that there would be one last excuse for indulging in another beating. Greg restrained himself and followed the ex-heavyweight into the brightly-lit office.

"God Almighty, Greg!" Vern's good-natured face was suddenly stiff with concern. "What's happened?"

"I ran into the Gestapo," Greg said, and didn't think he had ever been so happy to see anyone as he was to see Vern. "We made a mistake, Vern. They're not only in Germany, they've got a branch here."

The sergeant-major ignored Greg. "Do you know this man, sir?"

"Of course," said Vern, and looked at the four provosts with contempt wide open on his face. "He's Lance-sergeant Greg Morley, V.C. He's a section sergeant in my company, and he's on eight days' disembarkation leave which doesn't terminate till 10.00 hours next Monday. What's the charge against him?"

"There won't be any charge, sir," the sergeant-major said, and ran his tongue over his teeth, but nervously this time : "There's been a misunderstanding. He had no papers at all, not even his meat-tags, and we've been having a lot of trouble lately with soldiers going A.W.L.——"

CHAPTER FIVE

DINAH looked up as the two men came out of the bath-room. "There's bacon and eggs, and some apple pie. I'm sorry, Greg, it's all I could dig up at such short notice. Next time you're going to be done over, let me know and I'll have a seven-course dinner ready. How's the eye?"

Greg felt the swelling, now covered with a large strip of plaster. "Your old man should have been an R.A.P. orderly. He has the proper touch. A hand as sensitive as a bricklayer's, but still effective." He grinned at Vern. "Thanks, mate."

Vern gestured towards the table. "Better tuck in. Dinah and I'll have coffee with you."

He went down to the kitchen and Dinah sat down across the table from Greg, leaning forward on her elbows. "It doesn't seem credible. I thought that was supposed to be the sort of thing we're fighting against?"

"It is." Greg swallowed a mouthful of food. "I'll now go back into the war with renewed vigour."

Vern came back into the room carrying a tray on which were three large cups of coffee. "It's a thing about human nature that you only think the best about your countrymen, never the worst. You're afraid of condemning yourself by implication."

Dinah looked up at him and smiled as she took the cup he offered her. My darling, she thought. He can sound so

96

pompous at times, as if he's quoting from some editorial he's writing; and yet he's not pompous at all, and thank God it wasn't he the provosts belted.

"What will Sarah think when she sees you?" she said.

Greg didn't look up from his plate. "Probably think I've been in another pub brawl."

"Can't we phone her?" Dinah said.

"No, she's over at her mother's for the night," Greg said. "And the old lady hasn't got the phone on."

Dinah looked up, caught Vern's eye and shut up. Stop asking questions about Sarah, she told herself. He's on eight days' leave, after two years away, and she goes over to spend one of the eight nights with her mother. If Vern's mother was alive and *he'd* gone over to spend a night there, I'd kick him where the bullock got the knife. There's something wrong in the Morley marriage bed, and it's time the conversation was changed.

"Were these men, the provosts, all Australians?" she said. "I mean, the sort of people I see every day on the street?"

"Exactly the same," said Vern. "Cruelty isn't the prerogative of one or two races."

"Stop quoting euphemisms at me," said Dinah.

"Aphorisms, loved one," said Vern.

"Euphemisms, aphorisms." Dinah rolled her eyes and spread her hands: her mother was Jewish and she had inherited some of her gestures. "Do you quote aphorisms to your wife, Greg?"

Greg sipped his coffee, his good eye shining above the cup. Dinah had the idea he was already forgetting the provosts and what they had done to him: something that had been with him before was crowding back into his mind. "She does all the quoting in our family," he said, and Dinah thought, I'm right, there *is* something wrong between them.

"Righto, so I'm an aphorism quoter," Vern said. "But what

G

I'm trying to say is that the Germans and the Japs and our gallant allies, the Russians, haven't cornered the market on cruelty. We may not indulge in pogroms or purges or wholesale rape, but we've all got some cruelty in us. The Americans have it—the Ku Klux Klan was an outlet for cruelty. The British have it, though in a more refined form. Centuries of being on top have allowed them to be a little more tolerant and do away with the crudities of their early cut-throat colonisers. We Aussies have it, too."

"So I notice," said Dinah, and nodded at Greg's swollen eye.

"Oh, we had it long before to-night," Vern said. "We had it before the war, when Saturday afternoon pub crowds used to knock down a policeman and put the boot into him. You can see it in the crowds who go to fights and scream their heads off when they see blood. It's all cruelty, darl. These coves to-night were just worse than the usual because they had some authority that they normally wouldn't have. It's unaccustomed authority, unexpectedly being top dog, that often brings out cruelty."

"You don't sound shocked by it," Dinah said.

"Oh, I was shocked, all right," said Vern. "But more probably because it happened to Greg, someone I knew."

"You men." Dinah shook her head. "I'll bet you wouldn't catch women being as cruel as that."

"Maybe they're a little more subtle," said Greg. "You're like Vern says the British are. You've been on top so long you no longer have to be crude."

He's not generalising, Dinah thought, he's being particular. About Sarah. What's happened there? Has she fallen for another man while he's been away? I don't know him as well as I know her, and yet I don't really know her well. I like her, and I think she likes me, but we never got to the girlish confidences stage. I'd like to know what's wrong, even if I am a stickybeak. I just don't like to see things go wrong with a marriage.

"I'm on top in this family," she said, and hooked her shoulder under Vern's encompassing arm and pressed it against her cheek. "He doesn't know it, because I'm as subtle as hell."

"I haven't finished my aphorisms yet," said Vern. "May I go on?"

"Do, darling," said Dinah. "Our visitor is bored stiff, but he can't leave yet. He hasn't finished his apple pie."

"It's good pie," said Greg. "Better than the aphorisms."

"A man needs a streak of cruelty to be a good soldier," Vern said.

"Wonderful soldier, my husband," Dinah said to Greg. "Beats me black and blue regularly. Hasn't any subtlety, though. Do you beat Sarah?" she said, and thought, there you go again, Dinah, with your big loose trap.

"I used to," Greg said, "but I've got out of practice while I've been away."

"Despite the interruptions," said Vern, "I shall continue. What makes the Aussie such a good soldier, or at least a good fighting soldier, is that he usually saves his cruelty for the battlefield. The older, more civilised races practise their cruelty on the home front. The best bayonet fighters in the world are the Aussies and the New Zealanders, and there's nothing more satisfying to the sadistic-minded than shoving a bayonet into another man."

"I second that," Greg said with a grin. "I used the bayonet a couple of times in Syria, and I remember the nice feeling as it went home."

"Some of my best friends are sadists," Dinah said to her mother's photo on a side table. "I should have kept the children up."

Vern pressed her shoulder and blew the hair from behind

her ear. "Don't be surprised at the cruelty you find in anyone, darl. You know old Herb Nutter?"

"Of course." Dinah had met him at the station on the day they had arrived back. He was Vern's batman, a long-faced, buck-toothed man of forty with a friendly grin and a love of children. Vern had written her how old Herb was the delight of the Arab kids in Palestine, and everywhere he went was followed by a herd of chattering children, like a shepherd leading his flock. At the station he had dived into the depths of his kit bag and produced a bracelet for Jill and a wrist watch for Michael. "Don't tell me he's a sadist?"

"Not exactly a sadist. But I'll show you what I mean about being cruel when you're on top. One day in the Desert he was detailed to march a bunch of Eytie prisoners back to the trucks that were to take them back to the compound. There were about two hundred Eyties in the bunch, and there were Herb and three others to look after them. They split up the party between them, and went through them for all the watches and fountain pens and binoculars they could lay their hands on. That watch he gave Michael was one of them." Vern grinned. "But don't tell Michael. He'd rather think it came from a dead Eytie. Kids perfer a ghoul to a plain ordinary robber. It's more gruesome."

"A child psychologist, too," Dinah said to Greg. "Versatile as billy-ho, my old man."

"Tells a very good dirty story, too," said Greg. "He's very highly thought of in the battalion."

"Thank you," said Vern, and inclined his head modestly. "Anyhow, back to old Herb. Among his group of prisoners —or shall we call them victims?—he discovered a padre. This padre, a chubby little man who was quite out of place even in uniform, let alone at the front, was wearing a very beautiful pair of hand-tooled decorated riding-boots."

"What was he wearing those for?" Dinah said.

"He was going to Heaven on a mule," said Vern patiently. "Well. The padre pleaded and prayed and finally cursed, I'm told, but Herb made him hand over the boots, and the padre had to walk six miles over the desert in his stockinged feet. His feet were red raw when he finally got to the compound. And there was old Herb, his pockets crammed with loot and the boots strung around his neck, walking along beside him, grinning as if he were enjoying a Charlie Chaplin film."

"How did you know all this?" Dinah said.

"I drove up just before they reached the end of their march," said Vern.

"And what did you do?" Dinah said. "Make him give the things back?"

"I just kept driving," Vern said, and looked across at Greg and grinned. "You don't dress down your troops in front of the enemy, do you, sergeant?"

"Never," Greg grinned back. "You just ask for ten per cent of the take."

"I should have gone into a convent," said Dinah. "I can see I know nothing about men."

Then Greg said it was time he should be going home. "Bed will feel extra good to-night."

They walked to the door with him. "I'll drive you home," Vern said. "You'll never get a cab, and they wouldn't let you on a tram looking like that."

But Greg protested. "Heck, you've got better things to do with your petrol ration than drive me home."

"It'll ease my conscience to use some of it for a good deed," Vern said. "Otherwise we just use it driving around to visit Dinah's innumerable relatives. You've never seen such a fertile family."

"And they all think he's wonderful and tell him so," said Dinah. "He laps it up."

Greg put out his hand. "Thanks, Dinah. Coming here was the pick-me-up I needed."

"Come again some time," said Dinah. "We'll have another night of euphemisms."

"Aphorisms, beloved," Vern said, and slapped her on the behind.

When the men had gone, Dinah closed the front door and went in to look at the children. Jill was lying on her back, her head turned sideways on the pillow, her small face calm and slightly smug, as if she had already looked at life whole and decided it held nothing to frighten her. What a run-around you're going to give the boys, Dinah silently told her daughter. A few more years and they'll be ringing at the front door, their hair slicked down, broken-voiced, awkward as men on stilts, and the duchess there will spit on them from a great height and like all men, juvenile or senile, they'll take it and come back the next night, ringing at the door-bell for more. Oh, you'll do all right, Jill my girl: but you'll have to go a long way to do as well as your mother. I never spat on your father from a great height, I never had to, never wanted to. I loved him from the first moment, even before he told me I had a magnificent chest, and it's been that way ever since. Good night, Jill, and half my luck.

She went down the hall to Michael's room. He had kicked off the bedclothes and was lying on his side, his legs outspread, ready to leap out of bed at a moment's notice. My buccaneer, Dinah thought, one of the boys who are going to be spat upon by girls like Jill. She covered him up and walked slowly back to the door of the room. If we lose this war, God, keep him close to me. I'm one mother who doesn't want a hero in the family.

She went into the front bedroom, undressed and got into bed. The good old double bed, she thought, the basis of all successful marriages. I wonder if Greg and Sarah sleep in a double bed? Or have they twin beds, and the space between them has widened? A single bed is lonely and selfish-making and, in a marriage, downright dangerous. *Make sure you get a double bed*, said Mumma, who had conceived and borne seven children in the same sturdy one with the big brass knobs. *I've been married thirty years now and your father is still glad to climb in every night and cuddle up to me. While you've got a double bed, Dinah, you'll always have companionship in your marriage. You can't talk about dreams or laugh about your children or solve your worries in twin beds. The very first thing you buy, Dinah, make it a double bed.* But a double bed could be lonely, too. Big and lonely as a huge white desert, as it had been these last two years. Several times, feeling small and afraid in its imagined vastness, she had brought Jill in to sleep with her. She reached out a hand now, feeling the vacant space beside her. Come home, Vern darling, come home to this basis of our marriage, quick, quick!

He's long enough, she thought, and switched on the bed lamp and looked at her watch. He'd been gone forty minutes —did it take that long to go to Bondi and back? She switched off the lamp, looked out the window and saw it had begun to rain. Not heavily, but a thin autumn rain, just enough to make the roadway shine. What if the car skidded and he's wrapped around a pole somewhere? She felt suddenly nervous, her whole body prickling with apprehension, and her palms got clammy. She rolled over on her back, trying to clear her mind of the picture that had sprung into it, trying to be reasonable. Why should he wrap the car around a pole to-night, he's been driving for ten years or more, hasn't he? Two years he's been dodging bullets and shells and bombs and all the other things men have dreamed up to kill each other, and you worry about a silly old wet road.

Then at last she heard the car swing into the drive, and she sat up in bed and switched on the bed lamp. In less than a minute he would be here in the room, and God help him if he took his time hanging up his clothes and getting into bed to-night. There were only three more nights of his leave left, and time was running out. Hurry, my love, hurry, hurry.

Then he had opened the front door and come through into the room, rain glistening on his hair and shining on his face, smiling with the smile that hadn't changed in thirteen years, and she knew if this war took him she would never survive the sorrow.

CHAPTER SIX

"I THINK you should give up at least one Saturday night
for a cause like this," said Mrs. Bendixter. "I promised
faithfully I'd bring along two partners for these American
officers. I just took it for granted you would be the two."

"I'm sorry, Mother," Silver said. "I'm going to a party."

"I've had American officers for a while," said Mamie. "I
spent last week-end with a couple of them."

"What do you mean, you've *had* them?" said Mrs.
Bendixter. "Really, Mamie, you have some terribly loose
expressions."

"It's not only her expressions that are loose," said Silver.

"I know. I'm not exactly blind," said Mrs. Bendixter, and
did her best to look hawk-eyed and shrewd. The only shrewd
thing she had done in all her life was to marry her husband
when his wealth was still only potential, and she had done
that, not out of shrewdness, but because she had loved him
with a directness that she had never succeeded in applying to
anything else. "You really should pull your socks up, Mamie.
You're going to get into trouble one of these days and disgrace
the lot of us. God knows, I'm broad-minded, but I don't want
the place overrun with your little bastards."

"That *would* disgrace you," said Mamie, seeking a soft
chocolate in the box on her lap, a gift from one of her
Americans. "You'd have to resign from the Housewives'
Association."

"I don't happen to belong to the Housewives' Association," said Mrs. Bendixter, then looked doubtful. "Or do I? I've joined so many things since the Japanese bombed Honolulu."

"Pearl Harbour, Mother," said Silver.

"Well, it's the same thing, isn't it? I wonder if that lovely hotel on the beach there was hit?"

"I don't think so," said Silver, wondering if other people had as much patience with her mother as she and Mamie showed. "I think the Japs were only aiming at battleships."

Mrs. Bendixter seemed relieved and satisfied. "But I really must get Smithy to check on what groups I belong to. Perhaps I'm on committees I don't know about, and haven't been going to."

"You'd be more than just a committee member, Mother," said Mamie. "You'd be chairwoman, at least. Think of it, there may be meetings sitting down ever day all over Sydney with no one in the chair, simply because you forgot to turn up."

"Are you pulling my leg?" said Mrs. Bendixter, then lifted her skirt and put out her leg. "Do you like these nylons? An American brigadier-general gave them to me. He said I had legs like a middle-aged Betty Grable."

"What a lovely compliment," said Silver, and reached over and took a chocolate from the box on Mamie's lap. "No one ever flatters me that way. What about you, Mamie?"

"Never," said Mamie. "It's galling to have a mother who looks young enough to be your daughter."

"You should take more care of yourself. This new diet I have is doing wonders for me. And it's so convenient. None of the things on it are rationed. "Mrs. Bendixter stood up and walked to the window. They were in the large front living-room and from here they could look out over the front lawns and the roofs of the houses opposite to the harbour. Mrs. Bendixter stood admiring the view for a moment, then she said, "Whom do we know with a Rolls-Royce?"

"Us," said Silver. "We have one."

"I know, smarty. But ours is grey. This one is blue."

"Can't be ours then," said Mamie. "Unless Haddon painted it this morning."

"Did you tell him to?" said Mrs. Bendixter, still looking out the window.

"No," said Mamie. "I don't like blue."

"Smacks of innocence, does it?" said Silver.

"Why, of course!" said Mrs. Bendixter. "It's the Featherstone boys!"

"Meaning father and son," said Silver. "The Featherstone boys."

"Oh, God," said Mamie.

"Don't insult them," said Silver. "Just because they're not perverts doesn't make them unbearable."

Mamie looked up at Silver as the latter stood up. "One of these days, sister mine, I'm going to run a bodkin through you."

Their mother had gone out of the room into the main hall to welcome their guests, and the two girls were alone. Silver looked down at her sister and said quietly, "It would be better if you ran the bodkin into yourself, Mamie. I'm just glad Daddy died before you started on this career of yours."

She was surprised when Mamie lowered her head and said, "So am I."

She stood for a moment, for the first time in a long while feeling sorry for Mamie, unable to think of anything to say, then her mother and the Featherstone boys came into the room.

"Well, what do you know! All the Bendixter girls home together! The Featherstone boys are in luck, eh, Rog?"

Henry Featherstone was a man of middle height with a plump brown face, a toupee and, Silver was sure, a girdle. The family name originally had been Featherstonehaugh, but no one had ever been sure what to do with the last syllable and so Henry's father had discarded it. Henry's wife had died when their son Roger was six years old, a strong-willed invalid who had ruled him with a hand of iron, and ever since Henry had been trying to pluck up courage to ask another woman, any woman, to marry him. He had adopted a hearty air and, as time went by, the toupee and, if Silver was right, the girdle; but he still hadn't found the courage to adopt another wife.

"Hallo, Henry," Silver said. "What's this about a Rolls-Royce?"

"I bought it from Spike Sharpe," Henry said, and walked to the window and looked out at the car. "He's gone into the Air Force as an instructor or something, and he won't need it there."

"Hardly," said Silver. "How have you been, Roger?"

She turned her face up for Roger's kiss, wondering why she had at one time thought of marrying him. He was a nice-looking boy, without his father's false joviality and with a good deal more hair. And he looked as if he would never need a girdle. The Featherstones' money came from grazing properties in western New South Wales, and because Henry preferred to live in Sydney and had no interest in a sheep other than as a source of income, it had been left to Roger to run the stations, something Silver was sure he did well. He was tallish, with a dull lean face and dullish yellow hair. That was his trouble, he was dull all over. She had let him make love to her once or twice, and he had even been dull at that. But he was honest and hadn't a mean thought in his head and she liked him. Girls with less money than herself might find him a very good catch.

"You're looking well," Roger said.

"Better than the lubras out west, eh?" said Henry, and walked over to the drink cabinet and began to pour drinks. It was part of his joviality that he made himself at home anywhere and everywhere, although Silver sometimes suspected he was at home nowhere. "I keep telling Rog he should spend more time in Sydney. I've always liked it, but it's got really lively since the war."

"Someone has to earn the money," said Roger, and Silver looked quickly at him: he sounds almost fed-up, and that's not like Roger.

Henry laughed. "We've got damned good overseers on each of the properties. You could get away every now and again without the places going to ruin."

"Why are you down in Sydney now, Roger?" Mrs. Bendixter took the drink Henry offered her, and gave him a dazzling smile. Silver looked at her, then winked at Mamie: one of these days those two might elope. Although she knew that with Henry's lack of courage and her mother's vagueness, someone else would have to arrange it for them. Perhaps Smithy: it could be her first post-war job. "Are you going into the Army or something?"

"That would be an idea," Roger said, and sat down on the lounge beside Mamie. "No, I'm going up to Queensland. They're moving all the cattle and sheep away from the coastal areas, taking them inland. And right now they're overlanding all the cattle they can move out of the Kimberleys across to western Queensland. I'm going up to take over some of the sheep from one of the properties that are being evacuated. We're going to drove them down to Mullumbingi, about four thousand head of them."

"That will be quite a trek, won't it?" Mamie said.

Roger looked sideways at her, then turned to face her fully. He had always been scared of Mamie, Silver knew, and had never expected anything but sarcasm from her. But now he seemed reassured, and his dull, pleasant face lit up with a smile. "Yes, I reckon it will. But they did it in the old days, and we can do it again. I've got a good bunch of men, and we'll get the sheep down all right. We'll lose a few, but that can't be helped. It would have been worse if we'd had to do it a few months back, in the summer. But so long as we don't hit floods, this is a good time for it."

"I think it's wonderful," said Mrs. Bendixter. "Just like the pioneers. And you mean if the Japanese land in Brisbane—although I don't know why they should want to land *there*—there won't be any beef or lamb for them to eat? But I always thought they ate only rice."

Silver and Mamie lay back and laughed, and after a hesitant moment Roger joined them. Henry grinned, unsure whose side to be on, then he leaned across and patted Mrs. Bendixter's knee.

"Don't take any notice of them, Katie. The youngsters to-day are always a little too ready to laugh at us older ones."

"I'm sure I don't know what they're laughing at," said Mrs. Bendixter. "I just asked a perfectly simple question. Have you seen the Fergusons lately?"

Henry, like all of Mrs. Bendixter's friends, was used to her sudden switches in conversation. He parried the new question and the two of them settled down to a discussion of the Fergusons. Roger, loose-tongued in his pleasure at not being a butt for Mamie's sarcasm, was going too far and suggesting she should come out to Mullumbingi for a visit some time. Silver sat in her chair sipping her drink and wondering when Jack would arrive.

She was impatient for him to come. She hadn't been like this since God knew when. I'm not in love with him, she thought. I've had too many men and too many disappointments for love to happen that quickly to me.

But it was a long time since any man had excited her so much, but she knew from experience that excitement wasn't love. She had come to realise, not from experience but from observation, that contentment was a more necessary and lasting quality in love; and it was still too soon to know if Jack Savanna could bring her contentment. The war had speeded up everything, even falling in love; and he might be lost to her forever before she had time to know.

Mrs. Bendixter was leaning backwards in her chair, stretching her neck to peer out the window. "Surely the Army's not thinking of requisitioning *our* place? I know they're doing it, but I thought it was only if the houses were empty. I certainly wouldn't want to move out of here into some stuffy little flat, although I suppose we could go and live at the house at Bowral——"

"What the hell are you talking about, Mother?" said Mamie.

"There's a soldier standing out there in the middle of the lawn," said Mrs. Bendixter, "looking at our house as if he's already taken it over and wants it altered."

Silver got up and walked to the window. "It's Jack!"

"Jack?" said Mrs. Bendixter. "Jack who?"

"Jack Savanna, her latest," said Mamie, as Silver put down her drink and hurried out of the room. Mamie leaned across and patted Roger's knee. "Roger, old boy, you must get awfully sick of meeting all of Silver's latests."

"You get used to it," Roger smiled: his dull face didn't look capable of showing hurt. "It's like getting teeth pulled. After the first half dozen, there's no pain."

"You're a fool, Rog," said Mamie, "but quite suddenly I like you."

Outside on the terrace Silver was standing at the top of the steps looking down at Jack. The latter was standing in the exact middle of the big lawn, his hands on his hips, his hat on the back of his head, gazing at the house with the air of a prospective buyer.

"Well, do you like it?" Silver called.

"Too big," Jack shouted. "Whoever built it lost his sense of perspective." He came across the lawn and up the steps. "However, if you go with the joint, I'll take it."

She put her arm in his, excited and (yes, she thought) contented now he was here. "Hallo, Jack. I thought you'd lost your way."

"And you didn't think any of the natives would be able to direct me to the Bendixter château?" He bent and kissed the top of her head. "No, I was just late starting. My watch has gone on the blink."

"I'll buy you a new one as a going-away present," she said, and thought suddenly that he would be gone in a couple of days.

"You keep your hard-earned money," he said, and took a last look at the house before they went in the wide front door. "You need it to run this museum."

"Mother, you remember Jack Savanna, "Silver said as they entered the living-room. "You met him Wednesday night."

"Why, of course! You're the boy with that ridiculous moustache!" Mrs. Bendixter always identified people and subjects by their most salient feature; nondescript persons and abstract subjects only left her even more vague and slightly annoyed. She also prided herself on her memory for other detail, no matter how inaccurate: "You were one of the bodyguard for that happy war hero we had the other night!"

Silver pressed Jack's arm. "At least she remembered your face."

"What were you scrutinising our house for?" said Mrs. Bendixter.

"I was thinking what a wonderful headquarters it would make for General MacArthur," Jack said. "We've been told to keep our eyes out for possible locations."

"General MacArthur?" Mrs. Bendixter was already half-way out of the house on her way to Bowral: having the house requisitioned by a *general*, and General MacArthur at that, was something else again to having it requisitioned by the *Army*.

He fits in, Silver thought half an hour later, sitting in her chair and watching Jack with pride and affection. When that cynical streak of his isn't working, he's amiable and likeable and so much at home with people. I think he still resents our money, but that can't be helped: we have it and we're not going to throw it away. He doesn't seem to resent it as a Communist might, nor even as the son of an ex-rich man might. She remembered the couple of poor boys who had fled when they had learned of her wealth; but Jack looked the last man who would flee in the face of such misfortune. But he had made a couple of oblique remarks about her money, and she would have to find out why.

At last the Featherstone boys rose to leave. "We've got a dance on down at the yacht club," Henry said. "We've invited some of the American naval officers from those ships that have just come into port. I'm acting-host, since the commodore is away on patrol this week-end."

Silver knew that those harbour yachtsmen who hadn't gone into the Services had volunteered to do coastal patrol work in their own boats. Henry owned a 35-foot motor cruiser and though she knew he went out on patrol, she couldn't picture him being anything but a hindrance to his crew if they should sight any sort of Jap vessel. Henry was one of those poor unfortunates who were completely lost in a war and who unfortunately so often finished up getting themselves killed in circumstances that another man would take in his stride. She looked at Henry now, smoothing down his toupee, easing his girdle (she really must find out about that. But how?) and she wished him safe, uneventful patrols till the end of the war.

"I'm going along to the dance," Roger said. "I thought you may have liked to come, Sil."

"I'm sorry, Rog," she said, and thought he looked even duller beside Jack. He's nice, but I've completely lost interest in him. Even as a friend. Does that mean I'm finding Jack sufficient? Was that love, when there was only one man and all the rest faded away? "I already have a date with Jack. Next time you come down, give me some warning."

"I'll do that," said Roger, and again she noticed the slightly fed-up note in his voice. He looked down at Mamie. "You wouldn't like to be second choice, would you, Mamie?"

"I'm cut to the quick," said Mamie, "but in any case, Rog, I couldn't go. I have a date, too."

"Well——" Roger shrugged, shook hands with Jack, and followed his father and Mrs. Bendixter out to the hall. Silver, feeling a little sorry for him (he must lead a pretty dull life out there at Mullumbingi these days), went out after him.

Automatically she lifted her face for his good-bye kiss, as she had been doing for years, but she was totally unprepared for the kiss he gave her. Her mouth was bruised when he let her go and she could still feel the pressure of his hands on her shoulders where he had held her.

"My!" said Mrs. Bendixter. "They're passionate out Mullumbingi way, aren't they?"

"A chip off the old block, eh?" said Henry, who hadn't kissed a women like that in years.

Silver was angry with Roger, but she carried it off with what grace she could muster. A week ago she wouldn't have minded, perhaps been amused and kissed him back, but when she looked over her shoulder she saw Jack watching her through the big open arch into the living-room. He stared at her for a moment, unsmiling, then he turned to Mamie and went on talking.

Henry and Roger left, the latter showing no sign of smugness or triumph but only giving Silver a last-minute wink as they drove away in the blue Rolls. Mrs. Bendixter went upstairs for the thirty-minute daily rest recommended by her beautician as an antidote to the world's worries. Silver closed the front door and went back into the living-room.

"I'm coming to the party to-night," said Mamie. "Jack has just asked me."

"I thought you told Roger you had a date?" Silver said.

"I couldn't hurt him by telling him I didn't want to go to the dance with him," said Mamie. "But I'd had enough of poor dull Roger for one day."

"Would you say he was dull?" Jack said. "I shouldn't have thought so."

"You wouldn't look at him the way a woman does," said Mamie. "Will there be any dull men at the party to-night?"

"There may be one or two, but it will be lively enough." Jack looked up at Silver, and she could only guess that what she read in his eyes was cynicism. "There'll be plenty of men to go around."

"Good," said Mamie.

Silver sat down, picked up her drink and slowly drained the glass. She wasn't jealous of her sister and didn't mind her coming to the party, although she hoped she would behave and not disgrace her in front of Jack's friends. Two or three years ago Roger had often kissed her as he had just a while ago. And if Jack was cynical again, it wasn't the first time since they had met. Nothing new had happened in the last five minutes, yet somehow she felt the bottom had fallen out of the coming evening.

CHAPTER SEVEN

WHEN Sarah had come home on Friday morning and seen Greg's face battered, his swollen eye and cut lip, her first thought was that he had been in another pub brawl. She had been about to make a comment to that effect, but had checked herself: we're finished, she had thought, and it's not my place now for wifely criticisms. Ever since she had known him, he had been getting into fights, usually in pubs, and almost never coming out of them unmarked. He'd always had excuses, that the other fellow had started it or (with a grin) that his fist had been on its way before he had realised it, but she had soon grown tired of them. They had had several arguments about his behaving like some adolescent larrikin. He would storm out of the flat and she would lie down on the lounge, wondering if her mother hadn't been right after all in warning her that Greg would never amount to anything as a husband. Then an hour later he would come back, his arms laden with flowers, grinning sheepishly, and always she had given in and the row and the fight in the pub had been forgotten. Till next time. So that yesterday morning habit had almost made her commit a blunder.

She had been shocked when Greg had told her what had happened. He had made no secret of the fact that he had been drunk when picked up by the provosts, and she had noted he'd made no attempt to excuse his drunkenness. He had told her simply what the provosts had done to him, just because she asked and without trying for her sympathy, and she had felt a rush of the old feeling within her again. It's my maternal instinct, she had told herself; but she had decided that, instead of going out that afternoon as she had planned, she would spend the day with him.

She had changed the dressing on his eye, cooked him the best lunch and dinner she could dream up, and in the evening had suggested they go for a walk down to the beach. They had got through the day like a couple who had never been parted, who had been married for ten or fifteen years and now took each other's company for granted. When it came time for bed she felt her first discomfort.

"Are you sleeping in the spare bedroom?" she had said.

"I think I'd better." He had been unnaturally quiet all day. She knew there was a thoughtful side to him that only she had discovered, and she had cherished it for its unexpectedness. But it had come to the surface rarely and certainly had never before lasted an entire day. Even now, when she had expected another plea, some sort of outburst, he had been calm and matter of fact. "It will cut out the awkwardness."

"Good night, Greg," she had said. "Are we still going to the Browns' party to-morrow night?"

"Do you want to?"

"I think so. I've got a new frock that I've been saving for months. I told you about it in a letter."

"I remember. Taffeta, and the colour is American Beauty, whatever that is."

"You'll see to-morrow night. Good night, Greg."

Now she was getting ready for the party. The dress lay on the bed, rich and glowing under the light directly above it, and she was impatient to put it on. She had bought it six months before in a crazy moment when she had felt like spending money, buying something that was unnecessary and exciting and that at that time she had had no opportunity of wearing. She had seen the dress in one of the small shops in one of the arcades off Castlereagh Street and after thinking about it all night had gone back next morning and bought it. She had told Greg about it because, then, she had been seeking anything at all to put in her letters, to make up for what she had left out.

He tapped on the door. "I come in?"

Without thinking, having her husband knock on her bedroom door for the first time and being used to it, she said, "Of course."

She was wearing only panties and her suspender belt and was sitting on the boudoir stool pulling on her stockings when he came in the door. He stopped and looked down at her, and only then was she aware of her bare breasts. His eyes went slowly over her, not salaciously, not angrily, but only as if remembering, and she blushed.

"I'm sorry, Greg. I wasn't thinking. Throw me my gown from behind the door."

"It's all right," he said, and made no attempt to get her gown. He crossed to a closet, took out his uniform jacket and looked at it. "I'll have to wear this old job to-night. My other uniform needs cleaning after Thursday night's show."

"I'll send it to the cleaners on Monday." She was still conscious of her nudity, but it seemed ridiculous to get up and throw her gown about her now. It was too soon for them to be complete strangers just yet.

He hung the jacket over his arm, closed the closet and turned to walk past her to the door. Then he stopped and bent over her and she felt the weakness run through her and she thought, It's going to happen and I can't say no to him.

But all he said was, "I still love you, Sarah. Remember

that," then he had kissed her lightly on the lips and had gone out of the door.

She stared at the half-closed door for almost a full minute, then she dropped her face into her hands and wept. There was no future with him, she told herself, but I still have some of the past.

She dried her eyes, put on her gown and went out to the bathroom and vigorously washed her face again. By the time she had applied her make-up and finished dressing, her eyes showed no sign of the recent tears. She picked up her coat and the highly-decorative evening wallet Greg had brought back from the Middle East, and went out to the living-room where he was waiting for her.

"Do you like it?" She knew that the dress suited her better than anything she had ever worn before: the colour, style, fit, everything was just perfect. It seemed a shame and a little cruel that it was to be a sort of farewell gown.

"If I have to beat a Yank over the head for it," Greg said, "we're getting a cab to-night. You look too good to be riding in trams."

It had always been difficult to catch an empty cab on Saturday nights. Since the advent of the Americans, who had introduced some strange manna called tipping and therefore were objects of worship to local cab drivers, it had become almost impossible. One had to stand in the middle of the road furiously waving signs of profligate wealth, or sneak up in the dark with an American accent and be in the cab before the driver discovered one's treachery. Greg used the first technique, standing in the middle of the road, risking death and looking as profligate and promising as possible, and after ten minutes a cab pulled up.

"I'm on me way back to town, mac." This driver had spent a lot of time with the gods: his accent was Brooklyn via Woolloomooloo. "If it ain't outa me way, I'll take you."

"Vaucluse," said Greg, almost on his knees. "How about that?"

"It means I gotta detour," said the driver, "but okay, hop in."

"I appreciate this," said Greg, as he held open the door for Sarah to enter: cab drivers had given up opening doors when the sedan chair went out of fashion. "I wouldn't have asked you, but my wife has only one leg."

"'At's okay, mac," said the driver magnanimously. "I ain't got anything against Australians."

Greg closed the door, sat back beside Sarah and grinned. He seemed in a good cheerful mood, much like the old Greg before last Wednesday night at Katoomba but still with the quietness behind his cheerfulness, and she began to look forward to the rest of the evening. If he stayed sober and cheerful as this, they could both enjoy the party. She hadn't expected to enjoy even one moment with him till he went back to camp and their married life was over for good. It came as something of a shock that Monday morning, less than forty-eight hours away, would mean the end of everything.

The dark confines of the cab seemed more intimate than the flat had been, and she sensed an awkward atmosphere creeping in. She could feel his nearness: the warmth of his body, the roughness of his sleeve as it brushed against her hand, the vibrant maleness of him. He had been a good lover and she had always yielded to him willingly whenever he had wanted her. I'm not completely out of love with him yet, she told herself, and fought against the weakness. So she told him she had decided to take a job.

"You haven't got to," he said, and there was only a faint touch of rancour in his voice: he sounded more surprised than anything else. "You can go on drawing my pay from the office, and still keep my allotment from the Army."

"I think that had better go into the bank, and we'll talk

about it later. I'm taking the job because I think I should be doing something at a time like this. I haven't any children to excuse me——"

"We could have done something about that," he said, although he had been the one who hadn't wanted children immediately. Let's wait, he had said, let's enjoy ourselves for a while, then we'll settle down.

She could feel herself losing her grip on the evening, feel it falling to pieces around her like a jerry-built house shaken by the temblor of his mood. The cheerfulness was all at once gone and now he was angry and bitter. She shouldn't have mentioned the job. "It's too late for children now," she said.

He was silent for a while, then he said, "What are you going to do?"

She wanted to lie, to think up some new job, but her mind refused to work quickly. Knowing how so many of the returned men felt, it was like adding insult to injury when she said, "I'm going to work for the American Navy as a secretary."

He took it as she had expected. "You shouldn't be lonely for company, then. They tell me the Yanks look after their secretaries, twenty-four hours a day."

I should blow up, she thought, get angry, slap his face, but what's the use? After the way he used to play around, what right has he to suspect me of the same thing? He'd never understand that I chose to work for the Americans because they pay better, and I want to be independent, I don't want him to keep me. I want to do war work, but I may as well get what I can out of it. It's a selfish thought, but I've done enough self-sacrificing in the past. He probably wouldn't understand that, either.

They rode the rest of the way in silence. The cab pulled in at last in front of the Browns' house. "This is it, mac. You're outa your way over here, ain't you? This is officer territory."

But Greg couldn't be cheerful even with the driver. "No one asked for your comments. Here."

The driver took the money and instantly noted there was no tip. "No wonder we like to pick up Yanks," he said. "At least they're polite and know how to treat a guy." Then he reverted to pure Australian: "I hope you get your bloody head shot off."

CHAPTER EIGHT

"YEAH, it's tough on you boys being away. You miss a lot, don't you? War's a fair cow, ain't it? Say look, are you here with anyone? A girl, I mean. I come with Mick, but at the rate he's pouring the beer into himself I'll be on me own by midnight——"

Then Dinah came out and Vern said, "I'm afraid I can't make it. This is my wife."

The blonde raised her eyebrows, said, "Nearly put me foot in it that time," and went off to seek another possible replacement for Mick Kennedy. Dinah looked after her. "Making an assignment with her, mister?"

"Assignation," said Vern automatically.

"Well, you know what I had in mind. Were you?"

He grinned and put his arms about her. "I'm saving myself for you. I said to myself an hour ago, that brunette with no front in her frock is for me. What's your name—Chesty Bond?"

"Theda Bara." She kissed his ear and her hand played gently with the back of his neck. "Don't drink too much, mister. This is our second last night. I didn't buy this frontless frock for nothing."

"Steady on, Theda. This is no place for such antics. Let's change the conversation."

"Let's not."

"What are we going to do to-morrow?"

She sighed. "Righto, seduction postponed. To-morrow? Well, we're getting the car out, picking up the kids at Mumma's, and we're going out into the bush somewhere for a picnic. Even if it's raining cats and dogs, we're going to get away somewhere so people can't break in on us. To-morrow is *our* day. Mine and yours and the kids'." He kissed her, and she said, "Attaboy, Rudolph. Shall we take up where we left off?"

Then Dad Mackenzie came across to them. "Is this man molesting you, madam?"

"No," said Dinah. "Unfortunately."

"He's a fool, then," said Dad. "I never did have much respect for the initiative of officers."

"Who's running down officers?" Jack Savanna had joined them, his arm about Silver Bendixter. Several other couples drifted out and the group grew. Vern grinned and pinched Dinah through her girdle: their privacy was gone. "I have something to contribute on the subject of officers," Jack said.

"The other evening," said Silver, "he threatened to throw one down a lift-well."

He certainly knows how to pick them, Vern thought. This one seems to have everything and, what's most important, she seems to like him. You could expect a girl like her to be bored at a party like this, with all strangers about her and none from her own circle, but she's not. I wonder how interested Jack is in her? I'd like to see the old bastard settle down. He's too good a bloke to be wasted on the dizzy dames I've seen him with in the past.

"Hey, Jack," said Joe Brennan, "what was the name of the big fat reinforcement who joined us at Mersa Matruh?"

"King Farouk," said Jack.

"No, the bloke who was killed at Damour."

"Oh, *him*. Sid Hourigan. But whatever happened to Farouk?"

"He was boarded B-class," said Dad Mackenzie. "He got a job in Cairo."

Mick Kenedy was telling someone, "We'll beat the Japs in two years. You ain't got to be any military strategist to see that."

"Well, that lets you in," said Joe Brennan. "You ain't any military strategist."

"You wanna know why we'll beat 'em?" said Mick Kennedy.

"No," said Joe Brennan.

Mick ignored him. "We'll beat 'em because their lines of communication are stretched to breaking point. Nobody can win when his lines are stretched to breaking point."

"What about when *our* lines are stretched to breaking point?" said Joe. "When we chase 'em back to Tokyo? What happens then?"

"We don't win," said Bluey Brown. "They chase us back to New Guinea. Everybody's lines of communications get stretched to breaking point. How are your lines of communication, Jack?"

"Dry," said Jack. "Fill my glass."

Mick Kennedy took a gulp at his beer. "Righto, you bastards wait and see. I tell you, you ain't got to be a military strategist——"

"You said that," said Joe Brennan. "And we agreed you ain't one."

"Does MacArthur know about our Mick?" said Dad Mackenzie. "Maybe he could do with some help."

"I wouldn't work for MacArthur if you paid me," said Mick. "I'm one Aussie who can do without the Yanks——"

"He can do without the Yanks," Bluey Brown said. "How bout you, Jack?"

"Welcome them with open arms," said Jack. "I welcome

everyone with open arms. Yanks, Pommies, Irishmen, reffos——"

"What about the Japs, eh?" said Mick triumphantly. "Would you welcome them with open arms? You're the sort that ud throw this country open to the whole world. Me, I believe in Aussie for the Aussies!"

"He ain't no military strategist," said Joe Brennan, "but he oughta run for Parliament."

"There ain't any strategists in Parliament," said Mick. "Military or otherwise. They're just a bunch of mugs."

"He knows all about Parliament too," said Joe Brennan. "How's their lines of communication, Mick?"

The argument would get nowhere, like all arguments at a party, and Vern decided to get to know Silver Bendixter better.

"Would you like to dance?" A record-player had just begun a slow waltz, one of the few dances he could do with any degree of skill. He wasn't keen on dancing, preferring to save his energy for other things, but Dinah liked it and so he had done his best to learn a few steps. But Fred Astaire would never have cause for worry.

"I'd love to," said Silver. "I've been waiting for Jack to ask me, but all he's done all evening is talk."

Jack grinned down at her. "I'm trying to share myself equally among everyone. If I danced with you, there would be disappointment elsewhere in the room."

Vern looked at Dinah. "Am I excused?"

She looked at her watch. "Be back by supper time. No parking." She looked at Silver. "Watch him on the corners, Silver. He has a tendency to go round them dragging one foot as if he's riding a motor bike."

"I'm a highly individualistic dancer," said Vern.

Vern had had so few other women in his arms in the last thirteen years, even just for dancing, that he held Silver as if he were afraid of getting his face slapped. Being a one-woman man had its smaller drawbacks, besides the more obvious ones. He felt his awkwardness was conspicuous, and he held Silver a little closer to him.

"Not too tightly," she said, smiling at him. "Dinah's watching us."

"I'm out of practice." He felt sure she was the sort of girl one could be frank with. "Outside of Dinah, you're the only girl I've been near in the last two years."

"Oh, I thought you officers had a wonderful time in the Middle East. Nurses and V.A.D.s, and all those beautiful Jewesses in Tel Aviv. And the Lebanese girls in Beirut. Jack was telling me they were the loveliest women he'd seen."

"I'm the faithful type," he said, and meant it. Once or twice while overseas, admiring the ripe high-breasted girls in Tel Aviv and the nut-brown girls on the communal farms, their shorts rolled high on their provocative thighs and their breasts prominent beneath their thin shirts, he had had the sudden urge for a woman. But he had never succumbed and he had known if he had he would never have felt at ease again in bed with Dinah. "I'm one of the last repositories of old-fashioned morals," he said, and laughed and swung Silver into a gay whirl as the waltz came to an end.

"That last bit was very spectacular," said Dinah as he and Silver rejoined the group in the patio. "Have you been taking lessons from some Cairo dancing tart?"

Vern delivered Silver to Jack. A little later, as he and Dinah walked through to the front of the house, he saw Silver and Jack disappearing down the steps. "They must be going home. She's quite a dish, isn't she?"

"Now don't let's get lyrical about other women. I'm the dish in your eye. One thing I've always liked about you. You're not the sort of husband who's always busy admiring other women's legs and bosoms and faces."

"I do, actually." He drew her down beside him on the swinging canvas seat on the front terrace. "I just have a trick of looking at them with an inner eye you don't know about."

"So long as you keep it to yourself, that's all right. But I'll concede a point. Silver is quite a dish. Do you think it might come to anything with Jack. She's rather struck on him."

"How do you know?"

"I'm physic."

"Psychic."

She put her feet up on the seat and lay back with her head in his lap. "There, put your hand there. That's better. I've missed all that sort of thing. Did you miss it?"

"I used to get up in the middle of the night," he said, "and go for a walk, just to cool off."

"I love you, darling." He bent down and kissed her and she clung to him. After a while she said, "I can't get over my luck. Some of those other women inside there aren't as lucky as me. Sarah, for instance."

"There's something wrong between them," he said. "Greg's just sitting in there, doing nothing but getting drunk, and Sarah's hardly looked at him all night."

"Whose fault do you think it is?"

"I don't know. It could be hers. I know how keen he was to get back to her. He's a bit hare-brained at times, but he certainly loves her."

"That's just like a man, to blame the woman. Personally, I don't think it's her fault. She's too unhappy for it to be her fault."

"Well! Who was slinging off at me the other night about being a psychologist? Tell me more, Mrs. Freud. Do you think perhaps they're sexually maladjusted?"

"Did Greg get V.D. while he was in the Middle East?"

He laughed and patted her stomach. "I'm not his father

confessor, nor his doctor, either. We can't help them. Let them work it out for themselves."

"I just don't like to see nice people break up, that's all. I'm a great little believer in the permanence of marriage." She pulled his head down and kissed him again, then she said, "Have you made up your mind about the war corrspondent's job?"

"I'm not going to take it," he said, and waited for her reaction. But there was none, and he said, "Are you disappointed?"

She shook her head. "No. You know what you want, darling. It's easy for me to say it would be a good thing, but I haven't got to make the decision." She took his hand and put it against her lips. "Vern, you will be careful, won't you?"

He smiled, but in the darkness she couldn't see it. "I can only try, darl. But when you're in action, taking care is about the hardest thing to do. You're acting on reflex most of the time. If you're careful, it's because it's the natural, instinctive thing to do at the particular moment."

"Was Greg being careful when he won the V.C.?"

"No," he said, and smiled. "But I'm not going to be winning V.C.s."

"I wish I could understand the meaning of this war," she said. "There's more to it than just fighting Hitler or the Japs. What caused it in the first place? Why can't people live in peace with each other?"

"We could talk all night about that, and get nowhere. That's one of the few positive things about being in action— you don't have time to ponder the reason or sense of your being there. It's times like this, when you're out and away from the war, that the stupidity of it all strikes you. You see what you can lose, see it all in a new light. Everything you've built up and cherished——"

"Why don't people see it that way *before* they start wars?"

I

"I don't know, darl. Maybe they do see it, and yet in a way it contributes to war. Most ordinary people are pacifists by instinct and they're always ready to vote against rearmament." He looked down at the dim oval of her face. "The worst of war, darling, is that in the end it's only nobodies like us who lose."

"So long as I don't lose you," she said, "I haven't lost anything."

Then as they stood up Vern saw the searchlights down on the harbour break out in a rash of frantic beams, saw the sudden flash of guns and a moment later heard the roar of an explosion.

CHAPTER NINE

WHEN the first gun went off Jack took almost no notice of it. He and Silver had managed to catch a cab right in front of the Browns' place and had reached the Quay just in time to scramble aboard this ferry before the gangplanks went up. They were sitting on the outside of the ferry now despite the cold, he with one arm around her and the other hand exploring under the mink coat. He was kissing her when the first searchlights flashed on, so was only half-aware of them. When the gun went into action, somewhere behind them on the south side of the harbour, he heard it first only as a dull shock at the back of his mind. He had become accustomed to the sound of guns and his ears had learned to disregard them.

Then Silver stiffened in his arms, pulling her face away from his, and in that instant the other guns opened up. East of the ferry, towards the outer harbour, there was a succession of dull explosions. Searchlights flashed on all about the harbour, their ghostly beams criss-crossing each other like swords being wielded in a duel that had no purpose. The ferry suddenly ran into the centre of a beam and Jack saw the fear and bewilderment on Silver's face, close to his own. He turned his head and saw people rushing out of the saloon of the ferry, crowding along the side, shouting and frightened and puzzled. The ferry's siren hooted, a hoarse panic-stricken sound, as if complaining about being exposed in the glare of the searchlight, then the bright beam had swung away and gone probing west farther up the harbour. Jack stood up, pulling Silver with him.

"What's happening?" An elderly man, his arm about the frightened dumpy figure of his wife, grabbed Jack's arm. "Is it an air raid? Is it the Japs?"

"I don't know," Jack said, and tried not to sound irritable. How the hell did he know what it was? But the elderly man couldn't be blamed: he'd had no experience of war, possibly never even seen a gun fired till a moment ago. There would be a good many more like him on the ferry. The country had never seen a war: the people didn't even have history to help them. They were face to face with the unknown, and their bewilderment was as great as their fear. "I don't think it's an air raid. All the firing is horizontal."

Farther up the harbour, in the direction of Garden Island, there was a loud explosion. "They're after the Yank ships!" someone said. "The *Chicago* and those destroyers. Something just went up then."

"Don't tell me it's going to be another Pearl Harbour," a man said. "Jesus, we aren't going to be caught napping twice in a row!"

A burst of tracers went across the front of the ferry, and several women screamed. Again to the east there was a series of dull explosions, and Jack now recognised them as depth charges. A minesweeper suddenly appeared out of nowhere, swinging across the bows of the ferry into an intersection of searchlight beams, then plunging on into the darkness. The whole of the harbour seemed alive with guns, and Jack all at once became scared. There seemed to be no co-ordination about the fire, and no one appeared to know what the target was.

A ferry hand was moving through the crowd now, telling people to keep calm. "We're heading for the wharf at Taronga Park. We're right in the line of fire here, but we'll be out of it in a jiffy. Everybody please keep their shirts on, and we'll be all right."

"What is it?" Jack said to the man as he went past. "A sub raid?"

"I think so," said the man. "Dunno for sure." He moved on through the crowd. "Keep calm, everybody. We're putting in to the wharf at Taronga Park. A special night excursion to the Zoo——"

Jack looked down at Silver. "How are you?"

"Scared stiff," she said, then did her best to smile. "I hope you can swim well enough for both of us."

The ferry was swinging slowly, as if the captain was trying to sneak it away without being seen. Tracers were still streaking across the water, passing dangerously close, and once more there was the dull explosion of depth charges, much closer this time, so that the ferry shuddered a little as the tremors passed under it. From the direction of Garden Island, where most of the naval ships were anchored, there was now a steady stream of fire, most of it directed to a spot not a hundred yards from the ferry. In the dazzling brilliance of the searchlight beams water spouted like pale blue flowers. As they died slowly in a rain of spray, other flowers grew instantly in the same spot. Angry red bees of tracers whipped through the unearthly garden. There was a wild terrifying beauty about the scene, if anyone right then had an eye for beauty.

Then the heavier guns at the shore batteries around the harbour opened up and the water became just a seething riot of foam. Shells screamed over just to the port side of the ferry and went into the harbour in what seemed to be one continuous roar. It was like being caught in the middle of a naval battle in which there was no adversary, just an attacking force bent upon wreaking destruction on the sea.

"We'll all be killed!" a woman screamed. "Let me go! Let me go!"

Jack spun round. The woman had broken away from the young girl with her, and was trying to clamber over the rail. Jack left Silver, dived forward and grabbed the woman round the waist. She fought violently, moaning to herself, berserk in her panic. Jack turned her round, tried to reason with her, then drew back his arm and clipped her neatly under the chin. She went limp in his arms.

"Oh, Mum, what's the matter?" The girl, who looked no more than sixteen, was now beside Jack, clutching at her mother's shoulder.

"She's all right," Jack said. "I knocked her out. She'll have a sore jaw when she wakes up, but it was the best thing." He picked up the woman and laid her on a seat. "Sit here with her. She'll come round in a minute."

There were isolated signs of panic all over the ferry now, but generally the passengers were keeping themselves under control. The noise now was deafening. The air seemed to be full of screaming shells, bright tracers and spray that hung like blue rain in the glare of the searchlights. Closer to Garden Island there was now another concentration of searchlight beams, and there too the water was being churned into a cauldron of blue foam.

"There must be more than one of them!" Jack said. "Christ, we must be right in the middle of a pack of them!"

Spray hung all about the ferry now, wet and cold on the skin like the coldness of fear. Jack looked down at Silver and grinned reassuringly. He pressed her hand, feeling the fear in her. A searchlight beam detached itself from the skein on the harbour surface and moved east towards the boom defences across the outer harbour. It passed across the ferry, seeming to linger for a moment, and in that instant Jack saw the faces of the crowd as if in a newsreel close-up. Fear was there on every face, but the predominant expression was disbelief. These people had been reading about the war for thirty-three months now, aware all the time that it was getting closer to them, but still going on hoping that it wouldn't reach them, still showing the same complacent stupidity as they and millions of others like them had shown in the years before September 1939. He had been like them himself, he knew, only his awakening had come a little earlier and not quite so shatteringly as theirs was coming to them now. Hope for peace was a human failing that always left the individual unprepared. This moment had been coming for years, and now it had arrived the people still didn't fully believe it.

Then the submarine came to the surface astern of the ferry. It came up out of the water, out of line of the searchlights, black and glistening and deadly. It wasn't large, about twice as long as a good-sized motor cruiser, and it came up with a silence that heightened its effect of evil. A half-shout, half-scream, went up from the people at the rear of the ferry. They turned and began to scramble madly towards the front of the boat, pushing and shoving, women screaming, men shouting, and a young boy's voice calling fearfully for his dad. Then someone tripped and went down screaming. The crowd, unable to control its own impetus, kept coming forward, piling itself up on the people who had gone down. A mass of people was stuck between the outside wall of the saloon and the railing of the ferry, and the screams grew, pain now mixed with fear. The ferry's siren hooted frantically and the engines began to pound. The whole boat seemed to become a living thing, absorbing the fear of its passengers, and it strained with the effort to get away. The searchlights swung and focused, and the submarine was outlined, then lost in spray as the guns opened up on it. But the torpedo was already on its way.

It hit the ferry at the precise moment the submarine blew up under a direct hit from a shell. The two sounds merged and wreckage from both explosions fell in the one area of water. The ferry stopped suddenly, shuddering along its whole length, then as the roar of the explosions died away it began to settle at the stern. The smoke cleared a little, drifting slowly on the spray-laden air, and the back of the boat was exposed as a sickening scene of slaughter. The torpedo had hit just below the packed mass of people and now there was nothing there but the bloodied ruin of bodies. Moans and screams tore at the ears, and somewhere on the other side of the boat someone was laughing hysterically. Close by Jack and Silver a man was cursing violently and without purpose, and near him a woman was praying aloud in the one dull monotone. The smell of smoke and cordite was thick, and Jack recognised another smell: burned flesh. Panic was rushing through the sinking ferry faster than the water pouring in at its wrecked stern; and above it all the hooting siren added its urgent note.

"Can you swim?" Jack was pulling Silver's mink coat off her.

"Yes." She was frightened, but she was keeping control of herself. "But keep by me, Jack. It may be too far."

"You've got about four hundred yards. Take your dress and shoes off. Everything but your pants and brassière." He was already divesting himself of his own clothing, stripping himself to his shorts. He could feel himself shivering, and he wasn't sure whether it was from fear or the cold. "It'll be bloody cold. Yell to me if you feel cramp coming on."

"What about sharks?"

"Christ, this is no time to think about sharks! But with all this going on, they've probably all put to sea." He held up the mink coat. "This insured?"

"I couldn't care less," she said, and stood beside him shivering in her underwear. He put his arm about her. "We'll be all right, won't we, darling?"

He noted what she had called him and he bent and kissed the top of her head. "We'll be all right."

People were already diving overboard. Some had found life

preservers and were struggling into them. A man, holding fiercely to a lifebelt, was trying to persuade his wife to jump from the railing, but she was too scared to let go. He banged at her hands with the lifebelt, gave her a push and saw her fall in the water, then threw the lifebelt over after her. Then he turned and went back into the saloon, calling a girl's name, looking for a daughter he might already have lost forever. Another man was crawling across the broken bloody heap at the stern, looking for his wife or his girl friend, calling her name in a thin weeping voice no stronger than a child's. Some attempt was being made to launch a lifeboat, but the ferry had listed too far and the lifeboat had swung inboard.

Jack pushed Silver towards the rail, then felt someone clutch at his arm. It was the daughter of the woman who had tried to leap overboard.

"Please help me! Mum can't swim! I can't leave her!"

The woman was sitting up, looking about her with terrified eyes, her hand to her open moaning mouth. Jack looked down at the girl. "Can you swim?"

"Only a bit. I don't think I can make it. But save Mum, please!"

For a moment he felt stark fear, the paralysing effect of panic. Had he been alone, he wouldn't have worried: he knew he could swim to the shore with ease. He had felt fear before, practically every day he had been in action in the Middle East, but he had never felt the panic brought on by impotency. In action the odds had always been nearly even and he had had only himself to look out for. Now suddenly he had three women on his hands, only one of whom could swim. For a moment he had the urge to turn his back on the pleading girl and her terrified mother, to push Silver overboard and go after her; then he turned to the girl's mother and began to wrench off her coat.

"Take your things off!" he snapped at the girl; then he

straightened up and grabbed at a man as the latter went hurrying past. "Hey, can you swim?"

"Yeah." The man was fumbling with the tapes of a life preserver. He looked up, surprised that anyone should want to talk to him at a moment like this.

"Got anyone with you? A girl, your wife, anyone?"

"No, I'm on my own, thank Christ," said the man, then staggered as Jack snatched the life preserver from him. "Hey, what the bloody——!"

"You won't need this!" Jack was lifting the woman to her feet, trying to push her useless, paralysed arms through the tapes of the life preserver. The man grabbed at it and swung a fist at Jack. The latter suddenly snarled, let go the woman and brought his fist down in a savage chop against the man's face. He staggered back, blood rushing from his split cheek, then abruptly he turned and vaulted the rail and was gone out of sight. Jack turned back. Silver had ripped the woman's dress off her and now was tying the tapes of the life preserver, telling the woman not to worry in a voice that was chattering with the cold. Jack patted the woman on the cheek.

"Come on, Mum. We'll make it!"

The woman looked up at him, her eyes still wide with fear, then she allowed herself to be led to the railing. The deck was steeply slanted now and if they hadn't all been barefooted they would have had trouble standing up. Steam was billowing out from the interior of the ferry, warm and clammy, then suddenly cold against the skin, obscuring everything, reducing the whole panic-stricken world to Jack and the three women. He had never felt so lacking in confidence nor, looking at the woman and her daughter staring at him with trusting eyes, so sad. If he got both of them ashore it would be a miracle.

Silver stretched up and kissed him, then turned and went overboard in a clean neat dive, gone so swiftly he had not time to say good-bye to her. He hoisted the girl to the rail, gave her a push and then she had disappeared into the steam-filled darkness. Then he lifted the woman to the rail, sitting her on it, and clambered up beside her.

"Here we go, Mum. Keep your head, and we'll get there."

He gave the woman a push, then went after her, diving a little to one side. The cold water hit him as a shock that numbed him immediately. Pain happened in his head, almost blinding him, and his stomach contracted, so that for a moment he thought cramp had got him already. Then he came back to the surface, breaking through a film of oil that clung to his face and hair, and looked about for the woman. He was below the level of the steam cloud now and almost immediately he saw the woman. He swam towards her, turned her on her back, shouted to her to reassure her although he knew she couldn't hear him, deaf as she was with her fear, then he began to swim steadily towards the headland a quarter of a mile ahead of him. In a moment he caught up with two swimmers swimming close together, one aiding the other, and he recognised Silver's blonde head, coated now with oil.

A searchlight swung on to them, making a patch of brilliant blue unreal day on the surrounding water, and Jack glimpsed other swimmers, all heading for the frowning headland under the smiling moon. It was like some strange race, with safety the prize. Some were swimming with frantic speed, sprinting to get away from the horror behind them; some were swimming with steady patient strokes, and one knew the firm safe ground was as good as beneath their feet; and others were floundering with sickening desperation that left no hope for them. Even as Jack watched, he saw one head disappear, going down without a struggle and leaving no trace on the impassive water. Beyond the head of the woman behind him he saw the ferry suddenly rise on its end and go down, dying in a blaze of searchlights while a few black figures jumped like frenzied aerialists from her upper decks in the finale of the night.

He trod water, getting his breath. His limbs were stiff with the cold, and now for the first time he began to wonder if he could make it to the headland before the cold cramped him. The woman kept turning in his arms, unable to relax for her terror, and instead of floating she had to be held up in the water. He turned his head and shouted, "You all right, Silver?"

"I need help." Her voice was faint. "Hurry."

He stroked his way towards her, towing the woman after him. Silver was supporting the girl, who was making weak spasmodic strokes that barely kept her afloat. Silver turned a gasping strained face towards him; and again he felt panic race through him. He looked ahead, but now another searchlight was focused on the struggling figures in the water, and the headland was lost beyond the black edge of its beam. He knew the headland couldn't be much more than three hundred yards away now, but it might just as well be three miles. Some one of these three women, perhaps all of them, wasn't going to make it. He felt a coldness pass through him, colder than the water slowly freezing his limbs, and he felt both weak and savage at the same time.

He swam close to the girl. "Turn on your back! Let yourself float."

The girl did as she was told. He held her and her mother, rolled over on his own back and using only his legs for propulsion began to swim in the direction of the headland. Silver paused for a moment, getting her breath, then she began to swim after him. Something bumped against the back of his head, and a piece of wreckage floated past. Oil was thick on his face, running into his eyes, and each time he opened his mouth to breathe he got the sickening taste of it on his lips. His arms had gone dead now, charred stumps hanging from his burning shoulders, and his legs seemed ready to fall off. His breath wrenched its way out of him, as if taking part of his lungs with it each time he exhaled, and his head seemed to have swollen till it was big enough to float and support all four of them.

He stopped, looking back at Silver, seeing how weakly she was swimming, and he knew this was the end. There was no point in going on: if Silver was going down, they might as well all go down. The girl and her mother owed that to her, and he—he loved her.

Then a voice right above him said, "Give me the old girl, mate. Hey, Phil, you take the young 'un from him. Watch out for the blonde. She's almost gone."

Hands came down, taking the woman and the girl from him, lifting them up and relieving him of the weight of the world. He pushed away from the boat and swam towards Silver. He put an arm about her, feeling how spent she was, knowing she couldn't have gone another ten yards, and slowly they glided in towards the boat.

It was a rowboat, and already there were six people in it besides the two men who had brought it out. Other boats were coming into the circle of light, and it didn't matter how far it was to the headland. Silver was pulled aboard and collapsed into the bottom of the boat. Jack clung to the side for a moment, wondering if he had the strength to get out of the water, then with the men helping he clambered aboard. He flopped down on the cross-seat, hearing firing still going on somewhere in the harbour but not caring, looking down at Silver and the woman and the girl lying in an unconscious heap at his feet, unconscious but all alive, and gasped his thanks to a God he had never before bothered to acknowledge.

"We'll get you ashore right away, get you into a bed and something hot inside you," one of the men said. He and his mate took up the oars and began to row towards the shore. "How do you feel, mate?"

"Buggered," said Jack simply and accurately.

He came back into Silver's bedroom. It was Sunday afternoon and the sun came in the big deep windows in a broad mote-laden splash. Its golden warmth accentuated the rich furnishings of the room. A twisted silk coverlet lay like swirls of cream on the bed and the deep red carpet glowed with hidden fire. Expense dripped in heavy drapes beside the windows, and the three huge mirrors in the room reflected nothing but himself that wasn't elegant and luxurious.

"Well?" Silver said. " Did you get on to Bluey?"

"Yes. He was worried that we'd been on the ferry that went down. He said he went to church this morning and said a prayer that we weren't."

"Wasn't that nice of him?" Mrs. Bendixter lay on a couch under the window. "I do admire religious people. They go to so much trouble."

"Yes, he's a real devout," said Jack with a grin. "Uses the Lord's name every second sentence."

Mamie was in a negligée, lolling across the foot of Silver's bed. "Does he know anything about last night? I've been trying to get Henry Featherstone all day, but they must be out on patrol. I notice the harbour's been alive with boats all day."

Jack was in dressing-gown and pyjamas. He sat down on the bed beside Silver, leaning back against the thickly-quilted head-board. "Bluey has a friend at Garden Island and he was on to him this morning. Right now, they think three midget subs got in, but they're not sure if there were more."

Silver slid her hand under his. "We were lucky."

"I'll say you were," said Mamie, and Jack was surprised at the affection in the look she bestowed on both of them: maybe after all she wasn't the self-centred bitch he had thought she was. There was genuine relief and warmth in her face now, and he realised, also with a pleasant jolt of surprise, that she was looking on him and Silver as a pair.

"When Mamie called me at the dance and told me to hurry home," said Mrs. Bendixter, "I almost died. No one expects the war to land right at one's doorstep. Whoever would have thought the Japs would torpedo Silver?"

A little later Mrs. Bendixter and Mamie went downstairs. When the door had closed behind them Jack looked at Silver. "Do you feel too weak to be kissed?"

"No," she said. "Nor to kiss back."

He kissed her and she sank back under him among the pillows. Then he rolled away from her, propping himself up on his elbow and looking down at her. "Don't let's get excited. You're in no condition for it."

When they had finally got home in the early hours of this morning, after Haddon the chauffeur had called for them at the house to which they had been taken, Mamie, who was already home, had called Dr. Hugo. He had come out immediately and had ordered Silver to bed for a couple of days. He had said there was nothing radically wrong with her, but after the shock and exposure she would need rest. He had looked at Jack and said there was nothing wrong with him that a good stiff drink wouldn't fix.

"Don't you wish I were?" Silver said, her smile gently mocking.

"I'd be a liar if I said no." He looked down at her, knowing he had never felt like this before. He had stayed the night here at the Bendixters', sleeping in a pair of pyjamas much too small for him, lent by Haddon, and exhausted though he was it had taken him a long time to fall asleep. He had dreamed of drowning and of Silver going down with him and he had come awake with a distinct feeling of loss heightened by the strangeness of his surroundings, and it was with a weakening feeling of relief that he had at last realised where he was and that Silver was still alive. He had never felt like this before and it was time to confess it: "I love you, Silver."

The smile went from her face and her dark eyes glistened a little. "Really, Jack?"

"Really." He bent and kissed her again, tasting the salt of her tears.

After a while she said, "I've waited a long time for this."

He was puzzled. "Five days?" He grinned. "Heck, how fast did you want me to work?"

She smiled, reached up and took his hair in her hand and pulled his head down on to her breast. "I've waited all my life. This is the first time I've really been in love. And knowing you love me makes it perfect."

He lay there, feeling her heart beating beneath his temple, his face so close to hers that all he could see was the smooth curve of her cheek and her lips still moist from his kiss. Her body was warm and soft against the hardness of his own body, but his desire was quiet: just being there beside her gave him all the satisfaction and contentment he needed.

"I feel remarkably contented," he said. "Like an old married man."

"That's how I knew I loved you. I felt contented."

He hardly heard her: his idle remark about being like an old married man was still echoing in his mind. He hadn't really thought about marriage: five days was hardly time enough in which to get around to such a subject.

"What are you thinking about?" she said.

"Eh? Oh, nothing." Then because that sounded so inadequate, almost ridiculous for a man who only a minute before had confessed he was in love, he went on: "We haven't left ourselves any time to see what it's like being with each other. Now we're in love, I mean."

"We'll have time. When will you get leave again?"

"I don't know. If they don't pack us off right away, I may be able to get down again next week-end. Can you wait that long?"

"I'll try," she said, and kissed his cheek. "I can wait till the end of the war, if needs be."

"That may be a long time."

"I'll wait," she said. "I'm going to be in love with you forever."

He would have to think about marriage. Someone had once said that the basic quality of true love was selflessness; and now here he was, truly in love for the first time in his life and yet harbouring a reservation. Marriage didn't have to be a fiasco as his parents' had been: he had only to look at Vern and Dinah to realise that. Nor did every woman have to be like his mother. He had been jealous and angry yesterday afternoon when he had seen Roger Featherstone kissing Silver, but later common sense had returned and he had tried to be reasonable about it. After all she had known Featherstone for years and what could be more natural than that he too was in love with her? In an indirect way his mother still had a hold on him and it was time he broke loose.

"You're quiet," Silver said. "I didn't know you could go so long without talking."

"Actually, I'm a quiet chap by nature. I only talk out of nervousness."

"You're terribly nervous then. You're the most talkative quiet chap I've met."

"I'm glad you appreciate me."

"I'd appreciate you more if you shaved off that damned moustache."

"I can't do that till the war's over. It's half my strength in the Army. It gives me a more commanding presence."

"There's an Army word that answers that, but I'm too much of a lady to use it."

"You're no lady. I couldn't be bothered falling in love with a lady."

"Ah, it's nice to hear you say that. That you're in love with

K

me." All he could see now was the darkness of her eyes, just a glint in their black depths. "I wish I wasn't so damned exhausted."

He kissed her and sat up. "Cover up your chest. Just lie back there and let your blood pressure relax. I'll tell you some of my war experiences."

She smiled and put his hand under the coverlet against her warm firm breast. "There, my chest is covered. Now tell me all about how you won the war in the Middle East. I'd better get used to it. Like every soldier's wife, I'm going to hear it for the rest of my days."

CHAPTER TEN

"I HAD a bloody good leave," one of the men was saying. "They've built a munitions factory just outside our town and brought up all these girls to work in it. Talk about a surplus of sheilas! Gawd, I couldn't walk down the street without some bint smiling at me. I felt like Robert bloody Taylor."

"Yeah, you do look a bit like him," said Mick Kennedy. "You got a head and two legs."

"I never have that sorta luck," said Joe Brennan. "Whenever I come across a surplus of women, they're such a bunch of crows I'd sooner do without."

"That's because you don't look like Robert Taylor," said Mick. "Now me, I'm never stuck for a bit of skirt. I met a nice piece yesterday down the Domain——"

"Not the blonde you were with Saturday night?" said Joe.

"Her?" Mick waved a hand. "Nah, I let her go out with some sailor she knew. She was starting to bore me. I like to change me women every day, like me socks."

"You lying bastard," said Joe. "You only change your socks once a week."

"It was just a figure of speech, you ignorant mug," said Mick, and took a photo out of his pocket. "Anyhow, I met this sheila and she's gunna write to me. She gimme her picture. Here, take a squint at some real class."

Joe looked at the photo critically. "When was this taken, after an accident. What's wrong with her head?"

"Waddia mean, what's wrong with her head?" Mick snatched back the photo. "That's her hair-do, you bloody dope!"

"You mean," said Joe, "she walks around with her hair standing straight up on top of her head like that?"

"You wouldn't appreciate fashion," said Mick airily. "She said she copied it from that French sheila, Mary Antonette."

"Never heard of her," said Joe, then turned to look over his shoulder at Greg. "How much longer we gotta stay out here, sarge?"

"About another ten minutes," Greg said. "We're supposed to be on a five-mile march."

The party of fifty or so men was sprawled in a small clearing in the scrub. They had reported back to Ingleburn camp that morning and after lunch had been split up into parties and sent on route marches to keep them out of mischief. Greg had marched his party out of sight of the camp, found a convenient patch of scrub and ordered them to deploy for an exercise in concealment.

Fred Talmadge, the other section N.C.O., was lying on his back near Greg, his hat tilted over his face and his hands behind his head. He spoke from under his hat. "Heard any rumours, Greg, about where we're going?"

"Dozens," said Greg. "Everywhere from Fiji to the Panama Canal."

"My tip is we'll be up in New Guinea within a month." Fred had a slow bush drawl, slightly husky as if he had swallowed great quantities of dust and his throat now was as dry as the paddocks out around Barmedman way. "What do you reckon about New Guinea? Think it's going to be rugged?"

"I'm not looking forward to it," said Greg, and knew that was only a half-truth. He might not be looking forward to New Guinea in particular, but he was certainly looking forward to some place that was distant enough and would have enough distraction to keep his thoughts away from Sydney. The past few days ached within him like a wound that could only be cured by time and distance. At odd moments he had felt a hateful bitterness towards Sarah, but it hadn't lasted. He was still too much in love with Sarah for any other feeling to have come in and taken the place of that love. Till he was out of love with her, or the feeling was buried so deeply in him that it no longer worried him, all he could seek in the way of a cure was forgetfulness. New Guinea might help that way.

Yesterday he had avoided Sarah as much as possible. He had gone over to Harbord to see his father and mother and had spent the day there. He had told them Sarah was ill with a headache, and his mother had been most concerned: Sarah had always been her favourite among the four outsiders who had married into her family. When he was going home his father had walked down to the bus stop with him.

"You'll look after yourself, won't you, Greg?" his father had said. "We're both pretty proud of you, getting the V.C., I mean. But your mother worries now. I suppose she did before, but now it seems to be more so. She carries a newspaper cutting of the citation you got, has it with her all the time in that little black money purse of hers. I caught her reading it the other day. She looked up and said, ' Greg did *this*. He might have been killed.' She's frightened you'll try the same thing again."

"Not a chance, Dad." He had always been surprised at what he had done to win the decoration. He had started out to show off, to be the centre of interest, but once he had crossed the river all bravado had gone and everything from then on had been merely a matter of survival. He had rushed the machine-gun posts because there was nothing else he could do and his luck had held because the Vichy French had never expected anyone foolhardy enough to attempt to get near them. It was the main reason he had refrained from talking to Sarah about the action. He had been afraid that, knowing him as she did, she might suspect what had first started him on the way to glory. "There'll be no bar to my V.C. From now on I'm going to be the safety first type of soldier. I've shoved my neck out far enough for one war."

"I'll tell your mother. Well, here's your bus. Give our love to Sarah. Tell her to come over again, soon. We always like to see her."

"Yes, I'll do that."

He had dawdled going home, so that by the time he reached the flat Sarah was already in bed. He had knocked on her door, told her where he had been and then gone along to the spare bedroom. He had taken a long time to fall asleep, but at last he had dropped into a dream-racked slumber from which he had woken sometime during the night, thinking he had heard Sarah cry out. But he couldn't be sure and when it wasn't repeated he had told himself it had been only another part of his dream, another expression of the hope he no longer felt when he was awake. This morning their good-bye had been stiffly restrained, two strangers made awkward by their knowledge of each other. Now he was back with the Army and his married life was over.

When he finally took the party back to camp they were greeted with the news that the battalion was to move out in two days' time. Since the only destination that was ruled out was a return to the Middle East, he went up to the officers' lines to find out what he could from Vern. The latter was sitting in his room talking to another officer when Greg knocked on the door.

"Come in, Greg," Vern said. "Captain Putnam, Sergeant Morley."

The stranger stood up and Greg saw that he was an American. He was a wiry man of about Greg's own height, with a strong lean face, a slightly hooked nose and closely cropped curly brown hair. He had a quick friendly smile and a softer voice than those of other Americans Greg had met.

"I never know what's the right thing to do with you Aussies," he said, and put out his hand. "Am I breaking A.I.F. rules shaking hands with a sergeant?"

Greg returned the firm grip, liking this newcomer. "We just don't do it on parade, that's all. Mr. Radcliffe is a stickler for regimental decorum."

"Bull," said the stickler for regimental decorum, and waved Greg to a chair. "Sit down while I put you in the picture. Captain Putnam is joining us as an observer. His unit hasn't left the States yet, but he's out here to pick up some idea of the local way of winning the war."

"You'll learn a lot about that here at Ingleburn," Greg said to Captain Putnam.

"All these staging camps are the same. I was at Camp Kilmer in Jersey for a while." Captain Putnam shook his head. "Brother!"

"Well, we move out of this demi-paradise Wednesday morning," said Vern. "The rest of the brigade is going to Queensland, but we go out into a valley of the beautiful Blue Mountains, Nature's playground, and there we are to play silly buggers till they send for us."

"What the hell are we going out there for?" Greg said. "Out there in the mountains we'll freeze to death. Aren't we supposed to be heading for New Guinea?"

"Eventually," Vern said. "I think the whole truth is, they haven't the transport to move us north just yet." He looked across at Putnam. "You're in for some shocks, Alec. Things out here are in a pretty bad way."

"I've gathered that," said the American. "But you've still got one thing over the guys in my outfit. You've been in combat."

"Maybe," Vern said. "What do you reckon, Greg?"

"I don't know," Greg said. "I know what action is like and I think I've learned how far you can go before the margin of safety is passed. But New Guinea is going to be a different sort of war altogether. What we learned in the desert and Syria isn't going to be much use in the jungle."

Then a long stringy figure came in the door. "Brought you a cuppa, boss. And you too, cap'n. Or don't you Yanks drink tea?"

"We do," said Alec Putnam.

Vern took his cup and said, "Could you scrounge one for Sergeant Morley, Herb?"

Herb Nutter looked around. "Cripes, didn't even see you, sarge! You want a cuppa?"

Greg shook his head. "Thanks, Herb."

Herb turned back to Alec Putnam. "They tell me I'll be looking after you, too, cap'n. We're a bit short on batmen at present. You got any special likes or dislikes?"

"None that I can think of," said Alec. "Has Lieutenant Radcliffe?"

"Never asked him," said Herb, and made no attempt now to remedy the oversight. "Well, I'll fix up your beds later. They're just starting a two-up game down at the back of the kitchens. Am I dismissed, boss?"

"Dismissed," said Vern, and gazed after the retreating tall thin figure. "You'll find, Alec, that he's the most unregimental soldier alive. But I wouldn't swap him for any two other batmen in the battalion, in or out of action."

"All round," said Alec with a smile, "I think I'm going to

be kinda happy here. I might not even get to be homesick."

"Where's home, sir?" Greg said.

"Waquoit, Massachusetts. It's only a couple of dozen houses and one store on Cape Cod, and most folks have never heard of it. But it's God's choicest spot in," he grinned at them, "God's own country."

Greg looked at Vern, and the latter shook his head. "Don't say it, sergeant. After all, he is a visitor."

The movement order said the battalion would entrain at 10.00 hours. Experience had ironed out the wrinkles of movement within the battalion, but it still remained only a small component of the Army, which didn't seem to benefit from experience at all.

The train was drawn up at the station and the men got aboard. Ten minutes later Vern shoved his head in the window of the compartment where Greg and Jack sat.

"Righto, boys. Tumble 'em out."

"Out?" said Jack, who had just divested himself of all his paraphernalia.

"Wrong train," said Vern with a grin. "This train is to pick up some other unit."

"Wouldn't it?" said Greg, and began to pull on his gear. "How did they manage to make a balls of this?"

"Don't ask me," said Vern. "You know the Army."

He went away and Jack shouted for the men to detrain. There was loud grumbling but no surprise: after twenty-six months they had become used to such treatment. They pulled on their packs and filed out to the platform again, bleating like sheep. They stood there offering good-humoured obscene suggestions as to what should be done to the Army. Then it began to rain and that caused no surprise: the Army and the weather often worked together. Both had the same vagaries.

"We ran things better than this in the tribe," said Charlie Fogarty. "I got an uncle who would have made a bloody good movement officer. I remember once he took us from the Urapunga down to the Nicholson, and all he lost was one of me aunties. And he wanted to lose her, anyway."

It was another two hours before the battalion got aboard the right train, and another half hour before the train got under way. It was still raining, a steady drizzle, and the train crept through the drab countryside like a long brown slug. When it began to climb into the foothills of the mountains, its smoke rolled away down the banks to join the cold-looking mists oozing down out of the gorges. The trees were colourless, sodden and ugly as old crones in a funeral crowd, and the mountains through the rain had the look of huge burial mounds. They passed several small towns, dead under the pall of rain, and once a convoy went past on the road far below, disappearing under a bridge like ants scurrying in out of the cold and wet.

At last they pulled in at a small station. Its name-board had been painted out to fool any Japs who might pass this way: in the grey rain the platform looked miserable, an anonymous spot in the middle of nowhere. Vern tapped on the window and Greg opened it. "This is it. We've got a three-mile walk through the rain."

"What happens when we get there?" Greg said. "Can we expect our tents to be up?"

"You can expect bugger-all." Greg was always surprised at how Vern kept his good humour, even in the face of the most miserable prospect. "We start from scratch. The advance party has managed to put up only the kitchens and its own tents."

"Wouldn't it?" Jack said to the carriage at large, and the men agreed it would.

Along the muddy bush road that was little more than a

track hacked out of the scrub, it took them more than an hour to reach the camp site. The advance party had felled trees and done something towards making a clearing for battalion headquarters; but most of the unit was faced with virgin forest where its tents were to be erected. A groan went up that shook water from the sodden branches overhead.

"We should of stayed in the desert!"

"The Japs'll never find us here."

"Neither will anyone else. I'm glad I said ta-ta to the missus."

Five hours later, well after dark, the last tent went up. The men, covered in mud, wet and chilled to the bone, fell into their blankets and were soon asleep. Only the roving picquets, drenched unhappy creatures, roamed among the tents like lost souls. Quiet fell on the camp but for the steady patter of the rain on the tents.

"We're back in the Army," said Greg, and turned out the hurricane lamp. He kicked off his boots, hearing them drop with a soft plop into the glutinous mud that was the floor of his and Jack's tent.

"With a vengeance," said Jack, trying to get warm under his damp mud-spattered blankets. "Life gets rugged again."

They would only realise how rugged when to-morrow came.

CHAPTER ELEVEN

NEXT day the C.O. called a conference of officers. It had stopped raining and above the still dripping trees there were small lakes of blue sky. Weak sunlight filtered down into the camp like a stingy blessing, only highlighting the yellow morass of mud in which the tents sat.

The officers were standing around in groups when Vern and Alec Putnam came into the clearing around B.H.Q. Alec waved to everyone, a wide smile on his face, and all of them returned his greeting: in three days he had succeeded in becoming as popular as any officer in the unit.

"Hallo, Vern," said one of the officers. "I hear A Company has bad news."

"Such as?" said Vern, expecting some sort of ribbing.

The other officer smiled smugly. "The C.O. would carpet me if I spoiled his act."

"Here comes the Colonel now," said Alec. "Who's the guy with him?"

Colonel McInnes walked into the centre of the clearing, his bad news two paces to the rear of him. A murmur of astonishment went through the assembled officers, and Vern knew the war had suddenly taken a turn for the worse.

"Gentlemen, I have some good news for you." Colonel McInnes's face was impassive: he was just the voice of the Army. "Major Caulfield has rejoined us."

"Hurrah," muttered someone.

"He will resume command of A Company. I'm sure we're all as pleased as he is that he is once more back on active service." Colonel McInnes smiled stiffly, as if he had just had six teeth extracted. "Major Caulfield tells me a base wallah's life is hell."

"He should have felt at home then," Vern murmured to no one in particular.

"A little enthusiasm would be more seemly," said one of the officers from D Company. "After all, Radcliffe, old man, it's not every day your commander comes back from the dead."

Vern made a rude gesture with his thumb. He was aware of Alec Putnam beside him looking puzzled, trying to catch the drift of the ironic whispering going on among the officers. Well, he'll soon learn, Vern thought, staring across the clearing at the stocky arrogant figure behind the colonel, hands clasped behind the back, the legs spread wide, and the cap cocked at an angle over one eye. The United States Army probably had its quota of bastards, but it would have none bigger than Major James Caulfield.

As they walked away after the conference was dismissed Vern heard his name called. He turned and Major Caulfield was striding towards him. Vern saluted and Caulfield returned it with his abrupt casual movement that was almost an insult.

"There'll be a conference of company officers at eleven-thirty," Caulfield said. "Tell the other officers."

Here we go again, Vern thought, using his junior officers as messenger boys. Anything to show his authority. He hasn't changed, and he may even be a damned sight worse. I should have taken that job as a war correspondent.

"Yes, sir," he said, then introduced Alec Putnam.

Caulfield put out his hand. "Pleased to meet you, captain. Since you're attached to my company, I'll expect you at the conference. Right?"

Alec had been about to smile in greeting as he shook Caulfield's hand, but all at once his face closed up. "I'll be there, major. I want to be treated just like your regular officers."

"Good," said Caulfield, and turned to stride away. "Eleven-thirty, then. Make sure you let the others know, Mr. Radcliffe."

Vern saluted the retreating back, wishing he had the reckless nerve to plant his boot firmly under the muscular protruding buttocks that were somehow as arrogant as everything else about the man.

Alec looked sideways at him. "Is that what they mean by an arch-bastard?"

"That's what they mean," said Vern, and on the way back to their tent gave a summary of Caulfield's history. "None of us expected him to come back. We just took it for granted he'd been discharged."

Ten minutes later a runner came down from B.H.Q. to say the C.O. wanted to see Lieutenant Radcliffe. Vern went up to the C.O.'s office and sat down when Colonel McInnes waved him to a canvas-back chair. The C.O. was bouncing something in his hand, but Vern couldn't see what it was and took no notice. Colonel McInnes was the same age as Vern, with a blunt, almost ugly face and a restless energy that the rest of the battalion found hard to keep up with.

"Well, Vern, he's back."

Vern nodded, wondering why he had been chosen to discuss the return of Caulfield. "If I may venture an opinion on a superior officer, it wasn't a tumultuous reception."

McInnes laughed, tossed the things in his hand high in the air, caught them and rolled them like dice across the blanket-covered table in front of him. "If he hadn't come back, those would have meant more to you."

Vern looked down at the dark metal pips on the table. "Meaning I'm a captain now?"

McInnes congratulated him, then sat back. "Those extra pips might have meant you getting your own company in the next six months or so. My idea was that you would be 2 i/c of A Company and eventually take it over. We're going to lose officers now we're back here in Australia, to Division and Brigade. I think promotions will be coming pretty fast in the next few months. But as it is now, Haggett will drop down from commander of A Company to 2 i/c, and for the time being you'll have to remain as platoon commander." Just then there was a loud click of heels at the entrance to the tent. Jack Savanna was there. "Yes, sergeant?"

"Major Caulfield's compliments, sir. Could you spare him half an hour this afternoon at three o'clock?"

"Righto, three o'clock." McInnes stared out the tent after the retreating figure of Jack. "When will that man learn you don't use your sergeants as runners?"

Vern took a risk. Even in the so-called democratic A.I.F. it was not good form to discuss one's superior officer with the C.O. But Vern could see trouble coming up ahead like a mist out of the ground. In civilian life Vern wouldn't have had any worry in dealing with Caulfield: if one couldn't put him in his place, one could always walk away from him, escape from his sphere of influence. In the Army that couldn't be done. Caulfield had the company in the hollow of his hand and only he had the power to avoid trouble. And it was obvious he wasn't going to avoid it, but rather go out of his way to cause it.

"I'm afraid we're at the beginning of a hate campaign," Vern said, and went on to tell the C.O. of the incident at the Marble Bar last week. "We had no idea he was coming back. Otherwise we'd have been more discreet."

"He's been working at getting back to the battalion ever since he learned we were coming home from Syria," McInnes said. "When he came home last year he was graded B-class and got some job at Victoria Barracks. He's got some pull among the brass, and as soon as he heard we were on our way home, he went to work. I can't do anything about it. As far as Division and Brigade are concerned, he's a good officer." McInnes shook his head wearily. He was the sort of man who found the routine of running the battalion when out of a campaign more wearing than running it in action. "I can't tell him how to run his company unless he goes beyond regulations."

"That's his trouble," Vern said. "He interprets them too literally."

McInnes slapped his hands on the table and stood up. "We'll just have to wait and see. In the meantime you may have to act as buffer between him and the men."

"Yes, sir," said Vern, already beginning to feel the bruising.

That night Caulfield started in at his old tricks. While the rest of the battalion was given leave to go into the small town a couple of miles along the valley where there was a picture theatre, he announced there would be a night map-reading exercise for A Company. That was the first play in a pattern that the men soon recognised. Next afternoon, seeing some of the men who had been late having their showers queueing up for their evening meals in sandshoes, work trousers and sweaters, he issued an order that in future A Company would wear full field dress, complete to gaiters and web belt, to evening mess. That night leave passes, valid till 2359 hours, were issued to the men of A Company and they went into Frazer's Gully to the pictures. The show ended at eleven o'clock, most of the men stopped for a hamburger at the town's one café, and by the time they had walked the two miles back to camp it was well after midnight. Caulfield was waiting at the picquet tent, where the passes had to be handed in, and every man was told he would be confined to camp for the next three nights.

When Vern heard about it next morning he spat in disgust.

"How low can a man get? Hasn't he even a sense of dignity? A major, staying up just so he can catch the fellows creeping in half an hour late!"

"Something tells me the shine has worn off the war," said Alec. He and Vern were marching at the head of the platoon as the company swung along the road on its daily route march. The men were singing the Army version of "The Old Grey Mare," and it was possible to denigrate the company commander without lowering the troops' morale. The commander himself was right up at the head of the company, strutting along like a small-time Alexander, now and again glancing over his shoulder as if to satisfy his ego, lord of the long column that stretched down the dried mud road behind him. "Why does he carry on like this? Is the guy nuts or something?"

"He got off on the wrong foot when he joined us," Vern said. "The battalion had been formed two months when he came along. He came straight down from New Guinea, and I think he had some idea you run troops the same way you run Kanakas. And once he'd got started wrong, he was too pig-headed to try and correct it. He just went from bad to worse. Once I felt sorry for him. Now I just wish he'd drop dead."

Then the platoon in front came to a shuffling halt. Vern flung up his hand, the singing stopped, and the men behind halted. Then from the head of the column there came a blast on a whistle.

"Police!" Joe Brennan said, and there was a murmur of laughter.

"Come on," Vern said to Alec. "That's our rallying call. I feel like a bloody Girl Guide."

"Right behind you, Brown Owl," grinned Alec, and together they trotted up to the head of the column. The other officers were already there, waiting on the word of Major

L

Caulfield. The latter stood, hands on hips, gazing about him as if debating whether to sack Carthage now or do it over on the return trip. He turned round as Vern and Alec came running up.

"Want to move faster, Captain Radcliffe," he said. "Or have you got soft since I was last in command?"

Vern couldn't resist it: "That's about the strength of it," he said, and stared at Caulfield.

Caulfield reddened with temper, looked as if he was about to blow up, then abruptly changed his mind. He snapped open his map-case and jabbed at the map with a broad finger. "This is where we are now. We're splitting into two parties. You, Haggett, will take one and head for this point." The finger jabbed. "And you, Radcliffe, will take the other and head for this point. From each of those points you will make your respective ways back through the timber to camp. I'll be waiting there." He looked at his watch. "I expect you both in by 1200 hours."

Vern was about to protest, but he knew it would be useless. The men were not yet back in proper condition after the long lay-off since they had left Palestine to come home, and yet they were being ordered to do a cross-country run through timber in a time that would have tested them in the peak of condition. But it would be useless trying to reason with Caulfield.

A minute later the men, some grumbling, others baying like hounds, were on their way into the timber. At the edge of the trees Vern stopped and looked back. Caulfield was standing alone in the middle of the road, hands on hips, a broad cruel smile on his red freckled face. He always wore more equipment than any two other officers, and now Vern thought he looked slightly ridiculous, like a caricature of a military dictator. Binoculars hung by a strap from his neck, a map-case was attached to his belt, and at various other points about him were strung a compass, a whistle, a knife, a pistol, a machete, and a deloused grenade, the latter a final piece of affectation that was almost lost in the welter of other paraphernalia. He looked pompously arrogant and ridiculous, and Vern, taking a last look at him before he turned to run on after the men, hated him as he had never hated anyone before.

Not all the enemy was on the other side of the firing line.

Vern arrived back in camp with the last of his men twenty minutes late. He listened in silence to the sarcasm of Caulfield, then went down to his tent. The mail had been coming in each morning at eleven o'clock and he was looking forward to a letter from Dinah. There had been none from her for two days now and he was both annoyed and a little worried. There was no letter for him to-day, only a telegram.

Alec was lying stretched out on his bed, still exhausted from the run back through the timber. "At Boston U. I was on the track team. I was never very good, but I was enthusiastic. Every afternoon I used to run like crazy round and round the track, but I could never do better than a four-twenty mile. Then one day the coach tried to talk me into being a cross-country runner, said I had the makings of a champ in me. I didn't like the look in his eye and for some reason I said no. I'm glad I did now. The sonofabitch never told me anything about there being trees in the way in a cross-country run. I should've joined the Navy, like my dad wanted. He said any man who'd spent as much time in the water as I had, digging up quahogs, just naturally ought to go to sea in wartime." Vern had slit open the telegram. Alec looked across at him. "I wish I'd get a letter, even just a telegram. I haven't heard from my wife since I landed here in Australia. Not one goddam letter. It's a treasonable thought, but I am beginning to doubt the efficiency of the United States Army."

Vern had stood up and was already on his way out of the

tent. "My young daughter has pneumonia. Dig up Herb Nutter for me, would you? Ask him to get my things ready. I'm going home for a couple of days."

"Sure, Vern. I'm sorry about the news——"

But Vern was already out of earshot, hurrying up through the lines to the company headquarters tent. Caulfield was just coming out when Vern reached it. "Wanting me, Captain Radcliffe?"

"Yes, sir. I'd like two days' compassionate leave."

Caulfield shook his head. "Out of the question, Radcliffe. What's the trouble?"

"My daughter is seriously ill with pneumonia." Vern held out the telegram, but Caulfield ignored it. "My wife says the doctor recommends I come home immediately."

"I'm sorry to hear about your youngster, Radcliffe. But I just can't give you leave. In the last two days I've had four applications from the men for compassionate leave, and had to knock them all back. None of the reasons seemed particularly urgent, or in one case even genuine. I have no doubt your case is genuine, but after saying no to four of the men, I can't make an exception for an officer."

"I understand that," Vern said. "But each case should be judged on its merits. I'm not asking for favouritism as an officer."

"I'm sorry, Radcliffe," said Caulfield, and made a show of looking regretful. "Why don't you go into the town and call your wife from there? That should relieve your mind somewhat."

"I'm not interested in calling my wife to relieve my mind." Vern was fast losing his temper. "If my kiddie is ill and I can possibly get home to her, I want to do so."

Caulfield had only the one infuriating answer. "I'm sorry, Radcliffe."

Vern was aware of the company sergeant-major and the

clerk in the tent behind Caulfield, both of them trying to look disinterested in the conversation of the two officers but not missing a word. Vern out of habit, conscious of the indignity of arguing with his superior officer in front of the men, dropped his voice to a murmur. The quietness of his tone heightened the bitterness.

"I'm going over your head, major. I'm seeing the C.O." He stepped back quickly, saluted and had left Caulfield before the latter could speak.

The C.O. was understanding and immediately granted Vern the leave. Two and a half hours later he reached home. Dinah met him at the door, and young Michael was beside her. They both looked drawn and tired.

"The doctor just called up. He says the crisis will come to-night." Dinah leaned her head on his shoulder and wept. "Oh, darling, I'm so glad you're here."

Vern held her tightly and decided not to say anything about the trouble with Caulfield. It was unimportant now: nothing that had happened in his life before was as important as the next few hours might be. He tried not to think of Jill dying, and looked down at Michael.

"When did she take sick, Mike?"

"Yesterday morning. She was pretty crook when she woke up." Michael was on the verge of tears.

"I'll get the car out," Vern said. "We'll go straight up to the hospital."

On the way up to the hospital Dinah told him she and Michael had spent last night there. She had been afraid to leave there at midday to come home, but it was only an hour after she had sent the telegram last night that she remembered she had forgotten to name the hospital.

"You sent the telegram last night?" Vern said.

"About a quarter to five. I phoned it through from the hospital."

Vern cursed the Army. "It would have been all the same if I'd been too late."

"Too late? Oh, Vern, don't talk like that!" Dinah was biting her lips, her gloved hands tightly clenched in her lap; she looked on the point of breaking, collapsing into a helpless heap. He sensed all at once that her exhaustion didn't come only from worry over Jill: she had been worrying for two long years now and Jill's illness was another burden in the whole senseless sacrifice that a woman made in wartime. He felt a flood of thankfulness that he had been close enough to come home and share the strain of the coming hours with her.

At the hospital he was allowed to see Jill for a moment, and he was shocked at how ill she looked. Then the doctor led him out of the room. "We've done all we can for her. We'll know some time to-night how it's worked."

"How do you think it has worked?" Vern said.

The doctor shrugged. "We've come a long way with this type of thing since you and I were kids. We've got drugs that reduce the odds to about even money, maybe better. But things still depend a good deal on the patient as an individual. Kids usually want to live. That's why I think your girl has a good chance." He was a short broad man in his late thirties, with a large bald head and a happy, but tired, round face. "I've got to go out on another case now. I'll get the sister to make you all comfortable. It may be a long night. It's no use my telling you not to worry. You will, no matter how confident I try to sound." As they walked down the corridor he said, "I suppose you'll be headed for New Guinea pretty soon?"

"Any time now," said Vern.

"Things look pretty grim, don't they?" said the doctor. "But right now nothing looks as grim as back there in that room. Wars are unimportant beside your family, aren't they?"

He went on out through the door at the end of the corridor and Vern turned into the small ante-room where Dinah and

Michael were waiting for him. A nurse brought them dinner on a tray and they ate it all, not with relish but because none of them had eaten since breakfast. Then they settled down to wait. Michael fell asleep against his father. Vern stretched him out on the couch and a nurse brought a blanket and spread it over him. Vern sat there looking down at the small sleeping face, puckered as if worried in a dream, and felt a mixture of joy and sadness.

"I never thought I'd love kids as much as I do Mike and Jill," he said, talking to himself as much as to Dinah. "Before we were married I couldn't stand them, and even now I'm not enthusiastic about other people's kids. Not the way Herb Nutter is, anyway. I don't dislike them, but I can't work up much interest in them. But it's different with my own. I can't imagine life without these two now." He ran his hand gently round under Michael's soft jawline. "I've been lucky in the last thirteen years."

Dinah got up and walked across and kissed him. All her vitality had gone and there was no trace of the good-looking gay woman who had loved him so voluptuously last week. She was now a tired worried mother, her face made plain by weeping and strain. "You'll go on being lucky, darling. Don't let's even think it might be otherwise."

It was a long night, longer than Vern had ever before experienced. He was reminded again of his thought on waiting that morning when they had been held up just outside Central Station, when those last few minutes had been the longest time of the two years they had been away. Waiting was always painful, but to-night it was an agony. Several times the sister came in to tell them there was no change, then a long time went past when no one came. It was three o'clock in the morning when the doctor came in, grey-faced but smiling.

"She's going to be all right," he said. "She's sleeping now, but you can see her as soon as she wakes."

It was nine o'clock before they were allowed in to see her. Small and pale, her hair the only splash of colour in the coldly white bed, she smiled weakly at the three of them.

"You had us scared stiff," said Michael.

"Did you think I was going to die?" she said, her voice only a whisper but calm.

"We didn't think about that, darling," said Dinah.

"I did," said Jill, and Vern knew without surprise that she would have looked on the matter of death with the matter-of-factness of an aged sage. "I thought about it before I went into my coma, and I made up my mind I wouldn't die."

"Well, I wish you'd told us," said Michael gruffly.

Vern smoothed Jill's hair back from her forehead. "You'd better make up your mind not to get sick again while I'm away."

Jill looked up at him. "I thought about another thing, Daddy. I thought about you being killed in the war. And I made up my mind that wasn't going to happen, either."

Behind him Vern heard Dinah stifle a sob and felt her hand slide into his. He stood like that holding his wife's hand, aware of his son across the bed from him, gazing down at his daughter who had looked at death and said no to it, both for herself and for him, and a great and indescribable joy coursed through him. As the doctor had said last night, wars were as nothing beside one's family. Sweetness and sadness, laughter and tears, mingled within him and he knew, suddenly and very clearly, that no matter how the war went, he, Vern Radcliffe, could never lose. His victory was here in his family and he would come back to it.

He had never felt so sure of anything in his life.

CHAPTER TWELVE

"HAVE you heard from the boss?" Herb Nutter said.

Jack looked up from the letter he was writing. He wanted to finish it to-night so it could go out in the morning mail. In Vern's absence he was acting as platoon leader, and Major Caulfield had told him to prepare a lecture on gas precautions for to-morrow morning. Emphasis was being placed again on what was to be done in the event of chemical warfare, a bogey that hadn't cropped up in the Middle East and about which most units had become careless. The Army, suspicious of a new enemy, expecting the Japanese, because they were Oriental, to be more diabolical than the Germans, was preparing for that most hated of all forms of war, killing by gas. Their own scientists were already at work on such Occidental diabolisms as the napalm and atomic bombs, but such projects were still secret and did not yet worry the conscience, if any, of the Army. Jack, untroubled by conscience in the matter of warfare, prepared to kill the Japanese in any way that was effective and not blaming them if they chose gas as their most effective means, had already sketched out in his mind the familiar lines of his lecture. But chemical warfare would have to wait on its place in the scheme of things. The important thing right now was to get this letter off to Silver.

"I got a telegram this afternoon," he said. "His kiddie's out of danger."

"Ah, that's good." Herb's buck teeth came out in a relieved smile. "I hate to hear of kids getting close like that to croaking. Never seems right somehow. Cripes, I'm real pleased about that. And he's wrapped up in those kids of his, always telling me about 'em. Did he say when he'd be back?"

"He hopes to be in by lunch time to-morrow."

"He oughta take a bit more time. Still, I suppose if she's outa danger, he feels he oughta be back here winning the war." Herb leaned his thin length against the tent pole and expertly rolled a cigarette. "He's no bludger, the boss, eh? He's dead keen, without being one of them regimental bastards."

Jack set the writing pad down on the bed beside him and took out a cigarette. He liked old Herb and didn't want to hurt his feelings. I'm getting soft-hearted, he thought; there was a time, only recently, when he hadn't cared a damn about anyone's feelings. Herb obviously wanted to natter for a while.

"After the colonel," he said when he had lit his cigarette, "he's the best officer in the show."

"Yeah, easily," said Herb, confident in his judgment of good officers. "It's a pity he ain't the company commander instead of that other no-hoper."

It was time to change the subject. "What sort of leave did you have?"

Herb's face was seamed with lines as he grinned broadly. "Oh, bloody good. Went to the races on Saturday and won forty quid."

"How were the wife and kids?"

"Oh, good-o, good-o. The youngest one's got a broken arm and me eldest girl's just got engaged to an Air Force cove, but they're all fine. I took 'em all to the races Saturday, the missus and all six kids. Give 'em a day out. They all had a bet and all picked winners. We collected seventy quid between us. Yeah, I had a good leave."

Jack grinned to himself. Herb had two main interests in life, his family and racehorses, and sometimes it was to be wondered which came first. Melbourne Cup Day was a bigger day in Herb's life than his wife's birthday.

They yarned till their cigarettes had burned down, then Herb dropped his butt to the ground and stamped it out. "Well, reckon you wanna get back to your letter, eh? Thanks for the news about the boss, sarge. I'm real glad young Jill's all right again. He oughta take a ticket in the Lottery in her name. While her luck's in, he oughta cash in on it. Well, ta-ta, sarge. I enjoy a natter now and again with youse upper-class johnnies. Here comes another of youse."

As Herb walked away into the darkness Greg came into the tent. He was carrying his pack and when he set it down on his bed there was the clink of bottles.

"Going in for sly grog selling?" Jack said. "I never thought you'd turn into a bootlegger."

"I've got eight bottles of the best in here." Greg undid the straps of the pack. "I did a bit of smoodging to the wife of the pub owner in town, and she came good. Told her I had a mate out here in camp who had a broken ankle and couldn't get into town for a drink."

"Are you getting too stuck-up to drink with the boys in town?"

"No, I just felt in the mood for a quiet drink." Greg was drawing the bottles out of the pack and standing them on the earthen floor of the tent. "You are, of course, welcome to join me."

"Chawmed, I'm sure," said Jack. "I can't throw anything into the kitty till next pay day."

"The hospitality is on me this time." Greg snapped the top off one of the bottles and filled two thick china mugs. "For once in my life I happen to have a little extra change."

"I'll drink to that, if to nothing else," said Jack.

Greg drank, then nodded at the writing pad. "You writing to Silver?"

"Here it is Monday, eight days since I said good-bye to her, and this is my fourth letter. If someone had told me three months ago I'd be doing this, I'd have cracked him one. Thought he was insulting me."

"That's love for you," said Greg sententiously, nodding his head like a man who knew all about it. "The world changes."

Jack sipped at his beer. "I haven't noticed you writing Sarah."

Greg had already drained his mug and was refilling it. "I'm waiting for her to write first."

Jack sipped his beer again, wondering if this was any business of his, if Greg wanted to talk about it. He had guessed in the past week that something was wrong between Greg and Sarah. In the past two years Greg had never let a day go past without mentioning her in some way or other, and whenever they had moved into a new camp the first thing that had gone up in the tent had been Sarah's photo. There was no photo of her in this tent and there had been only casual mention of her since they had come back from leave.

"We're washed up," Greg said at last, looking down at his beer. "She's going to divorce me."

Jack hesitated for a moment: one didn't plunge feet first into other people's disasters. "This was sudden, wasn't it?"

"Too sudden. I only half believe it, still."

Jack reached across for the bottle and put a top on his beer. "Has she met someone else?"

"No. Maybe it would be better in a way if she had. Then I could let off some steam, go out and crown the bastard. But she says there's no one, and I believe her. Though I don't believe what she tells me is the real reason."

"What's that?"

"That she no longer loves me. Do people fall out of love

like that?" Greg took another long drink. "But how would you know? You reckon you've never been in love till this last week."

"I'm a novice at it, chum. I can't help you there. But I've seen other marriages break up, quite a few of them, so I guess people can fall out of love."

"I've been an unreliable bastard in my time, I know that. And I've played around more than I should have." Greg finished his second mug of beer. "But even when I was being a bastard, I never dreamed anything could come to a full stop between us."

"I'm not one who should moralise," Jack said slowly, "but maybe in a way you're only getting what you deserve."

"Oh, don't think I haven't thought about that!" Greg waved a hand, as if in disgust at himself. "But when I got off that train at Central the other week and saw her there, the first time in two bloody long years, I knew I'd never be able to look at another woman. I mean that, Jack. She doesn't know it, because once she dropped her bomb there didn't seem much point in telling her, but I'm more in love with her now than I ever was before. And Christ, I had it bad enough in those days! I mean it when I say I don't want to look at another dame. Without her, I don't want to look at anything!" He drank his beer, draining the mug in one long swallow. Then he looked across at Jack, his thin dark face flushed and tremulous, as if any moment it might break into weeping. "Get on with your letter, mate. There's no need for my belly-aching to break up your romance."

Jack picked up the pad and settled it on his knee again. "I've got only another page to go. Then maybe I'll help you get drunk. That was the idea, wasn't it?"

"Yeah. My mate with the broken ankle." Greg laughed, a little wobbly, and refilled his mug. "The pub owner's wife might have thought I was cracked if I'd told her I wanted it for a broken heart." He laughed again. "I'm getting maudlin. I'm going to be crying in my beer before the night's out."

Jack found he had more than another page to write. Now that he had told Silver he loved her, there seemed so much more he had to tell her. He had never been at a loss for words and though he was unaccustomed to letter-writing the old loquacity was there. He had gone from one extreme to the other: once he had even hesitated about writing a note declining a dinner invitation, preferring to phone, and now he was in the middle of his seventh page. He had bought a new fountain pen for the occasion, like a professional letter-writer setting up in business, and the words flowed out of the pen with the same fluidity as its ink.

When at last he was finished, Greg was more than half-way drunk. "Hold on, chum. You're getting too much of a start on me."

Greg smiled blearily. "Sorry, cock. Didn't realise. Here." He filled Jack's mug. "Catch up with me. I'll put the brake on."

Jack enjoyed beer and always welcomed it, but he had no desire to-night to get drunk. He took the mug and sipped at it.

Greg was staring moodily into the bottom of his own mug. "I'm a brave bastard, ain't—am I not?"

Jack was used to humouring drunks; he had no doubt there had been plenty of times when other people had humoured him. "You've got a medal to prove it."

"That's right. The *best* medal, too." Greg didn't look up from his beer. "But I'm not really brave, mate."

"No?" Discussing bravery even with a drunk was embarrassing.

"No, I got no real guts."

"Depends what you mean by real guts."

Greg sat still for a while, then he looked up. "Like blowing your own brains out."

It was a long time since Jack had had such a shock, twelve years, and he was unprepared for the jolt it gave him. "That doesn't take guts."

"You'd be surprised, Jack. You don't don't know anything about it. It takes all the guts in the world."

Jack knew he was contradicting what he had believed for twelve years, was destroying the idealised memory of his father, but he had never had to speak of it before. It had been easy to defend his father's suicide when arguing only with himself: the blame could so easily be shifted to his mother. But now, confronted again with the thought of it, knowing that Greg had hardly considered any alternative to it, he recognised suicide for the cowardice it was.

"It only takes a moment of guts, just long enough to pull the trigger."

"It took me only five minutes to win the V.C." Greg was drunk, yet one part of his mind, the part concerned with suicide, still seemed remarkably lucid. "They decorated me for those five minutes. They didn't say anything about going on being brave, having guts for the rest of my life. What's the difference?"

Jack put his mug down on the floor and after a moment said, "My old man committed suicide." It struck him all at once that he had never told this before to either Greg or Vern; and yet within an hour of meeting her, though he hadn't elaborated on it since, he had told Silver of it. It was almost as if he had known then that their relationship was going to be more permanent than any he had had before. "He blew his brains out because of my mother. His life wasn't finished, as he thought it was. He'd forgotten me."

"I haven't any kids," Greg said. "All I got to think about is myself."

"My dad got drunk, just like you're doing. I don't know whether he set out to get drunk so he'd have the guts to shoot himself. I like to think he didn't, that the idea of suicide came only after he was too drunk to think straight."

"You're only defending him," said Greg in a moment of clear sober insight. He refilled his mug and drank again. "I don't want anyone defending me."

"I wouldn't try to. If you shot yourself, I'd let people think what they liked. In my eyes you'd just be a weak gutless bastard."

Greg's face flushed and his dulled dark eyes flashed, then he grinned. "Sticks and stones—but I don't think you got to worry, mate. I know I'm not game to pull the trigger till I'm blind drunk. And when I'm blind I won't be able to see the trigger." He dropped his mug, the beer spilling and soaking instantly into the earthen floor, and buried his face in his hands. "Jesus, I wish there was some other way out!"

He wept and Jack sat across the tent from him feeling helpless and upset. Jack had never been capable of tears, not even when his father had died, and he had always thought of them as a sign of weakness in a man. But now, seeing Greg weep, knowing that Greg was weak and yet loving him none the less, he understood the tears and was saddened by them. For the first time in his life someone had come to him with their troubles and he was unable to help them.

"Why don't you write her?" he said, but he knew it was a futile suggestion.

Greg looked up. His face looked younger than ever with the tears on his cheeks; all the adult had drained out of his features and he looked as lost as any boy faced by his first tragedy. Jack suddenly doubted that Greg would ever find his way back out of this mess. He couldn't make it alone and yet Sarah, the only one who could help him, was the one who had caused it.

Greg stood up, reeling a little, and walked unsteadily out of the tent. Jack half-rose to follow him, afraid of what Greg might do if left alone, but then he heard him sluicing his face in the basin outside the tent, gasping with the coldness of the water. He came back into the tent and dried his face on a towel.

"I'm going down to see her to-night." He was still a long way from being sober, but he had evidently given up the idea of getting blind drunk.

"Will that do any good?"

"I don't know." Greg began to struggle into his greatcoat. Now he had made up his mind, he was going to lose no time. They were sixty miles from Sydney, three miles out in the bush from a station where the trains stopped only irregularly during the day and possibly not at all at night; yet he was rushing off as if he had only a ten-minute bus ride in front of him. Second thoughts had never been a part of his make-up: everything was done on impulse.

Jack stood up, reaching for his tunic and putting it on. "I'll come with you."

"I'll be all right, mate," Greg said, but his tone wasn't adamant: it was plain to see he would be glad of company. "It's a long way——"

Jack got into his greatcoat, picked up his hat, and blew out the lantern. "We'll have to move, chum. It's just on eight, now."

They trudged the three miles down the rutted road to the station, walking in silence through the cold still night. Occasionally a night-bird uttered a sharp cry, like some protesting spirit angered at being disturbed in its solitude, but most of the way the bush was silent but for the scuff of their boots on the dried mud of the road. The sky was thick with stars, cold and sharp as splintered ice, and the mountains were

M

black against the first glow of the moon. Jack dug his hands deep into his greatcoat pockets, feeling the letter he had written Silver and which he had absently shoved into one of them, and then he had his idea.

At the station they found a train would be coming through in half an hour. When the station porter invited them in to share his small office, Jack asked if he might use the phone.

Silver herself answered it.

"I wondered if I'd find you in," he said.

"I told you, I'm going to be a homebody till you come back from the war."

"That's my girl," he said. "Could you pick up me and Greg at Central in about two hours?"

"Why, what's the matter?"

"I'll explain later," he said. "Wait for us down in Eddy Avenue, near the Chalmers Street end."

"I'll be there, master," she said. "And master?"

"Yes?"

"I love you. And I'm not suffering from exhaustion any more."

He looked over his shoulder at Greg and the station porter both watching him with interest. "I'm very glad to hear that. I'll look forward to hearing more about it."

He heard her laugh, a sound he had been remembering so well this past week, then she said, "Righto, the car will be there. The Rolls or the SS?"

"Oh, the Rolls," he said, and hung up the phone and turned round. "Silver will meet us with the car."

"That's decent of her." Now Greg was on his way to see Sarah he had thrown off most of his morbidity; there even seemed a gleam of hope in his eyes. He's like a child, Jack thought, always ready to grasp at optimism. "Did you say she was bringing the Rolls?"

"A Rolls, eh?" said the station porter, visibly impressed. "That's not a bad car."

For the next twenty minutes the three connoisseurs discussed the merits of high-priced cars, then Jack and Greg bought two second-class tickets and went out and boarded the train. On the journey down to Sydney Greg once more dropped into a morose silence, and Jack left him to himself. At first he had been annoyed with himself for having allowed Greg to embark on this fool's errand: he should have slapped Greg under the jaw and put him to bed. But now, with the thought of seeing Silver again, the journey through the cold night seemed worthwhile. It might even be that Sarah would listen to Greg and they would make up.

When they got out of the train at Central they noticed at once that two military policemen were standing by the ticket collector at the exit gate.

"Provosts!" Greg said, and he sounded almost scared. "We've got to dodge those——"

Jack was surprised at the vehemence in Greg's voice, but he let it pass. He pointed to the men's toilet farther along the platform. "We can wait in the dyke till they've gone."

"That'll be no good," Greg said. "They come along the platform—here they come now!"

The two provosts had come through the gate. Jack looked about him, saw he and Greg were the only two soldiers on the platform, and knew that in a minute or so they were going to be asked for their leave passes.

"We'd better get out——" he said, but Greg had already gone, sprinting along the platform towards the outward end where it finished like a small cape jutting out into the sea of rails. Jack turned and followed, running with great loping strides, hampered by his greatcoat, and behind him he heard a shout from the provosts.

Greg went running down off the end of the platform and

Jack went after him. The tracks were a blue-silver maze in the moonlight, a swirling current of steel that stretched away like a great sheet of treacherous water. Jack remembered reading that more trains moved out of this station than any other station in the world: it was the city's only main line station and trains from here went to every corner of the State: and seeing the vast expanse of track before him now, Jack could well believe it.

He caught up with Greg and they ran together, leaping over the rails, stumbling sometimes, but gaining on the two provosts behind them. Then suddenly Jack looked up and saw the two trains bearing down on them. He grabbed Greg's arm and they pulled up, staring at the bewildering network, wondering on which set of tracks the oncoming trains were running. The noise of the trains came ahead of them, loud and terrifying, and heightened the effect of bewilderment, hammering the mind into a daze. Jack thought, what a bloody crazy way to die; then abruptly he stepped forward, pulling Greg with him, and a moment later a train went by on the set of rails where they had stood. Then the second train went by in front of them, its lights flashing on their faces, and they stood there, as if caught in a storm of lightning and thunder and wind, while the cheated wheels tore sparks from the rails and rolled on down the tracks.

When the trains had gone Jack looked back over his shoulder. The provosts had gone. He could see them climbing back up on to the platform in the distance: they had decided it wasn't worth risking their necks to nab a couple of A.W.L. soldiers.

"Let's take it easy now, chum," he said.

Greg took out a handkerchief and mopped his face: he was cold sober now. "I thought we'd bought it that time!"

They went on, moving across the tracks, and at last they came to a dark platform. Jack hoisted Greg up, then with

Greg's help scrambled up himself. They were dusting themselves down when a figure stepped up beside them.

"What are you two up to?"

Greg jumped almost a foot in the air and spun round. "Don't creep up on a man like that!"

"I said," the man's voice was as lugubrious as that of a natural-born grave digger, "what are you two up to?"

Jack fell back on the old defence of answering a question with a question. "Where are we?"

"You're on the Mortuary platform," said the man.

"Where the trains leave for Rookwood cemetery?" Jack said. "I might have guessed it. And you're the night watchman?"

"I'm one of the porters working overtime," said the man unhappily. "But you haven't told me what you two are up to."

Greg produced their tickets. "Here are our tickets, sport. Perfectly valid and paid for. We just came this way to avoid some friends."

"The provosts, is that what you mean?" said the man. "You might have got yourselves killed."

"There's no need to sound happy about it." Jack began to move along the platform towards the exit. Greg fell into step beside him and the porter trailed them closely. "Don't you get enough souls to dispatch?"

"There's a few more I wouldn't mind seeing on their way." It was too dark beneath the platform roof to see the man; they would remember him only as a mournful voice.

"Doesn't it depress you?" Jack felt they had to keep the man talking till they were out of the locked gates ahead of them. "Loading stiffs on a train every day."

"The dead 'uns don't depress me as much as some of the mourners," said the man. "And we don't just send off funeral trains all the time. We send troop trains out of here, too."

"An apt point of departure," Jack said, and the man unlocked the gates for them. "Thanks, chum. We hope you continue to have many happy years ahead of you, putting souls on the trains en route to a better world."

"Be buggered," said the dispatcher of souls, and closed the gates with a hollow clang behind them.

When they got round to Eddy Avenue, Silver was waiting patiently for them in the Rolls. As they got into the wide front seat beside her Greg said, "From dodging provosts to riding in this. Some people have meteoric rises, haven't they?"

Jack kissed Silver's cheek, the long cold journey and the stupid dangerous race across the tracks forgotten. "Take us out to Greg's place, would you?"

Silver handled the big car with the same cool lazy competence with which she did so many things. Jack sat and watched her lovely profile against the shaded street lamps as they went up through the quiet streets of the city. Even in wartime Sydney was a dead town at midnight: one could almost imagine aborigines wandering through its deserted streets as they had done through the bush that had been here two hundred years ago. Jack squeezed Silver's shoulder and she turned her head and gave him the smile that he had been remembering all week with a lift of excitement.

When they drew up in front of the block of flats in Bondi, Greg got out slowly. He had been very quiet the last part of the drive out from the city and now he seemed even reluctant to go in and see Sarah.

"We'll wait," Jack said. "Good luck, chum."

When Greg had gone Silver said, "What's it all about?"

Jack grinned, took her in his arms and kissed her, then told her of Greg's trouble. She lay against him and after a while she said, "Do you think it's Sarah's fault?"

"I don't think Greg could be in any sort of mess for which he couldn't be partly blamed."

"It's frightening to see marriages breaking up. I've seen it happen a lot in our set, and yet I never get over the shock when I hear of another failure." She looked up at him. "I look on marriage as something sacred, darling."

"So do I," he said. "That's why I've never rushed into it."

She was quiet for a while. In the distance he could hear the thunder of the surf on the beach, like guns on another front. A car started up and went by the end of the street, its gears clashing with an angry scream that jarred the still night. Jack sat there holding her tightly yet tenderly, thinking, this is like coming home, this is all I want and no more; and then she said, "Jack, why haven't you asked me to marry you?"

It seemed it was the hardest question he had ever had to answer and he took a long time about it. She stayed still nestled in his arms, not pushing away from him to confront him starkly with the query, and somehow that helped him. "I wanted to be sure——"

She raised her head sharply. "Aren't you sure you love me?"

"That, I am sure of," he said. "As sure as I've ever been of anything."

"Well, then?" Her voice was a puzzled plea.

At last he said, "I've never told you why my father committed suicide." She said nothing, and he went on to tell her of a disastrous marriage he had seen at close hand. "When it happens that close to you, it makes you hesitate."

"Do you think I resemble your mother?" She sat up away from him, pulling her thick polo coat closely about her. "You think I might go her way if I'm left alone?"

Oh, God, he thought, here we are on the verge of a quarrel already: the ghosts of that twelve-year-old tragedy hung about them in the cold night. "Of course not! But do you blame me for being cautious? For years now I've done my best to stop taking the first step towards getting married. Then when I do fall in love——" He stopped and ran his hand over the expensive upholstery of the car. "I fall for someone who belongs to *this*. Rolls-Royces, mink coats, a house big enough to be a museum. Other men, when they marry, have some hold over their wives other than just the lure of themselves. Their wives depend on them. For a home, for money to raise their children. A lot of women even depend on their husbands for small every-day decisions. But you would have to depend on me for nothing, Silver. Nothing at all."

"Is that why you've sometimes sneered about my money?"

"I don't know. Maybe. If I did, the intent was only subconscious. I'm not scared of your wealth just because of the size of it. And if we married I wouldn't be foolish enough to expect you to live on my earnings as an announcer. It's not that sort of old-fashioned pride that's made me scared of your money. It's——" He turned and roughly grabbed her shoulders, pulling her to him. "Can't you understand? I haven't a thing in the world to offer you that you haven't got or can't buy. All I offer you is myself. Do you blame me for wondering if that's enough? You've called me conceited —here I am being modest for the first time in my life——"

She smiled, not a quick wide smile, but just a gentle parting of the lips, the dimples hardly there in the smooth curve of her cheek. "Darling, why shouldn't I be satisfied with just yourself? Why shouldn't that be all I need in the world? I'm not the first rich girl who's fallen in love. Others have had everything before they were married, and still managed to stay in love with their husbands. Why shouldn't I stay in love with you?"

There were no words to answer her. He pressed her head back against the seat, feeling her mouth open under his, aware of the warm exciting body under the polo coat, and he knew that even if there had been words he would not have needed them. All the understanding between them was in the pressure

of lips against lips and the bodies tha[...]
in the cramped seat of the car.

It was another half hour before Greg[...]
He was alone and walking slowly. He ca[...]
and got in. "Sorry I was so long. I shou[...]
buzz off and leave me."

"How's Sarah?" Jack said.

"All right." Greg slumped down in the seat[...]
them back to the city. "We talked, but I don't k[...]
got anywhere. There doesn't seem any point at [...]
start. If there were another bloke—well, we could b[...]
there."

"Is she going to write you?" Jack said.

"I didn't ask her. All I said was, would she mind if I [...]
her." Greg blew out disgustedly. "It was almost as if I [...]
meeting her for the first time. Asking your wife if you c[...]
write to her. Wouldn't it?"

Silver dropped them at Central, Jack kissed her good night[...]
while Greg looked at the stars, then after a long wait they
caught the early morning paper train. It was almost daylight
when they got out of the train at the small deserted platform.
The stars were paling in the sky, but looking no less hard and
cold than they had last night; they were frozen for the winter,
splinters of polar ice always there in the vast silent space.
Some pools still remained by the sides of the road from the
rain of two days ago, white and glistening under their thin
masks of ice. It was a clear morning, sharp and glittering as
a new knife, and already last night seemed a long way behind
them.

"I don't know if it was worth it." Greg's breath trailed over
his shoulder like a grey-white scarf. "But thanks for coming
with me."

Jack just nodded. They cut up through the scrub from the
road and were ten yards from their tent when they saw Major

ng up at an angle
no avoiding him
of them met by
ce showed any
d, and went
as. "This

t hungered for each othe

y came out of the flats.
me across to the car
ld have told you to

as Silver drove
now that we
which I can
egin from

wrote
was
an

CHAPTER THIRTEEN

"HE was looking for you last night," Bluey Brown said. "Just after the signal came through. He came bellowing down the lines, wanting to know where the hell you were and who'd given you leave. He was like a bull that had just discovered it was a bullock. He bloody near burst a bloodvessel while he was yelling at me."

"When did the movement order come through?" Greg said. He and Bluey were sitting at one of the rough tables in the crude leaf-and-branches hut that was the sergeants' mess. They were at breakfast and Greg wasn't letting the possibility of a court-martial spoil his hunger.

"About nine o'clock. That was one of the things he was so crooked on. The C.O. gave orders that the movement plan had to be prepared last night, and the Ape didn't have a single officer or N.C.O. in camp. He had to do the lot himself." Bluey lit a cigarette and flipped the match outside the hut. "You're going to have the book thrown at you, mate."

"This time to-morrow I'll probably be Private Morley again. I'm just sorry Jack gets it in the neck, too. I'm to blame for the whole thing."

"He doesn't care about you. Jack's the one he wants, for what Jack said to him that day in the Marble Bar." Greg had been told of the incident and now he nodded in understanding. "If he hadn't copped Jack for this, he'd have got him for something else. He's been gunning for him ever since he came back to the battalion."

"Still doesn't make me feel any better," Greg said. "Where are we supposed to be going?"

"North Queensland, up around Cairns. Then the next hop is to New Guinea."

"What's New Guinea like at this time of year?"

Bluey shrugged and stood up. "They tell me it's bloody awful all year round. I think we've seen the end of the civilised war, mate."

On the way back to his tent Greg was stopped by Father Chase. "Hallo, Greg. I hear you're in a spot of bother."

"Looks like it, padre. Jack Savanna and I may be back with the hoi-polloi to-morrow."

Father Chase smiled, his long dark face with its strong nose and deep-set eyes suddenly losing the almost mystic quality it had when in repose. He had a deep melodious voice and a rare laugh that was as surprising as it was infectious. Walking about the camp, his head bent slightly forward and his dark face solemnly pensive, he had an aesthetic look about him that had at first deterred the men. Now they knew that he had a deep joy of living and a rare understanding of the weaknesses of men.

"Don't you ever feel remorse about anything, Greg?"

Greg looked over Father Chase's shoulder and saw Jack standing outside the tent cleaning his teeth. "I do this time, padre. I'm even capable of what you people call an act of contrition."

Father Chase pressed Greg's shoulder, still smiling. "I never thought I'd hear that. Something's happening to you, Greg."

"I'm becoming responsible," said Greg. "To-morrow I'll be the most responsible private in the A.I.F."

Then Father Chase left him and Greg walked on to the

tent. Jack said, "We're booked to see the Ape at one-fifteen right after lunch. He's going to demote us on a full stomach."

"I'm sorry about this. Let me take the blame when we get in there."

"It won't do any good, chum. He's not interested in excuses." Jack picked up his greatcoat and folded it to lay it on his bed. Then he felt in one of the pockets and drew out a letter. "How's that? Seven pages, and all of them now out of date."

"Out of date?"

"While you were talking with your missus, chum, I got involved in a delicate discussion with Silver. About marriage. Everything was smoothed out finally, but that letter is now just full of old theories."

"You're glad you went, then?"

"It was even worth being demoted," Jack said. "So don't worry your head about it, chum."

At midday Vern arrived back in camp. He had been back some time before he sent for them. Alec Putnam stood up as they entered the tent.

"I have a few things to check on," he said. "See you later."

When he had gone Jack said, "That was for our benefit, wasn't it? You're going to hammer us into the ground."

"You think I shouldn't?" Vern said, but he looked almost too tired to care.

"How's young Jill?" Greg said, feeling awkward and uncomfortable.

"All right, thanks," Vern said shortly, and lay back in his chair and looked up at them. "You're a couple of bastards, aren't you?"

Jack said nothing and after a moment Greg said, "I'm sorry, Vern. It was my fault."

"Balls, it was," said Jack. "We were in it together."

"I'm not interested in whose fault it was." Vern had a rare

look of irritation, as if he were thoroughly fed up. Lack of sleep and the worry of the last few days had stretched him to the point where his patience and good humour were no longer readily available to him. Looking at him, Greg was suddenly aware that he had involved not only one but both his closest friends in his troubles. Everything he did seemed sooner or later to have a burdening effect on everyone. Vern went on, speaking in a flat tired voice: "I've been protecting you two too damned long. You've got into scrapes before and I've got you out of them by hiding them from Caulfield. When you were demoted I got your stripes back for you, because when you behave yourselves you're worth them. Why the hell did you have to pick last night when I was away? You were acting platoon leader, Jack. Haven't you any sense of responsibility? You're not bloody schoolboys!" He slapped his hands savagely on the arms of his chair. "This is the last time, I'm warning you. After this, you're on your own."

"We see Caulfield at one-fifteen," Jack said. "I'm sorry, Vern. But you'll find someone to replace us. Fred Talmadge will make a good platoon sergeant. And Dad Mackenzie is worth a couple of stripes."

"That's all been fixed," Vern said, still without any friendliness in his voice. "We'll be back in action again within six weeks and I'd rather go in with the N.C.O.s I've already worked with. I've seen the C.O. and he's now having a talk with Caulfield—who doesn't know I've been to the C.O. The bloody intriguing that has to go on, because of you two stupid bastards and another bastard whose only idea is vengeance!"

"What happens then?" Greg said.

"Caulfield will tear a strip off you, but neither of you will lose your stripes. The C.O. is going to suggest to him that since you're a V.C. man, it mightn't be welcomed at Div if you were sent back to the ranks right now. Not after all the publicity you've just had. We never know when you'll be called on again to open another bond rally or something. And because you're not to be demoted, Caulfield can't do anything about Jack. But he'll tear into both of you and from now your life will be hell. And it will be all you deserve." Vern stood up. "That's all, you're dismissed."

As they walked across to the mess for lunch Jack said, "That's the first time since he got his pips that he's pulled his rank on us."

"I think we had it coming to us."

"I'm not complaining, chum. He called me a bastard, something I've been called lots of times. It just happens it's the first time I've ever felt like one."

Three-quarters of an hour later, on full stomachs, they listened to a vitriolic lecture by Major Caulfield. He ranted and roared like a caged animal, and down in the company lines the men listened with attentive ears.

"I remember Confucius once said to me," said Joe Brennan, lying stretched out on his bed, "Man who blow top only disturb dandruff."

"A Woolloomooloo philosopher," said Mick Kennedy. "What's it mean?"

"The Ape has somehow been blocked off," Joe said. "I'll lay even money Jack and Greg don't lose their stripes."

"I'll be disappointed if they don't," said Mick. "I've already written me mum to address her next letter to Corporal Michael Kennedy. How's it sound, eh? *Corporal* Kennedy. By jeez, you're gunna see some discipline then, I'm telling you."

"If they give you two stripes," said Dad Mackenzie from the other end of the tent, "I'm going over to the Japs."

"Please yourself," said Mick airily. "I don't want anyone in my army who don't wanna stay."

Major Caulfield was still going hot and strong. Dad Mackenzie sat up on his bed. "Listen to the drongo! Someone should shoot that man."

"That's the trouble," said Joe. "It's murder to shoot the bastards on your own side. That doesn't come under the heading of war."

"Who told you that?" said Mick. "Your mate Confucius?"

"How will he be when we get up to New Guinea?" Dad said. "He'll be back in his own territory there. I don't fancy the idea of him on our back all the time——" He frowned, and his heavy square-jawed face looked as pugnacious as a clenched fist. "It's going to be a long stoush up there and with him around all the time, chucking his weight about, never caring a damn about how any of us are making out—ah, why doesn't Greg or Jack just throttle him?"

"On second thoughts I think I'll knock back that offer of two stripes," said Mick. "I don't wanna be just a figurehead corporal."

"Talking about me?" said Fred Talmadge, and poked his head in the doorway of the tent. "I'm looking for some volunteers and you coves will do nicely."

"What's on?"

"Working parties. The movement order has been brought forward twenty-four hours. We move to-morrow instead of Thursday."

"You wouldn't read about it!" Joe Brennan rolled disgustedly off his bed. "Hasn't the bloody Army learned yet how to stick to schedule?"

"They're improving," said Fred. "It's *ahead* of schedule this time."

A little later Fred Talmadge's working party was joined by Greg. The men stopped stacking boxes and looked at him. "How'd you go, Greg?"

"We had a small polite conversation," said Greg. "Mostly one-sided."

"Are you still a sergeant," said Mick, "or are you now one of us?"

"Still a sergeant. I'm on a good behaviour bond till the end of the war."

"Tough luck, Mick," Joe said. "There go your stripes."

There was a bellow from the company headquarters tent. "Sergeant Morley!"

"Sir!" cried Greg, and went off at the double.

The men looked after him. "I dunno," said Mick. "Maybe I'm glad I'm staying a private. At least I got me independence."

"Righto, Private Kennedy," said Fred Talmadge. "More work and less talk."

"Up you, corporal," said Mick, and looked about at the others. "See what I mean?"

The rest of the day was a well organised scramble. Because no roots had been sunk in this camp, it was easily broken. There were further requests for compassionate leave, all of which were refused; two men from D Company went A.W.L and the battalion never saw them again; one of the cooks poured a dixie of boiling water over his arm and was carted off, moaning gleefully, to the nearest base hospital, which happened to be only two miles from the cook's home. By 1700 hours the battalion was ready to move.

Colonel McInnes called a rough assembly of the men, told them where they were going and expressed the hope that the battalion would soon once more be doing a constructive job towards winning the war. Then, a man with a sense of the fitness of things, he granted leave in the nearby town for a final booze-up. Everyone but the duty officer and N.C.O. and the essential picquets could go. It was Major Caulfield, making no attempt to lower his voice, who suggested that a picquet should also be placed on the railway station to prevent some of the men extending their six-hour local leave into an all-nightstay in Sydney. There was a growling murmur from the men, but no demonstration: Colonel McInnes was not one

N

who stood for lack of discipline, even in a rough assembly. It was left to Vern, the duty officer, to name the extra picquets, and the rest of the battalion went off to get ready for town.

Greg was the duty N.C.O. and Vern sent him looking for Jack. The latter was just buttoning up his tunic when Greg walked into the tent. "Righto, cock. You're it. N.C.O. in charge of the station picquet. You've got three blokes and the truck's waiting for you now."

Jack raised an eyebrow. "It's on, eh? We're being made to pay for our sins."

"Vern's hardly spoken to me all day. How's he been with you?"

"Sergeant Savanna this, Sergeant Savanna that. We're in the muck, chum, no doubt about it."

"Well, he's kept you with him on the rearguard. So maybe he's going to break down and talk to you."

"Or spend the time giving me extra kicks in the bum." Jack picked up his hat and clamped it on his head. "But I must admire the old bastard's sense of poetic justice. Putting *me* in charge of the picquet to stop coves going through to Sydney."

Half an hour later the camp was deserted. Greg sat in the large tent that was B.H.Q. and wrote to Sarah. He wanted to write and yet it was an effort; he had so much to say and yet there semed little that could be said. There was no longer any intimacy with Sarah: it was almost like writing to one's psycho-analyst: she was a stranger who knew all his secrets. He signed the letter *All my love*, wondering how much it would mean to her, and put the letter in an envelope. If she replied to this letter, the next would be much easier to write.

Last night she had been surprised but not annoyed when she had opened the door to him. She had had no make-up on, her eyes had been puffed with sleep and her usually well-groomed hair a mess, but when she had opened the door she had looked beautiful to him. She had shown no irritation with him while they had talked and he had succeeded in remaining calm beyond his own expectations. She had suggested asking Jack and Silver up to the flat, but he had said no to that and she hadn't insisted. When he had left, his only consolation was that they had got through the three-quarters of an hour without further bitterness; and now he was grasping at that frail straw with the optimism that was as natural to him as breathing.

At ten-thirty, Vern, who had been down in his own tent, came up to the office. "Anything doing?"

"Nothing at all. At least being stuck out here, we haven't got Brigade or Div on our neck all the time."

"We'll be back to that soon." Vern sat down, and after a while said, "How's Sarah?"

"All right. She had lunch with Dinah last week."

"They seem to get on pretty well together. How does she like her job?"

They had talked about that last night, and without ill-will. "Pretty fair. She says the Yanks are great ones for paper-work. They don't do things in just triplicate. They want nothing less than five copies. Always bigger and better."

Vern smiled for the first time since he had returned to camp and in a moment the strain between them was broken. "Don't be so crooked on the Yanks. You like Alec Putnam."

"Yes, but all Yanks aren't like him."

"How do you know? How many Yanks have you met?" Vern shook his head. "Americans are all right, Greg. That's the trouble with us Aussies. We haven't much time for anyone but ourselves. Most of us never get out of this country, so we never know what the rest of the world is like at home. The Yanks brag a bit, but they've got something to brag about. They aren't the only people who chuck their weight around when they're abroad. There's no one so bloody superior as an Englishman when he's abroad. And when I was in New York I met some Aussies who I wished had never been let out of Australia. Talking at the top of their voices, wanting to job everyone who disagreed with them. People look a lot different when they get away from home. Including us." Vern grinned. "I remember a cove who wrecked a café in Jerusalem and threatened to do over every Jew in the city. And after that he was going to take on the Arabs."

"I must have been drunk." Greg grinned back: the old relationship was back and he felt a warmth of good feeling. His marriage had gone on the rocks, but it was comforting to know that he still had the friendship of the two men whom he regarded with more affection than his own brother.

Then from down the road there came the sound of ribald singing that shook the stillness out of the night, crashing it down between the trees like falling branches. A few minutes later fumbling hands were lighting lanterns in the tents and tins were being kicked as men stumbled about the lines. There were curses and then laughter as some fell over guy-ropes, and a muffled roar as one tent, its ropes cut, collapsed on its occupants. The singing went on, sometimes just bawdy, sometimes obscene, often sentimental, and the battalion slowly drifted home. Men threw buckets of water over other men who had gone to bed, and the drenched ones retaliated in like manner. There was one serious fist fight and a tent was set on fire but quickly put out. There was wild drunken hilarity throughout the camp and psychologists would once more have had proven for them that only a thin line separates the boy from the man in all of us, and especially in soldiers. Bedlam reigned, and all that Vern and Greg could do was wander around and see that no one got seriously hurt.

It was 23.59 hours, the moment when leave officially expired, when someone threw a grenade into Major Caulfield's tent.

CHAPTER FOURTEEN

WHEN Vern called and said he was coming down to Sydney and would come out home for an hour, Dinah felt she had had an unexpected windfall, like winning the State lottery without knowing she had a ticket. She had said good-bye to him two days ago and had begun to prepare for the long wait till she saw him again. Something had gone out of her life as he had turned the corner of the street and disappeared on Tuesday morning. The good-bye had been even worse than the original farewell two years ago: now she knew the depths of the loneliness and the extent of the fear that lay in the months ahead. To know that he was coming home again so soon, even if only for an hour, was something she hadn't dared hope for.

He arrived just after lunch. She heard the truck pull up and when she went to the front window she saw him wave to Jack Savanna, who turned the truck and drove off again rapidly. She opened the door before he had time to ring the bell.

"Oh, darling!" She flung herself against him, pulled him into the hall and kissed him with a passion that shook her like a fever.

"Easy!" he said, grinning and gasping. "I'm supposed to be on duty."

"The moment you step in this house, the Army has no

197

they're both wild irresponsible goats, but they're not murderers! What on earth put that idea into your head?"

She listened impatiently while he told her about the trouble he had met when he had gone back to camp on Tuesday. "They had a reason. He hates their guts and they hate his."

"Yes, but Greg and Jack are decent men——"

He lay on the bed beside her and now looking down at him she noticed for the first time how tired he looked. There seemed as much strain on his face as there had been the night of Jill's crisis. Suddenly she felt ashamed of the eagerness she had shown when he had first entered the house. She had swamped him with her feeling and hadn't thought that he might not have been in the mood for loving her. This last half hour had been such ecstasy for her, so unexpected and therefore so much more exciting, that she hadn't noticed if it had meant as much to him.

"When I was a reporter on police rounds," he said, looking straight up at the ceiling, "one of the things I learned was that most murderers, to begin with, were decent men. After the murder they often go back to being decent as they ever were. They have one insane moment and afterwards they feel remorse, disgust with themselves, everything that you'd expect from a normal decent person. Greg and Jack and the rest of them have been at war long enough now to put a different sort of value on life from what you'd expect. Fundamentally, there's no difference between shooting a German or a Jap and someone on your own side, not if you have an equal amount of hate."

"That makes a nice aspect for after the war, doesn't it?"

"Prospect," he said absently. Then he grinned, pulled her down on to him and kissed her. After a while he pushed her away, rolled off the bed and began to dress. "I forgot to tell you. Jack is getting engaged to Silver Bendixter."

"Well, my God, isn't that just like a man!" She stopped

with her dress half-way over her head. "One minute you tell me you suspect him of trying to murder a man and the next you tell me he's getting engaged. Why, the two things are in—what's the word I want?"

"Incompatible?"

"Thanks. They're incompatible. A man who's about to become engaged couldn't be thinking of murder."

He grinned. "A woman's logic. Just as well there aren't too many woman detectives. The world would be a great place for criminals."

"Most criminals are men." She did up the placket of her dress. "And women, sooner or later, catch the men they want."

"It would certainly revolutionise the ways of detection. It raises infinite possibilities. Sex instead of justice hounding the criminal." He came round the bed and took her hands. He was suddenly serious again. "Look, darl, I didn't jump to conclusions about this thing. Someone in A Company did the trick. I checked on all the probables and none of them was near Caulfield's tent when the grenade was thrown. Jack had just come back to camp from picquet duty and Greg was somewhere out in the lines—and outside of myself they were about the only ones sober enough to throw a grenade into the right tent and then get away without being seen."

"You know," she said, "*they* could be suspecting *you*."

Obviously he hadn't thought of that. He stared at her, then looked annoyed. Tiredness suddenly fell down over his face like a veil and he turned away from her and looked out the window. The afternoon sun came in, thin and golden, striking in a broad band against the side of his face and his temple. It was only then, for the first time, she noticed the grey already beginning in his hair. Oh, my poor tired darling, she thought, and abruptly put her arms about him.

"Don't worry about it, Vern darling. It'll all straighten out."

"But I do worry," he said, still looking out the window. "I worry about Jack and Greg because, damn it, I love those two. I worry about every man in my platoon, because I feel responsible for them. And when eventually I get the company —*if* I get it—I'll worry about every man in it, the whole hundred-odd of them. I'm the greatest bloody worrier in the A.I.F."

A little later there was the sound of the truck's horn outside. When they went out, Jack's head was poked out the cabin window smiling like a boy setting off on a long-awaited holiday. "Congratulate me. I'm on my way to being an old married man."

"Did she say yes?" said Dinah.

"Did you think she'd say no?" Jack let out a roar of laughter, his happiness exploding out of him; Dinah had never seen him so gay and excited. "We'll be married next time I come home. Start saving for a bang-up wedding present."

They congratulated him, both almost as happy as he about the engagement. Then Vern kissed Dinah good-bye and climbed into the truck.

"I'll call in and see Jill. And Michael, too. Did he tell you he wanted me to bring him back a Jap sword?"

"Make sure you don't forget," said Dinah. "There's always room about the house for something nice and lethal."

Then they drove away and she felt again the crumbling inside her. The past couple of years had been as unreal as a dream: this last fortnight, having him back with her, had been like waking to a joy that had been almost as unreal as the fear and the loneliness. Now the dream was beginning again, and the cycle would go on for only God knew how long. It was hard to remember how beautifully safe their life had been before the war. Having him leave for the office each morning with the sure knowledge that he would be home again that night; having him beside her in bed each and every night, except those rare occasions when he had been sent away on a story; the week-ends when the four of them would go down to the beach or drive out into the country for a picnic. Some people might have called it a dull life; but it had been a beautiful practical fact and not a lonely dream.

That night she and Michael went up to see Jill.

"Mr. Savanna came in with Daddy," Jill said. "My, he looked happy. He said he'd just got engaged. Do you know her, Mummy? Is she nice?"

"She's stinking rich," said Michael. "That's enough."

"It helps," Jill said off-handedly, as if Michael was being childishly obvious. "It would be better if she was beautiful, too."

"She's stinking rich and very beautiful and a nice girl, all rolled into one," said Dinah. "Jack Savanna is a very lucky man."

"I'll say he is," said Michael. "I hope I marry someone who's stinking rich."

"Don't be so mercenary," Jill said. "You sound too predatory for words."

"Hey, hold on!" said Dinah. "Keep the words down to my level. Nothing over two syllables."

"You really should educate yourself more, Mummy." Jill was sitting up in bed with her hair in braids and with one of Dinah's bedjackets thrown about her shoulders. With the colour still not back in her face and her big eyes so dark and solemn, she looked like a little old lady offering advice to her daughter and grandson.

"I've got your father and you two," said Dinah. "Who wants education?"

"I've been thinking while I've been here," Jill said, "and when I'm old enough I want to go to the university."

"What are you going to be?" said Michael.

"I don't know," Jill said. "I just want to be educated enough to understand everything that goes on."

"We'll send you to the university," said Dinah. "And when you understand everything, you can come and explain it to your old lady. Because there are a good many things in this world I just don't understand at all."

And she thought of the war and what had caused it, and the sadism of ordinary men, and why anyone, who was as decent and likeable as the men she had met from Vern's company, should want to murder one of their officers.

CHAPTER FIFTEEN

SILVER had had to work back, and it was almost ten o'clock when she reached home. She let herself in the front door, threw her hat and coat on a chair in the hall and walked into the living-room. Her mother, having one of her rare nights without some war work engagement, looked up from the magazine she was reading. It was a famous fashion magazine whose writers were having difficulty in being ecstatic about wartime fashions: it was difficult to reconcile patriotism with the haute couture: General MacArthur and Maggy Rouf didn't seem to walk hand in hand. Mrs. Bendixter was wearing glasses with thick dark-blue tortoishell rims that gave her an intellectual look to which she hadn't the barest claim.

"Hallo, dear. You *are* late. I'll have to speak to Sid about overworking you."

Silver didn't demur: she knew that by to-morrow morning her mother would have forgotten all about speaking to Sid Hugo. "I'll get Julia to bring me dinner in here." When she came back from the kitchen she said, "I'm engaged, Mother."

"Oh, that was quick," said Mrs. Bendixter. "Did someone just call up?"

Silver sat down on the arm of her mother's chair. "No, Mother. I'm *engaged*. Engaged to be married. Jack asked me this afternoon."

"Jack?" Mrs. Bendixter took off her glasses and instantly

was her vague natural self again. "But I didn't know you——
How long has this been going on?"

"Just over two weeks. From the night I met him. It's
sudden, darling, but it had to be. I had to grab him before he
went away again."

"My God, I don't know what to say!" Mrs. Bendixter was
flabbergasted: it was obvious she hadn't given a thought
to Jack as a possible son-in-law. "You might have warned
me!"

"You were too busy to listen to me, darling. If you hadn't
been, you'd have seen I've been in love for the past week or
more. From the night he saved me from the harbour."

"Is that why you're in love with him?"

Silver knew that her mother could be irritating to outsiders,
but she had long grown used to her vagueness. It often
prompted questions that from someone else would have been
annoying, or sometimes, downright insulting. Mrs. Bendixter
was so vague that sometimes she missed the fact that her
daughters had grown up.

"I'm not a schoolgirl, Mother," Silver said patiently. "I
fell in love with him for sane, very adult reasons."

Mrs. Bendixter suddenly smiled, her eyes shining with
tears. "I get wrapped up in the wrong things. War work,
instead of my daughter's happiness. I'm really happy for you,
if he's the man you want."

"He is," said Silver, and felt it was the one perfect truth she
had ever uttered.

"I wish I'd taken more notice of him," Mrs. Bendixter said.
"It's going to be embarrassing having a stranger for a son-in-
law."

Silver laughed. "He's not that much of a stranger!"

"Oh, I know what he looks like. That awful moustache!
You'll have to get him to shave that off!" Mrs. Bendixter
flapped a hand, as if wiping a moustache from her own upper

lip. "But what's his background? Who are his people and what does he do in civilian life?"

"His parents are dead," said Silver, thinking that her mother, vague as she was, would never need to know any more than that. "And he was an announcer on the A B C"

"You mean he reads the news? But that doesn't sound very exciting. Those A B C men always make everything sound such bad news."

Then Julia, the cook, brought in dinner. She had been with the Bendixters for twenty years and when she was told of the engagement she burst into tears. "Oh, that's wonderful! Oh, I've waited such a long time for this! It's wonderful, isn't it, Mrs. B? Isn't it wonderful?" And another flood of tears coursed down the stout red cheeks. "I'm so happy! Aren't you, Mrs. B?"

"Yes," said Mrs. Bendixter, and suddenly she too burst into tears. She put her arms about Julia and the two of them stood together in the middle of the room weeping copiously and telling each other how happy they were.

Then Mamie came in. "Hallo, someone peeling onions?"

She was told the news. She let out a scream of delight and flung her arms about Silver. She had been drinking and there was the sickly-sweet smell of gin on her breath; but her joy was something completely removed from the effects of her drinking. She kissed Silver and when she stepped back her eyes too were glistening.

"Oh, my God, I'm happy for you! It's the first constructive thing anyone in this family has done since Daddy was alive. When will you be married?"

"Next time he comes down on leave," Silver said.

"When will that be?"

"We don't know. It may not be for another twelve months," Silver said, and suddenly the time ahead stretched before her like a vast empty plain. She had never had to wait for anyone before and she knew now that she was going to know real loneliness for the first time. Despite her conscientious efforts over the past months, the war had only just now become personal for her.

Jack's first letter since their engagement, written on the train going north, came three days later. She read it, and re-read it; then, feeling like a schoolgirl in the throes of her first crush, she put the letter away in the handkerchief box where she had placed the three others he had written. Life had taken on a new aspect and now she moved through it with a warm glow of complacency that caused joking but envious comments among her unmarried and unengaged friends. Mamie suddenly developed a proprietary interest in her, claiming that the wedding-to-be, being the family's first, was more than just Silver's affair, and the two of them went shopping for Silver's trousseau. There was some slight disappointment that in wartime she couldn't buy all the lovely things that would have been possible had her happiness happened three years earlier. But then she met other girls buying their trousseaux, saw the gladness and excitement on their faces even as they bought utility things, and she knew that a marriage lost nothing because silk was missing from it.

One night after work Mamie called for her in the low-slung S.S. As they drove out through King's Cross and down the long hill to Rushcutters' Bay, through the Yank territory that Mamie knew like an Indian scout, Mamie said, "I joined the W.A.A.A.F. to-day."

"You joined what?"

"I'm going into the Air Force. And starting at the bottom No influence or anything like that. I told them I wanted to be a driver or a clerk, anything but a cook. I thought the last should be avoided if they wanted to get the Air Force into the air."

Silver didn't know what to say for a moment. It was s

tally unlike Mamie to join anything, least of all a service
ganisation where she would be subject to regimentation and
scipline. "Was this something you did on the spur of the
oment?"

"No, I've been thinking about it for a couple of weeks now."
e took the car past a loaded tram, smiling at the two sailors
10 gave her a loud whistle. "I know this sounds unnatural
r me, but finally I got tired of wasting my time. Wasting
y life, if you like. I don't mean I'm turning over a completely
w leaf, though it's quite possible that may happen gradually.
don't know. It may have been your getting engaged that
1ally decided me. That was something constructive, as I said.
· it may just be that, like a lot of other people, I recognised
e war as a chance to make a new start. I'll have to work it
l out later."

"Mamie, when you first started playing around—you
10w——"

"I know what you mean," Mamie said with a slight smile.
Go on."

"This is a bit difficult to put. But—well, were you looking
r love? I mean real love, not just love-making?"

Mamie drove for a while in silence. At last she said, "It's
long ago, I don't really know. I'm twenty-six now and I
:nt to bed the first time when I was seventeen, just after
iddy died. I remember who it was, but I can't remember
I thought I was in love with him. Nor do I think I've been
love with anyone since. All I know is this—that after it was
over, I've always had the feeling I've still missed something.
iaven't any illusions about myself, Sil. I know I'm a good
al of a nympho, maybe more than a good deal. But I
ɔuldn't—and don't—laugh at real love when I see it. When
went to bed that night you told us you'd got engaged, I
ed, I don't know whether for you or myself." She swung
e car into the street where they lived. "I wouldn't laugh if

o

the real thing happened to me. But I have the feeling I'v
left it too late."

"It could still happen," Silver said, and felt closer to he
sister than at any time since they had been children. "I hop
it does."

Mamie pressed Silver's arm, then turned the car into th
drive and a moment later stopped it in front of the hous
"Now to explain to Mother what the W.A.A.A.F. is."

"Why don't you get her to join?" Silver said. "She's join
everything else in sight."

The winter dragged on. Everywhere the war got wors
In the Middle East the Germans had broken through as far
El Alamein; the Russians, about whom some trade unic
leaders were more concerned than about the Australian force
were barely holding their own; and along the east coast o
Australia Japanese submarine packs began to hunt with rapid
increasing success. Americans were pouring into Australi
but seemed to be going no farther: it began to look as
General MacArthur wouldn't make a move till all the od
were in his favour. Jack wrote her, giving her the troop
opinion of MacArthur, and she began to realise there was
great deal of difference between soldiers' and civilians' sent
ments regarding generals.

Mamie went into the W.A.A.A.F. and went to Roberts
for her training: "It's as cold as blazes and I'm putting c
weight," she wrote, "but I'm having the time of my life
Mrs. Bendixter went on joining committees, getting more an
more involved with organisations that couldn't have benefit
from her joining them. Silver's friends began to drift awa
some into the services, some into war work, others in
marriages that took them to other states where they could
near their servicemen husbands. More and more Silver fou
herself alone, her only interests the work at Sid Hugo's offi
and Jack's letters, which she read over and over as if each rea

ag, like an applied ointment, could do something to assuage
ae rawness of her loneliness.

One night, feeling lonelier than usual, her mother at one
f her meetings, she rang up Sarah Morley. Sarah said she was
ast going over to Dinah Radcliffe's and why didn't she come
ith her? Silver hesitated. She had met Sarah only twice and
inah once, and here she was forcing herself upon them.
hen she was aware of the house about her, big and lonely, and
ae said yes, she'd pick Sarah up in twenty minutes.

She almost ran out of the house, stopping only to comb her
air and put on lipstick, and she took the car over to the Morley
at in a good deal less than twenty minutes. Only when she
ot out of the car and went through the front doors of the
ats did it strike her that perhaps it was all over now between
reg and Sarah, and she and Sarah would have nothing at all
common. If Sarah no longer was in love with Greg, then
e would have no fear and her loneliness would be of a
fferent character from Silver's own.

Then Sarah leaned over the stair-rail and said, "Is that you,
lver? I'll be right down." And a moment later, coming
wn the stairs: "Greg wrote and told me you were engaged.
veral times I almost called—and Dinah is looking forward
seeing you——"

CHAPTER SIXTEEN

LIEUTENANT-COMMANDER ASBURY was what Sara
would have called a typical American. He was tall an
moved with a loose-jointed action that was neither awkwar
ness nor grace but was something of both. The bones of h
face were prominent and gave him a look of leanness, yet h
skin had a soft rubberiness about it that was quite unlike th
wrinkled leather that covered the bones of so many Australia
men. His hair was cut in what she now knew was crew-sty
and the back of his neck was always clean, as if he went to th
barber every week, perhaps even twice a week. He had goo
teeth and a voice that was crisp and took care with its word
and he recognised the fact that women meant more to a ma
than beer and racehorses, something that had so far escaped
good many Australian men. He had opinions on everythin
but they were only surface opinions and once one accepted the
as such they could be suffered.

"Mrs. Morley, for the seventeenth time, why won't yo
come out with me?"

"I've told you, Commander Asbury. I'm a married woma
with a husband up north."

"And I'm a married man with a wife in Westbury, Lon
Island. My motives aren't ulterior. I'm just a lonely ma
seeking company."

"There are plenty of other girls here who'd be glad to g

212

out with you. I might even say they're panting to go out with you."

"Panting women annoy me. They make me feel like a master of hounds."

"I didn't know you Americans hunted."

"You see? There's so much about us Americans you don't know. In the interests of international understanding, you should come to dinner with me——"

He was her boss in this sub-section and he had been asking her to go out with him from the second day she had been working for him. He was not the only one who had asked her to go out, but she had said no to all of them. She still wore her wedding ring and had never attempted to disguise the fact that her husband was still alive. She had an old-fashioned respect for principles that made her see it as somehow wrong to put herself in the way of temptation with another man while she was still married to Greg. She knew quite well that some of the other officers who had asked her to go out would be looking for more than just company.

"Look," said Tom Asbury. "Friday is my birthday. I shall be thirty-two years old, just a short step from the grave. Would you begrudge a dying man a small kindness? Come to dinner with me and I'll tell you all about my wife and you can tell me all about your husband, just to keep things respectable. At odd moments we may tell each other about ourselves, but for the sake of propriety we'll never let the ghosts of our spouses desert us——"

Suddenly, laughing, she capitulated. "All right, Friday night. But it isn't to be the first of many regular dates. It's just because it's your birthday——"

Friday morning there was another letter from Greg. He had written regularly once a week since he had gone north, calm restrained letters that were so unlike him. They had been composed of small news about the men she knew in the

battalion, descriptions of the countryside that seemed to catch
the lush warm landscape of north Queensland, and once or
twice several hesitant comments that hinted at a new maturity
in him. There had been no attempt to bring up the matter
of a reconciliation nor had the letters contained any passionate
protestations of his feeling for her. There was only the calm
yet poignant *All my Love* at the bottom of each letter. After
the second letter she had begun to answer him, and she was
not really surprised when she began to look forward to hearing
from him. She had known of people who had gone on being
good friends after their love had run its course, and there was
no reason why she and Greg should not continue as friends.

But to-day's letter disturbed her. She rang up Dinah:
"Have you heard from Vern this week?"

"I got one this morning," Dinah said. "I've just been talking to Silver. She got one from Jack. We think they're in
New Guinea."

"That's what I thought. Greg says nothing definite, but
he hints they've moved. And it's almost a fortnight since I
got his last letter."

"They're up there, all right." Dinah hesitated: "How do
you feel?"

Dinah knew of the rift between her and Greg: she had told
her of it, without too much explanation, the second time she
had gone over to the Radcliffe house. "Worried. How are
you?"

"The same. And Silver, too. It's the Middle East all over
again. Why don't you come over to-night? I'll call Silver, and
we can all console each other."

She almost said yes, then remembered. "Oh, I can't. I——"
She checked herself from saying, "I have a date"; right at this
moment it seemed flippant and uncaring, almost a little
promiscuous. "I have to go out. But how about to-morrow
afternoon?"

"Of course. Come early and stay for dinner. I'll try and et Silver. We'll have a nice long worry." Then the light note ropped from Dinah's voice and she said very quietly, "Greg ill be all right, Sarah. He's the sort that will always bear a harmed life."

"And what about your Vern?"

"For him, I'm doing what I've been doing for the last two ears," Dinah said. "Praying. Wives aren't left much more o do than that in wartime. I don't know that the women in talingrad aren't better off. At least they have their husbands eside them."

That evening Commander Asbury said, "I'm not taking ou to the usual American haunts. I've managed to get a car nd we're going to get out of the city. To-night I feel senti-nental—as distinct from romantic, bless your maidenly heart —and I crave peace and quiet."

They crossed the Bridge and drove through a chill starlit ight up through the North Shore suburbs. They pulled in at restaurant high on the crest of the slope that ran down to he Hawkesbury River. As she got out of the car Sarah caught he sharp smell of the bush, almost antiseptic in its purity. Down in the gorges that ran down to the river there was a ayer of mist that looked like liquid white gold under the full noon just coming over the ridges. The trees behind the estaurant and along the eastern ridges were black and sharp gainst the glowing sky. On the other side of the gorge that ell away almost immediately below the road, the trees and hick scrub were like a pale golden wave that at any moment vould fall into the shifting mist below. A hush lay on the ountryside like the stillness of the spaces beyond the rising noon.

"I couldn't have ordered a better night," said Tom Asbury. I always was lucky for weather on my birthday."

They sat by a window in the restaurant and Tom told her

about life in Westbury, Long Island, and his wife who love
to ride but right now was expecting their first child. "This
her picture, but I say without prejudice that it doesn't do h
justice. That's what I call her Wellesley expression. Wellesle
is a women's college in Massachusetts where all the girls thir
they have to be worthy of Harvard men. I'm a Princeto
man myself. Have you read Scott Fitzgerald?"

"No."

"A pity. It might have led you to a better appreciation o
me. I'm a more responsible Fitzgerald character." He grinne
and sipped his beer. "It's a failing among us Princeton me
to try and act like the guys Fitzgerald wrote about. Only tim
have changed, and what was okay in his day just looks dam
silly now. It occurs to me that you would be the sort of gi
who would appreciate a responsible man. Is your husband
nice responsible guy?"

"No," said Sarah, then had to add an afterthought: "A
least, I don't know. He wasn't, once."

"Neither was I. It's only recently that a sense o
responsibility has come to me, along with a few grey hairs an
a certain stiffness about my joints in the mornings. Oh, I wa
a wild 'un! I must have given a lot of folks a pain in the necl
I was the perennial college boy, still acting the undergradua
at thirty. Then I met Peggy. I remember distinctly—it wa
at a dance at the beach club at Southampton and she had com
with a Harvard man. He was six years younger than I, and th
most God-awful little punk. He looked and talked like he wa
first reserve for the Brains Trust, and I found out later h
was an assistant buyer at Macy's. I took Peggy away fron
him and fell in love with her just like that—— Am I borin
you?"

Sarah smiled at him across the table, thinking of the nigl
at the surf club dance when Greg had asked her to marry hin
"No, go on."

"Well, that was eighteen months ago," Tom said, and she knew he was talking to himself and his absent wife as much s to her, "and three months later we were married. The wedding was big stuff—— Did you have a big wedding?"

"Pretty big. I didn't want one, but Greg did. He said no irl should ever have a quiet wedding. He thinks girls getting married for even the third or fourth time should have big eddings."

"A man after my own heart. Some day I'd like to meet your reg. Well, anyway. Ours was a big wedding, about as big a Presidential inauguration, now I think back on it. We ad a bishop perform the ceremony and the Dean of Wellesley as there—and even the President sent us a present."

"The President?" Sarah laughed. "Oh, now, it wasn't *that* ig!"

"The President of Wellesley," said Tom. "President oosevelt wasn't asked. We Asburys are Republicans."

"Is there much difference between a Democrat and a epublican? There never seems to be to us Australians."

Tom looked pained. "Don't let's spoil a beautiful evening."

She looked out the window. "It is beautiful, isn't it? It's ard to imagine it belongs to the same world in which there's war."

"I wonder what your husband thinks of it?" She had told im that she thought Greg was now in New Guinea. "Or on't you see the moon when you're in the jungle?"

"I don't know," she said, and knew again there was so uch she would never know about war. However much she ad done before the war to help Greg, she had done nothing help him while he had been away in the Middle East nor ould she be able to help him in the coming months, maybe ars, in New Guinea. He was as much on his own there as she had never existed. Her ignorance and helplessness was uddenly a pain in her breast, and she thought of all the

irresponsible husbands all over the world who were fighti
without complaint for the women who would never rea
know the extent of their men's sacrifice.

Later as they drove home Tom said, "Our baby is due
November, around Thanksgiving if he sticks to schedu
It's funny to think about it—he may be three or four years o
before I get to see him. That's an awful long time to wait
see your first child."

"You think the war will last that much longer?"

"I'm pessimistic, but I can't see us winning it soon
Peggy's the one I'm sorry for—and you, too. It's a hell of
note for you women, all this waiting. Peggy will wait, b
I couldn't blame her if she didn't. But I know she will—
she talks about in her letters is, *after the war*. After the war—
he said, and the words seemed to hang in the warm closed
like a sad yet hopeful prayer. He turned and smiled at her, l
face wistful and with the dark hair and brown skin and wh
flashing teeth somehow not unlike Greg's. "Reunion will b
wonderful blessed thing, won't it?"

When he pulled the car up outside the flats he made
attempt to get out. "I'll let you go in on your own. This h
been an innocent evening and I don't want the neighbours
think otherwise." He looked at her, then he leaned across a
brushed his lips against her cheek. "That's for Peggy. And f
Greg, too, I guess."

She went into the flats and climbed the stairs slowly. T
tears were on her cheeks before she was aware of them, b
she made no effort to brush them away. She let herself in
the flat and went into the bedroom and looked at the photo
Greg and herself taken on their wedding day. She turned a
opened the front doors of the bedroom and stepped out on
the balcony. Down in the bay she could hear the sound of t
sea coming in like a vast gentle sighing, the sound of t
memories of the world, and she remembered her wedding d

nd the happiness she had tried to forget. She remembered
reg in all the moments when he had been good and kind and
oving, and she remembered they had both been young and
he young had faults that only experience could eradicate.
hey had still been growing up then, and in the last two years
reg had been through enough to put youth behind him
orever; but when he had returned she hadn't allowed herself
o look for any change in him, and had only thought of the
ast. Greg then hadn't known pain and fear and she hadn't
nown loneliness; and she now knew that love was com-
ounded of all those things besides the joy which was all she
ad once expected. The young would find or lose themselves
n this war; and perhaps it was she, and not Greg, who had
een the one in danger of being lost.

She was still crying when she began the letter that she
oped would recapture her happiness before it was too late.

CHAPTER SEVENTEEN

"I WISH we'd get some mail," Greg said. "It's been to bloody days now since we got any."

"There should be some coming up to-day," Bluey sai He had come up last night from B.H.Q. with four nativ carriers bringing rations. He hadn't arrived till just on dus and he had decided to stay at company headquarters rather tha go blundering down the mile of track in the dark. Vern hadn objected when he had asked if he could come out on this stan ing patrol with them: he had recognised it as the desire of a old soldier to pull a trigger again. "I heard twelve bags mail arrived at Brigade yesterday."

"I must have quite a wad waiting for me," Mick Kenned said. "I got four sheilas writing to me."

"All suing you for maintenance, I'll bet," said Joe Brennar

"There's too much talking." Vern's voice came out of th darkness, a disembodied whisper. "Shut your traps."

The darkness was so impenetrable that no man could s even any part of himself; their eyes were just aching nerv that saw nothing but the blackness that was worse than blin ness. There were no dimensions to the world about them b those offered by touch and sound; and they hadn't been blir long enough to be able to trust their other senses. The water mud in which they squatted sucked and squelched as th moved to ease cold cramped muscles; the rain dripped in ne steady stream through the invisible trees above them; and ways there was the cold smooth feel of leaves like dead fingers ushing against their faces.

The platoon had been out here since yesterday morning ting as a standing patrol in front of the battalion position. l day they had been watching the track along which the panese were expected to advance, but after twenty-four hours ere had still been no sign of movement. In another hour, st before dawn, they were to be relieved by a platoon from Company. A Company would retire down the track for rty-eight hours' rest—unless the Japanese moved again thin those forty-eight hours.

The battalion had been in action now three weeks without y respite at all. It had landed at Port Moresby and climbed the long tortuous Kokoda trail, through the rain forests the Owen Stanleys and down to join the single militia ttalion that had been fighting a desperate but losing battle ainst a Japanese force that outnumbered it four to one. ery day reinforcements had been expected, but none had rived. And every day the small force had been pushed ther back up the narrow trail that was the only way through Moresby and the key to the conquest of New Guinea.

Casualties had been heavy. Enemy bullets and mortars had ten their toll, but the Japanese were no more destructive in the jungle. Fifty per cent of the men evacuated had been ffering from malaria or dysentery or, in one isolated case, ub typhus. Haggett, the company 2 i/c, had been killed, d two other officers had been seriously wounded and sent ck. Vern was now 2 i/c of the company and Jack was acting atoon leader.

Vern, sitting in the mud, so cold and wet that he was aware of his sodden clothes clinging to him, felt someone de towards him.

"That you, skipper?" It was Jack.

"Yes. How's it?"

"Bloody, as usual." Jack's voice was another whisper
the whisper of the rain. "I've had the shivers all night. I thin
I'm in for a bout of malaria."

"You'd better get to bed as soon as we get out of here.
don't want to lose you, too."

"Bed? Christ, is there a dry spot anywhere in the worl
Three bloody weeks, and none of us has been dry in all th
time!" Vern heard him slap his hand against his tommy-gu
"This is no way to fight a flaming war!"

Jack's voice had risen slightly, hissing through the rai
Vern put out a groping hand and patted Jack's arm. "Stead
feller."

"Sorry, chum. I've got a touch of S.O.L., I think. I ke
thinking what a lovely war it was in the Middle East."

Then Vern heard him move away. Vern stood up, stretc
ing his aching limbs, and looked at the luminous dial of h
watch. He stood looking at the faintly glowing circle for
full minute, almost as if relieved to find that his eyes could s
There was another hour to go till dawn. He listened to t
soft mutterings of the men, vague sibilant murmurings th
were like the gentle escape of steam from valves. He knew mc
of them were like himself: too tensed, ready to explode
anger or hysteria unless some relief arrived soon. These pa
three weeks had been worse than the whole accumulated tir
in the Middle East. And what was worse was, that for t
first time in the experience of all of them but Joe Brenna
they knew they were losing. They had fought for three so
rain-drenched unending weeks and every day but yesterd
they had lost men and given ground. A feeling of defeat h
crept in and it was beginning to sap them more than t
chilling never-ceasing rain and the malaria and dysentery a
the fear that clotted each brain like a malignant growth.

Vern had listened to them talking among themselv

sterday. Mick Kennedy had started it. "Christ Almighty,
hat's the use of it all? Why don't they drag us out, get us
ck to the mainland and let's wait for the bastards there? At
ast we'll be able to see 'em! Three weeks, and I've seen the
istards once! That's all, just once. The day we used the
yonet down at Eora Creek."

"Where's everybody else, that's what I wanna know," Joe
ennan had said. "Even in Greece we always knew there was
meone else around. They didn't help much, but you didn't
el so bloody lonely. Outside of us and the 39th, who else is
this war?"

"The Japs," Charlie Fogarty had said, and the men had
ughed quietly and gladly, easing their nerves.

"I wonder where the flaming Yanks are?" Mick had said.
t's nine months since Pearl Harbour and we're still fighting
e war for 'em!"

"They're waiting to win it for us," Dad Mackenzie had said.
Ve'll start the roll-back and then Bullshit MacArthur will
p in and be the hero."

Vern had been glad Alec Putnam had not been around to
ar the next ten minutes' abuse of the Americans. Sometimes
had wondered himself what was delaying the arrival of
nerican forces in New Guinea. The Japanese had landed at
e and Sulamaua early in March and it must have been
cided weeks ago by the Allied Command that the battle for
istralia was to be fought in New Guinea. Alec had sometimes
nted at the extent of unpreparedness in the United States
d Vern had tried to be fair in his judgment. But for a man
10 had been at war for over two years and had been on his
ay to a theatre of war within two months of joining the
my, it was hard to understand or forgive the tardiness of
nation, some of whose spokesmen had criticised Australia's
rt in the war and asked if she was worthy of American aid.
rn would be glad to see the Americans when they arrived,

but he knew there would be some like Mick Kennedy whos
welcome would be tinged with bitter sarcasm.

If the Americans were here now, or even some mor
Australian battalions, which for some reason were still bein
kept on the mainland, these past few weeks might have bee
a different story. On the only occasion when they had had
hand-to-hand clash with the Jap, on the day at Eora Creek whe
they had gone at him with the bayonet, they had more than hel
their own. But two sadly depleted battalions, no matter ho
often they used the bayonet, couldn't go on holding their ow
with an enemy that never seemed to diminish.

He remembered what Joe Brennan had once told him abou
the Germans in Greece: "There were just too many of then
that was all. They licked the soul-case out of us. But man fc
man, all things equal, I think we could have licked 'em. Troubl
is, things ain't equal and haven't been since the start of th
bloody war."

That had been sixteen months ago and things were sti
not equal.

The Japanese came up the track with the piccaninny daw
ahead of schedule. There was still no hint of daylight in th
lattice-work of sky beyond the trees, but more just a lessenin
of the darkness. They had learned that the Japanese didn
like to move in darkness and usually waited for first dayligh
But this morning he was on his way early, possibly eager to g
going again after yesterday's respite.

"Someone on the track, boss." Charlie's voice was just
breath in the darkness. "A mob of 'em."

Vern strained his eyes till they pained him, but he coul
ee nothing but the black wall of trees that seemed only
yard from his face. Then suddenly he saw the dark wedge
greyness, almost a light blackness, that was the bend in th
track. He saw the black bobbing heads and heard the so
slush-slush of feet, then he opened up with his tommy-gu

Above the sound of the guns he heard the screams and
gh-pitched, almost girlish shouts of the Japanese and he felt
wild fierce exultation that swept away his fatigue and
spondency like the tommy-gun in his hands shattering the
visible bushes before him. The negroid silence had fled and
ow the paling morning was a welter of deadly sound. There
as the short snap of rifle fire, the deeper chatter of the tommy-
ins, the sharp flat bursts from the Bren; and still the shouting
d squealing that was so much like that of raped schoolgirls.

Abruptly Vern gave the order to retire. "Mick and Joe, stay
ith me on the Bren! The rest of you beat it!"

The men stood up and slid away. In the gathering daylight
tering down through the trees like a mist Vern saw them
. The Japanese had begun to return the fire now, but they
ere still seeking the target and the bullets were thudding into
e trees three or four feet above the men's heads. Fred
almadge took his section out, then Jack came slipping down
side Vern.

"Greg's taking the other section out now." He stopped for
moment as right beside him Mick opened up again with the
en. "Did you hear the firing over on the right flank? There
is now! The 39th must be copping it, too." All at once there
as a distant succession of thumps. "The bastards are using
ortars, too!"

"Righto, it's time we got out of here," Vern said, and gave
e word to Mick and Joe. "You two buzz off. Jack and I'll
ss a couple of grenades, then we'll be after you."

Mick hoisted the Bren to his shoulder, turned and went
uttling away in a crouch, followed by Joe. The Japanese fire
d dropped lower now but was still too far to the right of
ern and Jack, ploughing into the empty bushes where Greg's
ction had been a minute before. Vern and Jack pulled the
ns from a couple of grenades, tossed them, heard them explode,
en got up and went at a run up the track.

P

They hadn't gone fifty yards when they heard the firing i
front of them. They came round a bend in the track and Gre
was shepherding men into the bushes. "Come on! Get a mov
on!" He spun round as Vern and Jack came slipping and slidin
up the muddy trail behind him. In the grey morning his fac
too looked grey. "They got in behind us! They're right acros
the track, moving in on the company. We almost walke
into our own blokes' fire!"

"Can't we take them from the rear?" Vern said.

"There's too many of them. We'd never get through them
not with these other bludgers farther down the track trailin
us."

"Have you lost anybody?"

"Some. I don't know how many—look out!" Vern droppe
flat in the mud, seeing Jack fall beside him, as Greg let go wit
his tommy-gun above their heads. Vern swivelled round an
saw the Japanese coming up the track. Oh, Christ, there ar
millions of them, he thought; and felt his gun jam, clogge
with the mud in which he lay. Beside him Jack was firin
with a savage intensity and behind him he could hear Gre
slamming another magazine into his gun and cursing at th
moment's delay. Desperately he worked to clear his own gur
fear frantic as a flame within him, his fingers scrabbling lik
despairing claws. A bullet clanged against his helmet, jerkin
his head sharply, and then he heard Greg cry out.

"He's got it!" Jack gasped. "Get him out, for Christ'
sake!"

Vern swung on his belly in the mud, slinging his gun b
its strap across his back, and grabbed the cursing prostrat
Greg by the shoulders. "Can you get up?"

"No, it's my ankle! Leave me and get out yourselves!"

Vern didn't answer. He lifted Greg, rolled him over on t
his own back, then slowly began to crawl through the muc
off the track and into the thick bushes at the side. He move

lowly and with effort, Greg's weight pressing him flat into
he stinking black mud, so that he seemed to be breathing
nothing but the thick foul miasma that covered the treacherous
liding earth, a human tortoise crawling under its human
hell.

Then there was the roar of two explosions and he guessed
ack had thrown two more grenades. Then suddenly Greg
was lifted from his back and looking up he saw Dad Mackenzie
and Fred Talmadge staggering away up through the rising
bushes with Greg held between them. He got to his feet,
felt Jack fling an arm about him, and together they went
plunging up the hill.

At the top of the hill the rest of the men were waiting, eight,
ten, twelve, he wasn't sure how many. One or two were
wounded, and one man was sitting down holding his face in
his hands as if he were weeping. Below them in the jungle,
on three sides of the hill, firing was still going on. Away to
their right the mortars were still thumping away and nearer
at hand, where he guessed the rest of A Company to be, there
was the woodpecker sound of two or three Japanese machine-
guns. The firing was steady, and when more mortar bombs
began to fall with their dull door-banging noise only two
hundred yards away, he knew this was a major attack by the
Japanese.

"We'll keep moving," he said. "Down the hill and straight
ahead. Anybody hit?"

"I've got a slug in my shoulder," Bluey said. "And Charlie
copped one in the face."

Vern looked down at the man holding his face in his hands.
"Let's see, Charlie."

Charlie Fogarty brought away bloodstained hands to reveal
a smashed and bloody face. The bridge of his nose was broken,
the bone showing through as a jagged white fang, and it was
impossible to distinguish his eyes from the raw bleeding flesh.

that hung down over them. There was a gasp of sympath
from the men looking at him.

"I can't see," Charlie said, and his soft voice was numbin
and cold as a sliver of ice against the ears of the other mer
"They've shot out my eyes and I can't see!"

"Where's your field dressing?" Vern found it and ripped o
the covering. He wound the bandage round Charlie's heac
trying to be gentle but knowing he had to hurry. "That'll d
for now, Charlie. Soon's we get away from here, I'll dress i
properly. Come on, up on your feet. You lead him, Bluey
How's your shoulder?"

"It'll keep," said Bluey, and took Charlie's hand as he migh
that of a child. "This way, mate."

Vern looked at Jack. "Can you carry Greg on your back
just till we get off this hill? We'll see about making a stretche
later."

"Why don't you leave me?" Greg's voice was thin with pai
"Don't waste time——"

Jack swung Greg on to his back. "You talk too much."

Then the party had gone sliding down the other side o
the hill, slithering in the mud, tripping on roots, grabbing a
thick lawyer vines, crashing against trees; while from dow
on the track where they had been a few minutes before ther
was suddenly a chorus of exultant high-pitched yells, a fina
mad burst of firing, then silence.

Vern looked at Dad Mackenzie. "Sounds like our bloke
have had it."

Then he and Dad went sliding down the hill after the othe
men. At the bottom of the hill they were waiting in a strag
gling line along a faint native pad that ran roughly east an
west. "Which way, skipper?"

Vern pulled up, gasping for breath, hesitated a moment
then said, "We'll go east."

"That may take us back to the Japs, skip," Jack said.

"We'll have to risk that," Vern said. "I lost my map case back there on the track, but I had a good look at it yesterday. West of here the country gets pretty wild. If we get in there we might never get out."

"We mightn't get out anyway," Mick Kennedy muttered.

"We'll see about that," Vern snapped. "Anyone who wants to chuck it in, had better do it now. We don't want to be handicapped by bludgers."

"I'm no bludger," Mick said.

"Well, then, stop whining," Vern said, and looked around at the others. "Righto, on your way. You up front, Joe, as forward scout."

The party moved on. It had stopped raining now but the sky was still grey and sagging with water. The path was downhill and sometimes, when the screen of trees above thinned out they could see across to a spur of mountains in the west. There the sky was a trailing curtain caught in the grasping peaks; nearer, a small stray cloud or two floated above the mat of the jungle like grey carpet fluff. On either side of the narrow pad the jungle was a green wall covered with rotting fungus and tangled lianas: it was like walking down a back alley of some ancient forgotten city. Underfoot the path was a slop of mud that covered their boots above the ankles and in which thick leaf mould floated as a slippery trap for the unwary foot. Water dripped from the trees in a steady irritating whisper and always, so that it had now become part of the men's sense of smell, there was the heavy clogging stench of vegetable decay.

They had been walking ten minutes when Vern, at the head of the column, stopped and held up his hand. "Joe's coming back."

A moment later Joe came round a bend in the track with Major Caulfield, Father Chase, Alec Putnam and Herb Nutter. Caulfield had lost weight since they had been in New Guinea

and now looked a tired older shadow of his former strutting
self. Vern wondered if he himself had aged in the same time.
It seemed years since he had said good-bye to Dinah and the
kids.

"I wondered if you'd made it, Radcliffe." Caulfield hadn't
lost his arrogance of voice, even when he whispered as now.
"This all you managed to get out?"

Vern felt a stab of temper, but he checked his angry retort.
"This is the lot, sir. What happened to the company?"

"I don't quite know," Caulfield said. "Captain Putnam and
I were on our way down to you when the business started.
We could go neither backwards nor forwards, so we had to
duck into the bush. We were caught between two parties of
the Japs."

"Goddamned embarrassing." Alec's face was drawn with
strain, and blood flowed from a deep scratch down one cheek,
but he still managed to look wryly cheerful.

"I think the company's had it," said Father Chase. "Or
most of it, anyway. They were on us before we knew what was
happening, then they'd gone through us and were on their way
to B.H.Q. It was the same old story, but worse this time.
There were too many of them."

Herb Nutter moved past the officers. "What's the matter,
sarge? You cop it?"

"In the ankle." Greg was standing on one leg, leaning
against Jack. His eyes were dull with pain and his voice was
a shredded whisper. He had gone yellow beneath his tan and
looked ready to faint.

Herb patted the small extra haversack that hung on one
skinny hip. "I'm supposed to be a stretcher-bearer, only I lost
me stretcher. But we'll fix your ankle up later, sarge. And
Charlie, too. What happened, sport? Wasn't you looking
where you was going?"

Charlie smiled weakly but said nothing. There was some

ning unreal about the flash of his teeth below the bloodstained
ressing about his eyes. He was breathing through his mouth
n soft hissing gasps.

"Who have we here?" Caulfield said, and looked along the
ne. "Radcliffe, Putnam, the padre, Savanna, Morley, Brown,
Talmadge, Mackenzie, Kennedy, Fogarty, Nutter. And
rennan back down the track. That makes thirteen of us, a
ice lucky number. Have you got a map, Radcliffe?"

In the scrambling retreat of the past few weeks Caulfield
ad gradually lost or discarded most of his paraphernalia, but
Vern couldn't resist the slap. "Haven't you?"

The barb went home. Colour flooded into Caulfield's face,
ut all at once he turned away and went stumbling down
he path. Vern and the men stared after him in amazement,
hen they saw him lean heavily against a tree and begin to
omit.

"The poor bastard's sick," Bluey said.

"I didn't think his stomach was capable of it," said Dad
Mackenzie quietly and without sympathy. "He must be nearly
uman, after all."

In a minute or so Caulfield came back. There was a scum
cross his eyes and his freckles were black in the paleness of his
agging face. "Malaria, I think. A bad dose of it." He shook
is head and shut his eyes instantly in pain. "Christ, I've got a
eadache!"

"If he asked me for an Aspro," Mick Kennedy murmured,
"and I had one, I'd drop it in the mud and make him look for
t."

Father Chase looked at him and said softly, "Ever heard of
he milk of human kindness, Mick?"

"It curdles when I look at him, padre," Mick said. "I got
o Christian feelings towards that mongrel. So don't expect
m of me."

The men stood watching Caulfield swaying in the middle of

the path with his eyes shut. At last Caulfield opened his ey
and made an effort to draw himself together. "We'd bette
get on, Radcliffe. You take the rear. I'll lead. Ready, men
March!"

"Listen to the drongo," Dad muttered. "Thinks he's bac
at Ingleburn."

Vern stood by the side of the path watching the men fi
by him. There was a sameness about the look of their face.
the Japanese and the jungle had given them a common e:
pression: it was a look of exhausted resignation. They ha
lost their enthusiasm for the war and would fight now only fo
their own survival. Ideals and causes, patriotism and ant
fascism, were buried somewhere in the black slime of the pa
three weeks.

They were bent forward under the weight of their pack
some a little more than others. Herb Nutter was carryin
Greg's pack besides his own, and Father Chase was carryin
Jack's. Bluey's was hanging from his unwounded shoulde
canting him to one side. Vern took it from him as he wer
past.

"I'll take this for a while, Bluey. You look after Charlie

"Thanks, skipper," Bluey said. In action the men alway
stopped calling Vern by his first name. Out of action, on leav
or in the privacy of a camp tent, he was their friend; but a
soon as they were back in the serious business of war the
automatically looked upon him as their commander. It was
relationship that might not have worked in a good man
armies, but it seemed to work in the A.I.F.

Vern fell in behind the file of men. They went plodding
sometimes sliding, down the path, a line of indistinguishab
brothers. Some were in khaki and others in green, some i
shorts and others in long ducks tucked into canvas gaiters; b
sodden and mud-covered, hunchbacked under their packs, a
with the same glistening steel-topped heads, it was almo:

mpossible at a glance to tell one from another. The jungle had ompleted the Army's efforts at regimentation.

But in Vern's mind each man was an individual and he oved them all, with the exception of the stocky stumbling gure at the head of the column. But he knew that, much as e hated Caulfield, he was glad the major was here. Once nore he'd managed to dodge the full test of responsibility.

They did not see any more Japanese the rest of that day. hey had come to a swift shallow creek and there in the ice-cold vater they had bathed and dressed the wounds of Greg, Charlie nd Bluey. Greg's ankle had been smashed as if by a sledge ammer and it was useless to hope that it might mend enough or him to walk on. Charlie was completely blind: the bullet ad ploughed right through one eye from the side, across the ridge of his nose and seared the other pupil. Bluey's wound vas only a flesh one, but the bullet had lodged close to the one and it had taken Vern twenty minutes of careful probing o get it out.

"You see the advantages of carrying extra flesh?" Sweat vas standing out on Bluey's face: several times he had cried ut against the pain of the probing knife. "One of you skinny astards would have had a smashed shoulder out of this."

While Vern attended to the wounded men, Fred Talmadge nd Herb Nutter made a stretcher for Greg. They hacked own two slim saplings with their machetes, placed them on he ground a few feet apart, then joined them with a cross-bar t each end. Fred worked with a bushman's knowledge of vhat he was doing, and Herb was a willing and deft apprentice. hey used vines as ropes to tie the cross-bars, then swiftly they nade a cross-pattern of more vines to form a mattress between he two saplings. The other men brought armfuls of ferns and hese were spread on the interlaced vines. It would be a wet ed for Greg, but he hadn't known a dry one for three weeks.

Without any word of instruction, as if they were eager t[o]
help carry Greg, Fred, Dad Mackenzie, Joe Brennan and Fath[er]
Chase stationed themselves beside the carrying poles. Gre[g]
was lifted on to the stretcher and the men bent to pick it u[p]

"Wait a minute, Joe," Jack said. "You'd better stick to bein[g]
scout. I'll take your end."

"You're too tall, sarge," Joe said. "You'll only upset th[e]
level."

Alec Putnam had been sitting beside Major Caulfield. Th[e]
latter had vomited again coming down the track and now w[as]
lying flat on his back, his hand over his eyes and his stomac[h]
rising and falling like the flanks of an exhausted anima[l.]
Sweat was running freely out of him, soaking him, and ever[y]
now and again there was the faint castanet sound of his teet[h]
chattering.

Alec looked at him for a moment, then stood up and cam[e]
over to the men by the stretcher.

"I'll carry an end," he said. "I'm the same height as thes[e]
other guys." The men bent again and lifted the stretcher t[o]
their shoulders. "How do you feel, sarge?"

"Like an African chief I once saw in a film," Greg sai[d]
"Sort of regal."

"I've had some experience of this," Alec said as they bega[n]
to move off down the track. "At college I earned spendin[g]
money by being a professional pall-bearer. Carried some of th[e]
best people in Boston."

"You're a happy bastard," Greg said, managing a smil[e]
that was something like the one the men knew so wel[l]
"Captain Putnam, sir."

The other men moved on. Joe had gone on ahead again [as]
scout. Jack headed the column, behind him was Mick with th[e]
Bren, then the men with the stretcher, then Bluey and Charl[ie]
hand in hand. Herb Nutter, and bringing up the rear, Caulfiel[d]
and Vern.

By mid-afternoon Caulfield was stumbling along as if unk. His head was sunk on his chest and when Vern spoke him it was always some time before he could rouse himself reply. Twice he walked right off the track and fell forward to the tangle of vines and ferns and thick bushes. At four clock, when Caulfield had fallen for the third time, Vern lled a halt.

"This is far enough for to-day." The stretcher had proved a :ing and awkward burden for the men. They had rested equently and each man had been relieved after half an hour; it the day of staggering through the mud, often slipping to eir knees, tripping over hidden roots, had taken its toll of em. Their shoulders were chafed from the rubbing of the les, and Dad had a bruised and bleeding ear from a crack he d received from a pole end when he had slipped as they were ming down a steep grade. Vern knew even now that they ould never carry Greg to safety, unless safety was no more an a couple of days' march away; but he didn't let himself ink of the one and he had no hope for the second. "Get off e track. Try and find some spot where we can hide out thout being seen."

The men rested while Jack scouted around for a place to bed wn for the night. He came back in a few minutes and led em through the bushes to a small clearing about twenty rds from the track. Bushes and vines were thick here, but e trees grew less closely and there was room for the men to etch out in some sort of comfort. There even seemed to be s mud and the men sank down with grunts of relief on the ick carpet of leaf mould.

Vern and Herb had to carry Caulfield into the camp spot. was utterly spent now, too weak even to walk. They laid n down and Vern felt his brow.

"He's got a hell of a temperature."

"I got some quinine in me bag," Herb said. "I'll give him

a dose, but I dunno if it'll do him any good. If he's got malari
he looks a bit far gone for medicine."

It rained again all that night, but the men, exhausted
they were, slept through it.

Once Vern awoke and heard Caulfield moaning, but the
was nothing he could do for the man and after a while l
went back to sleep again.

Next morning Caulfield was worse. Vern took one lo
at him and knew he couldn't be expected to get to his fe
let alone walk. Caulfield stared up at him with scum-cover
eyes.

"I'm finished, Radcliffe." His voice was a faint croak.

"It's a bit early to talk about being finished," Vern sai
and tried to sound convincing. He turned to Fred Talmadg
"Could you and Herb make another stretcher, Fred?"

Fred hesitated, looked down at Caulfield, then back at Ver
"If you say so, skipper."

Vern was aware of the other men watching him closel
the atmosphere was charged with hostile suspicion. Th
Mick said, "Who's expected to carry him?"

"I'm hoping for volunteers," Vern said quietly. "If the
aren't any, I'll be ordering someone to carry him."

"I won't be volunteering," Mick said.

The others said nothing, and behind him Vern hea
Caulfield stir on the ground. "They've got me where th
want me, Radcliffe. They never had the guts when I was
my feet"—the harsh croak struggled vainly for the old tou
of arrogance—"all they could use was a grenade——" l
stopped suddenly and fell back, gasping for breath and his fa
saturated with sweat.

"Righto, Fred and Herb, get on with the stretcher." Ve
looked about at the others; responsibility had been thrust
him and it was proving more complicated than he had ev
dreamed. "I'm naming the men to carry Major Caulfie

here'll be myself, Captain Putnam, the padre and Sergeant
vanna. The others will carry Sergeant Morley."

"Why don't you leave both of us?" Greg was sitting up on
s stretcher. "Christ Almighty, it's too much to ask you coves
 carry us. Yesterday, with eight of you taking turns carrying
e, you bloody near wore yourselves to a frazzle. With two
 us, you'll get no rest at all. And Christ knows how far
u'll have to carry us."

"He's right, boss," Herb Nutter said. "If we had enough of
, it ud be all right, lugging both of 'em——"

"If we've got to make a choice," Dad Mackenzie said, "you
ow who we'd rather carry, skipper."

"Don't start making any choices," Greg said, and his voice
as surprisingly calm, as if he had lain awake during the night
d thought it all out. "I've got no more time for Caulfield
an you have, but I don't want his—him on my conscience."

"And neither do I," said Vern.

"He never had no conscience," Mick said. "What the hell
u're worrying about yours for——"

"For God's sake, stop nattering!" Vern's voice cracked a
tle with temper and strain: he felt the situation was slipping
ay from him. "Get the bloody stretcher made, and in a
rry!"

Twenty minutes later the stretcher was made and Caulfield
s lifted on to it. Vern, Alec and Father Chase took their
aces by the ends of the poles. As Jack took hold of the pole-
d across from Vern, Dad stopped him. "I'll better take this,
rge. You're too tall to be opposite the skipper. You'd do
tter to be with Herb on the other stretcher. He's more your
ight."

Jack hesitated. "Sure you want to?"

Dad nodded. "I don't feel quite as bad about it as Mick
es."

"I never thought you'd turn out to be a scab," Mick said

from where he stood by the end of Greg's stretcher. "Carryi
that bastard——"

Jack stepped across to Mick, standing close to him a
towering over him. "I could pull my rank on you, Mick, l
this is no place for it. But another word out of you"—
clenched his teeth on his words—"and by Christ, I'll flat
you!"

Mick stared back at him, a reply ready to burst out of hi
and one shoulder moved slightly as if he were about to throw
punch. It was Joe Brennan who saved the moment.

"Come on, mate," he said, and bent to take an end of Gre
stretcher. "While we're yapping here, the Japs may be sneaki
up on us. I don't want a bullet in me bum."

Mick glowered at Jack for a moment longer, then abrup
he bent and took hold of the stretcher pole. Then he and
others had pushed their way through the bushes and out
to the track.

Vern looked down at the now unconscious form of Caulfi
"I just hope it's all worth it."

"While a man's still alive," Father Chase said, "ther
always worth in keeping him that way."

"You're only arguing along the lines of your religi
padre," said Dad. "That's because you don't believe
euthanasia. But has religion got an answer for everythin

"It's got more answers than any other system," Father Ch
said. "And it teaches hope. It sounded to me a little wl
back that some of the men could do with more hope. Not
mention some charity."

"I'm not arguing with you, padre," Dad said. "I was j
asking. The skipper here is the one with problems, not n

The rest of that day they marched along the floor of a d
valley. The trail was comparatively flat to the one they l
covered yesterday but even so thay had to rest frequen
and by late afternoon they were dead beat. The stretch

emed to have increased in weight and the poles had become
unt saws that rubbed raw grooves in their shoulders. They
ound a good camping spot, well off the track and in the lee
f a huge fallen tree that had flattened out a narrow but
mfortable spot where there was more leaf mould than mud.

When they had set Caulfield down, Vern knelt down and
oked at him. His breath was coming in great retching gasps
d his eyes stared dully out of sockets that now seemed too
g for them. Even in the last few hours his body appeared
have got smaller, the flesh hanging loosely on the big bones.

"He's got more than malaria," Vern said.

Father Chase bent over him, peering intently at Caulfield.
saw the boy they took away with scrub typhus. I hope I'm
rong, but I think that's what the major's got."

Vern felt a spasm of shock and fear, but he tried to hide it.
That's contagious, isn't it?"

"Yes," said Father Chase, and behind him Vern heard one
the men stifle a shocked curse.

"What's the remedy?"

"None that I know of," said Father Chase. "All they
escribe is careful nursing. And prayer."

"That's all we'll be able to give him—prayer," Vern said,
d looked down at Caulfield, knowing the man was doomed
die and hating him no longer.

Later, when they had eaten sparingly from their rations,
x men to a tin of bully beef and one biscuit each, Father Chase
me back and sat down beside Vern. It hadn't rained since
idday and the sky now was a slow-moving curdle of red
ouds. Down here in the jungle night was already rising in
een-black wraiths, merging trees into each other and the
en into their background; but high above the trees and the
ttered lace of the vines the fiery sky still held the last of the
ing day. Water had stopped dripping from the trees and
e only sound was the far-off singing roar of a waterfall.

Father Chase sank down, his back propped against his pack
and shoved his long thin mud-covered legs out in front of him.
He had a stubble of dark beard and his black hair, badly in need
of a cut, hung in lank rats' tails on his neck and about his ears.
His fingernails were broken and thick with mud and a long
rent in his shirt showed a mat of black hair on his thin chest.
It was hard to keep in mind that he was a man of God; certain
sleek prelates in other parts of the world might have nominated
him for excommunication. When he took out a cigarette and
went to light up, it seemed to complete the identification with
the other muddy bedraggled figures in the clearing.

"All right if I smoke, Vern?"

"Better not, padre, it's getting dark," Vern said, and spoke
to the other men. "Smokes out, fellers. It's getting too dark."

After a few moments Father Chase said, "You've got
yourself quite a problem, haven't you?"

"What do you mean——" Vern said, then shrugged and
nodded. "Yeah."

"What are you going to do?"

"I don't know. What can I do? He won't live if we take
him with us—you don't get careful nursing when you're
having the guts jolted out of you on a bush stretcher. And if
we did take him, how will I feel if some of the other chaps
catch it?" Vern dug a furrow in the leaf mould with his heel.
"Yet I can't leave him here to die."

"I've been thinking about that," Father Chase said, and
looked up past the black trees at the last trace of rose on the
clouds. "I'll stay with him."

"Why you? Being a padre doesn't mean we have to call on
you first for this sort of sacrifice."

"Being a padre means exactly that, Vern," Father Chase said
quietly. "But I wasn't thinking so much about sacrifice. I
suggested it because I'm the only one in this party who doesn't
hate him."

The rose died on the clouds and the deep dusk climbed above the trees. Down here in the small strip of clearing it was already night, black and unknowable as eternity. The first mosquitoes were coming in for their feast; they sang past the ears, vibrating with gloating. Other night insects were murmuring and chattering and humming; the silence was being splintered delicately into fragments. A string of flying foxes went across the dim sky like leaves caught in some small wind that hadn't touched the rest of the jungle. Then abruptly the sky had gone and night and the blackness were complete.

"You think the others wouldn't care whether we left him or not?" Vern said.

"It's not my place to judge other men, Vern. I just thought I could relieve them of the responsibility of a decision."

Vern rubbed his hands down his sodden muddy thighs. Now there was no rain he was aware of the chill of his wet clothes and all at once he shivered. They were still in high country, still in the area of the rain forests, and there was little humidity at night: before they had arrived in New Guinea they hadn't believed one could be cold in the jungle. But now he was cold. He was cold and tired and still hungry, and suddenly he envied the other men who were settling down for the night. Their only worry was their own safety and all of them had now learned to put that problem at the backs of their minds when they wanted to sleep. They too were cold and tired and hungry, but in a few minutes they would be asleep. They had no other immediate problems but themselves.

"It's not their responsibility, padre. It's mine."

Father Chase was silent for a moment, then he said, "That was what I was getting at."

"You think I hate him, too?"

"I don't know. We priests are supposed to teach love, but I've come to know that in some cases love is a human impossibility. Sometimes even I have had trouble understanding

Q

the major. He's treated you as badly as he treated the other.
Even since we've been here in New Guinea he's done som
stupid unnecessary things. That business of keeping men i
the line when they were dead on their feet with malaria an
dysentery wasn't necessary. The C.O. had told him that whe
the situation was hopeless, he was to consider the men ahea
of any ground they might lose."

"We had an argument about that," Vern said. "I sent thre
men back, and he promptly ordered them back to me. He sai
that the motto of A Company was to be: Here we bloody we
are and here we bloody well stay. He'd just borrowed th
motto a little late, that was all. The men were too sick t
start thinking of mottoes. I called him a heartless bastard, an
he said he'd deal with me when we got out of the line." Ver
sighed. "Well, we're out of it."

"He's a bastard, all right," Father Chase said. "I'
understand if you did hate him."

"I don't know if I do now," Vern said slowly. "A couple (
months back I wished he were dead. It wasn't just an idle wisl
either. I really meant it. But now he looks like dying——
Vern slapped savagely at a mosquito on the back of his han
"I don't know, padre. Give me to-night to think it out."

He heard Father Chase stand up. "The offer still stand
Vern. Good night."

He slid cautiously away across the leaf mould, but he wasn
cautious enough. "Christ Almighty, watch your feet, yo
bloody drongo!"

"Sorry," said Father Chase with a soft chuckle. "Is th
you, Mick?"

"Oh, it's you, padre? Sorry about the language. But yo
trod fair on me hand."

There was silence again, deep and enveloping, then quiet
the insects began again. Vern lay back on his gas cape, his hea
pillowed on his pack, looking up at the darkness above hir

Near him he could hear the hissing laboured breathing of Caulfield, and at the end of the clearing there was the faint sound of someone already snoring. He could hear the other stretcher creaking slightly as Greg tossed restlessly on it, and then he heard a moan. He sat up.

"That you, Charlie?"

"He's all right, Vern," Jack said. "He's asleep."

"Has he got any fever?"

There was a moment while Jack evidently felt Charlie's brow. "No, he seems cool enough."

Half an hour later everyone seemed to be asleep, but Vern was still awake. Sleep was struggling at him, but his mind rolled and spun like quicksilver. He would have to make a decision on Caulfield by morning. The man was obviously dying, but there was something inhuman about leaving him to die alone that appalled Vern. And yet if they took him with them, he would probably still die and his illness might be communicated to the others.

He heard a gasping moan, then a faint appeal for water. He sat up and crawled towards Caulfield. He felt in his shirt pocket for the tin of wax matches he carried, struck one and held it cupped in his hands. In the faint yellow glow a death mask stared up at him. The black eyes were dull and sunken, like pellets of bitumen dropped in the sockets: they didn't blink or move in the glow of the match: there was no recognition or expression in them at all. There was no reminder now of arrogance in the hooked nose and flaring nostrils; and the pugnacious chin hung slackly under the gaping mouth. Vern felt for Caulfield's water bottle, lit another match from the first, then gave the major a few drops of water. His tongue licked greedily but without strength, almost of its own accord; then abruptly the bullet head rolled sideways and for a moment Vern thought Caulfield was dead. Then he heard the hissing breathing again and the momentary relief he had felt passed. If Caulfield died to-night there would be no problem.

But he was still alive at daybreak. Vern, who had at last managed to drop off to sleep, woke as the first light came slipping down into the clearing. He lay for a moment, numbed in mind and body, staring up at the dark rain-heavy sky. Then slowly he got to his feet and stretched his aching limbs. Both shoulders were raw and sore from the chafing of the stretcher poles yesterday, and for the last week he had had a pain across his kidneys each morning when he woke. He ran a hand over his face, feeling the dried mud on his cheeks and the thick stubble on his chin, and closed his eyes, dizzy with hunger and still half-asleep. Then he opened them and looked down at Caulfield and was fully awake.

He called the other men. Then he knelt down to look at Caulfield. The major looked already dead: only the faint pulse told that he was alive. Vern knelt, staring at the inert form in front of him, aware of the other men getting to their feet, aware of them as he had never been before. Eleven living men, still with a chance to go on living, and depending on him to help them all he could. He looked across at Greg lying on the stretcher that would need eight men, working in relays to carry it if Greg too wasn't to be left behind. He looked at Father Chase, the man who was willing to sacrifice himself to help the dying but who would be more help to the living. He looked at Jack and Bluey and the rest of them, then slowly he stood up, knowing what he was going to do and shocked a little at his own decision. All he could do was hope that the others would understand his reasons for it.

"We'll eat farther down the track," he said. "Joe and Dad, I want you to dig a grave."

"Is he dead?" said Dad.

Vern hesitated, then he sighed and said, "No, but he's that close to it, it doesn't matter. He may live only another couple of hours, or he may last out the day. But he's going to die and there's nothing we can do for him. Even if we get back to our own crowd in the next twenty-four hours—and frankly I haven't the slightest hope of that—I don't think they could save him. Even with the best of care, the percentage who recover from scrub typhus is very small."

"Why the grave then, skipper?" Jack said.

Vern looked slowly round the weary mud-stained faces, then he said, "I'm going to shoot him."

There was a gasp from one or two of the men, and shock quivered on the faces of all of them. Vern looked for a hint of understanding, but none of them yet was over the impact of his decision. Then Father Chase stepped forward. "You can't do that, Vern. I'll stay with him——"

"This has nothing to do with hate or revenge, padre." Vern felt suddenly and unutterably weary; it hadn't been easy to come to the decision and now he wasn't going to argue about it. "It's just the best thing, that's all. For all of us, including Major Caulfield."

"But I can't let you do it, Vern!" As Father Chase spoke, there was a distant swishing sound coming rapidly nearer and a moment later heavy rain broke above them. It fell with a steady hissing violence into the clearing, hitting the men and the ground with a flat sound and splashing off the fallen tree and the leaf mould in a swiftly drifting silver vapour. It ran down over Father Chase's face, streaking the dried mud on his cheeks, flattening his long black hair into a witch's wig, and he stood there with his arms out in an appeal, a wild and grotesque figure who looked more like a relative of the Devil. "You're a Catholic! We don't believe in this sort of thing, euthanasia, killing for mercy, call it what you like! The major's still alive—you haven't the right to judge——"

Vern had to shout against the rain. "I'm responsible for the rest of you! That gives me some right. The rest of you, even just one of you, may catch typhus from him. I can't risk that!"

"You don't have to risk it!" Father Chase cried. "I told you, I'll stay with him——"

"You'll be of more help to the other men." The rain ran like tears down over Vern's face; he suddenly wished for Caulfield's death even while they argued. "They're still alive, still have the hope you talked about yesterday! There's Greg to be carried——"

"I can't stand by and see you do it, Vern. It isn't your decision. I'm a man of God and I've got to abide by His laws——"

"That's where you're wrong, padre. It is my decision. I'm boss here, for what my rank is worth, and I'm saying you come with us!" He stepped closer to Father Chase, put a hand on his arm and stared with pleading at the thin dark mud-streaked face. "I haven't forgotten my conscience, padre. Leave me to face it—it wasn't easy to decide this——"

Father Chase stood gazing at him, his dark eyes searching Vern's face, then abruptly his look softened and he said, "May God have mercy on your soul, Vern."

Vern pressed his arm, then turned away and shouted, "Righto, Joe and Dad! Get that grave dug, quick. The rest of you move on—this rain will kill the sound of the shot, but just in case you'd better be out of the way with the stretcher. If the trail happens to fork, take the right fork—we'll know where you've gone then. Okay, get moving!"

The men moved off. Vern turned and saw Greg staring back at him from the stretcher, but in the screen of rain he couldn't tell whether Greg's look was sympathetic or shocked. Then the bushes closed behind the party as it pushed through to the track and the clearing was empty save for Dad and Joe digging swiftly at the leaf mould with their machetes, Caulfield lying still and unaware of the pelting rain, and Vern.

And Father Chase. When Vern turned back the padre was standing right behind him.

"I can't talk you out of this?"

"No, padre."

"Then I'll pray for him," Father Chase said, and Vern saw the wet beads glistening in the muddy fingers. "And for you too, Vern."

Then the grave was ready. Vern knelt down beside Caulfield and took the pistol from the holster on the latter's hip. He lifted Caulfield into a sitting position, stripped the shirt from him, took off his meat tags and went through his trousers pockets. There was nothing of sentimental value: Caulfield had been a bachelor, and Vern was glad of that. He put Caulfield's pay-book and meat tags in his own hip pocket, then put his hands under the unconscious man's armpits and gently slid him into the shallow grave. He wrapped Caulfield's shirt round the pistol to deaden the noise, then he looked up through the stinging rain at the other three men.

"You don't have to watch this."

"Go ahead." Dad Makenzie's face was stiff and impassive. Joe said nothing, standing with his head bowed against the rain, looking as if he were praying but his lips silent and unmoving: Vern knew he was a Catholic, though not a good one, and he wondered what he thought of this killing of Caulfield. Beside him Father Chase stood telling his beads: he had said the prayers for the dying and Vern wondered now if he were praying for the living. Vern stared up at the three of them, blinking as the rain beat in his eyes, then he looked down at the still figure lying in the mud at the bottom of the shallow grave and said a prayer of his own.

He put the pistol, wrapped in the shirt, against the faintly quivering temple and pulled the trigger.

It did not rain at all on the fourth day. On the fifth day the

sky cleared, the clouds curled away beyond the mountains, and
the sun blazed in the immaculate blue. They were down in a
valley now, still heading east, the mountains rising as a steep
slippery wall on their right, and under the hot sun the jungle
began to steam. Sweat sprang out of the men, so that their
clothes which had dried yesterday were now sodden again.
The stench of the rotten vegetable mould increased in the
steamy heat, and beneath the enveloping trees the air was thick
and suffocating.

The march had begun to show its effects. Fatigue was bitten
deep into every face, and every man walked with the same
plodding, stumbling step, like members of a road gang whose
ankles were bound by a chain buried in the shin-deep mud in
which they walked. They had eaten the last of their rations
yesterday and each man now was bent over around the hollow
of hunger. One or two were suffering slightly from dysentery
and hoping it wouldn't get worse. Weakened by exhaustion,
all of them within the last two days had had attacks of malaria,
but each man had come to accept it as part of the over-all
misery and neither complained nor asked for help. They were
developing a Job-like patience and resignation that was the
only defence against cracking up completely.

Even the wounded had taken to looking after themselves.
On the third night Greg and Charlie had talked, and in the
morning Charlie had hoisted Greg to his back and told the
others to throw away the stretcher. There had been an argument, with Vern trying to speak reasonably and not issue a
direct order, but Charlie had been adamant.

"This is me own idea," he said doggedly. "I suggested it
to Greg last night. He ain't got his legs and I ain't got my
eyes. We can help each other."

"But it'll be murder, Charlie," Vern said. "God, it's tough
enough when there are four of us carrying him——"

"I told you to leave me." Greg was clinging to Charlie's

ack, one arm about the aborigine's neck. "I'm just a bloody
hindrance——"

"We're not going to leave you," Vern said flatly. "Get that
into your thick stubborn skull, will you?"

"I can carry him," Charlie said. Blood had seeped down
under the dressing around his eyes and had dried on his cheeks;
he was still breathing through his mouth, so that his lips were
continually open in a half-gasp. He looked as if he too should
be carried. "He's no worse than a pack."

"Only about a hundred pounds worse," Vern said, but had
argued no farther. The two men obviously thought they were
a burden to the rest of the party and for a day or two it
might be best to let them have their own way. So Charlie
had carried Greg all day yesterday, only after further argument
allowing the others to relieve him for a quarter of an hour
every hour.

They were now on a wide track that wound along the floor
of this steeply-walled valley. Fred Talmadge was up in front
as the forward scout and the others were strung out in a
straggling file, with Dad Mackenzie bringing up the rear.
Mick was still carrying the Bren, but Vern was already thinking
of throwing it away. Twenty-eight pounds of lethal weapon
was only a useless burden to a man who was concerned with
avoiding death, not dealing it out.

Alec Putnam was walking beside Vern. "Where do you
figure we are?"

Vern looked sideways at him. The last five days had begun
to fret at his nerves. Each night, though he flopped down with
exhaustion, he had slept only fitfully: he was always thinking
of to-morrow, trying to anticipate it and yet afraid of it. And
though no one had since mentioned the shooting of Caulfield,
he had yet to see a hint that any of them understood why he
had done it. He was on edge waiting for criticism. "You
worried I shan't get you out of here?"

"Hey, now hold on!" Alec's lean hawk's face looked leaner still under the bucket of his helmet. His ragged dappled greens flapped on his bony frame and his carbine hung from his shoulder like the bone of a broken wing. He looked like some strange tattered bird that the men had caught and trained to follow them. "I'm just making with the words, trying to take my mind off other things. You think I'm trying to buy a fight?" He shook his head and the helmet wobbled.

Vern relaxed and grinned. "Watch out. You're going to lose your jerry."

Alec pushed the helmet farther back on his head. "I'm taking this tin bowl back to Waquoit, Massachussetts. Saturday nights I'm gonna get my wife to steam me up a mess of quahogs in it——"

"Why don't you call a clam a clam?"

"You don't understand us Cape Codders," said Alec. "We don't care what the rest of the world calls a thing. If we got our own word for it, then we use our own word."

"Stubborn bastards," Vern said.

"Salt of the earth, that's all," said Alec and grinned. Throughout the trek his good humour hadn't failed once. Most of the men were still in good spirits, better spirits really than over the past few weeks when they had been battling the Japanese. In the three weeks they had been in action the Japanese had never been more than a hundred yards away, often a good deal closer, and each man had been coiled tightly round the spring of his own alertness. Fear had lurked constantly in the back corridors of the mind, and any laughter had had to be smothered, a sign of momentarily relaxing nerves never of merriment but only of relief. To laugh sometimes had been as necessary as to breathe, but joking had been only a futile thumbing of the nose at the nagging migraine of fear. Now they were relaxed and their laughter, if sometimes tle bitter, was at least compounded of humour and not rvousness.

Vern knew there were one or two, himself included, who uld have felt better. Greg, riding now on Charlie's back, iding him as he might a horse, warning him of the sly nbushing roots, still felt he should have been left behind. e had said nothing more about it, but he rarely joined in e joking of the men and spoke most of the time only to narlie. A bond had grown up between the blinded man and e crippled one: in two days they had built up a dependence each other that excluded the other men almost completely. st night Vern had heard Charlie weeping to himself in the rkness and then he had heard Greg crawl over to him.

"What's the matter, mate?" he had heard Greg whisper. Your face paining you?"

"No worse than usual." Charlie had been quiet for a while, en he had said, "I'll never see again, Greg. That's what is irting."

"It's tough all right. I've lain awake a couple of nights, yself. Thinking that maybe I'll never walk again—or any-ay, never without a stick. I used to be such a lively bastard, o, remember? From now on I'll just have to sit and watch her people." He said nothing for a moment, then: "But at doesn't console you, does it? You can't even watch them."

"I never took me eyes for granted, like some people do." narlie's whispering made his voice even more poignant: emory and regret were a soft breath in the neutral night. took in everything I saw and enjoyed it and remembered "

"That'll be a help, then," Greg said. "If you can remember ings, their colour and shape, maybe you won't feel you've st them so completely."

"I dunno," Charlie had said. "Who wants to live in the past the rest of his life?"

Once while doing a general story on New York, Vern l
wandered into the old church, St. Mark's-in-the-Bouwei
while a deaf and dumb sermon was in progress. He had
in a rear pew, beside a man who had fallen asleep as if bo:
by what the preacher was saying with his fluttering finge
He had sat there, at first fascinated by the prestidigitoi
eloquence of the preacher, then by the rapt, almost deatl
attention of the congregation. There weren't many and m
of them were bums from the nearby flop joints; and th
had been no sound from them at all, not a cough nor even
shuffling of a foot. The church had been utterly silent,
preacher's gesticulating hands the only live things in a d
soundless world, and after a while Vern had been glad to esc:
into the street outside. There, the roar of the elevated,
tooting car horns, had been almost like music; and whei
bum had come up, panhandling the price of a night's r
Vern had staggered him by giving him five dollars. The bu
scooting away before the soft touch discovered his mista
had never known that his gravelly voice had just made a m
glad of his hearing.

Vern had some slight idea of how Charlie felt without l
sight.

He had heard Charlie and Greg still talking when he h
dropped off to sleep. He had dreamed of Caulfield, seeing h
lying in the mud of the grave, talking wordlessly and stari
at the rain, while the bullet had gone without a sound into l
brain and he had still gone on talking. Vern had woken ii
bath of sweat and it had been several moments before he h
realised that Caulfield was dead and two days behind th
along the track. He had tried to tell himself he had done rig
the sensible thing; but reason was a poor adversary for cc
science. What if Caulfield's time hadn't been up, if there h
been some miraculous chance that he would have surviv(
Father Chase had called it a mercy killing, said the Chui

n't believe in it; but what was even worse, had he been
owing mercy to Caulfield or had he been thinking not so much
 the other men's lives—of the other men—as of his own?
 valued survival as much as the other men did, and certainly
ore than did Father Chase. It had never entered his head that
 should sacrifice himself as Father Chase had offered to do:
at he had done had all the cold-blooded matter of factness
 the will to live: the desire for survival rarely touched the
gher emotions. It began to worry him that perhaps sub-
sciously it had been a choice between himself and Caulfield,
d he had taken the easy way out.

The thought had scurried and gnawed in his brain like a rat.
had been a time when he could have done with Dinah's
mfort. And yet he knew that if ever he got back to her, and
e was his main reason for wanting to survive, he would
ver tell her of what he had done. He was afraid that for
e first time she might not understand why he had acted as he
d.

He had taken his beads out of his pocket and said a rosary,
t prayer hadn't worked. He hadn't known whether he was
aying for forgiveness or for guidance for his conscience or
 the soul of the man he had killed. It hadn't helped to know
at he still had to learn how the men felt about what he had
ne.

He came out of his thoughts now, back to the steaming
uddy track and the plodding men behind him, to hear Alec
y, "Fred's coming back."

Fred Talmadge came round the bend in the track, slipping
 the mud as he ran. "There's a boong village about a hundred
rds up, skipper. Not a big one, and there don't look to be
y boongs there. But I think I saw a Jap."

Vern turned. "Okay, off the track, quick." The men
elted into the bushes, invisible in a moment, and the oily
ud of the track showed no trace of where they had stood.

Vern crouched beneath a bush, close to Fred. "You see any p
that goes round the village?"

Fred shook his head. "None. This track goes right throu
it, like a main road. But the village has a decent sort of gard
If we could get in there and sneak some tucker——"

"How many Japs do you reckon?"

"I don't know, skip. I saw only one. There may be th
or four more, but the place looked pretty deserted. I did
stay to look. I hopped back here before you could w
into it."

Vern tapped his knee while he judged the risk of going i
the village up ahead. If there was a good garden there, th
couldn't afford to by-pass it. Food was going to be a maj
problem from now on. "Righto, you and Joe slide back th
and size up the place. Make sure of the number of Nips, th
come back here and we'll make a decision then."

Alec was sitting beside Vern. "Wait a minute, Vern. I
me go instead of Joe. I haven't done anything yet to earn i
chow."

Vern looked at him, about to say no, then abruptly
grinned. "Okay. But leave your jerry here. That thing was
made for sneaking through the grass. Better leave yours to
Fred. Twenty minutes should do you to have a good look
the joint. Okay, beat it."

They slid quietly away, two lean mud-covered figures fro
the opposite ends of the world who looked like twins from t
same bed. They were back in fifteen minutes.

"Four Japs, that's all," Alec said. "They got all the st
from the garden neatly stacked up, ready to take away. I
say they were a foraging party out getting fresh vegetab
for the boys."

"That means there must be more Japs nearby," Vern sa
"No boongs in the village at all?"

"They've probably all pissed off," Fred said. "But th

an't have gone more than a day or two. The garden is still
retty neat."

"Well, we'll go in and take the Japs," Vern said. "But it'll
.ave to be a quiet job. Knives or machetes, no guns. We don't
vant to draw the crabs."

"Who goes?" said Alec.

"I do. Fred, Joe and——" Vern's glance flitted over the
ther men sitting motionless beneath the bushes.

"And me," said Alec.

Vern didn't argue. While they had been in action he had
een inclined to look on Alec more as a guest than an actual
ombatant, someone who was to be protected so his knowledge
.ained could be passed on to his own unit when it arrived;
ut the war had now become very private and small and outside
onsiderations meant nothing. Vern called Jack over and gave
im a quick summary of the plan. "Better have Dad stuck in
he bushes just outside the village. If things go wrong, he
an come back and let you know. If we run into real trouble,
on't hang around. Get to hell out of here. We'll pick you
p later."

"Good luck, skip," Jack said, and Vern felt the pat on his
ack as he led the other men through the bushes and out on
⟩ the track. Dad Mackenzie dropped behind and the other
⟩ur cut off the track to come into the village from the north.
'here, Alec had said, two large huts backed almost on to the
ingle and the native garden was only about fifty feet to the
ist of them.

The men had discarded their helmets and as they dropped
⟩ the ground and began to slide carefully over the leaf mould,
ithering quietly under the bushes and drapes of vines, they
)oked more than ever like creatures of the jungle. The three
ustralians carried their light automatic weapons slung over
ieir shoulders and Alec clutched his carbine in the crook of his
rm. All four carried heavy vicious-looking machetes.

Vern eased his way forward, pushing with his legs, hi body resting on his elbows and sliding gently and silentl over the soft wet floor of the forest. Insects darted away from under his sweating face. Once he looked right into the bulbou eyes of a lizard beneath a rotting log, then it was gone an he had crawled over the log and was flat on the ground agai The smell of the jungle floor, the mud and vegetable deca and the million creeping things that lived in the everlastin green darkness, was like a filthy stifling blanket against hi face. His legs ached from the unaccustomed action: the insid of his thighs seemed to be turned at right angles to each othe and he could almost imagine his thigh-bones scraping in th sockets of his pelvis. He had crawled no more than twenty-fiv yards, yet he wondered if he would have the strength to stan up when the time came.

Then through the screen of leaves before him, beyond a thi strip of kunai grass, he saw the two large huts of the villag He held up his hand and heard Alec, Fred and Joe stop. H turned his head, blinking against the sweat that rolled dow into his eyes. Alec was stretched beside him, breathing heavily his lips drawn back in a half-snarl over his teeth. His teet and his eyes were just flashes in his face: the rest of it wa black sweat-streaked mud.

"The Japs are the other side of the huts," Alec whispere "Hear them?"

Vern heard the rapid gabbling in the light womanish voice he had come to hate in the past month. The Japanese wer careless and unworried; they obviously believed they were mil from the nearest Australians. One of them said somethin a note of disgust in his voice, perhaps complaining about arm life like any soldier anywhere, and the other three giggle

"Joe and I'll get behind the hut on the right," Ver whispered to Alec. "You and Fred take the other. Wait for u to move first. And don't let them fire their guns! Okay?

He saw Alec nod, then he turned to Joe, jerked his head and
owly parted the bushes in front of him. He raised himself
owly, disturbing a brace of butterflies that floated away,
right flutters of colour in the sun, then he moved forward in
crouch towards the rear of the farthest hut. He could hear
ie Japanese still talking and giggling, the only sound in the
ick still silence; and then the hidden stick in the kunai
iapped like a fire-cracker beneath his boot. He stopped,
·eling every nerve freeze, and heard the sharp hiss of Joe's
itaken breath. The snap of the broken stick seemed to hang
ke an echo in the clearing at the moment the Japanese stopped
.ughing. Vern straightened up without moving his feet,
is ears stretched till they ached, waiting for the first quick
iovement of feet coming round the edge of the hut. Nothing
ioved or made a sound and in his mind Vern could see the
.panese on the other side of the huts rising silently with their
fles ready for action. Then a bright green parrot suddenly
ashed across the clearing, whistling past the huts with a beat
f swift wings, and the Japanese broke into an excited gabble.

Vern moved quickly for the remaining five or six yards.
e finished up against the thick sacsac wall of the hut, feeling
e breathing almost down the back of his neck. He saw Alec
id Fred reach the other hut, then cautiously he moved towards
ie gabbling, invisible Japanese. He felt the weight of the
iachete in his right hand and tightened his grip on it; then
looked round the edge of the hut and saw the four Japanese
tting on the ground not more than twenty feet from him.
heir rifles were propped against the front corner of the hut and
ie tools with which they had been digging up vegetables were
'ing in a small careless heap beside the rifles. It's too easy,
ern thought, then swung up his arm, giving the others the
gnal, and leaped forward with his machete already on its
ay down into the skull of the Japanese nearest him.

Three of the Japanese died with startled squeals that didn't

R

reach the edge of the clearing. The machetes flashed only onc
in the pitiless sunlight and life gushed instantly out of th
cleft skulls. The Japanese fell forward, as if in prayer, an
blood spurted in bright flowers out of the pods of their brain
The fourth Japanese, the one at whom Fred had aimed, ha
been about to rise as the raiders came round the ends of th
huts. He spun away and Fred's machete only grazed h
shoulder. Fred, off balance, fell forward and in that momer
the Japanese turned and fled.

Vern jumped the dead man at his feet and went after th
fleeing Japanese. He had never been a swift runner and h
heavy mud-caked boots didn't help him; but desperation ler
him speed and he caught the Japanese at the edge of the clea
ing. He saw the black bobbing head in front of him, th
white-eyed fear as the man glanced over his shoulder, then l
raised the blood-stained machete and brought it down wit
an animal savagery that he would remember with disgust lon
after. The Japanese staggered, blood spurting from him in
vivid parasol above his shoulder, then he plunged headlon
into the bushes and lay there. One hand struggled weakl
towards the back of his neck, as if to hold in the life flowing ou
of the gaping wound there, then he shivered convulsively an
was still. Vern stood looking down at him for a momen
breathing heavily, feeling nothing; then abruptly he turne
and ran back to the others.

"Drag 'em into the hut," he said. As the other three bega
to pull the dead Japanese into the hut, he ran to the centre
the clearing. He waved, saw Dad Mackenzie step out on to th
track, wave and set off back to tell the others. Then he ran ba
to the hut, picked up the Japanese rifles, pulled out the bol
and threw them well back into the trees, then tossed the rifl
into the bushes behind the huts. Alec and the others came ou
of the hut.

"What now, Vern?" Alec said.

"Everything's laid on." Vern gestured at the heap of sweet potatoes, yams, taro and wild bananas in the rough vine net. As soon as the others come up, we grab this and blow."

"Straight down the track, skip?" Joe said. "It might lead s right into the main Jap camp."

Vern nodded. "Head down there a couple of hundred yards, ɔe. See if you can pick up a pad leading off the track to the ɔuth. If you can't, we'll have to make our own. But I think his main track is going to be too dangerous from here on."

Joe went off at a run. Vern went down, dragged the ɪpanese he had chased farther into the bushes, and threw ferns n the bloodstained bushes where the dead man had lain. If ɪy other Japanese passed through the village they wouldn't now of the raid unless they deliberately went looking for the ɔdies. By the time Joe came back the rest of the party had ɪtered the village.

"There's plenty of signs of Japs down the track," Joe said. Trees cut down, bushes flattened. And where the mud isn't ɔo sloppy you can see their bootprints. They're somewhere round here, skip. And quite a mob of 'em, too, by the looks f it."

"You find any path leading off the track?" Vern said.

Joe shook his head. "I drew a blank there. There's bugger-ll but this track for the next coupla hundred yards. I didn't ːel like going any farther."

Vern looked around at the others. "The easy sledding is ver, fellers. It's the bush for us from now on."

"We have something to eat," Father Chase said. "At least hat's something to be thankful for."

Vern wondered how much they would have to be thankful ɔr in the days to come. He looked about at the ragged weary ɪen, seeing himself mirrored in their expressions, and for the rst time he began to doubt if any of them had any more future han the blood-covered Japanese in the hut behind them. The jungle and the mountains hemmed them in; and the other safe world was now as nebulous as a dream.

It was then he made up his mind that he would drive these men till they could be driven no farther, till death took their last chance of survival from them.

He owed it to the dead Caulfield, if to no one else.

CHAPTER EIGHTEEN

D AD MACKENZIE cut another small notch in the stock of his rifle. "That makes eighteen days now."

Jack stirred the stew of yams and sweet potatoes with his bayonet. It bubbled in Alec Putnam's helmet over the small fire in the centre of the hut. Over the narrow doorway of the hut two gas capes had been hung, shutting in the glow of the fire, and the smoke wreathed about the hut till it finally found its way out of the hole in the thatched roof. This was the fourth deserted village they had struck in the last week and in the weed-tangled, dilapidated gardens of each they had found enough vegetables to make a good warming stew. They had eaten wild bananas during the day and had lit the fire for the stew only after darkness had fallen. The thick sacsac walls of the hut hid the fire and the smoke climbed invisibly towards the black sky. It was Jack and Dad's turn to cook and the rest of the men were sitting out in the village clearing, talking desultorily among themselves as they waited impatiently and hungrily for the stew.

"After we've had a feed," Dad said, "there's nothing I'd like more than a good smoke. I'm dying for a weed."

"There's some sort of tobacco plant that grows wild up here," Jack said. "The boongs smoke it. But I don't know what it looks like."

"This is when we could have done with Caulfield," Dad said. "He probably knew it."

"I'd rather do without the smoke," Jack said. He stirred the stew and the thick aroma of it rose to tickle their nostrils.

"Smells all right, eh?" Dad said. "I used to be very finicky about food. Kidded myself I was a gourmet."

"You must have damned near starved in Sydney, then," Jack said. "They don't cater for gourmets there."

"My mother was a good cook. She used to put on a lot of Jewish dishes, real Yiddisher stuff. And she was good at French cooking, too. She had imagination." He grinned, his mahogany black-bearded face creased into a mass of dark wrinkles in the glow of the fire. "Maybe that was why I never married. Never found a chookie who could cook like Mum."

Jack took a spoon from the mess-tin by his side and tasted the stew. He smacked his lips appreciatively. "Ambrosia. Just a few more minutes."

Dad sat staring at the fire, his shadow dancing on the wall behind him. "Do you reckon we're going to make it, Jack?"

Jack stirred the stew again. "I try not to think about it. I get up each morning and say, well, another day. And that's as far as I let myself go. I don't think about to-morrow or the day after or next week."

"What gets me is that I never expected to run into anything like this. I thought if I was going to cop a ticket with my name on it, it would be a bullet or maybe a piece of bomb. Once or twice I thought maybe I'd be taken a prisoner. But I never thought I'd end up wandering around in the bloody jungle like a rooster with its head cut off. We don't know where we're going, every day we're getting weaker—sometimes, towards the end of the day, I wonder what the hell's holding me up." Dad looked down at the thin thighs showing through his torn trousers.

"We've been bloody lucky so far," Jack said. "We were lucky none of us caught the typhus from Caulfield, for one thing."

"It would have been consistent of him to have given it to us. What do you reckon about Vern? He rocked me when he said he was going to shoot the Ape. I didn't think he had it in him." Then he added as if to himself: "Though I shouldn't be surprised about anything now."

"It rocked me a bit. He'd always struck me as being too easy-going to be as cold and practical as he was about shooting Caulfield. It was the sort of thing you would have expected from Caulfield, if the positions had been reversed. But I think Vern did the right thing. I was just glad I wasn't the one who had to make the decision."

"It's preying on his mind, I think. Or something is. In the last week or so he's been a really rough-tempered bastard. Christ, I want to get out of this bloody jungle—who doesn't? —but he's got ——ing fanatical about it. A couple of times, listening to him yell at us when we'd stop for a breather, you'd have thought he was Caulfield."

"I wouldn't condemn him that much," Jack said with a grin.

Dad nodded. "No, maybe you're right. I've just got a complex about the Ape. It worries me. I'd hate to see Vern get like him."

"He won't," Jack said, and lifted the helmet of stew off the fire. "I'd shoot him first."

"Would you?" Dad said, but Jack was already heading for the door of the hut. Dad kicked earth over the fire, killing it, then took the gas capes away from the doorway and stood aside to let Jack carry the stew out to the waiting men.

"About bloody time, too," said Mick Kennedy. "I was just about to chew a piece of Brennan here."

"A cannibal," said Joe. "Takes all types to make an army."

"There'll be no second helpings," Jack said, "so take it slow."

"Do you say grace before this meal every night, padre?" Greg said.

Father Chase smiled. "I do, Greg. But it's testing m faith. I'm beginning to look on sweet potato stew as a devil' brew."

"Unless I've lost track," said Bluey Brown, "to-night' Saturday night. We always had corned beef and cabbag Saturday night. We used to invite all our Irish friends over I hated the stuff and so did the Irish. But they used to si there and gobble it up and say that no one had lived till he' eaten corned beef and cabbage and boiled potatoes. Great one for bulldust, the Irish."

"I'm seventy-five per cent Irish," said Mick.

"You're seventy-five per cent bulldust, too," said Joe.

Alec Putnam savoured a piece of sweet potato. "Saturda nights, we had baked beans and frankfurters. But first we ha clam chowder. Now you *really* haven't lived till you've ha clam chowder made from Cape Cod quahogs. Some Saturda night after the war I want you all should come over to ou house——"

"I'll be busy the first Saturday night after the war," Bluey said. "We're having the Irish in again."

"Make it some other Saturday, then," Alec said.

"We'll do that," said Vern. "What time does the last tram leave Cape Cod for Coogee?"

Jack chewed on the stringy vegetables of the stew. With a huge frame and a vast amount of energy that he had rarely conserved, he had always been a big eater. For the past fort-night now, hunger had been a constant ache and he had gradually felt himself growing weaker. Sometimes at the top of a long climb up a slippery tree-tangled hill he had felt his legs fluttering like an old man's, and once or twice he had retched violently but his stomach had had nothing to throw up. Most of the other men were also showing signs of weakness.

Charlie no longer carried Greg on his back: they had fashioned a crude crutch for Greg and he now hopped along supported by the crutch and with one arm around Charlie's shoulders. Bluey had lost so much weight that he was almost unrecognisable: the eyes of an old man looked out above the grey-streaked red beard. Some of the others, the naturally lean ones like Greg and Alec and Father Chase, were now thin almost to the point of emaciation: one could almost hear the scrape of their bones as they moved. Jack finished his stew and lay back against his pack, still hungry but knowing there was nothing to be done about it.

He wondered what Silver was doing right now. It probably would be too early for her to be eating just yet. She probably wouldn't even be thinking about it, just taking for granted all the rich and varied food he had seen in the big refrigerator in the Bendixter kitchen. He had a moment of sudden petulant anger, then he checked himself; it was only envy he felt and if he were home now he would be enjoying himself and not giving a thought to the men here in New Guinea. There were some people who could ally themselves with the privations of others, but they were few and far between and all they got from the world for their pains was ridicule. Gandhi had been a joke in Australia, even among those who professed to have some ideals. There would be sacrifices back home now, but no one would be going to the lengths Gandhi had gone to. Only fools, they would say, were extremists. And when it came to thinking of other people, he himself had never been an extremist.

Would Silver be going out to-night or was she perhaps staying home to write him another letter? It was—he thought for a moment—twenty-eight days since he had last heard from her.

I see a lot of Sarah and Dinah, she had written. *Sarah is unhappy and misses Greg more than she will admit even to herself.*

*She never says anything, but I can recognise a lonely woman when
I see one. I'm lonely myself—God, I am lonely, darling, so win this
war in a hurry and come home. I envy Dinah—she is lonely, too, but
she has her children and that's something. I am fascinated by
young Jill and Michael; or for that matter, any child fascinates me
now. I'm dying to be a mother, so come home and let me get started
on the way* . . .

"Thinking, Jack?" It was Father Chase, folding his bones
as he sat down, a thin angular heap in the starlit darkness.

"About my girl, padre. Wondering if she thinks I'm
dead."

"Don't you think it's too soon for her to think that?"
Father Chase linked his fingers and rested his hands on the
sharp peak of his knees; his knuckles cracked with a hard near
sound in the darkness. "Women don't lost hope as quickly as
that. What's she like, Jack? A nice girl?"

"I think so," Jack said slowly, luxuriating in the memory of
her. She was suddenly physically close, so much so that he
could almost feel the pressure of her against his loins, and he
felt an abrupt and weakening spasm of desire. He looked
sideways at Father Chase, glad the darkness hid the light in
his eyes. "But she may not be a nice girl by your standards,
padre."

"A priest is the last one who should have standards for a
woman, Jack. Every confessional taught me that."

"Priests aren't supposed to be cynical, are they?"

"I'm not being cynical. I'm just being practical." Father
Chase turned his head and Jack saw the long black hair that
now hung like a cap from the thin skull. "Women used to
come to me for advice and all I could tell them was to turn to
God. It was easy for me—I've never turned away from Him.
But with so many women, even as I gave them the advice
I knew it was useless. It's remarkable the number of women
who prefer a drunken faithless lover to God."

"And don't you ever despair? Don't you sometimes get tired of trying to save souls that don't want to be saved?"

Father Chase shrugged. "It's my job. Nobody conscripted me into the priesthood. I volunteered, just as you volunteered for the Army. Don't you sometimes despair of fighting a war that we've been losing now for nearly three years? Of course, you do. But you stick it out. You've got faith in ultimate victory. Well, so have I, though I shan't be here to see it."

He would be an extremist in thinking of other people, Jack thought. I don't know whether it's because of his vocation or because of the man himself, but sacrifice would be natural to him. "You have a lot of faith in human nature, haven't you, padre?"

Father Chase leaned back, looking up at the bright scatter of stars above the clearing. "I just happen to believe that man is greater than the sum of his disasters. He wouldn't have survived so long if he were not. He's been degraded, and sometimes he's degraded himself, but sooner or later he rises above it again."

"Come Judgment Day then, do you expect us all to be Christians again?"

"No. But I'm pretty sure God will find a good deal less wrong with us than a lot of cynics do to-day." Father Chase stretched his legs out in front of him. "What's your girl's family like, Jack?"

"Lousy rich, padre. They're the Bendixters."

Father Chase whistled appreciatively. "You're doing all right for yourself, boy. I used to read about them in the Society columns on Sundays."

"I didn't think you'd spend your Sundays like that."

"It was a sort of let-down after the sermons I'd deliver. I used often to wish I'd been posted to one of those rich parishes. I'd drink tea with the matrons six days a week, then tear hell out of them on Sunday."

"You'd have trouble tearing hell out of my future mother-in-law. She'd doze off as soon as you got into the pulpit. Vague —hell, you have no idea. She asks you something and you explain it to her. But that isn't all. Then you have to explain the explanation. If the Commos ever took over Australia, I think they'd keep her as a curio."

Father Chase's smile was a faint glimmer in the darkness. "I take it, then, you won't be living with your in-laws?"

"We'll see," Jack said, and looked about the dim clearing of the village. "Living with in-laws could never be as bad as the living we've had these past few weeks."

Next morning they were on their way again early. Vern had decided now to head south, straight up over the mountains. The trails east seemed to be leading them nowhere but into Japanese territory; certainly the going was flatter and easier but several times they had almost run into enemy patrols. Vern had called Jack over last night and told him of his decision to head south over the mountains. In the men's weakened condition it was going to put an almost impossible burden on them, but, Vern had said, it was the only thing to be done if they were to get out of this green hell. Otherwise they would finish up as prisoners, be killed or finally die of exhaustion. And none of those things, Vern had muttered with quiet vehemence, was going to happen if he could prevent it.

"If we head for the mountains," Jack said, "just take it a bit easy, Vern. Some of the coves are pretty knocked up."

"What do you mean?" Vern had said, sharp and edgy.

"Not so much of the Simon Legree stuff. A couple of times you've thrown your weight around as if the coves were bludging or weren't trying."

"A couple of them would have thrown in the towel a week ago if I hadn't stood over them. I'm telling you, Jack. No bastard drops out of this party while he's got breath in his body. That goes for everyone, including you."

Jack was surprised at his own patience. "I wasn't thinking of dropping out, chum. Just watch yourself. If you keep living on your nerves like you have been this past week, *you* might be the one to drop out."

Vern had said nothing to that. Jack had turned and walked away, wondering what had happened to the man who had once been so solicitous for those under his command.

Now in the hot steaming morning Jack watched the men stumbling ahead of him up the steep native pad. It hadn't rained for four days but the ground was still soggy. It yielded under the men's boots, giving them little leverage, and they had to clutch at vines and tree trunks for support as they scrabbled their way upwards. Mick was helping Greg and Charlie, and Joe was lending a hand to Bluey, whose left arm was now in a sling made from the sleeve of his shirt. Jack was carrying the Bren and he could feel the chafing weight of it against the bone of his shoulder. Vern had suggested throwing it away a week ago, but Mick, whose toy it was, had pleaded to be allowed to keep it. He, Joe and Jack had taken turns carrying it, and Jack knew it would have to be discarded soon.

Sweat bathed his back, sticking his torn shirt to him, and ran down his legs, irritating and stinging the dermatitis that had begun to appear in his crotch and down the insides of his thighs. Behind him he could hear Herb Nutter, sobbing for breath as he slipped and fell in the mud.

"I oughta stayed home," Herb panted. "Forty flaming three, I am, and trying to act like a two-year-old mountain goat."

"I used to think the hills in Syria were bad enough," Jack said. "But that was like walking up Martin Place compared to this."

Up ahead Greg suddenly slipped and crashed off the path headlong into a dense thicket of bushes. Charlie tottered for a moment, reaching out with a blind helpless hand for support,

while Mick above him turned quickly and tried to grab him
Their hands met, but, slick with mud, they couldn't hold
Charlie fell slowly back, almost as if deliberately, then abruptl
he spun round and fell face forward down the slope. Jack hear
him scream with pain, then he was rolling past and Jack
flexing his knees, digging his feet hard into the muddy earth
reached down and grabbed him. He felt his arm almost jerke
out of its socket, felt his body swing round and his feet slip
and for a moment he thought they were both going to g
crashing down to the bottom of the hill. Then Herb Nutte
put up his hands and pushed against him and a moment late
Vern, leaping and sliding recklessly down the path, ha
arrived to take Charlie from him.

Vern knelt in the mud beside the bloody moaning figure
"Charlie! Charlie, can you stand up, mate? Can you hold o
till we get to the top of the hill? I'll fix you up then. Can yo
do it, Charlie?"

Charlie was almost delirious with pain. His whole fac
and beard was a mass of blood: it was impossible to distinguis
the pulpy bandage from the raw flesh. But somewhere h
found the will to struggle to his feet. Vern put an arm abou
him and looked at Jack.

"Give the Bren to Herb. Give me a hand here!"

Between them they half-carried, half-dragged Charlie u
the rest of the steep slope. Someone had helped Greg to th
top of the path and now he and Charlie lay on the groun
moaning in pain, both on the verge of unconsciousness. Jac
leaned against a tree, pillowing his head on his forearm, an
gasped deeply for breath. His legs seemed to be on fire from
the muscular effort of a moment ago and his stomach wa
heaving and quivering sickeningly. He looked across the ba
of his raised arm, his eyes misty with salty sweat, and saw th
mountains stacked in countless ranks before him and abov
him. They stretched away to the high edge of the worl

heir topmost peaks cloaked in a burnous of white clouds, and
one could only guess at the narrow valleys and back-breaking
ridges that were hidden in the green overlay of jungle.

He had never doubted his courage before. He had been
severely frightened several times and while in action there
had always been the constant aching awareness of the sudden
closeness of death. But he had never weakened nor lost faith
in himself and had gone about the business of fighting with a
cold savage intensity that he knew had had the right effect
on the men under him. But all at once now he had no courage
and no faith. The war was futile enough, but this climbing
into these endless implacable mountains, not even knowing
if safety lay on the other side of them, had an utterness of
utility about it that suddenly left him empty and defeated.

He looked down at Vern gently unwrapping the blood-
soaked bandage from around Charlie's eyes. Dad was helping
him; and Herb Nutter and Father Chase were attenting to
Greg. The other men sat about in attitudes of dejected exhaustion, their mouths wide open in their bearded faces as they
gasped at the humid air.

"Is it worth trying, skipper?" he said. "Those bloody
mountains stretch for miles. We're buggered now. Do you
think we'll get over them?"

No man moved his head as he looked at Vern: weary
bloodshot eyes swung loosely in their sockets. Vern slowly
finished unwinding the bandage. Laboriously he stood up,
looked at the bandage, then flung it away down the hill. It
floated like a live thing in the sun, then came to rest on a bush
just down below the men. It hung draped there, a bright red
line against the green, and Vern stood staring down at it for a
long moment. Then slowly he turned and looked at Jack.

"I told you last night," he said. "I'm going over those
mountains and I'm taking with me every one of you bastards
who stays alive. There's no other way out of here but over the

mountains and if it takes me the rest of the war I'm going over them. And you all go with me, even if I have to walk behind you with a gun. You understand?"

There was silence on the hilltop but for the slight moaning of Charlie. The men had stopped gasping for breath and were gazing steadily and a little amazed at Vern. They had never seen him before like this, not even during his outbursts of the past week: he looked about at them with no sympathy, but only a cold nervous fury that none of them dared argue with. There had been times when Jack had thought Vern had had a certain softness in his character, a weakness that might crumble when the chips were finally down; but there was no hint of softness now and Jack knew that he himself had been the one who had been about to crumble.

"Righto, skip," he said quietly. "The mountains it is."

Vern stared at him for a moment as if he were about to reply, then abruptly he dropped to his knees and began to apply his own field dressing to the raw bleeding pulp that was Charlie's face.

Half an hour later, when Charlie and Greg had recovered sufficiently to move on with help, they got under way again. The hill dropped again slightly and ran south for almost a mile as a steep razor-backed ridge.

There was no trail, but on the top of the ridge there were no trees and Alec and Fred Talmadge were able to hack a rough way through the bushes with their machetes. It was still hot and sweat ran freely on all of them; but up here they were above the thick foetid jungle and the air smelt almost clean.

Jack was walking with Greg, supporting him with one arm about his waist and Greg's arm hooked round his own neck. Greg was still using his crutch, but it gave him only a rough unsteady balance, and with each hopping step he looked in danger of falling over again.

"Don't go arse-over-tit again," Jack said. "This ridge is too steep. You'd go right to the ground floor if you fell from here."

Greg glanced down at the tops of the tall trees fifty feet below. The top of the ridge in places was no more than three feet wide and fell steeply away on both sides. Bushes clung to the steep slopes like a thick fungus, but they wouldn't prevent a man from hurtling right to the bottom if he slipped and fell. "If would save a lot of bother if I did go down."

Jack tapped him gently in the ribs. "Quit that sort of talk, chum."

"Well, how do you think I feel?" Greg said. "Christ, no one likes to feel he's so bloody useless!"

Jack said nothing as he swung Greg off his feet and over a angle of grasping roots. From the very first day he had met Greg he had known that the latter had gone through life expecting people to help him. If he was late for parade he had expected someone to answer his name or cover up for him some way; if he had wanted to go on leave when he was slated for duty he had just naturally assumed that someone would be glad to stand in for him; if he had been short of money, as he usually was, he had taken it for granted that someone would offer him a loan. Someone had usually been willing to do all those things for him because, despite his irritating irresponsibility, the men had liked him and had known he would have done the same for them if they had asked him. Except that the rest of them had rarely asked him, being content to do their own tour of duty or go without money till next pay-day. Finding Greg now so bitterly desirous of being independent, when he needed help more than he had ever needed it before, was something of a shock. It made Jack aware of the extent of his weakness back there on the hill, and suddenly he felt a rush of shame. He couldn't remember when he had last had such a feeling.

S

Herb Nutter was walking ahead of them, just behind Alec
Putnam. "Ever follow the ponies, cap'n?"

"No," said Alec. "We haven't got a race track on Cape
Cod."

"No course?" Herb said incredulously. "Cripes, that's
crook. Waddia do to amuse yourselves?"

"Oh, we go sailing or fishing. And there's plenty of
swimming."

Herb wasn't impressed. "But no racecourse, eh?" He spat
and ruminated for a few yards on the lack of civilisation on
Cape Cod. "Look, cap'n. When we get outa this bloody
jungle and back to Sydney, how'd you like to come out to
Randwick with me one day? I'll give you a few tips on some
of the runners, and you can have a flutter. I'll introduce you
to some of the bookies——"

"Watch him, Alec," said Joe Brennan. "He works on
commission."

"Who asked you to poke your nose in?" Herb said. "I
just wanted to introduce him, social like. I know lots of
bookies, real friendly with 'em. You know Dinny Mulligan
I knew him when he was first starting out, when he ran a little
S.P. trade in a butcher's shope in Glebe. Now he's one of the
biggest bookies operating. And I knew him *when*!" Herb said
reflectively, as if he were a little astonished at how some people
got on in the world. "Matter of fact, I was best man at his
wedding."

"Who'd he marry?" Joe said. "A horse?"

"Ah, bloody funny," Herb said disgustedly. "Well, anyway
cap'n, when we get back to civilisation——"

Then the top of the ridge began to flatten out and slope
downward. A native pad suddenly appeared in front of them
and they went down again into the hot stench and green-gold
light and the Judas quiet of the jungle.

Jack saw the parrot shoot high across the track, a swift dazzle of blood instantly lost in the green, then the track was suddenly full of flying bullets. Even as he dropped flat in the mud, pulling Greg down with him, he was aware of them whipping through the bushes above him with the chittering sound of a startled plover. They thudded against trees, sending bright yellow chips fluttering through the air like disturbed butterflies, and vines whipped and wreathed as if they were attached to crazy kites whirling in a threshing wind high above the trees. The mud of the track spurted and splashed against his face and he could hear the shouts and curses of the other men as they plunged desperately for cover.

He and Greg had been lucky. They had fallen only a yard or two from a large log and they rolled swiftly behind it. Bullets stitched a seam in the log and a small rain of chips fell on them, but for the moment they were safe. The firing stopped abruptly and silence rushed in like an ice-cold wave. There was no sound but the faint creak of the trees and the soft suck of the mud as they cautiously moved their bodies.

"Where are the bastards?" Greg murmured.

Jack shook his head. The mud here was thick and deep and he lay almost half buried in it. He had to hold his head back to keep his face out of the stinking black muck and already he could feel the back of his neck beginning to ache with the strain. Insects floated as small black spots before his eyes and as he ran his tongue over his lips he could taste the sickening slime of mud. Cautiously, his beard brushing the mud, he twisted slightly and peered round the edge of the log. There was no sign of the Japanese: the bushes were blank and unrevealing as the dark glasses of a blind man. Then he saw the two figures lying in the centre of the track.

He jerked his head back. "Fred and Charlie have copped it! They're out there in the open."

"Dead?" Greg's voice was a hoarse gasp: they had both seen men die before, but this was different. In the three weeks they had been on this trek, the bond between all of them had thickened till it had become almost a sharing of the same blood a common pulse that quickened or slowed as each man was exposed to pain or danger that hadn't physically touched the others.

"I can't tell. They're not moving——" Jack's voice cut off as there was a sudden sharp burst of automatic fire from farther down the track. He heard a Japanese squeal and there was a wild scatter of shots that shook the bushes like arrows of wind. "That's Joe! He must have got past them."

Joe had been forward scout. The Japanese must have let him go past while they waited for the main party and then missed him when they had tried to cut him down. Now he was some thirty or forty yards away down the track, harassing the Japanese from the rear.

Jack suddenly decided on action. He turned quickly, flopping in the mud like a great seal, and dived behind a nearby tree. Bullets thudded into the other side of the tree, death beating its fists on a narrow door, but for the moment he was safe. He looked around and saw Mick and Bluey crouching behind a fallen tree about twenty yards to his right. He swivelled his head and picked up other men: Vern, Father Chase, Dad Mackenzie. He was surprised how widely separated they were: the ambush had scattered them in a wide arc on either side of the track. It was not a good site for an ambush, but evidently the Japanese had had little time to prepare and had had no choice of site. They must have been coming up the track as the Australians came down, and it had only been a matter of luck as to who was first aware of the other. The track here widened out into a small clearing and there were several logs and fallen trees behind which the Australians had been able to take cover. Only Fred and Charlie hadn't made

t and they now lay in the centre of the clearing like two
njured footballers forgotten by the rest of the players.

"Hey, Mick! Can you spot them?" His whispered shout was
ust a hoarse whistle.

Mick turned his head, his chin cradled against the Bren.
"They're on the other side of the track, up near that clump
of sugar cane. I ain't seen one of the runts yet, but that's where
heir fire is coming from."

Then Jack caught a movement out in the centre of the
clearing. He saw Charlie slowly raise himself out of the mud
and he waited with ice in his shrivelled stomach for the Japanese
o open up.

But they held their fire, and then he heard the sibilant
hiss. "This way!"

"No!" he suddenly yelled, his horror-stricken voice ringing
ike a cracked gong through the clearing. "No, Charlie!"

Charlie, on his knees, his hands held out in front of him,
urned his head in bewilderment. "Jack! Greg!"

Again there was the sibilant call from farther down the
rack, in a voice deeper than the normal Japanese voice. "This
way, quick!"

Jack heard Greg call out in a shrill frantic voice, "Here,
Charlie, this way!"

Then Charlie got slowly to his feet, mud dripping from
him like after-birth, as if the earth had just spawned him, blind
and lost and alone as a new-born animal. He stood, his head
twisting from side to side, his hands clutching with fearful
hesitation at the air about him; then like a child taking its
first frightened steps he began to walk towards the clump of
sugar cane.

There was a shout from the other side of the track and Jack
could hear Greg yelling with something of a sob in his voice,
then abruptly he saw Vern standing up behind his tree.

"Charlie, the wrong way!" Suddenly Charlie stopped, and

in that instant Vern gave the bush cry, something the Japanese could never imitate. "Coo-oo-ee!"

Charlie turned as Vern gave the cry again; then stumbling, crying incoherently, he began to run towards Vern. Jack saw Vern come out from behind his tree in a crouching run, then he stepped out into the open himself.

"Bore it up 'em!" he roared, and opened up with his tommy-gun at the clump of sugar cane. He heard the sharp stabbing sound of Mick's Bren, the crack of rifles, and the sugar cane waved and snapped and flew as the fire poured into it. Out of the corner of his eye he saw Charlie stagger and fall, but he didn't know whether he had tripped or been hit. He saw Vern and Greg crawling through the mud of the track, snaking along with the speed of men who had always moved that way, both headed towards the prostrate Charlie. Then he had gone running forward, flinging his first grenade with all his strength, diving into the mud while it burst before him in a dark red-centred flower, feeling the shrapnel whir over him; then he was on his feet again, still running forward and flinging another grenade. He went down behind a log, heard the grenade explode, then he got up on one knee and poured the remainder of his magazine into the clump of sugar cane. He saw Joe coming up the track, pumping away with his tommy-gun; then abruptly he stood up and yelled to cease fire. He slammed another magazine into his gun and moved cautiously forward.

But there was no need for caution. There were eight Japanese in the wreckage of the sugar cane, shattered bloody messes of men who had figured in their last ambush. Jack looked down at the small figures, twisted into the grotesque attitudes of their last agony, then he spat deliberately and venomously at the gaping red cabbage that had been a Japanese head.

Joe came panting up beside him. "All finished?" He looked

down at the dead Japanese, hating them as much now as he had a few moments before when they had been alive and trying to kill him. "The runts! It was my fault we walked into that. I didn't see their footprints till I'd got past them and then it was too late. You blokes had come round the bend. Christ, I must of been walking with my eyes shut!"

"You couldn't help it, Joe. We're all so buggered, we can't be wide awake all the time. Half the time I'm walking in a daze myself. Forget it, chum." He turned and walked back up the track to the centre of the clearing. The other men were there, some of them gathered about the inert form of Fred Talmadge, the others about Charlie. Greg was lying in the mud beside Charlie, taking the meat-tags from around the latter's neck and crying softly.

"The poor blind bastard! Jesus, if he'd only had his eyes he'd have been all right!"

Jack looked at Vern and the latter nodded. "Both of them."

Jack cursed softly. He looked down at the two dead men and felt an aching wedge in his throat that almost choked him. They had both been men of the bush, with the quietness and at the same time the strength of the bush, familiar with the seasons, involved with the pattern of rain and sun and the bountiful earth, men who had been aware of life in its simplest and most uncomplicated form. Politics and ideologies hadn't touched them, and they had been strangers to persecution. Charlie had known the disadvantages of race, but no one had hurled stones at him nor marked him for a gas chamber because of it. Life for them had been simple, and now they were dead in a way of dying which was as complicated as any to which man had succumbed. For they hadn't died just a moment ago with the last shudder of their hearts as the bullets had ravished them: their death had begun years ago and a long way off, a remote unsuspected cancer derived from people they had never known nor met but who had died for the same

things. This end here was a long-delayed climax that was no
more important than the beginning of their long death. For
the cancer was still at work, eating its relentless way into the
lives of men who still breathed and prayed and mourned for
those already dead. Fred and Charlie had died for freedom,
but their dying would mean nothing till the war was over.
Only victory could give their death any meaning.

The wedge broke and Jack waited for tears but there were
none. He had never had them and there were none now. He
felt a sense of loss, like a man who had never known laughter:
they would have brought a cleansing relief, like the letting of
blood in a swollen carbuncle of grief and sadness for the living
and the dead. He looked up and about at the men and loved
them as simply and completely as he loved the girl beyond the
mountains whom he might never see again.

Then Vern said, "Righto, we've got to get out of here. This
was only a patrol, but we don't know how close to home they
were. Joe, back down the track and keep nit. Herb and Mick,
you two dig a grave. We'll bury them together."

"Could someone else dig it, skip? I copped a slug in that
first burst." Only then did Mick lift his right arm and they saw
that the right side of his shirt was dark with blood.

"Oh, God," Vern said, and looked suddenly old and terribly
weary. "Anyone else?"

Dad Mackenzie said, "I got one in the thigh. I think the
bullet went right through, but I'm leaking blood pretty
freely."

With both hands Vern pushed his helmet back and stood
holding his head. There was a trickle of blood from a bullet
crease above his right eyebrow but he seemed unaware of it.
His face was haggard and lined above the red tangled mat of
his beard. The yellow flesh shone with sweat, and dried mud
accentuated the deep furrows about his nose and across his
forehead. His lips were parted on his teeth in a snarl of pain

and frustration, and his eyes were dull with the exhaustion of a man who had had more than just himself to carry. He was looking beyond Jack to the mountains, staring at them with what could have been hatred, and suddenly Jack knew that Vern had no more hope or faith than the rest of them that they would cross the peaks to survival.

As if he read Jack's thoughts, Vern said, "We've still got the mountains to cross. Do you two feel you can make it?"

"We can give it a try," Mick said flatly. "I bloody well don't want to be left behind, that's all."

"Righto," said Vern, and seemed to draw on new reserves of strength. "Jack, you and Herb dig the grave. Padre, will you help me fix up Mick and Dad?"

Ten minutes later Father Chase said a prayer for the dead, a rough cross was driven into the ground at the head of the small mound that was the last foxhole for the two men who were beyond the need of safety; then the living turned and moved on towards the mountains that waited for them like massive crouching beasts sure of their prey.

It was raining again.

"I'm glad Liz can't see me now," Bluey said. "She'd reckon I'd catch my death of cold."

"I used to complain about the desert," Mick said morosely. "There was never enough water for a decent bath, I used to say."

"When I get back to civilisation," Joe said, "I'm not even going to step outside the door if there's a cloud in the sky."

"My missus has a queer bloody habit," said Herb. "She *likes* to go walking in the rain. She reckoned it used to clear her head."

"You should have brought her with you on this trip," Vern said, then turned and looked back down the track to Jack. "How's Greg coming?"

"Making pretty heavy weather of it, I think." Jack plodded up to where Vern was waiting for him. "The poor bastard has just about had it."

Since the death of Fred and Charlie and the wounding of Mick and Dad, Greg had insisted on making his own way. He had made rough pads of leaves for his knees and hands, and for the last five days had been crawling at the rear of the party like a crippled but still faithful dog.

With a weary gesture Vern wiped rain from his eyes. He was still the driving force of the party, always urging them on, never letting them sink into that state of mind where there was no longer any will to move; but his driving now had compassion about it, a care for their beaten bodies and an understanding of the despair that every man carried within him like another burden. He was more like the old Vern. "Some of the others are pretty crook. Mick's cracking hardy, but he's in a bad way. And Dad is losing blood with every step he takes."

"How's Herb's dysentery?"

"You've seen him to-day. Every time we've stopped for a breather he's had to duck behind a bush. He was a stringy old bastard at the best of times, but there's nothing of him at all now."

"How do you feel yourself?"

Vern looked at him, then grinned without mirth, a ghastly expression in the bearded thinness of his face. "I try not to think. It's the only way."

Then Greg came in sight round the bend in the track. Vern waved to him, then he turned and went slowly on after the other men.

Jack waited for Greg to reach him.

"How's it going, chum?"

Greg paused, then flopped over on his back and lay there, oblivious of the mud and the rain, his chest rising and falling in great convulsions as he gasped for air. "It's no use, Jack. I'm finished!"

Jack knelt down, the rain drifting off his hunched body in a fine spray over the thin flattened half-buried figure of Greg. He could hear the gentle swishing of it on the tops of the trees and the louder heavier fall of it as it ran down over broad leaves and dropped in long slender silver falls to the bubbling mud. They were high in the mountains now and the grey miserable sky was just above their heads, tattered flounces of clouds drifting like smoke through the trees that were always too damp to burn. There was no direct light, just a grey-green gloom that reduced men and jungle to vague distorted shapes, like a scene caught as a reflection in a curved fragment of glass. In the dim half light, his black-bearded face merging with the mud in which he lay, only Greg's eyes seemed alive.

"Get up!" The rain hissed through Jack's voice. "Get up, —— you! You wouldn't let us carry you when we had the strength. You wanted to be bloody independent. Your independence didn't last long. Nobody thought it would. You're running true to form, chum. Get up, you gutless bastard, and let's see some of this independence you skited about!"

Greg's eyes flashed, lively agates in the mud of his face. "Christ, one of these days I'll get you for this, Savanna!"

"You'll have to follow me to do it," Jack said, and stood up. "I'm not staying here while you look for your guts."

He turned and went on up the track, not looking back. He hated himself for what he had done, but he knew it was the only thing left to do. For the five days now the men had been dropping behind, one by one, to talk to Greg in the gently chi-acking banter that was the soldier's embarrassed disguise for encouragement. At night Father Chase had talked to him in not too obvious terms of the limitless depths of hope. Jack had come in the last few days to have a humbling respect for man's capacity for suffering; but he knew now that Greg was beyond encouragement and hope. Only anger could now move him.

Jack walked a hundred yards before he briefly turned his head and looked back. Thirty yards behind him, like a relentless trailing animal, Greg was crawling doggedly through the mud.

An hour later they came upon the village. The ridge up which they were toiling suddenly flattened out and in a wide clearing in the trees were the six huts of the village. It had stopped raining, but the sky was still low and heavy. Small ragged clouds were streaking up the valleys, catching for a moment on the tops of the ridges, then spinning away to be lost in the greyness overhead. The village appeared suddenly out of one of these clouds as the party came up over the top of the ridge.

The natives were waiting for them in front of the largest hut, a glistening black group of frightened women and children and proud calm-faced men. Alec Putnam had been acting as forward scout and at the edge of the village he waited for Vern to catch up with him. Then the two of them went on and halted in front of the group. The native chief, a short skinny old man with a face and head like a scarred coconut, said something in a dialect none of the party could understand.

Vern looked over his shoulder. "Any of you coves speak pidgin?"

Bluey limped forward. He had lost his helmet in one of the streams they had crossed and his clothes hung on him in ribbons. With his bearded wrinkled face below his bald scalp and the stoop of his shrunken wasted body, he looked as old as the ancient chief before him. "I picked up a bit from the kanakas, Vern. What do you want?"

"Ask him can he give us food, and how far it is over the mountains to the coast."

Bluey put the question to the chief in halting pidgin. With the same difficulty the chief answered him.

"He can give us some food," Bluey said. "Sweet potatoes, taro, corn and bananas."

"Good," said Vern. "What about the distance to the coast?"

Bluey turned to the old man and a few moments later got an answer. "He doesn't know. He's never been over the mountains to the coast."

"That's a help," said Mick. "One of these bloody stay-at-home bastards."

"I wish I'd stayed at home," Joe said.

"Ask him if there are any Japs around here," Vern said to Bluey.

Bluey looked at the chief once more. "'Long this-pella place, Japan he stop?" he said, and instantly there was a stir and a murmuring among the natives gathered behind the old man. The chief himself broke into excited gabbling, pointing with a short thin arm to another ridge across a narrow misty valley. He made dipping motions with his hand, then dropped his arm and stood shaking his head and muttering to himself.

"What's that all about?" Vern said.

Bluey said, "As far as I can make out, there's some Japs camped just over the other side of that ridge. As soon as he's fed us, he'd like us to blow. He's scared the Japs will come back and do the joint over if we stick around."

Vern cursed. "That buggers it. I was hoping we could leave you wounded chaps here, while the rest of us pushed on to see if we could get help. But we can't risk it—and it's not fair to risk the lives of these kanakas either. Righto, tell him we'd appreciate the food and then we'll beat it. Ask him could we have a hot stew now, and could we take some vegetables and fruit with us." He turned to the men. "Make yourselves scarce, fellers, just in case the Japs are walking around on that ridge over there. We're not in any condition for any more donnybrooks. Nor have we got the ammo."

They had thrown away the Bren after Mick had been wounded. All they had now were their rifles and tommy-guns, and when Jack had added up their ammunition after the ambush there had been no more than thirty rounds among the lot of them. If they ran into another party of Japanese the fight would be over in a few moments.

Jack turned to follow the men into the largest of the huts, then stopped and looked down at Greg. "Want a hand, chum?"

There was real hatred in Greg's reply. "Not from you,—— you!"

Jack turned and went into the musty dimness of the hut, shocked and all at once afraid. An hour ago he had deliberately fired Greg to anger in an attempt to keep alive the latter's will to live; he hadn't for one moment considered that in the heightened distorted tension of their whole ordeal Greg's anger would flame into hate. He wasn't frightened for himself, although he knew that in a moment of blind anger Greg might be capable of killing him: Greg had never expressed any regret at Caulfield's death and he could quite easily have been the one who had tried to kill him months before. His fear wasn't for his own safety, since one way of dying now seemed no worse than another, but that Greg himself might die never understanding that his hate was all wrong and without real cause.

And yet to explain, to put out a hand in friendship, would dispel the anger that was keeping him alive.

CHAPTER NINETEEN

ON the thirty-fifth day they were just below the peaks of the mountains. They were not aware of it till suddenly in late afternoon the clouds drifted and the sun came out. The peaks stood out against the blue, glistening like dark green rocks, and on one they could see the silver rent of a waterfall. The rain-mist had gone creeping down into the valley, smothering the world below, and they were in a shining sunlit kingdom between the clouds and the sky. Nothing in the last five weeks had been more unreal than this sudden emergence into this high silent place that was neither heaven nor earth.

Greg stopped and lay in the mud and looked back. The track here was narrow and treacherous, a foot-wide ladder of roots and mud flung diagonally up the steep slope of a ridge. The trees had finished a hundred yards below and were lost now in the curdling milk of the clouds. Kunai grass waved gently along the face of the slope, brushed by the hand of a soft breeze that came down out of the pass ahead, and here and there clumps of bushes shook water from their heads in a flurry of glinting raindrops. The floor of clouds stretched for miles and the peaks jutted above them like thermal rocks in a vast snowfield.

Greg lay letting the sun soak into him. For the last week, continually sodden, never able to rise out of the cold slime of mud, he had hardly been able to sleep at night for the chill that had wrapped him like a dead skin. He had given up worrying about his temperature: the fever of malaria was now just another sensation of a body that was slowly getting beyond sensation. Both his legs, his arms as far as the elbows, and the deep hollow of his armpits were raw and running with sores, and his dysentery would have been worse but that there was nothing left in him for it to feed upon. His wounded leg was now dead below the knee, unless he happened to knock the shattered bone; the wound itself had a sickening smell and it was dressed now with the last strips of his shirt. The sun could do nothing for him, but he welcomed its warmth on his painful shrunken body as if it were some wonder cure-all that in a moment would have him hale and strong and walking again.

Vern came sliding down the track, clutching at bushes and the long waving kunai to prevent himself falling down the leaning wall of the ridge. "How are you making out, mate?"

"I'll make it," Greg said. "But it had better not be too bloody far."

Vern squatted down beside him. Like all the others he had at last thrown away his helmet as a hindrance, a weighty protection he could do without. His long auburn hair, dark with sweat and the mist through which they had climbed, merged with the brilliant red of his beard so that he seemed to be peering out at the world from behind a bush of rich autumn hues. His skin was yellow, hanging from the bones of his cheeks like dull silk, and when he opened his mouth one could see that his gums had begun to recede from his teeth, making them oddly fang-like, as if the last few weeks had begun to have an atavistic effect on him and he was slowly reverting to the animal from which he had sprung.

"That's the bind about all this," he said. "Christ knows how far it is. It may be just over the next hill or it may be a hundred bloody miles away."

"It would be a laugh if Caulfield turned out to be the lucky one. We've come all this way, and we may yet finish up just as dead and far from home as he is."

"Yeah." Vern pulled at a blade of kunai and carefully wound it round his finger. "Greg, how did you feel when I said I was going to shoot him?"

"A bit staggered. I just hadn't been expecting you to suggest anything like that."

"Do you think so now that I did the right thing?"

"Do you think so, yourself?"

"I don't know." Vern snapped the blade of kunai in two, then began to lace it between the thin sticks of his fingers. "If we don't get out of this, none of us, I mean—then I think I'll die knowing I did the wrong thing. But if we get out——" He broke off and stared out across the field of shining cloud. "Without meaning to, that morning I was playing God. The power may appeal to some people, but it didn't to me. I'd hated his guts, but I've never felt so sorry for anyone in all my life as I felt for Caulfield when I pulled the trigger. If that's having the power of God, then anyone else is welcome to it."

"How does Father Chase feel about it now—does he still think you're a renegade tyke for what you did?"

"We haven't talked about it, but I don't believe he does. Or maybe I'm just hoping he doesn't." He looked down at Greg. "I've always had a weakness, Greg, something that always stopped me from being fully confident. I was like it even as a kid. I've always wanted people to understand why I did whatever I have done."

There had been a time when Greg had never cared nor even thought whether people understood him or his actions. But that was a time behind him forever now, and he could recognise the pain that Vern had carried with him from the time of Caulfield's death. "Don't worry about Caulfield,

T

Vern. As far as we were all concerned, you did the right thing."

"Thanks," Vern said quietly. "The cove I'd like to ask is the one who tried to kill him before."

Greg looked up at him. "Do you know who it was?"

"No," said Vern slowly, "do you?"

Greg shook his head. "I don't think it's important now."

"It is to me," Vern said, and threw away the strip of kunai and stood up. And at that moment the two planes came out from behind a distant peak and came towards them. They rode on long rails of sunshine, the underside of their wings shining like the translucent wings of insects, and the hum of their engines came back from the peaks in faint echoing waves to set the air vibrating. Their shadows rode far below them on the clouds, vague swift shapes that merged off into rainbow-shot auras, and against the brilliant blue above the planes themselves looked deadly as arrowheads.

Vern and Greg stared up at them, and from the top of the trail and down below in the clouds there came the shouts of the other men. The plane went over, flying high, and Greg, twisting over on his back, looked up and saw the red-white-and-blue cockades on the underside of the wings.

"They're ours!"

Above him Vern began to wave frantically. Jack and Alec came plunging down the track, risking their necks in a mad scramble, and slid to a stop near Greg and Vern. The four men clustered together, waving and shouting in a frenzy of excitement. Jack slipped out of his pack, tore off his shirt and flapped it vigorously, a tattered pitiful pennant as ragged as the men's hopes. The planes went on, taking their sound with them through the pass above and disappearing behind the peaks ahead. The sky was suddenly achingly empty and the silence came back with the brutal stroke of a gong of doom.

The men slumped down, their excitement draining out of them, leaving them trembling and exhausted.

"We could have touched them!" Greg lay with his head pillowed on his arm, tears of rage and despair dropping into the mud an inch from his face. "The bastards were going home! Home!" Mud spurted beneath the pounding of his fist. "Home!"

Alec lay wearily back against the slope of the ridge. "I'd begun to think the war was over. We've been out of it for years now, and there's been time for someone to have won. I'd begun not to care who'd won, us or the Japs, just so long as it was over. I can't face the idea that even if we get out of this, we've still got the goddam war to win." He turned his face away from them and said, "Jesus. I'm homesick! It's only five months and I've forgotten the sound of my wife's voice."

Jack was staring up at the pass through which the planes had gone. "That's the way to fight a war. At one time I thought of joining the R.A.A.F.—I wish to Christ I had, now. The war is always clean—what do those bastards know about mud and dermo and dysentery?—and when you die, you die nice and quick. Christ, if I ever get out of this, and someone tries to compare them to us poor bloody mugs, I'll cut his ——ing throat!"

Vern grinned weakly. "Pull your head in, you happy bastard. What about me? I said no to a war correspondent's job, just to come on this hike with you bunnies. Right now I could be sitting on my bum back at Moresby, or even Brisbane, writing stories about how you coves are winning the war, and everyone thinking how brave I am to be right up here in the front line with you boys." Then he struggled to his feet. "But we'll get nowhere belly-aching. You coves go on. I'm going back to see how Mick and Dad are making out."

"Old Herb's just about on his last legs." Jack sat with his

elbows resting on his raised knees, naked to the waist, a large red swelling just below his ribs where a scorpion had stung him two days ago. His massive frame had lost most of its flesh and his big bones showed through like those of a skeleton under the draping of a thin cloth. But there was still a suggestion of strength about him and looking at him, hating him with the intense concentration of a man who found relief in his hate, Greg envied him his chance of survival. "Malaria and the jimmy britz have sucked him dry. He's got nothing in him to hold him up."

"Why don't you hold him up?" Greg sneered. "You're the one who wanted to help everyone early in the piece."

Jack was about to say something, but Vern cut in first. "Shut up, Greg! There are only five of us left in this mob who can still stand up straight. We've been helping you all we can and we'll go on helping you. But just because you're down on your knees in the mud doesn't mean you're the only one feeling the effects of this grind. We'll help you and Herb and the others, but just remember that sometimes it takes us all our time to drag ourselves up a hill." He looked at Jack and Alec and motioned them on. They climbed slowly up the track, and Vern looked down again at Greg. "I'm sorry, mate. But you asked for that. Jack has been carrying Herb on his back ever since we crossed that creek, about two hours back."

Greg stared up at him, feeling another pain stealing through the maze of pain that was already his whole being. Slowly he seemed to be losing his grip on the world, slipping away gradually from the friendship he had so much coveted into a limbo where there was only himself and a great saddening sense of loss.

"I'm sorry, Vern," he muttered, and turned and began to crawl up the track.

The crawling now tired him little more than walking would have—though he had forgotten what walking was like. He dragged himself steadily along, pulling on roots with his hands and pushing with his good leg, and on the hills lost little distance on the stronger members of the party. Going downhill he would often lie flat in the slick slime and go sliding down till a root or a log pulled him up with a jarring shock that would knock the wind out of him. Only on the flat stretches, where the others could walk with their normal stride, was he left behind.

That night they camped in the pass below the top peaks. The clouds climbed again, rose above the setting sun, and began to fill with rain. They hung dark and purple just above the pass and slowly caught fire as the sun went down behind a distant spur. The air turned bright red and the leaves on the trees flickered in the breeze like countless tongues of flame. The horizontal light struck right across from the distant spur and the valleys and ridges lay below it like a grid of green and black bands. The sky boiled with fire just above the men's heads and they moved through the hellish glare, bearded and thin and ragged, like damned creatures still making a pretence at living. The smoke from their small fire was a bright red column, a totem around which they seemed to be worshipping, and the stew of sweet potatoes bubbling in Alec's helmet might have been a potion which they hoped would return them to the life they had already left. The sun went down, leaving a splash of pure green sky between the top of the distant spur and the fading clouds, and for a thin stark moment some of them stared out at what might well be their last day. Then night came up from the valleys and rain came down from the peaks and the world was gone.

This small grove in which they were camped was in the bottom of the notch of the pass, an isolated stand of trees above the steep slopes of kunai. It was cold up here, but the trees at least broke the fall of rain, so that one got wet again only in stages instead of all at once. Most of them would be asleep before they were soaked again, and by then it wouldn't matter.

Against the brushing and pattering of the rain Greg heard Joe and Mick talking.

"How do you feel, mate?"

"Crook." All the cocky lightness had gone out of Mick's voice. "I've dropped me bundle, Joe."

"Don't start talking like some weak-kneed sheila," Joe said. "You've come this far. It's all downhill from here. You'll be able to coast all the way."

"Like riding no hands, eh? No, sport. It ain't gunna make no difference. I wouldn't care if Martin Place was just down the bottom of the hill. I couldn't walk from here to the G.P.O."

Joe was silent for a while and Greg could hear him moving restlessly in his gas cape, the mud sucking about him as he turned. The fire had been allowed to die under the drizzle of rain and the night pressed in on them like a cold damp hand.

Then Joe said, "Where do you feel it most?"

Mick laughed, a bitter gurgle. "Christ, I dunno even where it *starts*. I dunno whether it's the slug in me or the blood I've dripped or the dermo or the bugs I've got—I dunno, sport. I'm just buggered, that's all. I've been that way for days, but climbing up this last stretch to-day put the kybosh on it. Geez, Joe, I don't wanna toss it in! But I'm finished, I tell you. ——ed and finished, like an old crow."

After a while Joe said, "I'll carry you to-morrow. We'll make it, mate."

"You won't carry me," Mick said. "You're not going to bugger yourself for me, sport. There's no sense in two of us finishing up with our faces in the mud."

Greg lay listening to them. They had become friends almost from the day Joe had joined the battalion in Syria, hiding their affection for each other under the chi-acking that had never fooled any of the others. As mates on the Bren they had been a destructive force of which the rest of the platoon had been proud: at one stage of the retreat from Eora Creek it had been only their fire that had allowed the rest of the company to retire: the other Brens had been put out of action and Mick and Joe had sat astride the track and calmly held the Japanese in check while the remnants of the company drew out behind them. Joe might never die wittingly for a cause, but he would die willingly for his mate. And Mick would do the same. They were the ordinary decent men who fought the war for both imperialism and communism, and neither of the isms would ever own them completely.

And who will own me? Greg thought. If he survived this trek, the war would be over for him a lot sooner than for the others. He had already accepted the fact that if he did reach safety he would be a cripple for the rest of his life. He would be able to swim, but all the other things he had enjoyed— football, dancing, ice-skating—would be over for him. He wouldn't even enjoy parties any more: sitting slumped in a corner, drinking alone, would be no fun. Work? Maybe, but not likely. A clerk's job on the Water Board held little excitement, and promotion was slow. Nobody ever seemed to die on the Water Board, and one had to wait for a man to retire before one moved up. What would he do then to give him an interest? He had decided months ago, when they had moved north to Queensland and Sarah had begun to write to him again, that he would try and find another interest in life but himself. She had been his main interest, and now she was gone. But what could a cripple do?

Greg heard Joe turn over, his gas cape rustling like stiff taffeta, and suddenly the small unimportant sound brought Sarah back as an explosion in his brain. The memory of her in the bedroom that night before the party, the taffeta dress a blaze of colour on the bed, and she sitting with her honey hair falling forward over her face as she bent forward to pull on her stockings, and her breasts drooping slightly like soft ripe fruit—it all came back with such sudden clarity that he jerked nervously and felt a lance of pain drive up his leg as the bone of his shattered ankle struck against a root.

Sarah had hardly been out of his mind since they had landed in New Guinea. When her first letter had reached him in Queensland he had torn it open with frenzied haste. Even though he had been expecting no more, it had been like a douche of cold water to read the cool non-committal lines of the letter. The others that had followed had been the same: friendly and not abrupt, but as empty of love as news bulletins. One part of him had clung to the hope that this was the first step towards reconciliation, that she would weaken and one day the right letter would arrive; but as the weeks went by, reason with its cold unsympathetic frankness had told him that as her lover he now belonged to the irrevocable past.

For a while he had almost succeeded in forgetting her. There have been no mail for two weeks while they moved and in the bustling excitement of the journey from Townsville to Moresby, the turning to a new unknown brand of war after the months of inaction, there had been plenty to occupy his mind. He had listened to the lectures on board ship with more attention than he had ever been able to muster before, and when they had landed at Moresby he had known as much about the Japanese as one could learn in theory. In the two days at Moresby before they had moved out for the back-breaking climb over the mountains he had drilled his section with the intensity of a man fired by some personal crusade. When they had met the first shots of the Japanese he had known he was better prepared to lead the men under him than at any time in the two years before. He had no ideas of winning a bar to his Victoria Cross nor any other decoration; but for the first time in his life he was going about something with

the single-minded purposiveness of a man determining to
succeed in his allotted task.

Then two days after they had gone into action he had
received three letters from Sarah. They had been no more
committal than the others, but somehow the accumulation of
them had brought hope spurting warmly up inside him again
like a gush of blood. Two more letters had arrived from her,
still no more than friendly, but in the heat and panic of action,
every moment of the day and night now pregnant with death,
there had been no time for reason. and hope had continued to
flourish. Ever since she had been as tangible to him as the rain
that fell every night on his face, cool and soft as her lips had
been that last time he had kissed her, the night of the
party when she had worn the taffeta dress whose rustle was
so much like that of a gas cape here in the cold wet shank of
the night.

The clouds had all gone by morning and the sun blazed with
blinding brilliance from the rim of the peaks. It struck beneath the trees in the pass, flecking the bushes and grass and
mud with pale gold, and the chilled men came awake gratefully
to its warmth. Some stood up, moving out of the trees into
the full glare; but fewer men rose this morning than had risen
yesterday.

Herb, Mick and Dad lay like men waiting patiently for
death. Greg sat up and looked across at them and knew without
asking them that they had reached the end of their march.
Both Dad and Mick had bled again in the night, blood soaking
out through the almost rotten dressings and showing through
the rents in their clothing like scarlet strings binding their
white wasted flesh. Herb lay on his side, breathing only faintly,
a long heap of bones held loosely together by the torn shirt
and trousers he wore. None of them seemed aware of the new
day nor of the sun rising like a great brass warming-pan into
the blue bed of the sky.

Half an hour later Vern had made the decision. "I promised I'd take every living one of us over these mountains and down to the sea. But it seems I bit off more than I could chew."

"It's all right, Vern." Mick's words came out of his throat as if they were blobs of phlegm he was coughing up; he had got rapidly worse during the night. "You done all right."

Vern shook his head as if he didn't agree, but he didn't directly answer Mick. "Father Chase has volunteered to stay with you, and we're going to leave you all the food we can find around here. I don't think it will be much, but it may keep you going for three or four days. By that time I hope the rest of us will have reached an Aussie camp, or anyway a kanaka village where we can send back some boongs to bring you in." He had been squatting down beside the men and now he straightened up. "We'll go and scout for what food we can."

Greg, Bluey, Mick, Dad and Herb were left in the small clearing. Bluey gave Dad a drink of water, then corked the bottle and put it against Dad's pack. "A schooner of Tooth's KB would go all right now, eh? I've been licking my lips for days now, trying to remember what beer tastes like. Any of you coves remember?"

"I haven't had a beer since the night we broke camp in the Blue Mountains," said Dad. "I lost my taste for it."

"You were pretty pissed that night," Greg said. "I remember I had to lift you off a barbed wire fence and put you to bed. You were lucky you didn't rip yourself to shreds."

"I had all sorts of luck that night," said Dad quietly. "Real drunk's luck."

"Running into barbed-wire fences, you did," said Bluey. He and Greg were only talking to keep the others' minds off the farewell that would soon have to be said. "You should've tried your luck running into the grenade that went off in Caulfield's tent."

"I nearly did," said Dad, and looked around steadily at the other men, then back at Bluey. "I threw it."

Greg knew he should have felt shocked, perhaps even been horrified, but he felt nothing at all. There was surprise that Dad should have been the one who had thrown the grenade, but that was all. He looked at Bluey and Mick and Herb, and they seemed no more moved than he was. Now all at once Dad's confession was anti-climactic and almost unimportant. Caulfield was dead and so were Charlie and Fred, and by to-morrow Dad himself and the others might also have died. Death had become so familiar that an attempted murder months ago seemed to have lost its meaning.

"It's been worrying me," Dad said. "I hated the bastard and I still hated him when he died. But I'd never thought I'd had it in me to want to kill him. I was blind drunk that night, and yet one part of me knew distinctly what I was doing. I remember telling myself that he was only a Nazi under another name, that he believed in treating us just like he'd treated the boongs. I knew I was going to kill him and I went about it as if I were stone cold sober. I just forgot to look in his tent to see if he was there, that was all. I chucked the grenade and then I turned and ran—smack into the barbed wire. That and the explosion sobered me up completely. I wasn't drunk when you lifted me off the wire, Greg. I was just knocked silly by the thought of what I'd done."

"A man does a lot of silly things when he's blind," Greg said, but he didn't really believe what he had said and meant it only as a comfort for Dad. He was beginning to wonder if, silly as he had often been when drunk, he would have considered murder. He had hated people, including Caulfield, but never with that much venom.

"Yeah." Dad lay staring up at the peaks, looming like dark solid clouds beyond the screen of trees. A shaft of sunlight broke through, striking right into his yellow face, taking all the light out of his eyes and leaving them pale and stony as those of a dead man. His face had once been broad and muscular, flat and solid as a primitive carving, but now the only suggestion of solidity was the big skull showing under the wrinkled yellow skin. His beard was a thick black muffler round his chin and throat, only accentuating the yellow deathly pallor of the rest of his face. "Well, now you know. They'll have to come a long way to get me for it."

No one said anything, and a little later the other men came back. They hadn't been able to gather much, but Father Chase said he thought he had seen some coconut palms farther down the hill and would go down later to investigate.

"We'll leave you Alec's helmet," Vern said. "But look after it. He wants to take it home to Cape Cod and cook bloody quahogs in it."

"Yeah, don't burn a hole in it," Alec grinned. "Always keep plenty of water in your stew."

"We always got plenty of that," Mick said. "I never drunk or eaten so much bloody water."

Then it was time for going, for the farewell none of them had proper words to make. Greg lay and watched the shaking of hands, and the blaze of sunlight on the back of his neck had no warmth more than the green gold leaf mould on which he was stretched. Joe was talking with Mick, his voice husky and soft. Greg had heard him this morning, arguing that he would carry Mick the rest of the way, but the latter had been adamant, insisting that he wouldn't go if Dad and Herb had to stay. And they were both too far gone to be moved.

"So long, mate," Joe said. "We'll be back in a coupla days."

Mick shook his head slowly. "So long, you old bastard." He turned his head away from Joe, and Greg saw the tears glistening in the sunken pain-filled eyes. "Go and see me mum, will you, Joe?"

"We'll be back, I tell you!" Joe said hoarsely, but Mick only shook his head and kept his face averted.

Greg crawled towards him, pressed his shoulder and muttered good-bye. He shook hands with Dad, then dropped flat beside the still figure of Herb. The latter opened his eyes and tried to smile, but the effort was too much and Greg could almost hear the bones of the emaciated face beginning to split. Herb ran a black loose tongue over his lips.

"I backed a loser, sport." Greg had to lean close to catch the whisper that hardly seemed able to come up out of the dry gasping throat. "Tell me missus—and the kids——"

But he could manage no more. Greg pressed the withered arm and turned and crawled away. He felt someone put a hand on his shoulder and he looked up into the gaunt face of Father Chase. "Good-bye, Greg. I'll be praying for you."

Greg couldn't remember when he had last prayed, but he meant it when he said, "And I for you, padre."

"No, Greg." Father Chase shook his head, smiling with a gentle kindness that brought a wave of infinite sorrow sweeping up through Greg. "Pray for yourself. I think perhaps Vern was right about Caulfield, although the real answer still lies with God. But it's the living who should be prayed for. Not——" He pressed Greg's shoulder and looked across at the three men lying on the other side of the small clearing. "God will have mercy on them, Greg. They may have been sinners, but they are still good men."

"Too good to die like this," Greg said, and turned and followed Vern and the others down the track. Thirty yards down it swung to the left round a large vine-wreathed tree, then went on down across another broad slope of kunai. Half-way down the slope he stopped and looked back. Father Chase was standing in the middle of the clearing, his gaunt figure outlined against a slanting column of sunlight that struck through the leaves overhead as if through the stained glass of a church window. Behind him the three men lay stiffly like three bodies for whom the priest was about to begin a requiem, and from somewhere down the side of one of the peaks there came the light tinkle of water, like that of a vestry bell. A breeze came up through the pass, disturbing the trees, and water fell in a spray of golden tears through the column of sunlight.

Father Chase raised a long thin arm in farewell, and Greg lifted a hand from the mud and waved back. Then he turned and crawled on down the slope, tears mingling with the mud on his face, on his lips a taste he would always remember, the salt of sadness and loss. He knew he was leaving more than just the four men there in the sun-shot clearing.

He was leaving a part of himself he would never regain.

Four days later they were below the heights of the mountains, down once more in the thick suffocating atmosphere of the valleys. Dank curtains of air brushed against them, thick with insects, and in the rare open spaces heat rose in a dark vapour from the sun-warmed mud. Vines twisted gently against patches of sky as birds disturbed the trees in which they hung: yellow and pale green, they were like ropes of sun strung out to dry. Scalps of moss and lank fern, dark and stringy as hair, hung from the trunks of the trees. Roots rose out of the mud like striking snakes, and stinging bushes reached for the men with vicious fingers. The mud was thick with leeches and the men were continually stopping to scrape them off their legs and arms with the sharp blade of a knife.

Greg now crawled in a stupor of utter exhaustion. His limbs moved automatically: his hands never rose out of the mud but slid through it. He was hardly aware of his head: it was so light now that it seemed no longer to belong to him. His mind was completely removed from him: perched on he rim of insanity, it was somewhere high above him, looking down on his crawling pain-racked body with cruel detached contempt. Most of his senses seemed to have gone, too. He had no feeling and it was so long since he had eaten anything but sweet potatoes and bananas that he had also lost his taste. There was only one smell, that of the mud and the vegetable decay above which his nose seemed always to be hung like that of a jackal familiar with the stink of death, and he no longer accepted it as a smell: it was just the air he breathed, that kept him alive while he loathed every breath he took and every moment he lived. Sound meant nothing: the men had almost given up talking, and he had long ago forgotten the sounds of the jungle. Only sight remained and that was just a sweat-stung blur in which nothing had its true proportions.

The red-backed ants looked almost as large as crabs at first. He stopped and stared at them, the sweat streaming from his face and his mouth hanging slackly open as he gasped for air, and then he began to giggle. He flopped flat on the slick carpet of leaves that covered this part of the track and stared ahead at the ants that now crossed his ground-level gaze like a horde of red-backed armour-plated monsters. They seemed to stretch for miles ahead of him, crossing the track in a vast migration, blocking it as effectively as if a million pointed stakes had been driven into the ground ahead of him. They came out of the bushes to the right of him and disappeared behind a large tree to the left, and for all he knew their moving barrier might stretch for miles on either side. He lay with his face not two feet from the edge of the red shifting strip and watched them march past with a slowly gathering fit of hysteria.

"That's a good way of getting your nose bitten off."

At first the voice meant nothing. Then beyond the red-backed monsters he saw the muddy hills of a pair of boots. Slowly he raised himself, bringing the world back into some perspective, and looked up at the towering tree-like figure of Jack.

"Who asked you for an opinion?" he croaked.

"I've never waited before to be asked," Jack said, and with two long swift strides crossed the sea of ants.

"What you going to do?" Greg crouched back like a cornered animal. He had a sudden crazy fear that Jack was going to throw him to the ants. "Lemme alone—don't——!"

"Shut up!" Jack snarled, and reached down and lifted Greg to his feet. He bent, pulling Greg across his shoulders, then slowly straightened up. He wavered for a moment, as if Greg's wasted body was too much for him to carry, then he staggered forward across the ants. He kept going, his long legs in their tattered shorts plodding unsteadily along the trail that was nothing but a morass of mud, his body bent as if in pain beneath the hump on his back that was Greg, and ten minutes later they had caught up with Vern, Alec and Joe.

They were sitting on the bank of a narrow, deep-looking river. Jack slowly lowered Greg to the ground, then flopped down himself. Greg could see quivers of exhaustion shaking the big bony frame and could almost hear him gasping for breath against the noise of the river as it tumbled through a gate of rocks about twenty yards upstream. Greg looked at him, a turmoil of feeling within him as wild as the water boiling past the rocks, then he turned away because he had no words to express himself.

Vern raised his voice. "We'll follow this downstream. It's too fast to try and ride it on logs, but it should bring us to the coast. We can't have too far to go now."

Greg looked down at the river. It ripped through the rock upstream in torn white scarves, wove itself into a silken olive green whole and went plunging down out of sight through the leaning trees that lined its banks like poised divers. It was a way to salvation, a swift runner to the sea, but it couldn't wait for those who hadn't the strength to ride its currents. It couldn't wait, but at least it could show the way.

They moved on till sunset. The sun went down behind the mountains, and the clouds that boiled about their peaks turned violently sombre. Black clouds rose out of black mountain and the last of the sun showed as plum-purple streaks along the high horizon. Lightning suddenly grinned balefully above the peaks and the first rumble of thunder came like a landslide down out of the mountains. Beneath the trees the air was still and thick, almost having a solidity of its own.

"We're in for another wet ass," Alec said. "I'd almost got used to being dry. That is, except for sweat."

They lay on a grassy slope above the river bank. Mosquitoes hovered about them, but their humming was lost in the murmur of the river: they sucked at the men, but the men hardly noticed them. Alec had suggested the possibility of crocodiles, but they had then decided the river was too swift and they were still too far upstream yet to worry about that hazard. The grassy slope was comfortable and they were too exhausted to go looking for another spot.

"I wonder how the boys are?" Joe's face glowed yellowly as lightning quivered above the trees. The storm had already broken up in the mountains, and the peaks came and went like jagged knees under the fluttering apron of the sky.

Vern lay stretched on his gas cape, ready to wrap it round him as soon as the rain began to fall. "It's four days now. I wonder what Father Chase is doing?"

"You think he's on his own now?" Joe said.

"Don't you?" Vern said, and Greg could just hear his voice above the murmur of the river. Thunder fell out of the hills again and when it had rolled away Vern said, "I'd hoped we might meet up with someone and get them back there within a couple of days. Even then——" His voice was lost in another clap of thunder.

U

"You think we could ever find our way back to them?"
Jack said.

"I could," said Joe quietly. "Every time we branched on
to a new trail I hacked a mark in a tree." He stood up and
walked to the bank of the river. In another glow of lightning
Greg saw his stocky figure outlined above the black river. He
had lost weight and he had dysentery and malaria and dermatitis just as the others had; but some grim stubbornness had
kept in him a strength that was only just a shadow to the others.
Every man left back there in the pass had been a friend of these
here by the river, but there had been a bond between Mick and
Joe that Greg knew was only equalled by the feeling he himself
had for Vern. And had once had for Jack. "I told Mick I'd
go back. I'll go back, even if we don't meet up with anyone
for another month."

Beside him Greg heard Bluey moan sharply as he rolled
on to his wounded shoulder. Vern and the others, taking turns,
had been half-carrying Bluey now for two days. He was
constantly in a stupor of pain and exhaustion and unless they
reached safety soon Bluey wouldn't make it at all. Vern
made him as comfortable as possible each night, tending him
as a father might his sick child, and hand-feeding him when
they had their one meal of the day each morning before
beginning their trek. They were still eating only a stew of
sweet potatoes and yams, and had given up worrying whether
the smoke from their fire might be seen by any Japanese.
Yesterday morning they had passed through a stand of coconut
trees and after great difficulty had succeeced in knocking down
two coconuts.

The milk had brought on another attack of dysentery,
but it had been worth it: the change of diet had been as good
as a feast. This morning they had come on a thin patch of
sugar cane and that had been eaten with the same relish as if
it had been an expensive candy.

Jack got up and walked over to stand beside Joe. "I wonder what our chances would be of catching a fish or two?"

"I was thinking that," Joe said. "We'll try it in the morning, eh? We'll get the quahog specialist to give us a hand."

"That's me," said Alec. "There's no fishermen like a Cape Codder. My wife——"

Then thunder cracked right above them and lightning sprang out of the sky in a glittering leap. For a moment the jungle and the river and the men were a vivid bronze, then darkness rushed back in and the rain began to fall. It came in fat countable drops, hitting the leaves and the ground with a flat hiss, then they heard it coming across the tops of the trees in a deep swishing roar, and then it was on them. It fell with savage intensity, as if to beat them into the ground, lit as a thick screen of plunging lances by the quickening flashes of lightning, its sound all at once gone in the constant crash and rumble of thunder. It fell out of the sky in a drowning deluge, and Greg, huddled beneath the hammered skin of his gas cape, knew they hadn't met rain like this since they had landed in New Guinea. It slashed down through the trees, stripping leaves and fronds and vines that fell like dying writhing things on the men in the lightning-split darkness. It made the slope a sliding sheet of water and every time Greg moved he felt himself slipping closer to the river.

"You right?" Vern's voice was a scream against his ear in the torrent of sound.

He turned and saw the dark shape of Vern bent above him. Lightning vaulted along the tops of the trees and Vern's crouched figure seemed to fall in on him, black and huge. "Yes!" he shouted. "The others?"

Vern pressed his shoulder and was about to crawl away when there was a shattering crack right above them and a blinding burning glare. Vern fell forward over him and the next moment branches and leaves came down on them in a thick cloud. Greg felt a branch strike his shattered ankle, but his scream of pain was lost in another clap of thunder. He felt something strike Vern in the back, felt him shudder, then in another glow of lightning he saw the stricken tree falling. It fell slowly at first, smoke or steam melting off it into the rain, then suddenly it gathered speed. It came down through the rain, black and huge, like the limb of an angry mountain, the sky vivid and malignant behind it, and Greg lay waiting for his skull to be split and crushed about the dead horror of his brain.

He felt leaves scourge his face, heard a branch thump the ground just behind his head, then felt the earth tremble with the impact of the trunk. He struggled out from under Vern, in another glow of lightning saw Jack and Alec and Joe rising dazedly out of the wreckage of the tree, saw the boil of dark water leaping up the slope, then was alone and fear-stricken in the blackness again.

"The river's rising!" He had never shouted louder: his voice cracked in his head like another peal of thunder.

He felt the water wash over his feet and in the next splash of lightning he saw the river, its white-crested back humped like that of a buffalo, charge against the fallen tree and come over it in a wave that caught at him and spun him off the slope as if he were weightless.

He screamed again, threshing wildly, trying to find ground beneath his feet, but there was none. He could feel the water, cold and wild, carrying him along; he had always prided himself on his strength as a swimmer, but he had no chance now against this black flood. Then something smacked hard against his shoulders and he grabbed at it with desperate strength. He felt a branch or a root, something that held, and he clung on. He had forgotten his pain and exhaustion: terror raked up strength he hadn't known he still possessed.

Another flash of lightning lit up the river. Through the

silver sheet of rain, beating sharply against his face, he saw
Jack working his way along the bank. Then blackness fell
again and a moment later he felt something crash into the
water beside him and an arm go round him.

"Hold on!" Jack was beside him, kicking wildly as he tried
to stay afloat. "Get—my back!"

Greg swung round, feeling the river pulling at him,
tearing his rotting clothes from him, and clutched at Jack's
shoulders. He felt Jack heave under him, trying for a foothold
on the bank; then in the next lightning burst he saw Alec
right above them, his hand stretched out and his mouth
open in a shout that meant nothing. He reached up, felt
Alec's hand pull on his own, felt Jack get a foothold and rise
out of the water; then suddenly Alec slipped, the pull went out
of his arm, and he plunged forward over Greg's shoulder.

Greg grabbed frantically in the darkness, his hands closed
on a bush, and slowly he dragged himself up out of the river.
He heard Joe and Vern above him, reaching down to help
Jack; then the lightning blazed bright as day and he saw Alec
for the last time.

He was hung against a rock in the middle of the rushing
river, looking back at them with despairing appeal, his mouth
open in a shriek that was soundless in the crash of thunder
that seemed to rock the whole world. Then as the lightning
died he let go the rock, his hand a white star against it for just
a moment, and went on the plundering current of the river
into the darkness and his death.

Daylight came furtively like a frightened child. It crept
down through the broken wretched trees, prowled about the
flattened bushes, then as if gaining courage came striding
over the eastern spurs in clear red brilliance.

The sun was well above the trees when Greg woke. He
lay stretched flat on the ground, his arms flung wide as if he

were crucified, and he stared at the sun for a moment with dull sightless eyes, blind to the glare of it. Then abruptly he shut his eyes, feeling the warmth soaking through his drenched naked body, and after a moment he sat up and looked about him.

Vern and the others were still asleep, sprawled like drunks in a bed of broken branches, palm fronds, vines, and leaves that glinted in the sunlight like a quilt of broken glass. Somewhere down beyond the trees he could hear the murmur of the river, the purring of a wild sleek beast satisfied with its rampage during the night. Birds were chattering in the trees and once there was a deep-throated call like the ringing of a bell. A scarlet blizzard of parrots swept overhead, and a brilliantly-coloured leaf came floating down to turn itself into a large butterfly and be lost in a smashed thicket of wild ginger. A few shredded lianas and lawyer vines hung from the trees and even as Greg looked one broke away and fell as a black shiver through a thick golden beam of sunlight. Water dripped constantly, a tinkling pulse in one's head.

Then Greg was aware that Jack was awake and watching him. Nothing had been said last night after they had struggled up out of the river and through the undergrowth to this clearing fifty yards from the wild water. The sudden tragedy of Alec's death had stunned them: the shock had been a last overpowering exhaustion and they had collapsed into oblivion. It was almost another shock now to realise that the rest of them still lived and the agony of another day had to be endured.

"One of us will have to write Alec's missus," Jack all at once said, as if Alec had died only a moment before and not fifteen hours ago.

"Yeah." Greg could feel a surge of emotion rising inside him and it had nothing to do with Alec. "Thanks for last night."

Jack stood up and came over and stood looking down at him. "You'd have done the same for me, even with your bung ankle."

It might spoil it, but Greg had to be honest: "I don't know. Till I fell in the river, I hated your guts."

Jack grinned. "I know. I didn't think much of you, either." He reached down a large bony hand and ruffled Greg's hair. "You old bastard, Morley," he said, and everything was as it used to be.

Then the others began to stir. Jack went off down to the river and came back to say that it was almost back to normal level: the cloudburst last night had dissipated itself in one short ferocious splurge. But it was still flowing too swiftly for fishing and they would have to postpone their fish breakfast. All he had been able to find was a few sticks of sugar cane.

"Can any of you remember the taste of steak and eggs?" Bluey was sitting up: Alec's death seemed to have scared some strength back into him, as terror had done to Greg when he had been in the river. It might not last long, but at least it had shaken him out of the stupor he had been in yesterday. He looked about at the others now, but none of them answered him and after a moment he said, "All right, bugger you, I'm thinking the same as all you. It's a pity Alec's gone. It's a pity, too, that Charlie and Fred are gone. Yeah, and even Caulfield. And Dad and the rest of 'em may be dead, too, for all we know. The whole bloody thing is a pity. But it's all behind us and we've still got a way to go before we know for sure if we haven't bought the same tickets they had. I don't care a bugger about the taste of steak and eggs, but I've still got a taste for living and it isn't helped by thinking about the poor coots who are dead."

"You talk too much," said Joe bitterly.

"Take it easy," Vern said. "Maybe we all talk too much. I talked a lot about getting us over the mountains to the sea.

I had eleven of you when I said that. Look now"—he gestured and a spasm of miserable pain passed across his face—"None of us will ever forget the other coves. But Bluey's right. The time to start remembering them is when we get out of this ourselves."

Greg broke the tension that had settled for the moment on the group. They had been living on their nerves too long and the wear and tear was beginning to show. "How far do you reckon we have to go, Vern?"

Vern shrugged. "I'm lost without a map. But we're down on the flat, and as I remember it, there's not too much flat country between the mountains and the sea on the south coast of the island. I don't know this river, but I wouldn't mind betting it becomes a pretty big stream farther down. And if it does, we should find one or two boong villages along it." He looked at Greg, then across at Bluey. "We could save you two a lot of hard yakka by leaving you here with either Joe or Jack. Then the other one and I could push on——"

Greg looked at Bluey, saw the latter already getting to his feet, then said, "Another couple of days won't make much difference."

"I just don't like the idea of being left," Bluey said. "We've left too many on this trip."

Anger flared in Vern's face. "Do you think I wanted to leave them? You can't do the bloody impossible, Bluey, no matter how much you try. You can't make the dead walk——"

Bluey looked terribly aged, on the verge of death himself. His reddish grey beard only seemed to accentuate the thinness of the once-plump cheeks. Big veins stood out in his temples and his bald skull had the yellow-grey look of that of an old old man. His dull pain-filled eyes moved slowly in the sockets that were too big for them: they looked as if at any moment they might fall back into his head. His body was bony and bent, thin flesh hanging on him like soft bark ready to peel.

Even his plump chuckling voice was gone and in its stead there was just a harsh thin mutter.

"I'm not criticising you, Vern. I know—and the rest of us know it, too—that if it hadn't been for you, none of us would have got this far. Don't think we don't appreciate that. I just meant that all those we've left behind, we *had* to leave —we had to leave them, because as you said, they were dead. Or damned near it. Being left behind might start to work on me—I haven't got any resistance left, Vern. The only thing that's kept me going is the idea that maybe round the next bend——" His voice faded away and he stood there looking around at them as if they might not understand a man who was afraid of dying in an alien forest that had claimed so many others. Then he turned abruptly and went stumbling off towards the river, walking with the curious lop-sided shuffling gait that had become natural for him, his arm in its dirty ragged sling held tightly across his sunken chest.

"We'd better get moving," Vern said quietly, and they gathered up their few, miserable belongings and started off. The river last night had reduced their total possessions to two tommy-guns, one pack and two mess tins. Everything else had been swept away in the deluge.

To-night Greg knew he would lie down in the mud completely naked but for one sodden gaping boot which he still wore like a man clinging to the last vestige of civilisation.

It was late in the afternoon when Greg heard the yelling. He was well to the rear of the other men, nearly a hundred yards, and they were out of sight somewhere round a bend in the track. He stopped, crouching low like an animal scenting a trap, ready to dive into the bushes at the first sign of danger. Then he heard the stumbling running footsteps plunging through the mud, heard Jack shouting unintelligibly, then his long scarecrow figure came round the bend in the track and behind him were the dappled green figures of two Americans.

"Greg! Greg! We made it! Christ Almighty, chum, we made it!"

Greg felt a rush of feeling tear through him, a mixture of wild joy and crumbling relief and heart-breaking sadness for those who hadn't made it. He struggled up on his knees, a thin naked body in an attitude of prayer, and tried to smile; then the whole of the past few weeks fell in on him at last.

Oh, Sarah, he cried silently, and fell foward to bury his weeping face in the black mud he had cheated for so long.

CHAPTER TWENTY

IT was dark when they pulled out of Moresby harbour.
Lights from the hospital ship writhed on the water, yellow
snakes in a black oily pit, and down a hill across the bay a
jeep's headlights traced a swift spiral. A bright moon hung
above the harbour, but it no longer had the menace it once
had: the Japanese bombing raids had eased off considerably
in the last month, and to-night our own bombers were over
New Britain. Faintly across the water there came the sound
of amplifiers from an American camp on the shore: Bing
Crosby was dreaming of a white Christmas. Somewhere down
at the bows of the ship someone began to whistle the song,
sadly and a little out of tune.

Vern turned away from the open porthole. Greg was in
the next bed, the sheets humped over a cage that covered his
shattered ankle, and Bluey was sitting on the end of the bed
leaning on the cage. It was two weeks since the Americans
had found them and brought them up the coast to Moresby by
barge. Two weeks, but the time in the mountains still had
the immediacy of an echo.

Bluey was saying, "If you want an interest, why don't you
get into union work? You white-collar coves have never got
yourselves properly organised. You'll sit around on your
bums and when the war's over you'll find you've been taken
over by the Commos——"

Greg winked at Vern. "Listen to the capitalist giving advice."

"I was a bloody good union man before I became a boss," Bluey said. "I still am, except that I find it hard to talk to them now. In our country, as soon as you become an employer they start suspecting you."

"I can just see my old man, when I tell him I'm going to be a serious unionist." Greg laughed, the old bubbling life showing in the still-thin face. He was still suffering a lot of pain from his wound, but he rarely showed it. He would walk with a decided limp from now on, but there was no self-pity and he accepted it without a murmur. Sometimes in the quiet of the night he had thought of what he would be missing, the lively pleasures that had been so much a part of his pre-war life; but then the time in the mountains would come back into his mind, and he would be grateful for even being alive. The dead had less.

He tapped the folded letter sticking out of the pocket of the faded Red Cross pyjama jacket. "But first I've got to get my married life organised. As soon as I'm discharged, Sarah and I are going away somewhere for a long holiday. I'm going to forget the war and the world and everyone in it. I'm going to be a selfish bastard and think only of myself and my missus." He grinned. "Then I'll come back and see about setting the world straight."

Then Jack came into the small ward. He had picked up weight quicker than any of the others and he looked almost healthy beside the other three. He hadn't stopped eating since they had reached Moresby and now he leaned across Vern and flicked an apple core accurately out the porthole.

"Well, we've started to win the war at last," he said. "I've been talking to one of the doctors who came on board just as we pulled out. We've given the Japs their first beating, down at Milne Bay."

Vern felt no excitement. He still had to get into the feeling for war again: a first defeat of the Japanese meant little beside their own victory over the past few weeks. "A big show?"

"The doc seemed excited about it, so maybe it was. But he looked new to the game. I saw his Army number on the bag he was carrying, N X a hundred thousand and something. Even one dead Jap would look good to him."

"Stop sneering," said Bluey. "You old soldier."

"I'm not sneering," Jack said. "I'm just stating a fact. Christ, we've been in this war too long, that's *our* trouble. I'd like to have some of that bloke's enthusiasm. But one kick in the arse doesn't mean the Nip's going to toss it in. It's going to be a long war yet," he said, and wondered how he would feel about it now he had become interested in it. It had been more of an adventure for him in the past, a chance to rebel— against what, he had never been precisely sure: convention, monotony, perhaps even against the human race, so many members of which he had once despised. But when he returned to the battalion he would be an officer and a married man, two titles he would have jeered at not long ago; and his life would at last have taken on some meaning. He grinned at Greg and Bluey. "You two lucky bastards. Going home for good, while me and the company commander here have to go on fighting the war for you."

Greg looked at Vern. "Major bloody Radcliffe. If the blokes above you keep getting popped off at this rate, you'll be a brigadier by the time the show's over."

"How much does a brig make a day?" Vern asked.

"About the same as a Yank master sergeant," said Jack. "Think of me, trying to keep a rich wife on a lieutenant's pay."

"Never mind," said Bluey. "Now you've shaved off that bloody broom, maybe she'll make you an allowance as a reward. I know I would."

"I hope she likes me without it." Jack felt his bare upper lip. "I feel naked. And ten to one, her mother won't even remember who I am."

Vern said, "When we come back to the battalion, how would you like Joe as your platoon sergeant?"

"Couldn't do better," Jack said.

"I had a note from him to-day, up at the hospital," Vern said. "They're flying him home to-morrow."

"Old Joe," said Greg affectionately. "You know, I didn't take him seriously when he said he was going to lead those Yanks back to see if Mick and the others were alive."

"I don't know where he got the stamina from," Jack said. "I was dead beat when we ran into those coves. I'd begun to have visions of lying down that night and not waking up again."

"It knocked him when he found them all dead," Vern said. "He told me about that, the day he arrived at the hospital. He said he hadn't expected to find them alive, yet when they came on the bodies——" Vern stopped for a moment and looked out of the porthole at a distant star. He still couldn't think of the men they had left up there in the mountains as just bodies, always to be referred to from now on in the past tense. "He said the four of them were lying in a neat row, as if Father Chase had arranged the other three and then lain down beside them and just died. Joe said he took one look at them, and then the strength ran out of him. The Yanks carried him back to the coast. He said he felt bad about that, but he thinks they understood."

"We do, anyway," said Bluey.

Then a ward orderly came in, with a tray on which was a plate of biscuits and four cups of cocoa. "Here you are, sports. Health and strength."

"Get stuffed," said Greg conversationally.

"You couldn't make it four mugs of beer, could you, Oscar?" Bluey said.

Oscar twisted his mouth sourly. "When doctors start recommending grog as a cure, I'll get sick meself."

When the ward orderly had gone, Bluey said, "I wrote Liz to-day. Told her I wanted steak and eggs every meal for a week. And no vegetables."

"After the war," Vern said, "we should all meet once a year over a stew of sweet potatoes."

"You know what you can do with your sweet ——ing potatoes," said Bluey, and they all laughed and agreed with him.

After a while Vern left the other three and went up on deck. The lights of the hospital ship blazed about him: it was their passport, their guarantee of a safe passage home, but he had felt safer in the blacked-out ships of the convoys. Trust was a luxury one didn't allow oneself in wartime.

He leaned on the rail and looked out at the distant dark ranges. There it all was: the mud and rain, the malaria and dysentery and scrub typhus, the pain and fear of death. The fighting was still going on up there, but the Japanese had now been halted; the long-awaited reinforcements had at last arrived, and the battalion had been withdrawn for a well-earned rest. It was camped somewhere on the fringe of Moresby, and in a month or two he and Jack and Joe would be coming back to it. He would be coming back as a company commander, with more responsibility than he had ever had before, and he knew he would face the task with confidence.

The war was still to be fought and won; and it might be that young Michael, dreaming now only of glory, envying his father, would still be required to fight another war in twenty years' time. Everyone longed for peace, but war was a part of human nature, a recurring scab on the skin of the world. He held no hope that this was the war to end wars, but he wasn't altogether without hope. For he believed in the essential truth that man created more than he destroyed, that his dignity was greater than his folly, that the human spirit was not just a weak candle in the storm of time.

Up there in the mountains where the war still went on lay Charlie and Fred, Mick, Dad, Herb, and Father Chase, all dead; but they would not be forgotten and perhaps, when the next war came, he could mention their names to Michael. The mud of the jungle should not be their end, and Michael and his generation should know of them, should inherit from them the courage that made heroes out of the ordinary decent people who, despite dictators and imperialists, fascism and communism, still owned the world.

Down south now spring would be coming in: the time of the golden wattle, of new grass on the hills and the quickening pulse of blood, the time of hope after the sadness of winter. Dinah would be there waiting for him, and Jill and Michael; and for a while there would once more be happiness. It was something to be thankful for, no matter how temporary.

The ship went out of the anchorage into the slight swell beyond the point. New Guinea went backwards into the night: a string of lights, the hum of a speeding truck, Bing Crosby singing, and a black wall of mountains under the bright skull of the moon.